1

THE GALLOWS GIRL

Isaac and Harriet Curtis are in trouble. Their coaching inn, Green Gallows, is threatened by the rumours of a new turnpike stretching from London to Portsmouth which will take away all their important trade. They also plan to find a wealthy husband for their eldest daughter, Lucy, while keeping her sister Rachel as little more than a servant. Isaac does not hesitate to trade Lucy's virtue to pay his debts, but neither sister will submit without protest. Rachel may pay the price for Lucy's final act of defiance, but it will also be Rachel who seeks the ultimate revenge.

THE GALLOWS GIRL

To Judy
for believing…

THE GALLOWS GIRL

by

Melanie Gifford

Magna Large Print Books
Long Preston, North Yorkshire,
BD23 4ND, England.

British Library Cataloguing in Publication Data.

Gifford, Melanie
The Gallows girl.

A catalogue record of this book is available from the British Library

ISBN 0-7505-2495-2

First published in Great Britain in 2005 by Piatkus Books Ltd.

Published in Large Print 2006 by arrangement with Piatkus Books Ltd.

Magna Large Print is an imprint of Library Magna Books Ltd.

Printed and bound in Great Britain by
T.J. (International) Ltd., Cornwall, PL28 8RW

Chapter One

They called it the road of the dead, the people who came to our inn.

On a map it was little thicker than a hair. Outside our gates it was a rutted dustbowl in summer and awash with mud during most of the winter. But a long time ago, before my grandfather walked this land, the road swam with blood. And with tears.

All our years we'd lived under the shadow of the noose. My sister Lucy was seventeen. I was fifteen. Maybe sixteen. Mother wasn't sure. She never spoke much about my swaddling days, even in one of her softer moods.

Those moods were getting harder to find as if time was pinching her cheeks into sour lemons, running ahead of her ambitions as she grew older and less able to catch the swift, flighty years. Angered, she had a voice that could peel potatoes. When she gusted into a room conversation tailed off, people pulled their chairs closer to the hearth, candles seemed to flicker and dim.

The first thing you noticed was her mouth. Always on the move, always changing shape with the breezy currents of her voice. Words tumbled out of it like milk spilling over the lip of a jug. Oh she could smile, but it now took more to stretch the corners of that dry mouth. A new bonnet from Prestbury market was no longer enough, nor a silver trinket, nor scented ribbons. But when an eligible young gentleman looked twice at Lucy, aye, that blew the clouds from Mother's face.

Though we had our own bedchambers, Lucy and I had the pick of the guest rooms when business was slack, usually after heavy rain when the lykeway turned to a swamp. As toddlers we slept between Mother and Isaac in the square bed that filled their room above the porch, later moving into cots beside the window. When we grew too big even for those I told Isaac I wanted to be near the stables. Most of my chores took me into the yard and I never tired of watching travellers arrive. He painted out an old storeroom, laid planks across a few bricks and topped it with a straw mattress. Later he built me a proper bed, a small dresser and a wardrobe. I only ever needed two gowns. The one I worked the taproom in, and the one I wore to greet the carriages.

'Rachel, coach.'

Mother's voice rolled down the hall. I glanced at the clock then checked myself in the looking glass. Too tall, too fat. Dark haired instead of fair. Isaac joked that I must be the child of some travelling man but we all knew what he really meant.

We never talked that much about the family. Grandfather died before Isaac met and married Mother. His own wife had already lain ten years in Prestbury churchyard. I heard he was a thin man who never spoke much. He won Green Gallows in a fist fight and built it up from the gutted shell of an old posting house that used to serve the lykeway. Isaac spoke of his father as if he still lived in the inn or was just around the corner of the yard.

Harriet Wheeler was an orphan when Isaac took her to the altar. Her papa was a Portsmouth caulker who broke his neck when he tumbled, drunk, off a harbour wall at low tide. His wife died of grief, Mother claimed. Harriet herself was quite the belle of the town and a lure for the eye of every lad she passed. The ghost of that beauty could be glimpsed sometimes when she napped in the parlour armchair and sleep lifted the hardness from her face. I didn't know the name of the fellow who finally snared her heart. Isaac knew it but wouldn't ever say, not even when sharing a pipe and ale with the horsemaster. The subject festered like a blocked ditch, something that bubbled over every so often. But it was also slippery, like a thief. You rarely saw it except in a flash of anger from Isaac, or a glance full of bitterness from Mother. I knew that I was a part of this poison but I didn't talk about it either. It was supposed to be their secret, after all.

I leaned towards the mirror and grinned. My reflection grinned back. I was an unlikely cuckoo.

I scooped my hat off the bed and tripped out into the hall. The scents of cooking, fresh linen and fermenting ale mingled with the stink of piss-pots and burning peat bricks. Hannah scampered past, smothered in damp blankets. She'd not get those dry before the morning's rain returned.

I slipped into the Long Room. 'Lizabeth, never far from Mother, was using a tattered rag to wipe grease stains off the table. She frowned as I passed. I ignored her. Mother was checking ale barrels as they were loaded into the cellar beneath the taproom. Cool air from the stable yard gusted through the open door. I stepped, blinking, into the daylight and crammed my tricorne over my ears. Murky puddles dotted the yard. A night of heavy rain had washed all the colour out of the countryside. Bitter gales often hurled themselves like whooping ghosts across the Downs. Judd maintained it had been the coldest summer he could remember and he had been horsemaster ten years.

I shivered and took my place near the mounting block. It was something of an eyesore, our yard. Not sensibly square like most, but full of crooked angles and swallow-me-up shadows. Pedlars hawked wares and nostrums. Sometimes there was a tame squirrel or bullfinch. Usually there were ribbons, hand carved wooden trinkets or clothes pegs.

Green Gallows was the best pitch on the South Road. Not too close to Stonehill so that horses were changed when still fresh, nor too far towards the coast. Last summer things got so bad with hawkers jostling one another and squabbling with gypsies that scuffles broke out. One nostrum seller was pushed under the wheels of the Prestbury stage, snapping both legs. Passengers alighting from coaches were pestered and had their pockets picked.

Isaac closed the gate to the traders. He went among them as they stood in the lane, naming those who could work his yard and charging a penny a day for the privilege. Those with the best wares, Isaac let in. The rest, the vagabonds and beggars – those trying to peddle rags or badly carved baubles – were left outside to hawk their chattels as best they could.

Isaac moved among his chosen, inspecting goods, throwing out troublemakers. Men tugged off their caps. Women bobbed curtsies. Some offered gifts but Isaac took nothing.

In the middle of it all, Green Gallows Inn sat like a large felt hat stolen by a gust of wind and left abandoned at the side of the road. No one knew whether the walls held the roof up or whether the roof held the walls together. Cracked walls, strung with ivy and sagging outwards like old men's bellies. Upstairs, oak floorboards rose and dipped as if obeying some unseen, ancient tide. Chestnut panels were stained black with pipe smoke and spilled brandy. Windows were scattered reluctantly like loose chippings across the cream-washed walls.

It was always dark in Green Gallows, but never cold. Hot fires burned at its heart. The walls sucked in the warmth, held to it as a mother would a swaddled baby. Even in the depths of the most cheek-biting winter the place was as cosy as a womb.

Through the parlour window I spied Lucy seated at the cheap spinet Isaac had brought home from an auction in Prestbury. It had belonged to the old parson, he claimed, and what matter if the frame was a little warped or some of the keys chipped? Lucy's brow was pinched with concentration. Her corn-tinted hair had been bunched up behind her head and strangled with a blue ribbon. Isaac sweated behind her, mouth working furiously. Her fingers scrabbled up the keyboard, snapped back, scrabbled up again. Isaac said something else. She didn't look up. He wiped his brow, paced to the door then turned back and started shouting again.

I felt a familiar prick of irritation. The temptation to run up and bang on the window was strong. Why did she let him treat her like that? Why didn't she slam down the spinet lid, tell him to play the thing himself if he wanted it done so well, and storm out of the room? Isaac had never lifted his hand to her. She could stand up to him if she really wanted to.

I didn't go near the window. I was always full of ideas about what my sister should and shouldn't be doing and it hadn't brought me a day's peace. From the stables came the jingle of harnesses where Judd was preparing the team. Opposite, the kitchen door swung open and Matthew crossed the yard, a wooden pail dangling from his hand. He could balance a coach on a pin but could not call his own body to heel. He moved like an oak tree in a gale, limbs swinging. Often buckets went flying, people were knocked off their feet and no door could be passed through without his bony hips thumping against the frame. He bumped his head, barked his shins, lost tufts of hair when he climbed down the hayloft ladder and shut the trapdoor on his skull. Sally banned him from the kitchen when his rump sent a tray of freshly baked tarts, made with raspberries it had taken her half that morning to pick, crashing to the tiles.

Sally didn't believe in a gentle clip round the ear. She went after him with a cake knife and Matthew was lucky to escape with nothing more than a slit in his breeches and raspberry juice caking his boots.

Most thought Matthew a surly pup but I knew better. His face had high cheekbones spiked with a long nose and black tufted eyebrows. Local girls mocked him. I had done my share of laughing too.

But his eyes smiled all the time, the smiles sometimes leaking into the tiny cracks that lined the corners of his eyelids. He had woman's hands, with restless fingers that fiddled with cuffs or buttons when not busy elsewhere. His knuckles were scabbed where he kept punching the wall. Every time he did something foolish: 'Thwack!'. Every time he lost an argument or was told off: 'Thwack!'. Whenever he tripped over his own feet: 'Thwack!'. At least he hit the brickwork and not someone's mouth.

Sometimes Lucy rode to Marrin's Ridge with Matthew acting as groom.

'D'you trust them together?' I'd asked Isaac, irked that my duties prevented me from joining them.

He was sitting on an upturned pail, sun playing over his tanned skin. He swallowed the lump of bread he'd been chewing and washed it down with a swig of ale.

'With a man, no,' he said, grinning. 'I don't see there's aught to worry about with Matthew.'

I waved from my place by the mounting block. Matthew's thin face peeled into a grin. I returned the smile. I wanted the changeovers to go smoothly. Isaac was always in a foul temper after tutoring Lucy and it would go bad with Matthew if one of the horses was skittish or he couldn't balance the coach. His cheeks coloured. Stupidly, he started to whistle.

'Shut that racket up,' Judd boomed from the open stable door. 'If ye're as jolly with the harness as ye are with that tune we'll both have plenty to sing about before the day is done. Bring it over here and hold this beast while I slip it on.'

A clattering of hooves from the lane, a voice barking orders, the crack of a whip. I straightened my hat. Six times a week we'd get the Portsmouth stagecoach packed full of merchantmen and naval officers bound for the coast. Some greeted me by name and gave me pretty trinkets from the London shops.

Lucy never had much to do with the carriages. 'You'll snag your petticoats,' Mother warned, 'or put blisters on the ends of your fingers. Then where will you be, eh? Let Rachel do it. She has the knack.'

Lucy never got mud on her cheeks or straw from the hayloft caught in her skirts. Her glossy hair had never been blown by the strong westerly winds into a wild tangle about her cheeks. The smell of horse dung was foreign to nostrils suffocated by lavender and jasmine.

Once I found her standing beside the old gallows from which our inn sign hung. She was staring down the lane in the direction of Prestbury village. I was helping Hannah unload eggs from the tradesman's wagon. One burst apart in my hands and, amidst coarse laughter, I had gone to wipe them on the grass beside the gate. Longing, such longing casting shadows across Lucy's face, as if she wanted to hitch up her skirts and just run and run down the lane, not stopping or looking back, ever.

'Why don't you just go if you hate it here so much?' I'd blurted.

She looked at me and frowned. 'Why don't you?'

I shrugged. 'I like working with the horses, I suppose.'

'You like working with the horses.' Lucy turned back towards the house. 'There's no world for you beyond our gate, is there?'

That afternoon I tried to sit and read with her in the parlour. I was too slow and stumbled over the sentences. But I'd glean odd words and phrases from Lucy and use them without thinking. Sometimes it surprised me how much I could match her. It surprised our guests too, being greeted at the carriage door by a country girl with a fancy mouth. Mother seemed put out, though Isaac laughed and dismissed it as harmless parrotry. I think Mother was worried that if I could learn pretty words from Lucy then she could pick up bad habits from me. The ostlers had notoriously foul mouths and I was always in their company. Yet every coach that clattered into Green Gallows was a different world, a wooden egg ready to hatch a flurry of faces – laughing, chattering, scowling – into my busy life.

The drumbeat of hooves slowed. The carriage heaved into the yard, horses snorting in the sharp morning air. Faces peered from the windows while on top another half-dozen wind-battered souls clung to the roof.

From the driver's seat, Gregor winked and tossed down a penny, which I caught with practised ease. Matthew began unharnessing the foam-flanked leaders. Judd joined him, wiping his hands on his leather breeches.

'How are the roads, Gregor?'

'Not too bad, considering.' The coachman looped the reins around the iron hook beside his seat. 'Summer's baked 'em hard and the water's just sluicing off.' He peered up at the sky. 'Weather's just about spent, I'd say. This dirty lot will have run its course come afternoon. Should stay dry 'til the end of the week, maybe longer. Tell your pretty wife she can wear her best bonnet to church this Sunday without fear of a drenching.'

Judd laughed. 'My Sally ain't got a best bonnet and if she had you'd have to nail it to her head. Now, how are the horses?'

Gregor nodded towards the snorting animals. 'One of the wheelers has thrown a shoe. I drove the team as easy as I dared, but she was pulling badly by the time we reached the Ridge.'

Judd bent down to take a look. 'She a lame 'un, right enough.' He straightened up. 'Isaac won't like that. You know how he feels about swapping good horses for limpers.'

Gregor chuckled. 'I know how he feels about not getting his customers on time.'

Leather springs creaked as the passengers clambered off the roof. Gregor's darkie coachman started handing down sacks and baggage. His name was Sammy and he was as big as a mountain. The luggage was unloaded in less than a minute. Gravel crunched when his big feet thumped onto the ground. He grinned harsichord keys.

'Are you a slave?' I once asked him.

He'd bent over, his big flat face looming in my vision like an avalanche of coal. 'Are you?'

I swept forward, placed the mounting block and opened the carriage door. The smile slipped easily across my face.

'Welcome to Green Gallows,' I said to the first pillow-cloud of petticoats that feathered down the steps. An old woman in a young dress. I bit back a giggle and held out my hand. She grunted before accepting my help, red-rimmed eyes blinking in her withered face.

I took one gloved hand after another, searching for regular travellers. Perhaps Robert who smelled of sour apples, or Geoffrey who never shaved except on Tuesdays. Most were good for a penny tip, maybe more if I was lucky. Five grumpy faces followed one another, squinting, into the daylight. Clothes were smoothed down and aching limbs stretched in the blustery yard.

Don't bring 'em in straightaway, Isaac told me on the day I ran out to greet my first coach. My twelfth birthday, or was it my thirteenth? *Let 'em shiver a bit. They'll spend a few more pennies on hot food, linger a little longer in front of the hearth. More time in my inn is more money spent. Don't forget.*

There, at last, Sailor Ben. Always good for sixpence, or perhaps a chip of toffee if his sweet tooth had itched during the journey. He travelled regularly between his London house and the Portsmouth docks. Long white hair ran in a plaited rope to his waist and buckles the size of window frames silvered his boots.

'Bless me if it isn't a little wood sprite come to greet us,' he declared, rolling on his stout legs like a cannon full of damp gunpowder, 'all tucked up in her green dress with an enchanting smile on her lips. What about a bit of silver to deepen that smile, eh, my young enchantress?'

He held out a sixpence, a tempting sweetmeat pinched between thumb and forefinger. An old game, but I was now the quicker. I plucked the coin out of his grasp before he had time to pull back his arm. He stared at his empty fingers for a second and then exploded into laughter. 'Blow me if you're not as quick as a cat. Quicker I'd say. You'd make a dandy pickpocket my dear – have my watch out of my waistcoat before I could sneeze, I don't doubt.'

I grinned, one eye on the passengers, making sure their patience wasn't wearing too thin. Those who'd clambered down from the roof, the wheelwrights, coopers and sailors, had already disappeared into the taproom in search of ale and a hot potato. I led my group through the porch and into the Long Room to be served boiled fowl and French beans followed by cheesecake or gooseberry pie.

Once they were settled I headed for the taproom. Hannah was already serving armfuls of foaming ale jugs to the chattering customers. I slipped around the tables and joined her in the narrow space between barrels and counter.

'This lot behaving themselves?' I asked, tying a hessian apron over my gown. 'They seem a lively crowd today.'

Hannah grunted and dumped half-a-dozen empty tankards onto the counter. 'Their thirst is keen enough, but some don't want to pay. They think that because they've stumped up a couple of shillings to cling to the outside of a coach then that entitles them to free ale at every lodging house they call at. Well I've had that trick tried on me before and the horse trough is hungry for any wastrel that don't want to dip into his pocket.' She pushed the tankards over the counter. 'Fill these for me, will you, Rachel. I've men screaming for mutton pie and Sally's threatened to throw their potatoes into the yard if I don't go right away and fetch 'em out of the kitchen.'

I nodded, pouring ale into the first tankard before Hannah had finished speaking. About two dozen people filled the smoke-gutted room. Some would be clambering back onto Gregor's coach once the team had been changed. Others would be travelling locally, often hitching rides on any wagons that travelled around the farms between Stonehill and Prestbury. Working men often stayed overnight in our cheapest rooms but some labourers or sailors would drive a harder bargain still. Judd laughed when he thought of the number of times someone had offered him a penny to sleep in the hayloft.

I placed the brimming tankard onto the counter and started filling the next. At one table a dice game was in progress and in the far corner a cluster of dowdily dressed men squabbled over cards. Not for them the sophistication of hazard or piquet, but local games, brewed in the alehouses clustered around the south coast docks. Games with crude stakes where the aim was to deal the cards quickly and win or lose in an instant. As I watched, one fellow roared with glee and scooped up a pile of coins while his companions sullenly looked on. Trouble there later, perhaps.

I filled a third tankard. Judd and Isaac once caught a footpad working the lykeway and beat the fellow, who was built like a shire horse, to within an inch of his life. Afterwards, they tied a cut-off noose around his neck as a warning and booted him in the direction of Prestbury. The road between the village and Marrin's Ridge miraculously cleared of criminals though it was Will Davey, the local constable, who got the thanks.

A customer with a laugh like a dog's bark approached the bar, scooped up the ale pots and winked at me before carrying them back to his friends. With Isaac tucked away in the Long Room trying to impress his better bred guests, I was happy pouring ale for the next hour or so. Hannah and I held our own, filled them up, kept them happy. The man who'd won at cards kept his luck and tipped me a shilling. Hannah got sixpence, and thought herself ill-used. 'I'll give you half,' I said to shut her up.

The door to the Long Room blustered open. 'Lizabeth rushed in, her cheeks flushed and ripe with sweat. 'They want more port,' she said. 'Rachel, help me fetch some bottles from the cellar.'

She swept the keys off their hook and clunked open the cellar door. From the Long Room I caught a snatch of a song – Lucy entertaining the gentry with her high, dove voice. Sometimes Isaac pushed the spinet through from the parlour and she would play for hours at a time, usually when Sir this or Lord that was accompanied by his son, nephew or younger brother. With the song came laughter and raised voices.

'Lizabeth fumbled around in the light spilling from the taproom. A clinking sound, and two bottles were pressed into my arms. 'Take these upstairs and leave them on the counter,' she said. 'Don't let any of that rabble filch them.'

I ran back up the stairs. I didn't want to be alone in the cellar with 'Lizabeth. My arm still hurt from the last time. I placed the bottles on the bar near the cellar entrance. 'Lizabeth returned with two more clasped in her skinny hands. She found me peering through the Long Room door, which I had prised open a crack.

'Here, you know you're not allowed back in there, not until after breakfast.'

She caught me by my apron string and yanked me out of the way. 'Wait here and mind you don't go peeking again. I'll take these in now and you hand me the other two when I call back for them.'

'Yes, 'Lizabeth.'

The rain returned to drown the remainder of the morning. The rest of my time in the taproom passed by in a cloud of pipe smoke and barter. More dealing was done by traders in roadside houses than in any fashionable London coffee house, I suspected. London gossip was stale by the time it reached my ears, but local news straight off the coach was usually fresh, and merchantmen thought nothing of spilling stories to one another in front of a bar wench.

The call came to rejoin the coach. Most of our customers shambled out good-naturedly. Hannah could cope with the rest. I untied my apron, folded it and stowed it behind one of the ale barrels. The rain had eased into drizzle by the time I stepped outside, and Judd was checking the harnesses on the new team under Gregor's critical eye.

Matthew was waiting beside the carriage door. We had lost some passengers and gained new ones. The coach would need to be rebalanced if the journey was to be comfortable. A fat vicar had been joined by a weedy banker, and two women – one stout, the other as thin as a pole.

I shut the taproom door. Isaac was standing in the porch with a man in a blue velvet coat. They didn't notice me.

'Your accommodation is scant at best, sir,' Blue-coat was saying, 'and the price of the meal was scandalous. I would never be held to such a ransom on the Great North Road.'

'Then ride to York,' Isaac guffawed, 'and save yourself five shillings.'

'You are mighty impertinent for an innkeeper.'

Isaac's tone sobered at once. 'Green Gallows is mine, as is the land it stands on. This is an inn, not a posting house, with food, beds and horses better than any you'll find at a by-your-leave along the roadside. You are welcome to bring your own sheets if you wish. And while you're about it, you can bring your own brandy, your own supper and a basket of logs for the fire. If you are not satisfied with that, there's another coaching inn at Stonehill, twenty miles up the lykeway.'

Blue-coat pulled his hat down over his forehead. 'The turnpike will put paid to such extortion.'

Isaac's eyes widened ever so slightly. 'The turnpike is a rumour, used to cheapen food and pull down the price of a bed. Go about your business and pray don't detain me any further from mine.'

Blue-coat looked as if he might argue then thought better of it. He strode across the yard to the coach. Isaac turned and caught me watching. 'You mustn't pay heed to stupid tales about a new road,' he said. 'Now get on with your duties, lass.'

Matthew was already loading the carriage. 'I want to sit by the window,' the barrel-bodied clergyman protested as he was guided up the steps. 'Can't abide people's damned knees knock-knocking against my legs all the time.'

'Sit by the window, sir, and you'll end up tumbling out of it, along with your fellow passengers.'

The man regarded him sharply, searching for insolence and finding none in Matthew's genial grin. Spluttering, he squeezed himself between Blue-coat and the banker's ancient, powdered periwig.

'Obliged to you, sir,' Matthew said, tugging his forelock and stepping back so that I could close the carriage door. Satisfied, he gave the nod to Gregor, who clicked the reins and sent the team rumbling out of the yard.

I headed for the stables. No more regular coaches until the afternoon when the Stonehill carriage would be due, but I had to stay nearby in case any private traffic called. At the height of the season, Green Gallows boasted as many as twenty or thirty horses on call, with chaises and single mounts available for rent. There was plenty of casual work to be had for local men most weekends.

I crept into the stable's musty womb. Judd was in the far stall, examining the lame horse and muttering under his breath. I clambered up the ladder into the hayloft. I'd made a bed for myself beside the narrow window with some old, dust-suffocated straw and linen that was too ragged to be used on the beds. It wasn't a window really, just an old hatch once used for chucking out bales. Judd had fixed some scraps of coloured glass bought at the market for tuppence into a crude wooden frame and fitted it into the hole. I was sure the first decent storm would blow it out, but it gave a good view of the stable yard and the gate beyond, painting the world in livid hues of yellow, red and green.

Settling back into the straw, I heard Matthew's lopsided steps as he strolled across the cobbled stable floor, the clunk of a pail, the jingle of a harness.

'How's the mare?'

Judd's voice, edged with frustration. 'Tell Isaac we'll have to call the Prestbury smith out again. A new shoe and a couple of nights' rest will fix this beast, but it was a close thing. If Gregor pushed this another few miles he'd find himself at the side of the lane with a coachload of passengers and a dead wheeler between the shafts.'

A moment's pause. I could imagine Judd shaking his blond boulder of a head. 'That man is the finest driver I know but he has the sense of a donkey at times. He should have known better than to push that team. And I never thought I'd find myself sorry that Isaac tossed out Colly Bruce.'

Matthew's voice. 'Gregor wants his tips. People have been known to pay extra to be driven by him.'

Judd grunted. 'I asked Isaac again if we could have our own forge. That old outhouse near the gate is beggin' to be used.'

'He won't do it. Not after Colly.' His voice took on Isaac's deep, booming tones. '"This is a respectable establishment; I'll not have tinker trash like you on my land!"'

I giggled into my sleeve. Judd, however, was less than amused. 'Every time I call the village smith out it costs a ransom. Curtis would save a good few guineas if he swallowed his pride a little. Respectable this place might be but it's a working inn, not some landowner's folly. And don't go making fun of your employer either. One of these days he'll hear you, my lad, and they'll be naught I can do to spare you a hiding.'

Feet scuffed on the cobbles. 'Have you seen Rachel?'

'Don't bother her. She's worked hard this morning.'

They talked some more, about the horses, the morning's customers, the leaking roof at the far end of the stables. A last flurry of rain pattered against my multicoloured window. Sitting up on my makeshift mattress, I dipped my hand into the special pocket Mother had sewn into the folds of my gown and took out the morning's haul. Scraping a clear patch amidst the straw, I spread the coins out on the dusty floorboards. More copper than silver. I struggled to count them. Lucy could have added them up with a quick flick of her fingers, but even working the taproom had done nothing to improve my sluggish head for figures.

Two shillings and eightpence, including the tips from the bar. I slid aside a tarnished sixpence, as much as I dared take, and returned the rest to the safety of my pocket. I shimmied on my knees across to the window, checked that no one was watching from the yard, then fumbled underneath the crude window ledge. There was an inch gap between the wood and the stonework. Risking splinters, I edged my hand along until I found it: a hole between two good-sized blocks, which I had scooped out of the soft mortar with a teaspoon filched from the kitchen. I shoved the sixpence inside and was rewarded with a soft 'chink' as it joined the other coins. Almost nine shillings the last time I had dared count it. My fortune. Mother always took the rest of the tips. She used them to buy hats for Lucy.

Content, I lolled back on the straw for half an hour, watching as the first of the post boys entered the gate and crossed the yard in quick, busy strides. There! Always the snatched glance upward towards Lucy's room as if she would be waiting for them at her window, a flaxen-haired Juliet with a face full of kissing smiles. Even to wink at her took all of their daring. The first one to pinch her rump had found himself in the horse trough with an empty slop bucket over his head. The next one had been taken by Isaac into the stables and shown the axe.

'Touch her again and you know what you'll lose,' he growled. 'My daughter ain't for the likes of you, and if you don't want to spend the rest of your days squawking like a wench you'll tell your friends that too.'

No one had laid a finger on her after that, though they stole glances often enough and scurried to find some business that would take them inside the inn so they could be near her.

I would've exchanged heated kisses with any one of them, either in the hayloft or the musty green space between the nettles and the stable wall. But a man with a thirst for sweet wine has no desire to sup sour milk.

'Go kiss one of your horses,' a lad said, laughing, when I would have made a whore of myself just to feel his leather-chapped hands fumble with my petticoats. Maybe he thought I'd cry. Instead I bit him on the arm. The taste of his flesh, salty with sweat and lightly powdered with dust from the lane, filled my stomach with shivers. He slapped me to the ground and spat in the dirt. A boot in my ribs would have followed had Matthew not got a hold of the lad and sent him packing.

At fifteen, or perhaps sixteen, my body terrified me. It hurt and bled, and peppered my face with grisly red craters. Other times it clawed at my innards with a hunger I didn't know how to satisfy.

Only last week, Judd asked me to bring a pail of water to the stables. For no good reason I burst into tears and fled the yard. My face cried itself pink seemingly of its own will. I found myself snapping at people I liked. To make matters worse, everyone exchanged knowing winks and said something about 'that age'.

And want, want, every waking hour of the day.

Solace in the warm pitch-bucket of my bed-

chamber. Fumbles in the dark. I felt guilt. Shame.
Alive.

The Stonehill coach rumbled into the yard. Only four passengers inside and six on top. Still good for a couple of shillings if I could charm them enough. Another company worked this route and each day a different driver winked at me from his perch, impressed at my ability to squeeze a tip out of the most lemon-faced passenger. I smiled butterflies, saw my charges off the coach and, with a new team snorting between the shafts, on their way again. Above, the sullen carpet of cloud rolled up and blew itself towards the coast. The countryside sparkled in the gratitude of the newly released sun.

I spent a couple of hours in the coach house sweeping out one of the two post chaises we kept for hire. Then it was off to the kitchen for bread and a slab of cold mutton pie. Hannah had saved me some bramble tart from lunch and stood by in goggle-eyed wonder as I crammed the lot into my mouth and washed it down with a swig of milk.

'You're bursting out of that dress,' she observed drily. 'You'll never have Lucy's sweet figure if you don't even let your food touch the plate before scoffing it.'

I stared at my plate, pink rosebuds blooming on my cheeks. The food suddenly felt like rocks in my belly. Hannah looked beyond me to the window.

'There's a coach in the yard. Lord preserve us, it's Sutcliffe. You'd better run, girl.'

I fled the table and stumbled outside. A wooden monstrosity was waiting near the stables.

Lord Sutcliffe's carriage was a patchwork quilt of teak, oak, walnut, mahogany and whatever other woods could be pressed into service. I felt that were I to pull out the proper nail from the proper place, the whole thing would fall open like a box with loose hinges.

His visits were becoming more frequent, and each time he tarried a little longer, claiming the replacement horses were unsuitable or that their harnesses were worn – sending Judd or Matthew back to the stables on one useless errand after another.

'Hallo there!' he called over. I closed my eyes and dug deep to find a smile. Working my mouth into happy shapes was a game I played very well.

I halted a respectful distance from the door. Sutcliffe's withered face peered down at me. Burgundy curtains flapped loosely in a rogue breeze. The door hid him from the neck down.

'Good afternoon, Lord Sutcliffe,' I said. 'You seem in agreeable health today.'

'Pah, I look like a leper and well you know it. Don't lie to me, girl, or you'll feel the hard side of my hand across that mare's behind of yours.' He leaned forward. Loose strands of horsehair poked out of his powdered wig, giving his head the appearance of a white pincushion. 'Or perhaps you'd like that, eh?'

I could feel the blood rushing into my face. Behind my back, my hands curled into fists. I didn't hear what he said next. A full half-minute passed before I could bring myself to look at him again.

How could anyone be so old and still draw

breath? When he moved, his body shuddered the way a tree does on feeling the first bite of the axe. And that carriage must be a hundred years old. Matthew told me it had most likely started life as a simple box thing on wheels. But over the years it had been added to, the way a modest house can sprout granite wings, grand staircases and glass conservatories.

They were well matched, those two. I wondered if he ever stepped outside that tomb on wheels. I wondered if he even had a real body beneath that grizzly, pockmarked chin.

I swallowed. 'And where is m'lord bound today?'

'Oh.' A flick of his lace-cuffed wrist. 'I am merely riding the lanes, watching the traffic and commerce. It amuses me. This is a busy stretch of road, would you not say?'

'Aye, m'lord. Fifty coaches a week or more, not counting the farm wagons and gypsy vans.'

He nodded. 'They tell me it was originally built to take corpses to the parish churchyard.'

'That is true also.'

'Do you suppose my peers would prove so eager to travel this route if they knew it once ferried plague victims?'

'I can't say. It was a very long time ago.'

'No, no of course you cannot say. An urchin like you can hardly be expected to know what the gentry do and do not favour.'

The sharp bite of nails into my palms. 'No, m'lord.'

He perched round spectacles on his nose and peered about the yard. 'They used to hang criminals here, too.'

'Aye, that is how Green Gallows got its name. Our inn sign hangs from the old gibbet. There are other things we keep for novelty – a set of stocks, a scold's bridle. Our visitors find them interesting.'

'Indeed. And where is your pretty sister today?'

I stared at him for a few seconds before answering. 'Lucy is indoors. I think she's practising the spinet.'

'Tell her that I enquired after her, won't you, child?' He flipped a coin out of the window. It landed in the gravel at my feet. A sovereign, a whole sovereign, glittering like dragonfire on the dull ochre chippings.

'Yes m'lord, I will.'

'See that you do. Now fetch your father. I would have words with him.'

I ran, because the sooner Sutcliffe's business was done the sooner he would be off our land. Isaac was at the tradesman's entrance near the back of the kitchens. He and Mother were checking the bread delivery while the flustered baker looked on. For some weeks there had been a suspicion that he was selling us yesterday's loaves while the fresh bread went to the kitchens of Marrin's Hall. Isaac scowled as he sniffed and prodded. When I told him who was waiting he scooped up half a dozen loaves in his big arms and threw them into the dirt.

'Take your mouldy bread and go,' he told the baker. 'Don't bring your wares within half a league of my inn again.'

'B... Beg your pardon, sir,' the tradesman

stammered, 'but I am owed for this past week. Most of that bread was straight from my oven, I swear.'

'You'll not get a penny from me. Be thankful that I don't force you to eat your own rotten food.'

The baker rescued his battered loaves and tossed them into the back of his cart. A few tumbled back onto the dirt as he drove off in a flurry of gravel.

'So,' Isaac declared, wiping his hands on his breeches. 'Lord Sutcliffe wants a word, does he?'

'Why doesn't he come inside?' Mother protested. 'Do our hearth and our wine not suit?'

'Lord Sutcliffe dines, travels and deals in that carriage. You go to him, or you don't do business.'

'And what business could he have with you if it is not our hospitality he wants?'

Isaac stooped and kissed Mother on the cheek. 'A turn in our fortunes, wife, that's what I aim to deal in.'

Judd caught me on the way back across the yard. He stood beside me, thumbs hooked into the waistband of his leather breeches.

'I don't know why Sutcliffe comes here,' I said quietly. 'He's always trying to find fault with the place. How many times will he make you change the horses today, d'you think?'

Judd squinted into the lowering sun and shrugged. 'Oh, once or twice. On his last visit we brought the first team he dismissed back out and hitched them again without his noticing. If it were up to me, I'd have given him the same team he drove in with, 'cept that wouldn't be fair on the horses.'

Any other time I would have laughed but my

stomach felt like lead. I shielded my eyes against the light and stared towards Marrin's Ridge where the treetops bit into the late afternoon sky with rows of jagged, green teeth.

'He tipped me a sovereign. Why do you suppose an old man like that would give someone like me a sovereign?'

Judd placed a hand on my arm. His fist could break a man's jaw but it was like a butterfly landing on my sleeve. 'I wouldn't like to say, lass. The gentry think money can buy them anything. You should know that, and your sister too. Come on now, we've another two stagecoaches coming in before the day is done.'

All that afternoon Isaac remained within the stuffy bowels of Sutcliffe's ancient carriage. His horses were fed and watered, his coach axles greased, the harnesses cleaned and oiled. At five o'clock Hannah went out with a tray of bread, fresh thankfully, and a selection of our best cheeses. The burgundy curtains twitched when she tapped on the crested door. It swung open, the tray disappeared. Hannah returned empty handed.

'Could you see inside?' I asked, grabbing her as she tried to swill out some tankards in the tap-room. 'Does Sutcliffe have no legs as some say?'

She shook free of my grasp. 'Couldn't rightly tell. 'Twas dark and hot, and thick with cigar smoke. A wonder either of them could breathe.'

Around eight o'clock, Isaac climbed out of Sutcliffe's carriage and trudged across the yard. Perspiration slicked his hair and spread dark patches across his shirt. His clothes hung in loose folds as if he had shrunk. Odours clung to him. Spilled wine, stale tobacco. I ached to know what had happened.

'Go tell Judd to hitch Lord Sutcliffe's team,' Isaac ordered me, jerking a thumb towards the stables. 'If you see Hannah, tell her to bring a pail of water upstairs.' He wiped his brow with the back of his hand. 'I need to wash.'

The rest of the evening dragged by. I crawled into my bedchamber, sick with exhaustion, as the last light was leaking out of the sky. I didn't bother to light a candle. Instead I sat on my bed, opposite the cold hearth, and nudged off my shoes. My feet sighed with relief. After a few moments I flicked my tricorne onto the bedpost and padded over to the dresser to pour cold water into the basin. I washed my face of all the muck that I'd picked up in my workings between yard, kitchen and taproom. I scrubbed my hands, crone's hands, all calluses and broken fingernails. I couldn't imagine Lucy having hands like these.

I towelled myself and slipped still-aching feet into my old slippers. My belly wanted supper and wasn't going to let me sleep until it was fed. I shuffled down the hall past the Long Room. Muted conversation and a ripple of laughter came from behind the door. Guests would be smoking, drinking or playing cards. Sometimes, if the inn was full, Isaac hired a quintet and there was dancing until two or three o'clock in the morning. Hannah was most likely in there now, bringing up fresh bottles of port from the cellar or serving pipe fills from the tobacco box. If someone wanted food she would have to open up the kitchen and prepare it herself, Sally having long retired for the night.

A small chamber off the passage served as our family room. Mother was seated by the fire, her back to me, sewing needle glinting in the orange firelight as it dipped in and out of her embroidery. Lucy sat opposite in a tall leather armchair, a book open in her lap. She looked up as I entered and tipped me a very unladylike wink.

'You're late,' Mother said, eyeing me over the top of her sampler.

'Judd asked me to help with the horses,' I replied. 'He had trouble unhitching the team from the Prestbury stage. One of the harnesses got caught and needed to be cut free. The animal grew skittish and had to be coaxed into the stables.'

'Your father tells you what jobs to do and when to do them, not Judd.'

'Yes, Mother.'

'How much did you get today?'

I dipped into my dress pouch and scattered coins across the table top. Mother put down her sewing and pattered over to the table in short, quick steps, like a hen scratching across a farm-yard. 'Is this the lot? From the taproom too?'

'Yes.'

'Mmmm. It will buy a new hairbrush for Lucy.'

'It's mine,' I said, almost in a whisper. 'I earned it.'

'Hoarding money is wrong. Your work pays for your keep. We all have jobs to do, Lucy more than most. Now eat your broth.'

She scooped the coins into her apron and shoved a wooden bowl across the table. Steaming liquid slopped onto the chipped surface. Lucy kept her eyes on her book. A flush had crept into her cheeks.

I ate supper in silence. Vegetable broth was followed by boiled potatoes and a slice of cold beef. I was too hungry to care what I shoved into my mouth. Isaac appeared, bathed and wearing a change of clothes. He dropped a sheaf of papers onto the table. Excitement glimmered in his dark eyes.

'I am expanding Green Gallows,' he declared. 'Bigger stables, more horses and hire carriages, new rooms indoors to accommodate more guests. The kitchen and taproom will have to be extended and extra staff hired to cope. Stableboys, ostlers, chambermaids – even bar wenches to serve ale. We need them all.'

We stared at him. 'Better use will have to be made of our outbuildings,' he continued. 'Perhaps we can turn them into servants' quarters to free up space in here. That shed behind the tack room hasn't seen decent work since I was a lad.'

'Whose scheme was this?' Mother said, dropping her sampler.

'Lord Sutcliffe has a friend in London, a Lord Grays, who is keen to invest money in coaching properties. Bait has also been cast for one or two other investors to nibble. He's confident we'll hook a sizeable catch.'

'And what is your share in these grand designs? How are you to pay for your slice in this rich new pie?'

'Lord Grays is willing to advance a handsome sum, interest free for the first year. Lord Sutcliffe has vouched for me and his word is good in any part of the city.'

'Not without security he won't, so don't try to fudge my head with talk of good names. These men are not your friends. My cousin was a banker and wouldn't risk a penny against a pot of gold without bricks or stock to back it up. A loan is what you are speaking of, Isaac Curtis. You have nothing to your name except Green Gallows, so I daresay it is Green Gallows you are willing to sign away.'

Isaac shrugged. 'Hardly a risk. Lord Grays is a respected man of business and must follow the rules of his trade. He'd be obliged to ask for security against tomorrow's sunrise if it came to it.'

'Take care, husband, that your ambitions don't lose us our home as well as our livelihood.'

'You have ambitions too, Harriet. You've always hankered after a place in society even if you believe society is undeserving of you. If you want to sup off silver and ride around in a landau then save your mockery for those women who will one day be beneath you. We have to work towards prosperity and sometimes that means taking risks. A thriving business will also better Lucy's chances of catching the right husband.'

'Your head is as empty as your pocket. Ashes, that's all your hopes will turn into. You will sweat and bleed and spend, and have nothing to show for it but empty stables and empty beds.'

'This will be the best coaching inn between London and the coast. Expansion will improve our trade – bring us the custom we deserve. The London *Charger* will stop here. I swore to my father that I'd see the day when it would, and it'll be my doing. Mine. Why don't you believe in me, Harriet? It's what you wanted, ain't it?'

'Ain't it.' Mother shook her head. 'Listen to you. A glint of gold and you're talking like a ploughboy. We could give up our beds, empty our cellar, pave our stable yard with silver shillings and the *Charger* would still throw mud in your face. A highwayman couldn't stop that coach. The last one who tried got a belly full of shot and a rope around his neck at Tyburn.'

'Face the truth, Harriet. This proves that the turnpike was just a rumour. I've been talking to Gregor and he agrees. The South Road has always been at the heart of travel in this county.'

'Gregor will say anything to please you if he thinks there is a free tankard of ale at the end of it.'

'I give the drivers free food and ale to encourage them to stop their coaches here. The practice is well known.'

'And how do you know they wouldn't stop anyway?'

They talked like this for a while longer. Lucy seemed to be trying to push herself into the back of her armchair. I prodded the last of my supper around the plate. This was not like their other arguments where Isaac always told Mother to go and boil herself, then gave in and did just what she wanted. I was reminded of a brittle old oak standing in a gale which, unable to bend, eventually snapped.

'Green Gallows will grow,' he said. 'We can either grow prosperous with it or wither away like unwatered weeds. You can't win a shilling without first gambling a penny.'

'Even if it is our last penny?'

Isaac put his hand on Mother's shoulder. 'It won't come to that. You'll see.'

Chapter Two

I woke, blinking, into a plank of sunlight thrown across my room from the narrow window above my bed. The mantel clock said half past eight. I had slept late but it was Sunday with no coach until noon.

I swung my feet out of bed, splashed my face with some stale water from the ewer and shrugged into a serving gown. Sunday morning brought a special peace. Most guests were still in bed sleeping off last night's party. Only the most pious hired a horse for morning service at Prestbury parish church.

I slipped into the hall and glanced up the stairs towards Lucy's room. The door hung ajar.

Every Sabbath Judd drove Lucy, Mother and Isaac to church in one of the post chaises, with Matthew and Sally following in the curricle. No one pressed me to go. Parson Buseridge's sermons sent parishioners to sleep but the women liked to gossip in his churchyard. While they swapped stories, Isaac hung around the tombstones drumming up business, sniffing around for a good deal on a horse or barrel of ale. They wouldn't be back until ten o' clock at the earliest.

Going to church with Mother was an ordeal and I ducked out whenever I could. After the service she always promenaded between the gravestones, twirling the parasol Isaac had bought her. Ladies smiled and nodded when she spoke to them. In the carriage afterwards she was full of, 'Oh Mrs Updike said this and Mrs Musgrove told me such and such.' But she only ever heard what they said with their mouths, never noticing the stories their eyes told or the slow, spreading smiles behind their gently wafting fans.

If I'd said anything Mother would have cuffed my ear, told me not be foolish then gone and cried her eyes out for the rest of the day. And next Sabbath there would have been a terrible scene for Mother wasn't one to let things lie (not even the dead, someone once joked) and it would all have fallen down around Isaac's ears and, eventually, mine.

I put a foot on the bottom step.

You can't go up there, I told myself. *You can't. Lucy will find out. Don't know how but she will. You don't go into her room. Ever. You wouldn't like it if she sneaked into yours.*

I fled into the kitchen to breakfast on whatever leftovers had been brought in from the Long Room. Isaac didn't mind if the servants helped themselves. 'Too good for the dogs,' he said, 'and it saves me a few pennies if I don't have to fill the maids' bellies once in a while.'

I stuffed my face on cheese, cold ham and soggy lettuce. Guests never left cakes or sweetmeats. What they couldn't eat, they pinched. One visitor was so keen on Sally's raspberry flan he stuffed it, cream topping and all, down the front of his velvet riding jacket.

After washing the food down with half a mug of flat ale I checked the taproom, the yard and the stables. One or two private carriages might pull in before the morning was over.

Green Gallows squatted heavily in the gathering heat. Insects buzzed. I batted at a wasp that got too close to my nose. I couldn't get my mind off Lucy's open bedroom door. It was usually locked when she was out. Though she could sleep wherever she chose, that was her private place. A quick peek through the door would be enough. I didn't have to put a foot inside. 'Were you in my bedchamber?' she could ask and I'd put my hand over my heart and say, 'No, not at all.'

I scurried back inside and ran up the stairs. I pushed. The door whispered wide on oiled hinges.

There was the four-poster, swathed in muslin. Flowered wallpaper, lemon yellow drapes, a full-length looking glass peering at me from one corner. At the foot of her bed, a small engraved walnut chest. Lucy's Happy Box. Whenever she was feeling glad she wrote down all her good feelings and locked them away. If she woke up melancholy or had a difficult day she opened the box and took something out. A snippet of a love song. A snatch of a poem. Often just single scribbled words like 'love' or 'laughter'. Sometimes she brought it into the parlour or sat with it in the paddock if the weather was good.

'I promised myself that I would try to add something every day,' she told me. 'At the end of my life I want a hundred Happy Boxes, perhaps a thousand, filling every room in my house. You should have one, Rachel.'

I suggested it to Isaac. 'A Miserable Box would suit you better,' he said, laughing.

My gaze flicked over to the wardrobe taking up most of one wall. I stepped into the room. She was my sister. It wasn't as if I was going to steal anything.

I tugged at the catch and moved back as the door swung open, revealing a rainbow of velvets, silks and taffeta. I plucked out a gown. Red velvet whispered through my hands. My fingers were trembling.

I pulled off my garments. The cotton petticoat snagged on the corner of the dresser and tore. Impatiently I tossed it over the back of a chair, unfastened my stays and shrugged them onto the sheepskin rug. My skin tingled. I wanted to feel it, feel that lovely, gossamer material against my bare flesh without a petticoat or corset getting in the way. I stepped into Lucy's gown and slid it up over my shoulders. I was taller than her and the hem lifted well above my ankles, but I didn't care. Matching my sister's waspish waist was impossible. Even with my stomach sucked in I could only manage half the fastenings.

I admired myself in the tall looking-glass. It was like stuffing a potato into an eggshell but I was convinced that kings and princes would fall breathless at my feet. I had always been proud of my long black hair. 'Lizabeth sometimes gave it a tug and called it a witch's thatch. 'Just like the feathers of a rook, Rachel. One day I'll pull it all out by the roots.' I believed she would do it too.

'Lizabeth had a way of looking that made you believe.

'What are you doing?'

I spun round. Mother, still in her best Sunday clothes, stood in the doorway. Her face was a thunderstorm. I hadn't heard her carriage in the yard. I found out later that she'd left the service early with a headache and had ridden back on Farmer Blankerton's gig. (Only time you'll catch me in church, Bill Blankerton once said, is at my own funeral.) He'd dropped her off by the gate.

'Nothing. I only wanted to try it on, to see if it suited me.'

''Tis bad enough I have to lose one daughter to this frippery without you willingly following suit. Take it off and get out of your sister's bed-chamber.'

'No.' I took a step backwards. 'Lucy has all the nice things.'

Mother strode across the room, her fingers hooking into claws. I hugged myself for protection, squashing the precious velvet. She made a grab for the top of the stomacher but I twisted away.

'No!'

I'd seen Mother in a temper before but this time I thought she'd lost her wits. She got me out of the dress all right. She pushed me onto the floor and tipped me out of it as though she was emptying a sack of oatmeal. The garment ripped in at least three places. I scrambled to my feet, snatched up my old clothes and fled the room.

Lucy found me in the scullery, sitting on an upturned pail and nursing a fat lip.

'Don't wear my clothes again,' she said.

'Are you going to shove me around too?' I asked bitterly.

She spread out an empty flour sack and knelt beside me, slipping her cool fingers into my hand. 'Tears don't suit you,' she said gently. 'You like my clothes? Let me tell you, they're a prison. I'd burn them all if I could.'

'I only wanted to look pretty.' I gazed into her face. 'To look like you.'

'Pretty? Yes I'm pretty and that's all Mother and Father think about. I'm not sure what I really look like any more, under all the rouge and powder.' She smiled thinly. 'Perhaps we *should* exchange clothes. You can stay here and look all grand while I run out of the gate.'

I fingered my cheek. 'Look at what she did to me.'

'I heard her in the parlour crying. She's afraid, that's all. Your face will get better. Come on,' she helped me up, 'I don't have to play the spinet today, and Father is talking to some men who rode back with us from church. We can go to the meadow by the pond. We're not wanted, either of us, this morning. We can be together for a while.'

Being together with Lucy was something I had to fight for. I didn't have much in the way of friends. The children at Marrin's Hall were too busy being little lords and ladies. Prestbury, the nearest village, was two miles down the lykeway. My life was full of come-and-go people.

Many summers ago Lucy found an old harness buried under some sacking in the corner of the coach house. We scampered across the yard to where some empty barrels were stacked up outside the back of the taproom. Together, we rolled four of them together to serve as wheels and laid half a dozen planks on top. A carriage fit for the King. We spent an hour or more hitching and unhitching imaginary teams, taking it in turn to be driver, horsemaster or pampered passenger. Lucy even wore her cloak inside out and pretended to be a ruthless highwayman while I, as lady of the largest estate in England, begged him to take my jewels but spare my virtue. Then, in a sudden change of role, I became a dashing hero intent on saving the coach and its unworthy occupants. Lucy and I grappled with one another in the dirt, growling threats and brandishing imaginary pistols. Finally we collapsed, laughing, into one another's arms. We spent the rest of that day scrubbing our faces and trying to shake the dirt out of our petticoats.

I was usually the one who took the lead in these games. If I told Lucy to jump in the pond I'm sure she'd do it. We spent all those childhood days together yet most of the time I had no notion of what went on inside her head. If I questioned her she'd let out little snippets of herself, like snatched glimpses through a window.

Then she went away.

Isaac tried to explain it to me, a difficult task for someone who spent his life shouting at the world as if it was something he could wring by the neck until whatever he wanted fell out of its pockets. He was a big man. The biggest man I ever knew. He filled my vision, smothered me in shadows. I only felt the sun's rays when he stepped aside. Squat neck, round barrel-bottom chin squaring off as it rose to the dark, close-cropped plateau that was his head. Dark-skinned too, like a gypsy, though he'd kill any man who said so. His mouth never smiled, never seemed to move even when he talked. I was often afraid of him, afraid of his black eyes. But in his company I was afraid of nothing else.

Lucy had not physically gone. She was still at the dinner table or in front of the parlour fire, or walking with Mother around the grounds. But my Lucy had been snatched away and replaced with some starched-faced poppet buried in embroidery and books in Greek or Latin. All because of something one of our guests said. A politician from London who'd come south to check on his rotten borough. Lucy had brought his valise out from the Long Room. He cupped her chin, gazed into her blue eyes with a father's love and said, 'An angel is what you are. One day you'll marry someone fine and take supper with princes. Mark my words. If I had a son I'd marry him off to you myself.'

That was the start of it. The more charming Lucy became the more the gentry loved her, the way they'd love one of those pampered pups ladies sometimes liked to keep on their laps.

Some sort of thorn seed stuck its barbs into Isaac's head, its thickening roots slowly strangling his mind.

Robbed of Lucy, I stomped around the yard, pretending to be Isaac, barking orders, cuffing the ears of imaginary post-boys, dealing in meat and brandy – wringing the best prices out of tradesmen who prided themselves on their own cunning. I didn't know whether Isaac really loved me.

Sometimes it was difficult to imagine any feelings at all lurking under that tree trunk of a body. I pictured those big arms encircling Mother's waist, drawing her in for a rare embrace. And Mother snapping in two like a dry twig.

I didn't hear much of what he tried to tell me that day. I loved my sister. And I missed her. When I wanted to play I was told that Lucy was practising the spinet, or improving her dancing, or had a sampler to finish in the parlour. We had to steal moments together like secret lovers.

The pond lay in a cleft punched into the chalky soil of the paddock. A ringlet of spindly trees surrounded it like a tuft of hair on an otherwise bald head. Jutting out from one side were the grey, brittle bones of a jetty, fifty years old or more. Its purpose was long forgotten as there was no place to send a boat, and nothing to fish for in the pond's murky depths save frogs and dragonfly larvae. There was never a time, even in the crystal depths of winter, when the waters turned clear. An inch from the reed-choked bank and it was impossible to see the bottom. Summer turned it into a green-topped sludge. Flies wheeled and dipped in fuzzy black clouds. Matthew teased me by saying that if you fell in, the murky waters would drag you down into the bowels of the earth.

Usually I strolled up the slope and crossed the grazing paddock, a small field that marked the edge of our property. Most of the gentry in these parts could stand at one end of their land and not see halfway to the other. But here I could perch on the drystone wall and view acres of farmland, an ocean of greens, golds or browns, depending on the season. And the lane, a dark artery cutting southwards through the sward. Winter brought the clearest days with air sharp enough to cut your lungs. The muggy veil lifted off the fields and the world suddenly became big enough to make my head swim.

'Mother was in a foul temper before the service began,' Lucy explained as we stood, hands linked, beside the pond. 'Lady Marrin baited her in front of the parson and Father nearly got into a fight with the Marrins' coachman over it. You know how he blusters.'

I nodded. Lady Marrin's tongue could slice hearts and reputations apart with ease. 'They ought to put a scold's bridle on her,' I said. 'What hat or gown was it over this time?'

Blue ribbons rustled like dried leaves as Lucy shook her head. 'Father was bragging about his plans for Green Gallows. Lady Marrin suggested to Mother that he might not make such a show of it once the turnpike opened to traffic. She spoke to her as if she was a kitchen maid.'

'Ouch.'

'Yes, I know. You can imagine the look on Mother's face. Worse, Father overheard. He told Lady Marrin that Mother had every right to feel pleased. Their coachman warned Father to respect his betters or he'd get a whip across his back. Father invited him to try it and I thought they would start a ruckus right there in the churchyard. Everyone turned to stare. All over a stupid road that's not even going to be built.'

I studied Lucy's face under the rim of her bonnet. Blue eyes blinked in the pollen-choked air. She could not scent the danger. She would not share the worry that tightened the corners of Isaac's mouth and had him out working before dawn, checking everything before the ostlers had roused from their beds above the coach house. A stupid road she'd called it. Yet every coach brought fresh rumours. The Trust had already been formed, some said. Plans were in hand to lift the first sod at the beginning of August to get the work done quickly while the season was still kind. Toll-booths would be in place by October or Christmas at the latest. New roadhouses and posting inns would sprout up.

Judd shrugged them off. 'Stories,' he said, parroting Isaac. 'Tales to keep tongues oiled and heads empty.' But there was concern in his eyes too.

Lucy swooped down and plucked a daisy from its green nest. She stroked its tiny petals. 'Let's cool our feet in the water,' she said.

We kicked off our shoes, hitched up our skirts and sat on the bank, letting our feet dangle, stockings and all, into the brackish water. Tiny minnows squirmed around our ankles. Lucy squealed. Catching her mood, I let go of my skirts. Petticoats wafted like white clouds into the dark water.

'Mama will go radish if you return home in a wet gown,' Lucy warned.

I didn't reply, revelling in the soft coolness between my toes. Impulsively I swept cupped fingers through the water and brought up a dark, wriggling raindrop that tickled my palm in its bid to flee the tiny pink pond which had for a moment become its new world.

I held it up to the sunlight. Golden teardrops showered from my fingers. Lucy sploshed over, made ungainly at last by the water, and peered into my hands.

'Let it go.'

'I will, in a moment.'

'Let it go. I hate to see anything trapped.'

Some unspoken feeling chiselled her face. I lowered my hands into the water and let my fingers flower open. The minnow wriggled off into the reeds. Lucy watched it go. Her features softened. 'Sorry,' she said.

Later, sitting soggy and contented on a soft patch of grass, we made garlands out of summer flowers. 'This will soothe Mother's temper,' Lucy said, her gown encircled by blooms.

'Lord Sutcliffe asked after you yesterday.'

A grimace. 'Hannah warned me that his coach had pulled in. I was an ace away from hiding in the linen cupboard. What did he want this time?'

'He was just being nosy. I was in no mood for chat.'

'Did you see inside his carriage? Have you found out what he keeps behind those drawn curtains?'

I shook my head. 'I'd sooner put my leg in a gin trap than go near that awful thing.'

Lucy gazed across the meadow. 'You can smell his coach when the wind is right, even before it hoves into view. A horrible stink of soiled linen, stale food and dried-out leather. Old men always smell like that, have you noticed?'

We spoke in guilty whispers though we had only flowers and insects for eavesdroppers. I had the better of Lucy because I heard the stories fresh from the London coaches.

'They say he never leaves his carriage. A footman takes out a pot and fetches it back once it's full. He owns a house in which no one lives except servants, while his coach is parked in the stable yard with him eating, sleeping and who-knows-what else inside. I've heard that when Sutcliffe dies his men have orders to nail the doors shut, board the windows and brick him up – carriage and all – inside his own stable. It will become his tomb.'

'But why does he never leave it? Are his legs as bad as they say?'

I leaned forward. 'I doubt he's walked more than a hundred paces in any one go. He eats and drinks too much in that stuffy wooden hole, and doesn't care if idleness leaves his legs rotten with gout. He's poxed too, that's no secret. Gregor said his coach is often spied near the London docks where the Bad Women are.'

'But why does he shut himself in there? Answer me, Rachel. Don't tease.'

I picked at my flower chain for a few moments. 'As a lad he was walking across some open fields on his father's estate in Sussex. It was December and he wasn't supposed to be out on his own, though rumour had it he'd slipped off to visit a farmer's girl he'd fallen for, a love affair for which his family would have disowned him. A blizzard got up, heavy, not often seen here in the South. The world turned completely white. Nothing to be seen in any direction. Young Sutcliffe didn't know up from down. Nothing but emptiness and silence in all directions. He called out but the snow just swallowed up his words. Imagine it Lucy, totally lost and alone. A boy who'd always had the best of everything. How terrifying it must've been.'

'What happened? Tell me.'

'The gamekeeper's dogs sniffed him out less than half a mile from the house. He must have stumbled around in circles for an hour or more. They found him curled up on the ground sobbing for his mama, and her more than six years in her grave. The cold had got to his legs so they had to carry him home. Another half-hour, the surgeon said, and he would have frozen to death. As it was he caught a fever in his limbs that had him bedridden for a month. Afterwards he refused to leave his bedchamber. Nothing could be done to coax or bully him out. The surgeon said that it was just in his head, that he would get over it in time, though his legs would be weak for the rest of his life. Sutcliffe's father, a strong man in both body and will, gave up on his son in disgust. But the father died less than two years later, thrown from a horse, and the son inherited everything. Now he travels up and down the country in that coffin on wheels, never leaving it. Some say he doesn't bathe or change his clothes. Once a week he lets his driver inside to sweep out all the rubbish.'

'I don't like the way he keeps touching me,' Lucy protested. 'Any excuse and his fingers are there – on my hand, my chin, brushing my cheek, tickling my ear. Father keeps sending me out to speak to him. His eyes are like two mouths, roving over my body, eating me up bite by bite.'

'Is an old person's touch so horrible?'

'No. Of course not. Most are as tender as babies. But him? It's like getting scratched by tree bark. I wish he would leave me alone. I wish someone *would* nail him up in that old coach and drive him away from here for good.'

Lucy had a right to feel irked. Sutcliffe didn't need to come here. He was always drawn by a team of six. More than enough to take him to the next posting house, or perhaps even all the way to the coast without a change.

She knitted the last stems together and held up her garland for inspection.

'Yours is by far the prettier,' she admitted. 'Mother is sure to love it.'

We took them inside. Praise for Lucy's ragged effort, which Mother immediately draped around her shoulders. Then she saw my necklace. The smile that lit up her face was so rare, so genuine, I thought my heart would burst. She tried to give us a ticking off for our damp gowns but it was hopeless and we all knew it.

Later I found our handiwork amidst the stale food, offal and broken barrels littering the yard outside the kitchen door. The chains were broken, the blooms fractured. I don't know what had happened. Mother worked hard, as hard as Isaac most days. Perhaps he wouldn't let her wear them around the inn. She wouldn't have just thrown them away. Would she?

Lucy rescued the remains. She sat on the patch of grass behind the stables and smoothed out the bruised petals. Then, with a steady hand, she threaded the stems back together until our necklaces were whole again. She wore them to supper that evening. Not a word was said. I never loved my sister as much as I did that day. Lucy in her best clothes, wearing my dandelion necklace as a queen might parade rubies and sapphires.

That night, long after Isaac's heavy tread had thumped across the ceiling to bed, she slipped into my room and shook me gently awake. Finger to lips in the semi-gloom, she took my hand and stole me away to the forbidden territory of upstairs. We were pale, fluttering moths in white cotton nightshifts, scampering barefoot across polished boards until – here! – Lucy halted outside the finest room in the inn, reserved for the very cream of the gentry.

She held the key in her small palm, letting me glimpse the glimmering brass treasure before slipping it into the dark mouth of the lock. One silent twist granted us entry.

That night I lay in sisterly warmth, locked within Lucy's arms. We whispered secrets within a four-postered palace, a rippling sky of indigo velvet above our heads.

'I envy you, Rachel,' Lucy murmured into my disbelieving ear. 'You can be whoever you want, do whatever you wish and no one will care. I dance like a marionette to Mama and Papa's every whim. They have stuffed my head full of Latin and music. I can quote the greatest poets and eat at the dinner table as though my knife and fork were made of silver instead of pewter. They think that just because they have forgotten that I am an innkeeper's daughter other people will too.'

Seduced by silken sheets and the soft feather pillow beneath my cheek, I only half heard her. For once I was led willingly, not dragged by exhaustion, into sleep. Lucy may have said something more but the darkness snatched her words away.

I wasn't naive enough to believe my sister would share all her inner rooms, the entire sprawling mansion that comprised her life. I never resented that. She was a private creature, full of will-o-the-wisp thoughts and flitting shadows. But one door she firmly slammed in my face. That door was called Jeremiah Cathcart, the muddy-cheeked bastard son of a ruined farmer. He walked barefoot into our stable yard one wet August morning to beg a job, any job even if it meant shovelling shit out of the stalls from noon to midnight.

'Ain't none in our village will take me in a respectable trade,' he explained. 'Thirty miles I've walked for the chance of honest work. I'm good with my hands. I don't each much and I'll sleep in your stables.'

He showed Isaac the cuts and blisters on the soles of his feet. I stared in awe at this brute. His eyes caught mine, wide mouth breaking into a grin. Not here the foul-breathed jumble of rotting tombstones that filled the mouths of common folk. His teeth gleamed like polished ivory and his lips were soft and full. A thick mat of brown hair sprouted from beneath his felt hat. Eyebrows grew in a wiry hedge across the ridge of his forehead. And the eyes themselves? Now there was a place to lose oneself. Eyes that at first glance seemed half-sleepy, the lids drooping over twin pearls of polished jet. Swim in those waters and you'd drown quickly enough.

He was a young man, maybe not even twenty, yet a sliver of grey threaded through his hair just above the temple. He gestured with both hands as he spoke. Palms were gnarled bark, his fingers wind-stripped twigs. Hands that had never known a day's rest from hard, bitter work. I imagined them gently stroking my bare arm, or a callused fingertip chasing the line of my jaw. It had never taken much to bring the blood to my cheeks. As Jeremiah stood pleading his case to Isaac, I dawdled in the yard, staring at my battered slippers. When he smiled at me I felt as if I'd been stabbed.

Now here's a dangerous one, the growing-up part of me thought. *A smile like that could do a lot of mischief.*

Judd stood by, listening carefully, sometimes nodding. I didn't know how Isaac's mood would turn. He might send this Jeremiah Cathcart packing into the lane.

Let him stay. Oh please let him stay.

Isaac silenced Jeremiah with an impatient gesture. 'Tuppence a day and your keep in the tack room behind the stables. In bad weather you sleep with the horses. Take it or leave it. I ain't a charity and there's not so much work that I have real need of you.'

Jeremiah tugged the brim of his hat. All that morning the yard echoed with the tireless slap of his bare feet. He mucked out, changed the straw, did the jobs that no one else wanted. Too proud to take the boots Judd offered him, to wear anything he had not earned with his own hard sweat.

I fluttered around the stable yard like a green-gowned moth, hoping always for another glimpse of him amidst the endless rumblings and chatter that was daily life at Green Gallows. I opened carriage doors. I placed footstools. I took the satin-gloved hands of ladies, pretty and poxed alike, and helped guide their pearled slippers onto our soil.

Gregor rumbled in on the stage, a stream of rank smoke leaking from the oversize pipe he sometimes smoked while driving. Sammy was perched, coat flapping, on the seat beside him. A blunderbuss was slung loosely under one arm. When the carriage hove to he vaulted onto the roof and started passing down luggage.

I helped my charges, pocketed my pennies, and saw them safely into the inn. I returned, coins jingling, to find Gregor alone with the carriage. Matthew had already unharnessed the team.

'Where's Sammy?' I asked.

'Sent him into the taproom for an ale. His throat's so dry it sounded like rocks grinding together whenever he spoke. Drove me half out of my mind.'

I glanced across the yard. Jeremiah had been set to work clearing the nettles away from the coach-house wall: a forest of stinging green that would have taken a gang of men an hour at best to dig out. He'd stripped off his leather jerkin. Snatches of wiry torso peeped through ragged holes in his shirt. His brow was pinched in concentration as he plunged the spade into the unyielding soil.

I ran my tongue along my lower lip. 'Gregor, might I ask you something?'

'Aye, sure.'

'Am I pretty?'

Shadows rippled across his face. Somewhere beyond the line of trees a jackdaw was cawing.

'Of course you are. As pretty as a blossom.'

I dropped my hat into the dirt. 'Don't fib. You waited too long before answering. Enough to tell me you don't mean what you say. That, and the look in your eyes.'

I was going to start crying but I was too upset and too sick of myself to care what he thought any more. I felt ugly and stupid. Donkey Rachel, turnip brain, face that could crack a china plate. I wallowed in my wretchedness.

'Wait now.' Gregor vaulted off the driver's seat, his booted feet landing with a soft thud on the packed gravel. I tried to turn away but he caught my shoulder with a leather-gauntleted hand. 'What's brought this on?'

'Let me go.' I squirmed.

Gregor sighed. 'All right, you want me to be honest? Think about it, Rachel. You gorge yourself on roast beef and mutton pie. You don't wash or brush your hair so it turns to greasy string. You walk like a duck instead of a lady and get covered in shit from the stables. Even your breath could kill a horse. All these things can be fixed, Rachel. But you've got to want to fix 'em.'

'Mother will be upset if I try to ape Lucy. I sometimes think she wants me ugly so Lucy will look all the prettier.'

Gregor shook his head. 'I've known your mama for years. She's a hard woman but she don't hate you and it's wrong to think ill of her. What started all this anyhow? Some lad caught your eye?'

I swallowed hard and stared at his boots. I was scared he would laugh but that wasn't Gregor's way. 'Look,' he said, 'Here's the *Charger* just crested Marrin's Ridge. Best go, else they'll wonder what's become of you.'

I was grateful for the escape and dashed for the gate. There was no fence here. Instead the ground formed a six-foot-high grassy embankment which ran into the ditch at the side of the lane. Every weekday I scrambled to the top, ready to wave and wave until my hands felt as if they would fly away from my wrists like swallows.

The London to Portsmouth coach, which was pulled by six horses and never stopped, ever. A walnut-panelled clatter of wheels and hooves, groaning under the weight of travellers and far-bound, leather trunks.

Every day it passed and every day I stood in the same place, in all weathers, smiling like a happy idiot. Once, in the pouring rain, I even dipped a cheeky curtsy in my sodden gown.

'You'll go down with a fever,' Mother warned, 'then burden us all with coughing fits. Stay away from the lane. You'll make fools of us all.'

'Where's the harm in it?' Isaac had said, supping a long draught of ale from his tankard. 'Who's to say that grin won't bring the *Charger* in one day?'

The sharp crack of a whip. The thunder of hooves. I stood tiptoe, craning my neck. Six horses let loose and galloping for their lives. Another second and they rounded the curve in the lane, wide-eyed and foaming with sweat, the whip flicking expertly above their backs. Light caught the walnut panels so that they shone like burnished gold. A storm of dirt billowed along in its wake. It seemed as if the very ground it passed over had caught fire.

I stared as it ate up the distance between us. The *Charger* seemed to fly above rucks and potholes, moving smoothly on well-oiled metal springs, not the creaky leather straps on which the older coaches wallowed. And it had come all the way from London. The biggest city in the country. Perhaps even the world.

I jumped up and down like an excited child at the local fair. My tricorne tumbled from my head. Hair fell unheeded around my face. The *Charger* seemed even bigger than before. A whole shipload of passengers was perched on top, hats tied to their heads with scarves or stuffed under their arms. Most seemed too intent on clinging to their places to notice me, but I waved anyway.

Now close enough to almost touch. The driver's coachman shifted on his perch, one hand resting on the butt of his musket. He eyed me warily, perhaps thinking me a beggar or a highwayman's doxy sent to distract him from the danger ahead. I had an instant to glimpse the powdered faces of the travellers inside. Clumps of dried mud struck the embankment and rolled down into the ditch. One or two landed at my feet. My mouth and nostrils filled with grit.

It was gone.

I lingered as the hoof beats receded into the distance. They had not stopped. They had not waved back. No one had even smiled.

'A waste of time,' Judd once said, shaking his head. 'They'll not wait for you, lass, whatever Isaac might think.'

I scooped up my hat from where it lay on the

grass and scrambled back down the embankment. Gnats fluttered around my head in a whining cloud.

'They will stop,' I whispered. 'One day.'

For the rest of the afternoon I dunced my coach duties, earning curses instead of pennies. One lady passenger stumbled on the step because I let go of her hand too soon. Only her husband's quick thinking and firm grasp stopped her tumbling face first into the dirt.

'You stupid lump of a girl,' she bawled, face colouring even beneath the layers of powder. 'My heel has snapped, and on my best pair of slippers. I'll have that out of the price of my accommodations.'

I tried to help but she smacked me across the arm with the hilt of her fan. 'Get off. Get off me. Josiah, give me your arm. Take me away from this creature.'

She walked lopsidedly across the yard, clinging grim-faced to her husband. I dissolved into thick, gulping tears. Judd, having supervised the unhitching of the team, ambled over. 'Go and help Matthew in the tack room,' he said. 'You can't do any good out here today.'

I tarried beside the coach. 'That woman will tell Isaac what happened. I'll fetch a thump. He'll take my dress away and I won't be allowed to greet the coaches again. 'Tis all I have, Judd. I don't want to work in the taproom all day.'

'Women like her have a hundred pairs of slippers. She's angry because you made her notice you and the gentry don't like to notice common folk until it suits them. I wouldn't fret. Now go and help Matthew.'

The sun was throwing long shadows across the yard when I finished in the stables. Beside the coach house the forest of nettles had been dug out and cleared away. Fresh whitewash was already drying on the stonework.

Jeremiah was crossing the yard, a sack of oats slung loosely over one shoulder, when Mother and Lucy rounded the corner of the inn. They had been walking in their pretty gowns and shawls. Lucy held a parasol. Crimson ribbons fluttered from her straw bonnet. Mother had her fan open, a bone-handled fancy with coloured pictures printed on the thin material. Flies, attracted to her scent, buzzed around her head. She swatted them absently.

The walk was a regular afternoon ritual. Green Gallows lacked the sprawling gardens, fountains and sculpted arbours of Marrin's Hall. The lane was always treacherous, the paddock peppered with horse dung. Lucy and Mother had to stick close to the inn. Quite the little rabbit track they had worn with all their strolling.

Jeremiah halted. He slid the sack off his shoulder and dropped it onto the ground. He pushed back his cap and wiped the perspiration from his brow with a wire-muscled forearm.

Lucy glanced at him, looked away, then found him with her eyes again. Jeremiah caught her gaze. His chest swelled as breath filled his lungs. I heard a soft, low sound like stream water running over sand.

Lucy's face turned carrot-red. Her normally blue eyes had widened into shining black pennies.

The air in the yard thickened and turned suffocatingly hot. Tongues of lightning seemed to flicker over the few yards of gravel separating them.

The exchange couldn't have lasted more than a second. Jeremiah was already swinging the bulging sack back onto his shoulder. Lucy had begun to fiddle with the handle of her parasol. She followed Mother inside.

Last job of the day was to take water into the stables. This was an hour before I could expect supper and my belly was growling like a demon as I lugged a brimming pail across the yard. Jeremiah was already inside laying fresh straw out in the stalls. I was looking forward to asking him about his day. He had worked so hard.

Halfway across, Lucy called to me from the porch. I put the bucket down, frowning. Water slopped over the edge and splashed onto the dirt. I wiped my pinched hands on the front of my apron.

She ran over in a flurry of petticoats. 'Let me take it,' she said. 'You have done enough for today.'

'No more than usual,' I retorted.

Her fingers were already reaching for the handle. 'Sally will need you in the kitchen and the evening stage to Portsmouth is due within the half-hour. Is that not so?'

It was so, but to have Lucy lecture me about coaches was like having a scullery maid preach religion to the parson. I eyed her critically. She was wearing one of her prettiest gowns, a confection of saffron velvet and cherry satin bows. The white curls of a powdered wig cascaded from beneath the generous brim of a feathered bonnet.

Rouge made bright apples of her cheeks.

'You're not dressed for humping buckets around. Aren't you afraid of blistering your hands?'

'I can do what I please,' Lucy replied tartly. 'And it pleases me to help in the stables.'

I glanced across the yard. Judd had taken a pair of skewbalds to the smithy at Prestbury to have them reshod and Matthew had gone with the wagon to stock up on feed. The other two lads were up in the paddock warming up the team for the Portsmouth stage.

'Fine, but if you're going in there then I'm coming too.'

I reached the stables first, the bucket forgotten. Lucy couldn't run in those satin vices Isaac made her wear and her petticoats dragged on the gravel. Jeremiah had his back to me. He was whispering something to the horse, one big hand stroking its flank. I batted a fly that seemed hell bent on buzzing inside my ear. Jeremiah turned at the sound, eyes widening as they settled on me. His other hand reached for his forelock then stopped as he took in my battered dress and the scuffed shoes peeking from under the hem. Or perhaps it was the way I stood, legs apart, hands on hips, hair falling in oily black rivulets over my shoulders. Isaac once joked that I had a face fit to frighten a hunting dog when my temper was up.

Lucy arrived, a gasping bundle of lace and ribbon. Now there was no hesitation. Jeremiah gave her a respectful nod.

'Miss.'

I stepped between them. 'I'm not her servant,

you know.'

Uncertainty flickered across his face. He glanced at me then stared past my shoulder at Lucy.

'This is Rachel,' she explained, a smile in her voice.

He smiled back. I wanted to thump him. 'Mr Isaac Curtis is landlord here,' I blurted. 'We are both his daughters so you can show a bit of respect to me too.'

He guffawed. 'Very well, m'lady.' Turning to me he bowed low but his eyes quickly settled on Lucy again. 'Jeremiah's my name. Jeremiah Cathcart.'

'Well, Jeremiah Cathcart,' Lucy said, 'do you know much about horses?'

'A bit,' he admitted after a pause. 'My pa kept a couple of old nags but I wanted to work in proper stables, wear riding boots, maybe one day be a horsemaster or groom.'

'A groom? You'd like that, would you, Jeremiah Cathcart?'

He gazed at her levelly. She matched his stare, tossing her head back so that her yellow tresses tumbled off one shoulder. Jeremiah reddened. He probably did have a lot to learn and not just about horses. I suspected that as a lad he had felt the thick side of his father's hand too often. It was in his face, simmering resentfully beneath those dark eyes.

'Yes I would,' he said.

I snorted. 'A farmer's boy.'

His eyebrows arched. 'You've a sharp tongue. I didn't think you the type.'

Lucy chuckled brightly. Such an innocent sound yet it drove spikes into my rapidly spoiling humour. 'And what type would I strike you as?' I retorted, blushing to my roots. 'Weak? Flabby? A half-wit? If so you'd best get used to my empty head because you'll see enough of it if you go on working here.'

He regarded me darkly for a moment, a handful of oats clutched in his fist. Lucy had stopped laughing and was watching us. I stood my ground, fuming.

'You've left a bucket out there in the yard,' he said. 'Perhaps you'd best go and fetch it.'

Both stood there looking at me expectantly. Of course I had to go and get it. My job, as I had said. I walked out of the stables thinking that if either one of them so much as snickered I would die right there on my feet. It was a horribly long walk to get that pail. I had never felt so much a girl and so less a woman in all my life.

I took the bucket, dumped it outside the stable door and ran inside the inn. It was half an hour before Lucy returned. Each long minute screamed inside my head. She came through the door with her bonnet off and her rouge smeared. I caught her in the hall, grabbed her arm.

'Isaac won't like it,' I said. 'You know what I'm talking about, Lucy.'

She shook herself free. Her voice was almost a whisper. 'Best keep your mind on the coaches then, hadn't you?'

Chapter Three

I had a feeling the day was going to start badly and I wasn't disappointed. Isaac had an argument with a passenger from Gregor's stage. Sailor Ben, no less. Both men had a knack for scratching one another's temper.

'You'd do well to sort your politics out, sir,' Ben said.

'My business is innkeeping, not government,' Isaac growled. 'Kindly leave your own politics at the gate.'

'I hear Lord Grays is visiting these parts at the end of the week. He is a staunch Whig. He will not be too well disposed to an establishment which does not share his ideals.'

'If he likes the cut of my beef I'll be happy enough.'

Sailor Ben flipped open the lid of his watch, scowled, then returned it to his waistcoat pocket. 'One day your strong-mindedness shall bring you ill, Curtis.'

'Aye, but that day ain't come yet.'

I stood beside the carriage door and kept my mouth shut. Ben might act kindly towards me but I wasn't about to forget my place, even if Isaac forgot his. One day, years ago, I'd learned a harsh lesson. Mother used to open the doors when I was little. She wouldn't trust it to one of the maids. 'Got turf between their ears,' she said.

She clucked and fussed around the passengers. Her busy, darting eyes swallowed up their clothes, their jewellery, the style of their wigs. It had rained that day. Hard enough to strip the bark from a tree trunk. Mother's hands turned pink when the weather got too cold. Pink and fat, and they spited her for the rest of the day. Sometimes it was so cold your skin would stick to the brass doorknobs. She borrowed a pair of Judd's gloves. Big, leather things, scuffed and cracked with work. They were like bread puddings sprouting from her wrists. She went out and opened the door, holding out her hand, forgetting about the gloves. A lady stepped out. A fine lady. White gloves. Satin maybe, or a very soft kid leather, that creamed her arms right up to the elbows. Mother reached out and ran her fingers along the material. The lady jerked back a little, the way a polite person might when a passing horse kicks up a dollop of mud and they don't want to get their dress streaked. Then she slapped Mother across the mouth.

Mother staggered back, hand to bloody lips, eyes wide. I knew, little sprat that I was, that she would never hold open a carriage door for anyone again. The lady didn't say anything. She stepped off the mounting block and walked past Mother like she wasn't there. Mother went on standing by the door, hand out, like she was a beggar, and perhaps that's just how she felt. Then she shook herself and walked back towards the kitchen leaving the other passengers to get out as they pleased. She didn't look back. She thumped through the door and hurled the gloves across the table. I was eating some leftover cheese from the Long Room. Isaac sat opposite, quietly sucking on his pipe. One glove clipped my ear. The other smacked into my plate and knocked the cheese onto the floor.

'Rachel opens the doors from now on,' she said.

Later, Mother and Isaac had a row in the parlour. It wasn't much of a fight. Mother had it won before the shouting even started because she knew what was in Isaac's heart even if he didn't know it himself.

She got a splinter. Maybe it was the look the woman gave her. Perhaps it was just those gloves. Mother got a splinter like the kind that gets stuck under your nail when you're clumsy opening the gate. The kind you can't winnow out. That splinter was in her heart but it was through her eyes that you could see it. Hard eyes make a hard face.

Next day I was with Lucy in the small garden behind the kitchen. Mother appeared at the door. 'You're too old to be playing games with one another,' she said, and took my sister inside. Lucy never came out again.

I stole back bits of her. When I could. A smile, a wink. I fought hard for every grin she slipped me.

Isaac emptied his purse on tutors to teach her music and Latin. After the first awkward lessons they found something charming in her and worked hard to make her shine. Isaac just worked her. Day after day at the spinet or the dance floor, or with the books he bought from Stonehill. She sang until her throat turned hoarse and danced until her feet went leprous with blisters. When the money got low and the tutors didn't come any more, Isaac kept at it, teaching her in his own crude fashion.

Out in the yard, opening carriage doors in the rain, I got drenched and splattered with mud.

Sailor Ben went on his way and Isaac returned to the Long Room in a foul mood. I hated it when he argued with passengers. Sailor Ben boasted he was in charge of a man-o-war that had seen off six French frigates. Isaac told me he ran a merchant ship to the Indies. I never knew whom to believe. Green Gallows was a place where stories thrived. I'd met other sailors off the coaches. They carried the smell of salt in the creases of their shirts. Wind had carved lines into their faces and roughened their hair into brittle mops. Leathery skin sometimes carried scars from the bite of the lash. On a dare, one had shown me his back. Ragged welts criss-crossed his spine. 'Got that for falling asleep on watch,' he said, winking. 'Doesn't take much to feel the lick o' the cat.'

'Did it hurt?' I asked stupidly.

'There's worse to be suffered on a ship at sea, lass.'

Sailor Ben had milk pudding skin. His eyes were bright, his ribboned hair always perfectly groomed. Clouds of expensive cologne seemed to drift in the air around him. He moved like a city dandy. Other sailors walked slightly crouched as though a wooden deck still swayed beneath their feet. When I asked after Sailor Ben these grizzled men shook their heads and claimed never to have heard of him.

'There's some never got their toes wet what call

themselves seamen,' one said, laughing.

I followed Isaac inside and volunteered to take the empty plates back to the kitchen. In the washroom at the back, 'Lizabeth was loading a large basket with linen fresh from the tub.

'I'll hang that out,' I said, having stacked the soiled breakfast things on the kitchen table.

'Lizabeth raised an eyebrow. 'Well now, 't'ain't often you're so keen to do washerwomen's work. You'll never shift this basket in any case. 'Tis almost as big as you are.'

'I don't have time to argue. Other coaches are due.'

'I should have that job,' 'Lizabeth said. 'I'm prettier than you. You're a potato in that gown. You'll fall flat on your face in the mud and everybody will laugh.'

The trembling started in my hands and slowly worked past my wrists into my upper arms.

'Go back to your washing. You can run doe-eyed after my mother all you like but Isaac will never let you work the coaches.'

She laughed and flicked her long tawny hair. 'I see we have a new stableboy.'

'What of it?'

'*What of it?*' she sneered. 'As if I don't have two good eyes in my head.'

I felt like grabbing her shoulders and shaking that hateful smile from her face. 'Why say these things, 'Lizabeth? What d'you hope to gain from it? Your ill thoughts will bring you trouble one day.'

Her head cocked to one side. She looked a bit like a spaniel. 'Not from your woolly heart, Miss Rachel.'

I wracked my mind for some witticism, a cutting retort to shut those poisoned lips and chase away that smile. But my brain had turned to mutton. Some people were just born with nettles twisted around their hearts.

'Lizabeth saw my reddening cheeks and laughed all the harder. I knew fine well why she devilled me. She occupied the worst room in the servants' quarters, a poky little cupboard tucked in the corner of the attic, and she blamed me for getting her put there. I'd spotted her fumbling with one of the post-boys behind the coach house. They were drinking wine that I recognised as coming from Sally's larder so I told Isaac and, despite Mother's protests, 'Lizabeth got a thrashing. Being a parish girl she had no choice but to accept her beating and get turfed out of the room she shared with Hannah. 'I don't want thieving parish trash mixing with the other girls,' was how Isaac put it. So, blaming me for her new circumstances, 'Lizabeth thought it was up to me to repair them. The inn was too busy and Mother too fond of her for Isaac to kick her into the nearest ditch, which was the only place she'd have to go if she lost her position here.

I filled my pocket with pegs and scooped up an armful of linen. 'I'll come back for the rest,' I said.

A square of lawn beside the vegetable patch served as our drying green. I filled my mouth with pegs and started to hang up the sheets. My work was slow and clumsy. Every time I thought I had one safely pegged a rogue breeze snatched away a corner and flapped the wet cotton mockingly in my face. My fingers were damp and the line kept slipping out of my grasp. There, got one! Beaming a wooden grin of triumph I started to unfold the next. A pair of hands squeezed my waist.

'I have 'ee!'

The sheets tumbled to the ground. I spat out pegs and rounded on my tormentor. 'Ow, Matthew, gerroff you daft fool. Now look what you've had me do.'

I took a swipe at his grinning face. He dodged the blow and stepped back, hands raised, fingers spread.

'You'd cuff me for the sake of a bit o' washing?' he laughed. 'No doubt you'd see me hanged had I tramped on 'em as well.'

''Twon't be your fingers rubbed raw in a bid to get them clean again,' I said. 'You might've felt Judd's boot now and again, but I've had the sharp end of Hannah's tongue and I'd think it a fair trade should you wish to go and tell her why the sheets she spent all morning scrubbing have suddenly found themselves dirty again.'

I started to pick them up. Matthew moved to help but I batted his hands away. 'No, leave be. I don't want your grubby fingers making matters worse.'

He watched, amusement in his eyes, as I shook the worst of the dust off the sheets and struggled to get them pegged up. It seemed to take forever. *That's the last time I offer to do this*, I thought. When the job was finally done, Matthew strolled back across the stable yard with me, chatting easily, his hat perched on the back of his head. I was only half listening. My hand fumbled with two spare pegs in my pocket.

'Race you to the stables,' he said suddenly. 'I'll give you a good start.'

I ran half-heartedly, only doing it to humour him and because I felt guilty about snapping at him earlier. I won, or he let me beat him. I flounced onto a pile of straw in the corner, grateful to take the weight off my aching feet. Matthew landed beside me, sending clouds of chaff into the air. He started laughing. I laughed along with him. Then I saw something on the floor it wasn't funny any more. A cherry satin bow lying amidst the scattered straw like a dead butterfly. I'd seen lots of bows just like it. On Lucy's gown. The gown she had been wearing yesterday evening when she collared me in the yard and we argued over a bucket of water.

'What's the matter, Rachel? You've gone as pale as buttermilk.'

A tear slid down my cheek.

'Here now, what's this?'

He reached for me. I shoved his hand away. 'Get off.'

Matthew, who didn't know the meaning of the words 'give up', tried to hug me. I fled his arms and ran choking into the tack room. Harnesses dangled leather entrails from hooks in the ceiling. I pushed blindly through the jingling forest, fetched up against the back wall and sank onto the floor.

Matthew picked his way to where I was slouched in the shadowed corner.

'I've had a bad day,' I said. 'Where's Jeremiah?'

He hunkered down and slipped his arm round

my waist. This time I didn't care. We had played games together as children, tussled in the grass, chased and teased one another until I bawled or he tripped and fell into the dirt. There were no secrets. There had never been any secrets. This was Matthew. He was as much a part of the stable yard as the horse trough.

'Jeremiah? Oh, our new muck shoveller? Judd has taken him to Prestbury to fetch something from the smithy. Why d'you ask?'

I could sense his helplessness, his foggy attempts to understand. What had Judd told him about women as they sat in the stables at dusk, maybe supping on slops of ale begged from the taproom or sharing Judd's pipe, a boy indulging in man's talk amid clouds of tart blue smoke?

His fingers brushed the back of my hair, lightly, not his usual clumsy proddings. His touch sent tingles through my scalp.

Something warm and moist pecked the back of my neck. It moved softly upwards towards the tender area beneath my ear. Drugged with misery, lulled by his attentions, I didn't notice or care at first. Then panic shivered through me.

'No Matthew! Glory, no!'

I dodged his awkward kisses and pushed him. Startled, he fell back onto the flagstones, hands grasping air.

'What's the matter with 'ee? It's what you want, ain't it?'

'Don't touch me.'

He rolled over onto his knees. Straw spiked his hair, clung to his breeches with coarse yellow fingers. 'I'm not good enough for 'ee, is that it?

You're just like your sister, though you won't admit 'tis so. Well there's none better'n me would have 'ee, Rachel Curtis, and you'd be as well to mind that before going all coy.'

I clambered to my feet, shook the straw from my petticoats and spat out dust. Matthew. Dear, stupid Matthew. 'We've been friends long enough,' I said, wiping my mouth with the cuff of my sleeve. 'Can't you be happy with that?'

'You've teased me well enough these past few years. Played a right little game. Well you've had fun enough, Miss Curtis, and I'll not trouble 'ee again.'

A world of hurt lurked within his eyes. He stood up and pushed his way towards the door. Harnesses tumbled from their hooks and clattered onto the cobbles. The door was flung open then slammed. Dust thickened the sweltering air.

'I'll get what I want,' I whispered. 'You'll see.'

At the end of the week, Lord Grays and his private banker arrived to talk to Isaac about his plans to expand Green Gallows.

'Once you've seen them off their carriage,' Isaac told me, 'I want you in the taproom. If anyone calls for more port, fetch it from the cellar but give it to Hannah to bring in. Help Sally with the food if her hands are full. Otherwise keep out of the way. Later I'll let you sit at the table. I'm hoping we'll have cause to celebrate.'

I grimaced. His hand thumped the table. 'Don't make faces at me, girl. Do the job well and there'll be a pretty ribbon or pair of gloves at the end of it for you.'

Towards early evening, clouds spread across the face of the dipping sun. The horses fidgeted in their stalls, scratching at the cobbles with restless hooves. The old gypsy mongrel that frequently sniffed around the rubbish outside the kitchen door squeezed itself between a stack of ale barrels and lay there, whining, tail flat on the ground. Hannah tried to coax it out with a scrap of mutton. It regarded her with rheumy eyes and refused to budge.

'Well if it wants to stay there all night, let it,' she said, disgusted. 'I'll more'n likely find it dead in the morning, stupid old thing.'

The air was porridge-thick. My hair felt like it was standing on end. Everyone kept snapping at everyone else. Sally and Hannah, who had been friends for years, got into a row over a broken plate and Hannah fled the kitchen in a flood of tears.

I dealt with two coaches, both nearly empty. The drivers, keen to finish their journey, harried Matthew to get the teams changed quickly. I thought he would swing a punch at one of them but Judd pulled him aside and took him off the boil. Later I caught Judd looking at the sky and shaking his head.

'She's going to blow a good 'un,' he said. 'The stable roof will likely lose a few tiles tonight. I'll stay in with a lantern and watch the horses.'

'As bad as that?' I asked. Storms both frightened and excited me. I once saw a lightning bolt split a three-hundred-year-old oak tree in two as easily as a woodcutter's axe slices a log.

'Bad enough,' he said. ''Tis the rain I'm worried about. Summer has baked the road brick hard. If the ditches fill up it'll run a river. Might even flood the yard. Lord Grays won't get his carriage any further than Marrin's Ridge.'

'Isaac won't be happy.'

The poisoned sky painted Judd's face a dreadful pallor. 'Don't I know it.'

Later that evening, with the storm still threatening, Isaac ordered me to help in the taproom. As I passed the kitchen door a hand grabbed my arm and hauled me inside. 'And where might you be going, young miss?'

Puzzled, I turned to face Sally.

'I'm to work in the taproom.'

She eyed me critically. 'You smell like the wrong end of a horse. I'll have Hannah fetch the hip bath down from the attic.'

I stared at her in horror. 'You're going to wash me?'

She nodded. ''Tis the custom with baths.'

'All over?'

'Well I ain't going to lug buckets of hot water from the kitchen just to dab the end of your nose.'

Sally wasn't like any cook I knew. I had seen enough of those in taverns and posting houses up and down the South Road. All apple-dumpling matrons who were too fond of their own food. Sally looked half starved despite the generosity of her helpings, which led some to believe that her meals had a magical quality, that food touched by her hands could be shovelled down and not an ounce gained. This made her the envy of many.

Isaac, taking the notion that it was bad for guests to be served their supper by a skinny cook, banished her to the kitchen. Instead, Hannah was ordered to take the plates in.

'Is he sayin' that I'm fat?'

'Nay,' Sally said, 'just that you're more comely than me,' and they'd both laughed.

I made a dash for the taproom door and ran straight into Judd, who had chosen that moment to come in from the yard in search of some cheese and ale. Sally wasted no time in explaining the situation. I was given a choice. A bath in front of the kitchen hearth or a ducking in the trough.

I chose the bath.

I was scrubbed pink and had the dust rinsed out of my tangled hair. While I stood dripping on a towel in front of the stove, Hannah brushed down my green dress. A cluster of pretty gold ribbons from Prestbury market were pinned to the back of my tricorne.

Meanwhile, Isaac closed the Long Room. Grumbling guests found themselves crammed into the taproom with a cold supper and a dozen bottles of our not so best wine.

He'll lose custom because of this, I thought, but Isaac had his eyes on bigger fish.

Lord Grays's coach arrived an hour later than expected. As Judd predicted, the skies had split apart, spilling an ocean of rain onto the suffering land. He hauled an old coat around his shoulders and dashed out into the downpour, lantern swinging in his hand. Grays's horses, a team of four, neighed and scuffed the ground as Judd fumbled for the leader. Rain whipped the animals' flanks, plastering their manes to their necks.

I was at the kitchen window and bit my

knuckles as Judd grabbed the harness. He barely had it in his grasp when a vicious bite of wind sent the team lurching forward. Judd leapt out of the way. A second longer and he'd have been trampled.

'Dearest God,' Sally whispered behind me, 'Did you see that?'

Wind rattled the windows and shivered through the cracks in the door. I jumped when it banged open. Isaac, face dark.

'Rachel. What are you doing standing there? Get outside. There's a carriage to see to.'

I stared at him. Sally stepped between us. 'You can't send a girl out in that. Her gown will be soaked. Surely 'tis a job for Matthew or one of the stable hands?'

Isaac eased her out of the way. 'She's not wearing that dress to dance in. They're working clothes, as much so as your apron, and I won't send out a milk-faced boy. Rachel has been out in worse. Is that not so, girl?'

'Yes,' I squeaked, 'much worse.'

'See? Now tend to your cooking and let my daughter earn her keep.'

I would not meet Sally's accusing stare as I shuffled to the door. As soon as I was outside rain bit into my face and plastered my gown to my shivering body. Cold rain, blown out of the frigid north, that had no business visiting these summer meadows. I splashed across the yard to where Lord Grays's carriage was waiting. Another flash of lightning, another bellow from the gods. I reached for the carriage door. Numb fingers slipped on the dripping brass. Before I could try again a liveried footman stepped between myself and the coach. His face was a dark mask beneath his sodden, feather-trimmed tricorne.

'Out of the way, you.'

A hand thumped into my chest. Arms windmilling, I fell rump-first into the deepest puddle in the yard. Soaked, spread-eagled and whimpering like a pup, I watched as the footman lowered the steps and opened the carriage door.

A clutch of figures, huddled against the weather, hurried by. Hannah, in her best apron, held open the Long Room door until they were inside.

Furious, I dragged myself out of the water. The driver and coachmen splashed past, heading for the taproom. From the opposite direction two figures, blurred by the rain, hurried from the stables. Matthew and Judd. They started unhitching the team. A pause. Both men bent over, shouting at one another above the thunder. I hurried over. Old habits.

'Trouble?'

Judd was examining the lead horse's leg. He looked up at me, face swimming with raindrops. I had to listen carefully to catch his words before the wind snatched them away. 'Three blind 'uns and a bolter,' he shouted.

My hand flew to my mouth. Bad horses.

'Will Isaac exchange them?' I yelled back.

'Reckon so, the way he's been preenin' himself for Lord Grays's visit this past week.'

'Can we do anything with these?'

Judd dropped the leg and straightened. 'They've been flogged near to death. 'Twas a miracle they made it this far. A few weeks, maybe more, and they'll be fit for work again. I hope your father keeps his temper, Rachel. Barely through the door and his guests have stitched him already.'

I ran inside. Two steps into the kitchen and Sally had my sodden dress up over my head and a towel tossed into my shivering arms. Seating me in front of the blazing hearth, she took the dripping garment into the scullery.

'Dry yourself off,' she called through. 'I'll see if I can wring some prettiness back into this thing.'

'What about our guests?'

'Let them wait.'

My teeth were clacking together like old twigs. 'Did you see the way that man pushed me?'

'I saw. Those sort like to push their way through life, them and their masters.'

I towelled the rain from my body in long strokes, then covered my modesty and slipped out of my sopping undergarments. Stockings joined them on the tiled floor. My shoes, turned into unrecognisable mud cakes, were thrown into the log basket. Warmth from the sparking grate spread through my chilled flesh. A sip of hot tea helped bring me back to life.

I padded barefoot to the oak panelled L-shaped partition which separated the kitchen from the Long Room on one side and the taproom on the other. One of the panels was hinged. Pulled back, it revealed a rectangular peephole through which most of the Long Room could be watched. The hole was supposed to be used for passing signals to the kitchen. More wine for her ladyship, the sauce dish needs a refill, take away the fowl and bring out the apple tart. Of course everyone used it for spying on the guests in the hope of catching a whiff of scandal or seeing a drunken gentleman make a disgrace of himself.

Three guests, seated at a table fit for twenty, a trail of rapidly fading raindrops marking their progress from the stable-yard door to the point where cloaks were surrendered, boots or slippers stamped clean, chairs dragged back then pulled forward again. At the head slouched a rugged bull of a man. He was stuffed into a button-bursting waistcoat that, with every movement, seemed determined to escape the lightly embroidered summer jacket that struggled to keep it in check. Real hair, not a wig, aged a horrible grey, stabbed his forehead in a brutal widow's peak.

On his right sat a young peacock in a blue and silver coat, powdered cheeks bruised with rouge, wig a pile of summer clouds stitched together and trimmed with velvet. A glimpse of his shoes beneath the tablecloth revealed silver buckles the size of window panes. I supposed this was Augustus Rand, Lord Grays's personal banker. Glory! He even sported a paper heart glued suggestively to the right cheekbone.

And on the left, a powder puff of a girl who had to be Lord Grays's wife. I squinted to get a better look. A high forehead, pert nose. Teeth all there? Maybe. Beige gown dripping with jewels, bone-handled fan resting on her lap, an easy familiarity with cut glass crystal and silver tableware. Yet something about her suggested the gutter. The laugh perhaps, or the hard glint in her eyes. Lady? Not likely.

Mother flitted around the table in her very best

gown – a sack compared to Lady Grays's lace-trimmed confection. I couldn't make out what she was saying. Her words dribbled into one another like melting butter.

And Lucy, dressed as a bride, standing by the spinet, hands clasped together as if in prayer. Our honoured guests joked and chatted as she sang in a nightingale voice, ballads and love songs drowned in Lord Grays's bellowing laughter. She looked too perfect to exist, a brittle ice-thing that would shatter at a touch.

The parlour door swung open. Father swaggered into the room, proud in his best Sunday clothes. And *the wig*. Made from real human hair ('Only from fine English heads sir, I guarantee it', the shopkeeper had assured him) the thing lightened his pockets by six whole shillings and made him scratch like a flea-bitten cur. For three days he'd paraded around the house, wearing it at the dinner table, in the privy, probably even to bed. Matthew fetched a warning clout around the ear from Judd for snickering.

Now Isaac swaggered around the table like a city fop, seemingly plucking flies from the air with his thumb and forefinger.

'We expected you an hour ago, Lord Grays. No doubt the storm was the cause of your delay.'

The affected voice rumbled coarsely in his throat. Lord Grays glanced at him and frowned.

'Damn road more like. 'Twas like trying to run a carriage through a ditch.'

Isaac swallowed. Smiled weakly. 'How fares society this season, m'lord? And politics? I am a staunch Whig myself.'

He took a pinch of white powder from a cheap pewter snuffbox and made a great show of snorting it up each nostril. Only I knew that it was chalk.

'Fetch my supper and less of your impudence,' Lord Grays retorted. He toyed with a deck of cards. Gold rings, sweet with jewels, sparkled on his fingers.

Cracks spread across Isaac's face. He didn't move. His lace cuffs fluttered gently in the warm draught from the fire.

'Maids will bring your supper in directly,' he said at last.

The young peacock touched his wine glass to his lips and took a gentle sip. His Adam's apple, visible through his loosened neckcloth, bobbed as he swallowed.

'I would have your daughter serve me,' he said smoothly.

'I beg your pardon, sir, but my Lucy isn't accustomed to serving at table.'

'If she can handle silver half as prettily as she sings then I daresay a drop of gravy on my breeches can be overlooked.'

'Lucy doesn't serve,' Isaac repeated. 'Rachel can bring in your supper if you like.'

'Rachel? Was that her outside, floundering like a drowned pup? Well if your precious girl cannot serve us she must join us. And we'll have the mudlark too. Make room at the table. They shall sit either side of me. Beauty on my right, and on my left ... well, no matter.'

''Lizabeth, go and fetch Rachel from the taproom,' Isaac instructed.

Lord Grays's eyebrows arched. 'You'd have a scullery wench sup with us, Augustus?'

'It should amuse, m'lord. We cannot have one without the other. Where would be the sport in that?'

'Lizabeth headed towards the kitchen. I hurriedly closed the hatch. 'You are to go out,' she told me, looking as if she'd just swallowed a toad, 'to sit at table.'

Sally fetched my gown from the laundry room. 'Nothing for it,' she said. 'You'll have to go. I don't have anything pretty enough to lend and it wouldn't fit if I did.'

'I can't put that back on. Look at the sleeves. They're still dripping.'

'Come on girl, up off that stool. We can't have Isaac coming in to fetch you. Here, arms up.'

The slither of damp cloth against skin. 'Now,' she stepped back, 'a quick brush of your hair, a new ribbon, and you'll pass.'

I squirmed and tugged at the bodice. 'It's cold. I'll catch a fever.'

Sally shook her head. 'Isaac had Hannah stoke the Long Room fire. You could bake bread in there, it's that hot. Five minutes and you'll be as dry as paper.'

'Lizabeth grunted and made to return to the Long Room. She got a hand on the doorknob before Sally called her back. 'Not so fast, you. Wait until Rachel has joined our guests then you can take out the soup. And it's no good looking at me like that either.'

'Lizabeth glared at me instead. Soggy dress or not, I'd go now just to spite her. Heat smothered me as I entered the Long Room. I paused by the hearth. It was pointless to light anything but a huge fire in that yawning stone maw. The chimney swallowed up the flames, sucked them into its huge gizzards and threw its power into the sky. Isaac claimed it was one of the first parts of the inn to be built, finished even before the floor was boarded and the last piece of thatch stitched into place. You could stew an ox under it and still have room to warm your feet. Tree trunks, chopped into fat logs, barely blunted its appetite. When they put the fire out to clean the chimney it took two days, sometimes three, for the last of the embers to go cold.

Eyes were on me. Amused? Bemused? Not much welcome either way. And what was Lucy thinking, already seated beside Augustus, napkin a crushed dove on the table in front of her?

'Welcome my dear, welcome. Sit down. Here, we have reserved a special place for you.' Augustus gestured.

Isaac slid the chair out for me. I seated myself awkwardly, causing him to fumble. 'Lizabeth appeared and banged down a soup plate.

The only thing worse than wearing wet garments was sitting in a warm room clothed in damp ones. To my crushing shame, wisps of steam began rolling off the material. The clammy feel was horrible, like having a dozen frogs slithering down the back of my neck. My body itched everywhere. Worse, I began to smell like mouldy linen.

Augustus eyed me curiously. His cologne was overpowering. I picked up my napkin holder but my finger got caught in the ring and the napkin slithered onto the floor. Mother, in the middle of serving bread rolls, winced.

Lucy, bless her, kept them distracted, enchanted, talking. She could draw a conversation out of a rock, switching subjects with the ease of a rake changing lovers. The heart of a lady and the smile of a whore was how Isaac once put it.

In came a platter of cold beef, a basket of puffy white bread, steaming pheasant and potatoes drowned in butter sauce. Lady Grays had a talent for eating and talking at the same time. I watched, fascinated, as sauce dribbled down her chin and dripped yellow spots onto the table cloth. She spoke of London, of fashion and finance, palace scandals and roisterous theatrical shows, dropping people's names into the conversation as easily as she slipped her spoon into the potato dish. Her words were sincere enough, but was that contempt in those blue eyes?

Only once in my life had I met a highwayman face to face, a dashing heart-swooner robbing under the unlikely nickname of Lord Jack, who made the unusual mistake of holding up the Prestbury stage. He wore an expression just like that as he relieved Gregor's passengers of their purses and trinkets. A wolf's grin. A second later the local constable, who had been tipped off and was hiding in the trees at the side of the lane, put a musket ball between his shoulder blades.

Hannah was circling the table with the wine bottle. She filled Lucy's glass. Lucy gulped it down and continued talking. Augustus leaned towards her, seemingly rapt, the fingers of one hand curled under his chin. Except he wasn't listening. He had not taken in a single word. Lucy's sentences picked up momentum until they started rolling into one another. As she spoke (no, this was not speaking, it was a babble) her hands worked furiously – one moment folded across her breast, the next fluttering apart like frightened sparrows.

Augustus's other hand was not visible, had not been for some few minutes now. Lucy's voice was now like an out of tune spinet, notes and pitch all jumbled up.

How could you? I thought. *Here, in front of everyone?*

The edge of the tablecloth rustled, shifted. Lucy flinched. Her smile never wavered though her eyes were screaming. She was either very brave or very frightened. A cruel part of my mind said: *You deserve it, Lucy Curtis. This'll teach you not to be so fancy with men. I bet you smell of Jeremiah the way a whore stinks of a dandy's cologne.*

Then the thought was gone. She was my sister and I had to do something. Nudge him, pretend to faint, spill my supper onto the floor. Lord Grays was flicking playing cards onto the table, watching with heavy-lidded eyes as Lady Grays ate and drank and droned on and on. Hannah went to fill Augustus's glass for at least the third time. Her hand slipped, or she stumbled, I wasn't sure which. A cupful of ruby liquid flew from the bottle neck and splashed down the sleeve of his jacket.

'You stupid girl.'

Before Hannah could stutter an apology, Augustus stood up and slapped her hard about the face. The sound was like a whiplash. Hannah screamed and dropped the glass, which shattered into glittering shards.

Augustus flapped his hands impatiently. 'Oh get out, get out you wretch before you do any more damage. Go on!'

Hannah fled to the kitchen. A minute later Sally, pale-faced and grim, came in to sweep up the mess.

'The cost of a new coat shall be deducted from my account, of course.'

Isaac, face shadowed beneath that monstrous wig, nodded. 'Of course.'

I put down my fork. That jacket must have seen off the best part of twenty guineas. Grays's account with us would barely notch up five, perhaps ten if they continued to eat and drink like pigs.

'And that girl,' Augustus continued, waving his fork as if making polite after-dinner conversation, 'such clumsiness would not be tolerated in any of the better London establishments. You have been too lenient, Curtis.'

'I don't normally have cause to strike the servants, sir.'

'There you have it!' The fork clattered onto Augustus's empty plate. 'If a dog fouls your floor you do not let it off with a scolding. Do you not agree, m'lord?'

Lord Grays looked up from his cards. 'I expect the girl will be dismissed.'

On the floor, Sally stopped sweeping up the broken glass. Lady Grays gazed at Isaac over the rim of her own wine glass. She sipped the liquid delicately, licked her lips and swallowed. Muscles twitched in her long, pale throat.

'As you wish,' Isaac said.

'Well, that's it settled.' Augustus beamed. 'Now fetch me another glass.'

Isaac turned and shuffled towards the kitchen door. Powder erupted into the air as he tore off the wig. When he returned a few minutes later with another glass and a fresh bottle of wine his waistcoat had been replaced with a grease-stained apron.

'Lizabeth served me raspberry tart. Her knuckles were white on the cake knife. Augustus spooned up his portion without another glance at Lucy, who sat tight-lipped and staring at the tablecloth. Finally the port came in and I left as quickly as politeness allowed. I fled to the front door, taking in lightning-scorched air in huge, animal gulps. Blue-white fireworks continued to dance in the sky above the rain-lashed yard. The taproom windows were bolted and shuttered. Trees, whipped into fury by the gale, shed twigs and leaves onto the rooftops. A forlorn light glimmered weakly beneath the stable door. Judd would be trying to settle the horses. He'd not have eaten since the storm broke. Someone ought to take out supper, bread and ale at the very least, or something hot.

'I thought I would find you out here.'

Augustus stood beside me, port glass in his hand.

'Have you come to take the air, sir, or to insult my family further?'

'Ah, what's this? Where is the mouse who squeaked around my table earlier? You could not lift your fork without quivering. Has a sip of wine gone so easily to your head?'

'No,' I replied, resting my head against the doorpost. 'I don't care for the way you treated my sister, or our servant.'

The scratch of a tinderbox. A flicker of orange, a ghost face in the darkness. The rich, choking scent of cigar smoke before it was snatched away by a gust of cold air. 'Ah, the little milkmaid. I looked twice, I don't deny it. Many men undoubtedly have, whatever their class. It must be very hard for you.'

'Not really.'

'Hah. You lie as crudely as you dress.'

The storm moved south towards the coast. With its dying breath it lit up Augustus's face. White, grotesque, the visage of some demon. He had been smiling at me in the darkness. In that fleeting instant of illumination I caught it pinned on his mouth.

'She is a remarkable creature,' he continued. 'Were she introduced to London society, one might never guess that she was an innkeeper's daughter.'

'There must be hundreds of pretty ladies in the city. Why pester Lucy?'

A soft chuckle, barely heard beneath the rumbling thunder. 'London is full of vixens eager to clean out a fellow's purse. A mistress can be bought to measure, the same as a shirt or pair of boots. Peasants come cheap and, like hot metal, can easily be beaten into shape.'

'Isaac owns this land. He is entitled to be called "master" or "sir".'

'A couple of bedraggled acres and a few flea-bitten nags don't add up to much. Your sugar-tongued sister would do well to put her charms to good effect otherwise she will find herself back in the mud where she belongs. You are stupid to think otherwise, as stupid as that oafish father of yours who seems to think he can leap generations of quality breeding simply by pairing off his brat to someone with a title.'

'He's not stupid.'

Augustus turned to go back inside.

'Why are you saying these things?' I demanded. 'How d'you know I won't tell Isaac?'

He paused, hand on the latch. 'Because you have a face no one notices, a voice that is never heeded. Even out here, in the darkness, your sister's shadow swallows you up. Your father has the glint of gold in his eyes. The mewlings of a scruffy kitten are hardly likely to turn him from his course. Tomorrow he will show us around this rat's nest and try to convince us that it is worth our investment. I have no doubt at all that he shall succeed.'

'How can you be so sure?'

But Augustus had gone.

Chapter Four

I was going to church whether I liked it or not. I had to wear the same gown, dry and crinkled now, the same hat, the same shoes. I looked like a tinker girl and smelled of old sacks.

The kitchen door slammed. It had its own

sound, like most things in the inn. Both hinges squealed, each in a different pitch like two out-of-harmony cats yowling on the porch. Then the thick 'kerchunk' that only a solid oak door can make as it closes. Even in the Long Room you could feel it shiver through the walls.

I edged towards the window. Sometime in the night the sky had sent its grumbling belly towards the coast. The rain had lightened into a clinging drizzle. Behind me, my bed was rumpled through hours of restless squirming. Last evening's events stuck in my mind like a rotten potato souring the gullet.

The yard was Sunday-quiet. Hannah passed in front of the stables. She dragged her right foot slightly as she walked, the result of some horrible ulcer that had eaten up part of her leg as a child. Only a cat's-whisker miracle had stopped the local quack from lopping it off. Halfway towards the gate, she stopped and turned. A bruise jaundiced her left cheek. Her fingers fluttered over it before clasping the shawl around her throat. A cheap straw bonnet sat on her head.

She spilled that wine on purpose, I realised. *I ought to go to her. Say something. By the time I'm dressed she'll be gone.*

Hannah shivered. The drizzle pricked her face with thousands of tiny, wet diamonds. Her eyes were hollow, haunted looking. They flicked over the familiar angles of her former home. A gesture, perhaps a shrug.

The kitchen door opened again. Sally ran into view clasping a bundle. The world seemed to hold its breath for a moment, then the two women squeezed into each other's arms. They stood like that for a minute, eyes closed, saying nothing. Then Sally thrust the bundle into Hannah's hands and ran back inside, her fingers covering her face.

Hannah tugged the gate open and stepped into the lane where Judd waited with the gig to take her to Prestbury. She tossed the small bundle into the back and climbed onto the seat. She might manage to hitch a wagon ride to Portsmouth where she had a cousin who worked in the harbour. He'd likely look after her for a while. Once the Grayses had gone, Isaac might take her back. If she would come back. Hannah was proud.

Visiting gentry usually attended the service at Prestbury parish church. I'd hoped the Grayses would keep to their beds, but no such luck. 'Have to keep up appearances for the rabble,' Lord Grays said. Breakfast had already been ordered for their return and Matthew was out readying one of the hire chaises. Isaac had set Jeremiah to cleaning out their own carriage, I discovered. Lucy was to ride with the Grayses. We would take the other chaise.

We arrived at the churchyard ahead of the others. The drizzle showed no sign of letting up. Water gathered into pools, hiding the treacherous nature of some of the lane's deeper potholes.

Old Buseridge was late opening the church. He kept the building bolted after losing too many candlesticks to local footpads. Someone joked that not even the Second Coming would persuade him to leave the door open. We were forced to shelter under the large beech tree that dominated much of the churchyard.

Ten minutes later the Grayses' party arrived. Augustus was out first, followed by Lady Grays and then Lucy. Augustus held out his hand to help her down the step. Lucy ignored it. Parasols mushroomed above the two women. Mother had forgotten hers and we both got wet.

It was the custom here to allow the gentry to enter the church first, to sit when they sat, rise when they rose, and keep a respectful silence throughout the service. But old Lord Marrin hadn't shown his face here since last Christmas and the rest of his brood were on the Grand Tour – at least until their inheritances fell due. Parishioners had taken to sauntering in at will, to rise whenever they chose or not at all, and to gossip before and after the service.

This Sabbath, however, Parson Buseridge kept his flock grumbling in the churchyard until Lord Grays was ready to enter. Lady Grays walked elegantly on the arm of her tardy husband. But there again was that smile, that ghost in her eyes which seemed to say *this is a game*, a bit like the crude charades Mother played in the parlour with Lucy when she was younger. A game I resented, not because I wasn't asked to join in, but because another piece of Lucy, another chunk of her precious time with me had been stolen away. I'd peek in from time to time and watch them pretend to be princesses, pirates or dancing bears. Lucy was a natural trouper and always kept Mother guessing, but there was a ring to her voice, as hollow as a rotten tree trunk, and a falseness in the way she held herself, an exaggeration of every little gesture that betrayed even the most convincing performance for what it was – an act, a mask to be cast aside after use.

Watching Lady Grays tread the cinder path I saw Lucy on the parlour carpet and the act was on again. I could not take my eyes from her. She was at once fascinating and horrible.

Go away, I thought. *Go away and leave my family alone*.

Her face passed into shadow as she walked under the arch, eyes roving from villager to villager. Men nodded, women dipped shallow curtsies. One or two hesitated, frowned.

By the time we were seated, the old pipe organ in the corner was already blowing cobwebs towards the vaulted ceiling. The Grayses and their banker took the front pew. We settled for our usual place two rows behind and on the other side of the aisle. Lucy buried her face in her prayer book as Buseridge mounted the pulpit and cleared his throat. Lord Grays's chin sank slowly to his chest. His eyelids blinked once, twice, then settled closed. Lady Grays looked around as if she had never seen the inside of a church before.

About halfway through the service, Lucy nudged me and pressed a piece of paper into my hand. She sat still as a rod, expression stony.

I unfolded the paper. She regularly passed me notes when Buseridge was droning on. Tucked away in her reticule was a supply of paper cut into small squares, along with a stub of charcoal. Usually these messages were nothing more than a comment on someone's new bonnet, a remark on the weather or a village lad who had caught her eye.

I smoothed the note out on my knee. It was brief enough.

He keeps looking at me.

Lucy's eyes burned like sapphires in her pale face. I folded the paper up again and slipped it between the pages of my prayer book. Twice I summoned up the courage to steal a peek at Augustus. Twice I caught him staring at Lucy. There was nothing I could do. Nothing. We sat in the house of God and God wasn't helping, wasn't keeping this demon away from my sister. I looked at the parson ranting in his pulpit and felt sick.

A finger poked into my ribs. 'What ails you?' Isaac whispered in my ear. 'Why'd you keep fidgeting?'

'Nothing,' I lied. 'Just a bit of cramp.'

Lucy was first out of church. This was an achievement. In the back pew, nearest the door, sat the Bennetts and their five children. The family ran a notorious smallholding just on the other side of Prestbury, fretted over the well-being of their pigs, the state of their farmhouse and the always-on-the-verge-of-bawling baby swaddled in Ma Bennett's hairy arms. Always last in. Always first out.

Not today.

Buseridge had barely finished saying the 'n' on 'Amen' and Lucy was gone. By the time we pushed through the chattering throng, the parson had slipped out through the vestry and was waiting for us at the door.

'Your daughter was in an uncommon hurry to leave, Mr Curtis,' he said. 'Haste sets a bad example.'

'She was ill,' Isaac replied evenly. 'An attack of the vapours. This church gets as stuffy as a chicken coop.'

The parson fiddled with the sleeves of his clerical garb. 'An attack of something. Not the vapours methinks.'

Isaac let go of Mother's arm. 'The Bennetts also left early. All but ran out of the church.'

The parson's gaze was unwavering. 'The Bennetts have no example to set.'

Outside, the sun had scratched a thin gap in the rain clouds. A temporary wound that would heal by the time we arrived back at Green Gallows. Lucy was waiting in the churchyard, standing some way back from the cinder path in an older part of the grounds where broken, time-wiped headstones sank into a thick clump of nettles. The hem of her gown was dark from the wet grass.

'I want to ride back with you,' she told Isaac when he went to fetch her.

Isaac glanced at Lord Grays, who was outside the lichgate talking to his coachman, and shook his head.

'You go back the way you came.'

He rejoined us. Mother's face was dour under the brim of her straw bonnet. They exchanged unreadable glances. Isaac took hold of her arm again and led her away. Lucy hadn't moved from the overgrown graves. I wanted to go to her but Isaac beckoned me to follow him instead. A shadow fell across the cinder path.

'Curtis.'

Colly Bruce, who beat his woman, whose drunken fists broke teeth in the Coach and Horses tavern. Isaac had kicked him off Green Gallows six months ago. He now plied his trade around the local markets, and we had to trail our horses into Prestbury every time one threw a shoe.

'I hear you still need a farrier,' he said, kneading his felt cap between his fingers like a piece of old dough. 'I'm the best in these parts. You know it to be so.'

Isaac nodded. 'That I do. But I also know you drink, you thump your lass and you've an unhealthy eye for my daughter.'

'If you packed off every man who gave a wench a slap you'd have no one working for you.'

'I found Jenny huddled in the stables, her face beaten so black I only knew her from her voice. You've got good hands when you've a mind to use them right, Bruce, but they're too thirsty for blood. I don't want hands like that touching my stock. Or my girls. Stay off my property.'

Colly pulled his cap back on and planted his fists on his hips. 'The dandy in the silk coat standing in the lane. He's a guest of yours?'

'Aye. What of it?'

'I shod three of his nags. He's owed me since April.'

'Don't start anything, Bruce. Not with my wife and daughters watching.'

The farrier thought about that for a moment. 'You should choose your company more wisely, Curtis.'

'Lord Grays is here on business.'

Colly stared over Isaac's shoulder at Lady Grays, who was chatting to the parson. Most of the congregation had already drifted off home, with only one or two stragglers talking quietly between the tombstones. But it was not the weather for exchanging gossip and soon they were also heading for the lich-gate.

'I've worked with metal all my life,' Colly said, 'I can tell a silver tureen from a pewter pot that's not fit for pissin' in. I won't be ill used, Curtis. The time's comin' when you'll need friends.'

On the way back to Green Gallows a deep rut knocked one of our wheels out of kilter and we arrived half an hour behind the Grayses. I ran upstairs and tapped on Lucy's bedchamber door. No answer. She was not in the parlour or in any of the common rooms.

'Not been in here so far as I could tell,' 'Lizabeth informed me tartly from behind the taproom counter.

Through the window, I spied the Grayses' groom walking across the yard from the stables. I ran out to meet him.

'Where's my sister?'

He eyed me as if I was a bit of dirt stuck on the end of his polished boot. 'I saw her going into the coach house.'

Over the years I'd worn my feet out crossing that yard. I knew every kink and rut in the gravel. Three dozen steps would take me across it. I'd counted once, as a little girl, then counted again as years passed and my gait had lengthened. My childhood, girlhood and early womanhood were taken in measured steps from kitchen to stable door.

Laughter from one of the upstairs windows.

Coughing from another. Above, patchy cloud. A sliver of sunlight barely made an impression on the weary sky.

Nothing now but the steady whisper of my own breathing and the crunch of gravel under my feet. I rounded the corner of the stables and skirted the remains of the nettle patch. Ahead lay the coach house, one unshuttered window punched into the whitewashed wall.

How stupid, I thought. *They don't care who sees them.*

'Maybe they won't be there at all,' I said aloud.

They stood together in the light from the window amid the junk and old carriage bones littering the coach house. I pushed a fist into my mouth. I thought he was attacking her. She, locked in a brutal embrace, moaning gently. His face buried in her hair, which was all windblown and crooked haystacks. Mouth open-close, open-close, his eyes scrunched up. Hands wandering, touching, moving on.

At first I wondered why he did not say anything, then realised he *was* talking to her – with his face, eyes and fingertips. The quiet air around them was filled with language – words no interpreter could translate. I was on the edge of a thunderstorm and peeping into its heart.

Release. Air whooshed out of her. A breeze that carried a lingering sigh. Smeared rouge made a cherry tart of her face.

Sated, they gently embraced. Jeremiah nuzzled Lucy's cheek. His eyes opened and stared into mine.

I fell away from the window. My footsteps

seemed to boom around the yard as I fled back to the taproom.

The afternoon dragged. I had many of Hannah's chores to do as well as my own. Being Sunday, only two coaches demanded my attention. Even then the passengers, sensing that my mood was off, were reluctant to tip me and all I had to show for my sullen greetings were two pennies and a bent farthing.

Later I haunted the stables. Lady Grays had sent to Prestbury for some fancies. Judd also needed something from the village and he had gone with Matthew in the cart. Jeremiah was in the lane clearing out the ditch so I had the place to myself. I didn't want the day to end. Dusk meant supper and having to face Lucy. Twice I found myself on the landing outside her door. Twice I skulked back downstairs. If I confronted her I wouldn't be upset if she lied to me. It was the truth I was afraid of.

I remembered the look on her face. How could I spoil the one sliver of happiness she'd found? Jeremiah was of the earth, like me. Solid, rough-hewn, basic in his drives yet gentle as dandelion petals. He was the one act of defiance Lucy was capable of. She could use him, but not love him. Never love him.

But oh glory, she did. *She did.*

The sun turned orange and dipped out of the sky. The wagon rattled into the yard, Judd at the reins, Matthew perched grim-faced beside him.

I cornered Matthew in the tack room. 'Why so glum?' I said. 'This isn't the first time you've been packed off to town to fetch a few lady's trinkets. You've done it for Lucy often enough.'

Matthew ran a leather harness between his fingers, checking the fastenings. Satisfied, he hung it up and took down another.

'The woman with Lord Grays,' he said at length, 'she's not his wife.'

'Who, Lady Grays?'

Matthew tossed the harness onto a pile of sacking. 'She's a whore. Judd once spied her with a guest at the Stonehill posting house. He had her in his carriage with her skirts up about her waist and did not care who saw, even with all the drapes drawn wide. Afterwards he handed her a purse and another coach took her away. It was the same woman, Judd's sure of it. She's been in these parts at least twice before, always different, always with the gentry.'

'Have you told anyone else?'

'I thought I'd fetch a clout for prying.'

It made sense. Such terrible sense. Isaac fought an ongoing battle with travelling prostitutes who slipped down from London to ply the South Road, enjoying a brisk trade with too-long-at-sea sailors, merchants and weary farmers with mutton-faced wives. What was the difference, after all, between selling favours or selling a chaffinch in a cage, a potion or a tuppenny ribbon? The gentry often brought their own faceless women to rumple our bed sheets and it wasn't fair for Isaac to chase a gaggle of jeering harlots off his land while a painted tart at double the price tripped brazenly through our front door.

'Gregor often sees her up in the city when he takes a stage there, dallying around the better taverns and posting houses.' Matthew glanced out of the window. 'But it don't make any difference. No matter how much perfume and face paint you use, you can't put a dog in a velvet gown and call it a lady.'

Later, Lord Grays and his banker borrowed a pair of geldings and went to Marrin' s Hall to pay their respects to the squire. They returned after dusk and strode right into our parlour, shaking rain from their cloaks. They were shadows within shadows in the cramped room. Candles flickered on the table and along the mantel.

Augustus asked for wine. Isaac sent 'Lizabeth running to the cellar to fetch it. I was to serve.

'Lucy will sing for you,' Isaac said, geniality pinned on his square face. But these men were itchy for business and had no time for songs. They unrolled plans and spread them across the table. A sheet of vellum, the size of a rug, on which Green Gallows had been dismembered with an ink-dipped quill and rebuilt again.

I lingered in the corner, wine decanter in hand, filling their glasses when bid and then filling them again. Isaac frowned at the plans, hand rubbing his chin. The men spoke in turn as if this had been carefully rehearsed, making suggestions, quoting figures, tapping the paper with busy fingers.

Isaac questioned the cost of labourers, the transport of materials, the amount of space required.

'Extending the stables that way will gobble up half my paddock,' he said. 'My horses need that land.'

'Come now, Curtis,' Augustus said, 'you struck

us as an ambitious fellow. You will need good business sense if you wish to make your mark in the world. In anticipation of the problem we have negotiated with Lord Marrin. He is willing to lease you the fields bordering your inn. 'Tis a fair-sized acreage and the rent not unreasonable.'

Doubt flickered in Isaac's eyes. 'I ain't leased nothing in my life. I own land, I don't pay to borrow it off another man.'

Each objection was persuasively swept away until they had Isaac believing he could build the Tower of Babel in his own stable yard and still show a profit. Flush-faced, he signed their documents, no sound now but the rustle of paper and scratch of quill. I wanted to snatch the pen out of his hand and crush it.

Isaac tapped the base of his glass on the table. 'More wine, girl. Don't stand there looking at me.'

I brought the decanter to the table and filled his glass. The other men had barely touched their drinks.

Earlier in the month, Judd had taken me to Prestbury in the gig. Matthew was languishing in his bed with some sort of ague and the horse-master was grateful for a pair of hands, anyone's hands, to help him buy the feed.

On the far side of the market square a horse lay sprawled in the dirt, tongue lolling out of its flyblown mouth. A sack of bones, its flank criss-crossed with badly healed scars. I had seen many such nags. They were the dregs of the market, bought cheap by farmers to haul carts until they dropped. This one probably died between the shafts and was abandoned where it lay. Soon it would disappear; its shoes plundered, its meat cooked by gypsies or starving paupers. Even its bones could be ground into trinkets or fashioned into crude tools.

Ravens circled in the air above the carcass, cawing, flapping dark wings. Emboldened by hunger they dropped like black snow onto the corpse, pecking between the ribs, inside the ears. The eyes.

Isaac picked up his wineglass and toasted his new friends. They smiled, teeth glinting wetly in the candlelight, and raised their own glasses in return.

All I saw were ravens.

Lord Grays took his banker and his harlot and left for London in the rain-lashed dark. 'We cannot stay another night,' Grays explained. 'There are pressing matters in the city that require my attention.' They drove off with our fresh horses, as Judd said they would.

Lucy shut herself in her bedchamber and did not come downstairs until Isaac called her. She picked at her supper but her eyes were bright and I caught her smiling to herself. Isaac glanced at her curiously a couple of times, then shrugged and went on devouring his food.

Before going to bed I paused at the door leading to the yard. I lifted the latch then dropped it again.

'Aha,' I said under my breath.

I sat on my bed with my back to the wall, a blanket wrapped around me. The fire slowly flickered into ashes. My body was all wrung out but I felt wide awake.

Around midnight I heard a noise in the hall. I didn't move from my place on the mattress. An hour or so later there was another sound. I waited a few moments then blew out my candle. Even after crawling between the sheets it was a long time before I fell asleep.

Next morning I found Lucy alone in the parlour. She had risen late. A bowl of beef soup sat on the table in front of her. She looked up when I came in.

'Would you like some?' she said, gesturing at the soup pot on the sideboard. 'It's nice and hot.'

I held her gaze. 'I heard you go out. I heard you come in. Oiling the latch was a nice trick but you'll have to nail some of those floorboards down if you want them to stop creaking. Your feet must be black as plum puddings from creeping across the yard in your stockings. Or did you even bother to dress? Did you meet him in your shift?'

Lucy put down her spoon and rose from the table. 'You need help sleeping at night. I'll ask Sally to fix you a draught.'

'Did you find warmth in the darkness, Lucy?' I called after her. 'Did you? *Did you?*'

The ink had barely dried on Lord Grays's credit note when Isaac set off with our biggest wagon. He clutched the note in his fist as if it could crack open the world. He was gone the whole day, not returning until dark smothered the inn. The wagon groaned with timber which took an hour to unload, even with Judd and Matthew pitching in. Isaac fidgeted all through supper.

'I've employed labourers and a foreman,' he

told us, food tumbling off his fork. 'Had to go to Stonehill to find men willing to start work right away. Paid them in advance so they've nothing to gripe about. They'll be here at the end of the week. Let's see anyone try to build a turnpike now, eh?'

He disappeared the next day, and the day after that, returning with a wagon so laden the nag could barely haul it. Building materials were left in huge piles around the edge of the yard. Isaac was so worn out he could hardly stand, but nothing seemed to dim the hard, glassy light in his eyes.

Other tradesmen started turning up at our gate. Stone was delivered, mountains of it, and roof slate brought all the way from Wales. Isaac paced out imaginary walls, measured for partitions and spent minutes at a time standing at the end of the paddock, looking down on his as-yet imaginary kingdom. A smile was always on his face, though it looked as though someone had drawn it there. Sometimes he forgot to eat or shave. His grumbling belly sang out-of-tune songs to us when darkness finally forced him back into our parlour.

The hired labourers turned up, then promptly left again.

Isaac went scarlet. 'They say I need better plans,' he blustered. 'The ones Lord Grays had drawn up aren't good enough. I have to get a proper architect. Where will I find an architect around here? I'll have to go to London. Bastards won't give me my money back, say it's not their fault things haven't been done properly, that it's not safe to just go ahead and start work. What can be so difficult about putting up a few walls and knocking through a couple of windows? My grandfather built most of this place with his own two hands and it hasn't fallen around our ears, has it? Not only that, they told me I've bought the wrong kind of stone. How can you have the wrong kind of stone?'

Next day he was off again. The quarrymen wouldn't take the stone back so it lay in heaps around the inn, getting in everyone's way. Another storm arrived to blow the muggy air apart. It lifted the tarpaulin off the stack of timber and soaked everything. The wood warped, rendering it useless. Isaac's curses coloured one day after another, especially when he checked the shrinking accounts.

'I'll have to go cap in hand to Grays and ask for more money,' he said. Nobody answered him.

With all the commotion we were lucky to have any guests left, but by the middle of the following week things had started to settle down. The gentry breakfasted in the Long Room while next door the merchants devoured thick slices of Sally's ham before shaking out their cloaks and facing the day. Usually there were a few stragglers – lone horsemen who'd put in for the night, the odd drover, farmer or tradesman in search of an early sup of ale.

A small grove of tables faced the bar, stools upended on top. Empty of smoke and chatter the taproom could be a gloomy tomb of a place.

I yawned and glanced at our only customer, seated in the far corner beside the window. A jug of cider (a rancid local brew, but it was cheap) grew stale on the table in front of him. A horse dealer from Middlesex called Rodgers.

The yard door thumped open. Startled, I knocked a bottle over. Quick reflexes saved it from shattering on the floor.

Three men, shaking dirt from their felt hats. Thick mud caked their boots. Dark and rich, not the washed-out muck of the lane. They'd walked across the fields. From where? Sally and I exchanged glances. 'Lizabeth would bite the rafters when she saw the trail they left across her scrubbed floor.

'Three jugs of ale,' said the tallest in an accent that pinned him within three miles of St Paul's. (That was the trick of working a coaching inn. You could tell in a sentence where a fellow hailed from without ever venturing six steps outside your own front gate.)

Three foaming tankards were slugged down in less than a minute and banged back on the counter. 'Cat's piss,' the long-legged man said. 'You country turnips brew concoctions that aren't fit for washing breeches in.'

'Don't have to drink none if you don't have a mind to,' Sally said evenly, 'though it seems to me that you put those three away willingly enough.'

Long-legs laughed. 'Here we have a clothes peg in an apron lecturing us about beer.' He tapped the rim of his tankard. 'More. I reckon after a barrel or two we might get a taste for it.'

Sally drew the ale. One of the men lit a pipe and snorted blue smoke. Another pushed a wad of tobacco into the side of his mouth and began to chew. Their manner was easy, confident. I doubted they were farmers.

From his corner Rodgers scowled at the newcomers. His chair scraped as he got up. He strode across to the bar and thumped his tankard down on the counter. *Uh oh*, I thought, wiping my soapy hands on a dishcloth. Rodgers glared at the three men then turned to leave. Pipe-smoker grabbed him by the sleeve.

'You have a problem, friend?' he asked in a singsong lilt, lips working around the pipe stem.

'I don't drink with road monkeys,' Rodgers spluttered, 'let alone Irish. These places are for respectable travellers, not mud-grubbers like you.'

'Is that right now?' said Pipe-smoker genially. 'And what would a fellow like you – a gentleman – have against the likes o' us?'

'My brother lost his farm to a turnpike. They paid him half of what it was worth then threw him and his family into the ditch.'

'As I see it, a man in this country don't give up his home unless he wants to.'

'Then you have a turnip between your ears. He was forced out. The Trust's agents bribed local merchants to raise the price of feed so his stock grew thin. They diverted the local stream so his well dried up and undercut his prices at market so he couldn't sell his produce or was forced to let it go at a huge loss. One morning he found a dead cow dumped in his barn. It was crawling with pestilence, which spread through his herd. Their hide was ruined, their meat not fit for pigs.'

'Serious things you're saying there.'

'Aye, serious enough.' Rodgers tried to shake himself free of the Irishman's grasp. Pipe-smoker exchanged looks with the Londoner who shook his head. The grip was released. Rodgers straightened his coat and left.

'A sorry state of affairs,' Pipe-smoker observed after the door had slammed, 'when a man can't get a friendly drink in a roadside inn.'

He winked at Sally. I folded the dishcloth and hung it from its hook beside the sink.

'What road was he talking about?'

His eyes settled on me. 'Hallo. Here's another who's forgotten how to be polite.'

''Tis only a wench, Liam,' Long-legs said. 'Don't make sport of her.'

'A wench with a tongue, Jack, and a look on her face I don't like.'

'Are you building a road?' I pressed. 'Are you?'

'We don't build roads, my sweet. We sort of make them happen. We look at a hill, a marsh, a forest and say to ourselves, "Yes, there's a way through there," or "That needs a bridge, that a causeway." You can whip the land if you're hard and clever enough.'

'That man was talking about a turnpike. I heard him. Is that what you fellows are working on? Is that why you are here? How far have you come? How far away is this thing from Green Gallows?'

But Pipe-smoker slid a brace of dice out of his pocket and they took themselves off to the corner, to the same table Rodgers had left only minutes before, and set about their game. Soon the room was full of coarse laughter.

I put down the bottle I'd been holding. 'Sally, can you look after the counter on your own for a while?'

'You're meant to stay here for the rest of the afternoon.'

'We're not busy. You can manage.'

Matthew jumped up when I walked into the stable. He'd been sitting on an upturned pail, his head resting against the door frame. Breadcrumbs were scattered across the front of his jerkin. Judd was nowhere to be seen.

'Saddle up Mistral.' I nodded towards Lucy's chestnut mare.

Matthew plucked the stalk from his mouth and flicked it into the corner. 'Is Miss Lucy going riding?'

I gestured irritably. 'Don't be an oaf. Get the saddle. I'll fetch a harness.'

'Where are you going?'

'Not your business.'

'Isaac won't like it. I'd better come with you.'

'No. You'd be missed. Go back to your day-dreams. If Judd asks where Mistral is, smile and tell him I wanted to blow the cobwebs out of my hair.'

Uncertainty flickered across his face. 'What's the matter, Rachel? You're shaking and look fit to be sick.'

I sat down on a straw bale, kicked off my shoes and crammed my feet into a pair of Judd's old riding boots.

'I am, Matthew. Glory, I am.'

Chapter Five

The sun slipped out from behind the clouds and beat down on the open meadow. Holding Mistral's reins with one hand, I used the other to shield my eyes against the glare. Ahead, Marrin's Ridge was a dark, tree-capped backbone of rock and soil. Mistral fidgeted. Flies buzzed around my face. I brushed them away. Grasshoppers rustled in the grass.

The common rippled away, cut by tufts of briar, coarse grass and boulders sprouting like grey mushrooms. It dipped slightly before rising to meet the Ridge. On the far side of the Chase – the very edge of Lord Marrin' s estate – water glimmered amidst banks of reeds. A small patch of marshland, barely two acres, but deep enough to swallow a horse or small cart. To the right stretched a tumbledown drystone wall where some long-ago tenant farmer had tried to enclose the land. The chalky soil was too poor to farm, too plagued with clover, thorns and poison berries to be safe for grazing animals, though gypsies sometimes camped there during the milder winters. The best stones had been plundered from the wall years ago. Only moss-stained chunks remained, half-buried and scratched with bramble.

Mistral snorted. A shimmering of foam coated her flanks. Far behind me, a wagon lumbered down the lane, the grind of its wooden axles sounding broken and disjointed.

Half a mile distant, moving figures dotted the open ground. Long ditches had been cut into the turf. The grass either side was muddy and trampled. Soil was heaped loosely in uneven piles.

I clicked the reins. My mount picked her way across the uneven ground. A team of men were shovelling dirt at a blistering rate. Their backs were bare, the skin grimy and damp with sweat. They hardly spared me a glance. Other labourers were taking the soil away in handcarts down a track worn in the grass. On either side, boulders had been stacked in untidy heaps.

Two men in shirtsleeves pored over a sheaf of papers spread out on a small folding table. A third was bent over some contraption perched on three wooden legs. Coloured poles had been driven into the ground at regular intervals.

I nudged Mistral forward. 'What are you doing?'

The men at the table looked up. Curiosity flickered across their faces. Behind them the excavations continued.

'Tell those fellows to stop,' I persisted. 'They shouldn't be working here. This is common land. You've got no right.'

One of the men slipped off his neckerchief and mopped his brow. Three of his front teeth were missing, two on top and one below. It gave his face a lopsided look.

'Rights are not my concern, little lady,' he said, air whistling through the gap in his upper jaw. 'There's a fat bonus for us if this job is finished quickly and it's my aim to collect it. Are you one of the local farm girls?'

'No. My name's Rachel Curtis. My father, Isaac Curtis, is landlord of Green Gallows Inn.'

The two men exchanged glances. 'Green Gallows? Is that on the South Road?'

Mistral shifted beneath me. I tugged gently on the reins until she settled. 'Yes, about six miles from here between Prestbury and Stonehill. It's the best coaching house in this part of the country.'

'We're Londoners, miss, so we wouldn't know about that. But if your papa runs an inn on the South Road then he'd best find another trade.'

'Why? You still haven't told me what you're doing here. This is common land all the way to the Ridge.'

'Not any more. The Southern Counties Turnpike Trust owns everything you see, including the ground your nag is standing on. That means you're trespassing, miss.'

Panic bit into my stomach. Mistral, sensing my distress, snorted and pawed at the ground with her foreleg. 'There is to be no turnpike here. It was just a rumour. Everybody knows that.'

Again the two men glanced at one another. One shook his head. 'A turnpike, all the way from London to the coast. Planned and paid for by the Trust. From what I heard that old South Road was little better than a cart track anyhow.'

'I don't believe you.'

He unfurled a map and passed it up to me. 'See for yourself.'

I stared at the ink lines dividing up the rolling hills and meadows of my world. I was no expert but everything was clearly marked. A thick, dark gash cut from north to south.

'Three of those meadows belong to Bill Milston,' I said. 'It is his best pastureland.'

'Milston Farm has been bought by the Trust. The farmhouse will be torn down and its stones used for laying the foundations of the new road. Post horses shall graze the fields. 'Tis the same story all along the planned route. Farms and taverns bought up, new coaching inns built, toll booths and gates to be erected. Most folk have either sold up and left or changed their trade. Your papa must have known.'

I followed the line on the map with my finger. It carved through villages that had stood for centuries. Neither forest or river seemed to halt it or force it to change course.

'You can't build a turnpike here. It shall take all our business. No one will use the South Road except drovers and pedlars. My father has just signed papers for a loan to expand the business.'

The workman shrugged. Not his life that would be ruined, his sister thrown into paupery, his parents into a debtors' prison.

'He must have known,' the workman repeated. 'Why don't you go home, lass. Men are working here. More will follow soon. It is no place for a girl.'

All I could hear was the beat of ravens' wings.

I don't remember the journey back to Green Gallows. Mistral used her nose and plodded home. Clouds smothered the sun again, turning the countryside gunmetal grey. Marrin's Chase sat like a black wart, the trees limp and unmoving.

Everything had a violated look.

I hoped to slip quietly into the stables but Matthew was in the yard, lifting hay bales from one wall and stacking them against the other. Stalks of chaff drifted like yellow knife blades. Mistral's hooves sounded unnaturally loud on the gravel.

Matthew put down the bale he'd been carrying. 'You weren't gone long,' he said casually. 'Not long enough to ride to Prestbury, or even as far as the base of the Ridge.'

I dismounted and threw him the reins. He caught them without taking his eyes off me.

'Take her inside,' I ordered. 'Stow her saddle and brush her down. She hasn't been worked too hard and should settle quickly.'

'You were not seen so far as I could tell,' Matthew continued, still clutching the reins. 'None need be any the wiser about your trip.'

'Fine. Let it stay that way.'

Still he held his ground. 'Those are Judd's old boots, and they're clean. You've not been out of the saddle since you left.'

I clucked in irritation. 'I've given you work to do. Stop idling and take Mistral inside.'

'Idling? I've been shifting hay bales as you can see.'

'Those bales didn't need shifting. You've been waiting for me, that's what. You were angry because I wouldn't let you come along, and you're put out that I won't tell you where I've been. And what if I still don't tell you, Matthew? Will you go and tattle to Judd?'

'Naw, I wouldn't do such a thing.'

'Yes you would. Not straight out, perhaps, but you'd say that Mistral was missing from her stall and I was nowhere to be found. You always want to know where I've been, what I've done, who I've spoken to. Would wearing a cowbell around my neck make you happy?'

'Quit shouting, Rachel,' he said quietly. 'Everyone will hear 'ee.'

I pulled off my gloves and threw them onto the floor. 'It doesn't matter. After today, nothing much matters any more.'

Isaac knew.

Maybe he bumped into the labourers. Likely, given how free they were with their tongues. Or Sally might have told him. She had a scold's mouth at times. Certainly she'd have mentioned it to Judd. He'd know what a turnpike meant.

Pride still smarting from my tantrum in the stable, I flounced into the parlour. Isaac was pacing the rug. Mother was seated by the cold hearth, hacking bitter tears into a crumpled strip of lace. Isaac paused when he saw me.

'You know about the road,' he said straight away.

'Yes,' I said. 'Labourers came into the taproom, started swilling ale. They were full of talk.'

'Where have you been hiding?'

'Matthew wanted help in the stables.'

'Why didn't you come to me when these men started talking?'

'I was frightened.'

Isaac sat down wearily on the bench beside the table. 'It can't be true.'

Mother shifted on her chair. 'If you had spent

more time building friendships instead of planning extra bedrooms then you would have listened when men with more sense tried to warn you,' she said, voice muffled behind the lace.

'I'll ride out this afternoon. Maybe it's not so bad as we fear. Men like that are always full of stories. Lord Marrin has long wanted that common land cleared. Talk of a turnpike is a jest. It must be.'

I bit my tongue. If he rode out, if he told them who he was, barked it out in his bullish voice, one of the workmen might tell him about the girl on a chestnut mare. I could imagine a leathery face breaking into a brown-toothed grin. 'Got in a proper strop she did. Told us all to go home. Said she was the innkeeper's daughter and we had no business here.'

They'd laugh. Isaac's face would colour. He'd forget how many men were working the area. He'd forget they had picks and spades.

'City labourers are not brought in to drain a marsh,' Mother said. 'Don't go, Isaac. You will never hold your temper. You'll get us all into trouble.'

Isaac stared at the palms of his hands. 'I must see for myself. Lord Grays said there would be no turnpike. He said there were deeds – covenants – protecting the common land. He said they would not build a road because of the marsh.'

'Covenants can be broken,' Mother said. 'The only common land that ever stayed common were the barren plots the gentry had no use for.'

'They'll do more than drain the marsh. Woods will be felled, game scared away, fields carved up.

Those purse-proud merchants of London will block up wells and build bridges where no bridge has a right to be. I know all about turnpikes. You can't take so much as a step down these filthy devil's tracks without having to empty your pocket for the privilege. It will kill the land. I can't let it happen.'

That afternoon, Isaac rode out towards the common. Judd followed on one of our posted horses. Both men returned an hour later, grim, boiling with unspoken thoughts. I was waiting inside the stable door, tolerating Matthew, one eye on the gate which I could just glimpse from the end stall. Matthew, badly judging the mood, made some jolly greeting. Judd pushed him aside and went through into the tack room. Isaac followed and closed the door. I listened for voices – Isaac's sharp bark, Judd's low, normally amiable rumble. Nothing. Not a sound. I waited until Matthew unharnessed the horses then went back inside the inn.

Both men emerged as the sun was dipping behind the Ridge. I found an excuse to go into the hall. They brushed past me, smelling of gin and tobacco. Sally often said she suspected Judd of having a jug tucked away in there. Isaac's eyes were black, Judd's looked broken. Later in the kitchen Judd had an enormous row with Sally. The inn shook with it. Isaac sat on the bench at the parlour table and did nothing to interfere. As twilight spread over the hushed countryside, he put on his riding jacket and fetched Apollo, his hunter, from the stables. He galloped off in the direction of Prestbury. From the parlour window,

Mother watched him leave. Her face was as grey as the dusk. Lucy dragged out the sewing box and tried to persuade Mother to sit by the hearth and do some embroidery. I puttered about with the cutlery, but gave up when I found myself cleaning the same knife twice.

After about ten minutes Mother threw her sampler aside, lay back in her chair and pressed her fingers over her eyes.

'I think I'm growing a headache,' she said. Isaac still hadn't returned by the time the soft evening blackened into night. We all went to bed, leaving a candle burning in the parlour.

I dozed fitfully, conscious of every lump in my mattress, every creak of this sad old house. Sounds drifted through the woodwork, the nocturnal slumberings and shiftings of our guests. Somewhere a man coughed in his sleep, a wet sound, thick with phlegm. Elsewhere, bare feet padded across the ceiling, followed by the glassy trickle of water into a pot. I could only guess the time. It was too dark in my room to see the clock.

The slow clop of hooves on gravel. I rolled off the bed and scampered to the window. A glimmer of light from the taproom stabbed a yellow finger across the yard. Isaac, on foot, and behind him, Apollo being led by the reins. Other figures shifted in the darkness. The light caught their faces as they filed through the taproom door, shaking the night from their woollen coats. A dozen men, maybe more. Isaac tethered his horse and followed them inside.

I hugged my shift around me, slipped out of my room and padded along the hall to the parlour, hoping to find some warm embers at the bottom of the hearth. Mother was buried in Isaac's armchair, a candle stub spitting out a weak yellow halo. She looked up as I entered. In her lap was the half-finished sampler she'd tried to work on earlier.

Sighing, she leaned forward and patted the leather footstool beside the chair.

'Come sit with me, Rachel,' she said wearily. 'I have use of your company.'

I gathered up the hem of my shift, tiptoed across the rug and seated myself at her feet. Immediately the gentle scent of lavender surrounded me. Mother's breathing whispered in the quiet room. Regular, a little dry.

In the frantic bustle of each day our lives seldom touched with much tenderness. Without thinking, I reached up and was glad to feel Mother's fingers slip into mine. Cold, so terribly cold. I squeezed, wanting to warm them, wishing if I could that the warmth would spread – seep along her arms, into her chest, her heart.

With her other hand she began stroking my hair. Her face was heavy.

'What are they going to do?' I said finally.

'What those sort always do,' Mother said. 'Think with their fists instead of their heads.'

'Will there be trouble?'

The hand ceased its gentle movement. She tilted my head upwards and gazed into my eyes. I knew right away what she was searching for, or rather *who* she was searching for.

'It was the boots I noticed first,' she said. 'Thick brown leather with nails driven into the soles so that he kicked up a shower of sparks whenever he walked. Clem Baxter was his name. I never told you that, did I? He was tall like you, and round-faced with a burst of dark hair that always seemed to be falling into his eyes. He could scramble across cargo netting like a spider and got his share of gambling, fist fights and harlots. No saint was Clem, but no worse than any other man who worked the Portsmouth docks. He had a way of looking at me, of touching, that made me the centre of the whole world.'

She chuckled thinly. 'When Father found out he refused to give me supper. He said if I was set on being Clem Baxter's doxy then I had to learn what an empty belly felt like. Clem didn't have a home, just one flophouse room after another and, believe me, the bugs bit deep. I lost both my parents within a month of each other. Clem thought he'd have me for sure, but I was a well-educated girl and knew what I wanted even then. When Isaac Curtis came south on business for Green Gallows I all but forced a proposal out of his mouth. He was my last chance at respectability, I suppose. Of course I always knew I would go on seeing Clem, even after the birth of Lucy. Some hooks are in too deep. You can't cut them out or the wounds would fester and kill you. I never thought for a moment that God would punish us.'

She began stroking my hair again. 'He was crushed between the hull of a ship and the harbour wall. Rotten netting had split under his feet. I never saw his body, never said goodbye, but there was life in my belly again and that gave me something to cling to. You have his hair,

Rachel. You have his eyes. But I made another mistake. I thought Isaac would be content to have a beautiful daughter in Lucy, but he wanted everything. He stole you away from me. Every day I had to watch you get more and more like him. Those horses. That precious yard.'

She leaned over and kissed the crown of my head. 'Yes, I think there will be trouble.'

Next morning a raggle-taggle group gathered in the yard. Most held staves or pitchforks. One wielded a sword, a clumsy double handed monstrosity that was almost as tall as the bearer. In another pair of hands was an old rusty musket that looked more likely to blow up in its owner's face than send a ball hurtling anywhere with a hope of accuracy.

They talked quietly among themselves. One or two lit clay pipes and blew wisps of smoke across the yard. From time to time each man glanced towards Marrin's Chase and the open land beyond. Tattered kerchiefs hid faces for the most part. The eyes above were slitted, unblinking.

Before going outside to join them, Isaac knotted a strip of red linen behind his neck and tugged it over his face.

'Look at you,' Mother scoffed, 'a highwayman without a horse. Or a head for that matter. What can you hope to do? The milkmaid told Sally that a dozen men from Prestbury have already joined the workings and more are set to follow. They have to depend on it for their living now. What will they think of you coming to try and break things up?'

'Parish trash,' Isaac grunted through the cloth. 'They take the dirty jobs, the ones no clean-living man would touch.'

'I heard Will Briggs has gone to the road, and Jake Culvert from Boxhill Farm. You'd be as well to go too, Isaac Curtis. 'Twould put shillings in your pocket and bread on this table.'

'And what of our debts? I could work on a road from Portsmouth to the tip of Scotland and still not earn enough to cover them. What will these men you speak of do when the turnpike is finished? Those who sold up their land, or let themselves be bullied into giving it up? They will want to throw their lot in with us soon enough after the work has dried up. I've been my own man for too long, Harriet. I'll not call another my master.'

'Then you should've gone last night instead of ranting in the taproom. 'Twas a wonder our guests were not disturbed. How many barrels of ale did you open for those fools? Only a man with a sozzled head would set off on such a doomed errand. At least wait until it's dark again.'

'And blunder around in the Chase? Or lose men to the marsh? We're not poachers. One of us would most likely stumble and split his skull open.' He shook his head. 'Nay, Harriet. It has to be stopped. It has to be stopped now.'

A familiar shape hobbled across the yard. I squinted through the parlour window. Barnabas. Barnabas Pegg. For pity's sake, what did Isaac think he was doing letting him join this unkempt mob? There was no mistaking him, even with the thick coat and that useless mask over his face. Barnabas 'sticky-shanks' Pegg who had a left leg three inches shorter than the right and a strawberry birthmark sprouting on his cheek. I might've known he'd come. Looking the way Barnabas did, you couldn't grow up without black eyes and bloody knuckles. Barnabas was the one who had to climb the trees higher than anyone else, who plunged into a fast flowing river to fetch Matthew's makeshift rod from the bottom when they both went fishing together, who took on the dog – some hoary cur with the blood of half a dozen vicious breeds roaring in its veins – that was worrying Geoff Cullins' sheep, fought it with his bare hands because he could not find rock or stick, and who earned himself a bloody crescent on his forearm where the brute sank its fangs before Barnabas twisted its neck. He was as strong as a bull, and as slow, walking with a permanent list to the left that even the wooden block nailed to the sole of his boot could do little to fix.

I moved towards the door.

'Rachel, where are you going?' Isaac said.

'Outside.'

'No you're not. This is men's business. Drop the latch on the door. Stay away from the window. You're not wanted there.'

Not wanted here. Not wanted there, nor anywhere. I returned to my bedchamber. I owed sleep a big debt and it was scratching at my eyes. I slumped onto my lumpy bed, not bothering to take off my dishevelled gown. I turned onto my left side, I turned onto my right. Outside, the crunch of boots on gravel faded into the distance, then silence.

I lay on my back, staring at the ceiling. Above

my pillow, two spiders circled on gossamer strands so thin it seemed they were walking on air. Long spindly legs tapered into needlepoints, clinging to an empty web.

I often kept my window closed. The post boys used to tease me by scooping newts out of the pond, leaning through the window and dropping them into my bed, and if it wasn't newts it was strips of bramble. 'Lizabeth probably put them up to it. Besides I couldn't stand flies buzzing around the room.

My eyelids drooped. The spiders continued to circle one another, legs reaching, touching, drawing back. Then one spider climbed onto the belly of the other and sank its fangs deep inside its body. I screamed and jerked upright, knocking off a slipper. The victor began to spin. Before long, a silken cage bound the victim's limbs together. I wanted to snatch the spider out of its web, squash it between thumb and forefinger, and rub until nothing was left.

It was too far away. Even standing on the end of my bed, I couldn't reach it. Finally, a well-aimed pillow knocked it out of its lair. I went for it, heels stomping, but the cursed creature scuttled under the crack at the bottom of the door.

Exhausted, I returned to my rumpled bed, lay down and fell into a deep sleep.

It was raining again by the time Isaac returned. His head was a strawberry cake of blood and matted hair. Mud coated his breeches. The sleeves of his shirt were torn and stuck with thorns.

Mother and I were waiting for him in the kitchen. It was past two o' clock. He had returned alone.

'Did you put a stop to their fancy road?' Mother said quietly. 'Did you scare the city boys? Show them what men you are?'

Isaac ripped off his waistcoat and tossed it over the back of his armchair. Bruises yellowed his forearms, and the back of his hands were criss-crossed with scratches.

'We never made it to the road, never made it within sight of the first diggings. They were waiting for us at the edge of Marrin's Chase. Wood's so thick they were on us before we knew it. All we could do was run. When we broke through the trees they came after us. They had guns, Harriet.'

'Someone must have told them. Who's the Judas? Who?'

Isaac shook his head. 'Maybe they heard us crashing through the woods. We thought that would be the best way, that we wouldn't be spotted until we were close. Took us better than an hour to blunder halfway through. More than enough time to be ready for us. We can't try it again. They'll have posted watchmen.'

I couldn't keep quiet any longer. 'Was anyone hurt?'

Isaac looked at me. 'Barnabas. The cooper's lad.'

Mother's hand flew to her mouth. 'Oh Lord. Not Barnabas. He was barely fourteen.'

'They had horses. Not shires or any other kind of cart-puller but fast hunters. We couldn't outrun 'em. They jumped the old dykes like they weren't there. Barnabas tried to hide behind one, but a hoof clipped him across the skull and another brought some of the stones down across his legs. I tried to fetch help but everyone had scattered. Barnabas was moaning. God help me I had to press my hand over his mouth in case our pursuers should hear. Blood was gushing out of his nose. I managed to haul him into the ditch beside the lane. Marsh water had been drained into it. 'Twas all I could do to keep his head up, and all about us there was yelling and shooting. Four hours we stayed in there, shivering and groaning like old women. That water was cold, Harriet, colder than any water had a right to be at this time of year. And all the time I'm whispering to Barnabas: "Hang on, lad. Hang on." But the ditchwater went red with his blood and flies kept buzzing about his head like he was a piece of scrap meat someone had tossed into the lane.

'Finally, when I thought things had quietened down enough, I dragged Barnabas out of the ditch. What a sorry, sopping sight we were. I got the boy onto my shoulders and tried to carry him, but I could hardly feel my legs and kept stumbling. Once I heard hooves clopping down the lane and hid in a bush with him a dead weight sprawled over me. It was just a farm cart heading towards Prestbury. A cat could've crossed my path and I'd have swooned like a maiden. Finally I got him to Bill Blankerton's farm. Beth Blankerton said some men had come with constables from Stonehill. They said they were looking for troublemakers and just about pulled the farm down about her ears. She'd spent all afternoon trying to clear up. Bill had been taken to Prestbury for questioning. Beth had her dander up about that too because

Bill had told me to my face that he'd wanted nothing to do with us, that the road was here to stay and, with a wife and farm, he'd no notion to feel a hangman's rope kissing his neck. I thought Beth was going to turn me away but she fears God more than she fears the bailiffs and took Barnabas in. "There's a priest hole beneath the scullery floor," she told me. "If the constables come back I can put him in there."

'I knew she could an' all. I've seen that woman with a calf slung across her back and walking just as merrily as you please. I fussed by the window while she bathed the lad's wound and put him in Bill's bed. Barnabas had stopped moaning but his breath had a ragged edge and I didn't care for what was in Beth's eyes when she bent over him. She told me to go in the end, said there was no point in risking us both getting caught and just looking after Barnabas was trouble enough.'

Isaac stared at his open hands. 'What am I to tell his mother? What will I tell his da? He's just a boy. Young Jane Acre over at Meadowcroft is sweet on him. There was talk of a wedding next spring.'

'You shouldn't have taken him.'

'I couldn't get enough men.'

'Then you should not have gone at all.'

Isaac wiped his brow with the back of his hand. 'I'll have to tell his da,' he repeated.

'You must burn your clothes,' Mother said. 'No amount of scrubbing will wash his blood out of your shirt.'

Isaac smacked his fist down on the table. We both jumped. 'Quiet yourself, wife. I'll do a lot more before I see that road finished.'

‘I will not be quiet. Those men will come looking for you. They’ll come here.’

‘They’ve no reason to come here. They know we won’t go back.’

He shambled over to the hearth and stared into the empty grate. ‘The other lads managed to slip away. Those bailiffs are too fat to put up much of a chase and there are places horses can’t go.’

Outside, a dog barked in the muggy afternoon air.

Isaac curled his fingers. ‘They’ve already brought in travelling masons to build their toll-houses. I’ll go to London to see Lord Sutcliffe. This must be a mistake.’

‘You’ve already seen for yourself. A hundred men digging up the common and carting rubble is no mistake. And even if you were allowed anywhere near Lord Sutcliffe what would you say to him?’

‘He counselled me to expand Green Gallows. ’Twas his friends who loaned the money. An investment, that’s what he called it, those very words. There must be something I can bargain with.’

He sat back down, touched the back of his head and regarded his bloody fingers. ‘Rachel, fetch me a basin of hot water and some brandy.’

I scurried towards the kitchen. ‘There must be something,’ he said again.

Barnabas Pegg died in his hiding place at Blankerton’s farm. There was a hole in his skull you could push two fingers through. The linen which had covered most of his face was thick with dried blood.

Harry Pegg fetched his son home and laid him out on the bed he shared with his brother. Mother told us. She was on gossiping terms with Catherine Pegg. Their other son, Joshua, drove the barrel cart to Green Gallows. He was sitting in our yard, still on the driver's perch, bawling his eyes out. Mother filled a wicker basket with bread, wine, mutton and some oatmeal cakes. She threw her shawl around her shoulders, clambered up onto the seat beside Joshua and made him drive back to Prestbury.

'Got barrels to deliver,' Joshua said. He sounded as if he had been forced to swallow his own heart. 'Mr Isaac won't take kindly to not gettin' his barrels.'

'The barrels can wait,' Mother said. 'And so can Mr Isaac.'

They drove off, swallowed up by the drizzle. Mother didn't return until dusk. Her face was pinched, her basket forgotten. She blustered into the parlour, asked 'Lizabeth to fetch her some broth from the kitchen, and thrust her sopping feet in front of the fire.

Harry Pegg had not been at home when Mother arrived. He'd spent an hour praying by his dead son's bedside then had stormed back out of the house, taking neither hat nor coat, marching in the direction of Marrin's Chase. Catherine Pegg had been frantic, thinking with good reason that he'd gone to seek revenge against Barnabas's killers.

'They'll kill him too,' she said.

'We must find him,' Mother replied. Joshua was

no use to anyone so she made Catherine collect her wrap and together the two women had set off towards the woods. They found Mr Pegg just inside the Chase, squatting in the lee of an old dyke. His face was raw from sobbing. They couldn't get him to unclench his fists. His nails had cut bloody 'u's into his palms.

The women sat with him for more than an hour until he was ready to come home.

'Even then we had to support him,' Mother said. 'You should have seen us, stumbling the three miles to Prestbury with him clinging to our skirts like a child. I'll go back tomorrow and see how Catherine is.'

'Tell her I need those barrels,' Isaac said.

Next morning Harry Pegg was discovered hanging, blue-faced, from the rafters in his workshop. His mouth was twisted as if his son's name was forever mortared onto his dead lips.

Even in death he would be denied a reunion. Taking his own life condemned him to a burial outside the churchyard at a cold, noisy corner of the lykeway.

Catherine Pegg had his coffin laid out in the workshop. After the carpenter and his apprentice had gone, she covered some barrels with pitch and set fire to them. The blaze quickly spread, consuming the building along with her husband's tools. Then she packed what belongings she could onto the cart, took Joshua with her and drove out of Prestbury, leaving her house to the turnpike.

Thunderclouds billowed above Green Gallows' chimneys. The air thickened. Each breath had to be dragged into the lungs. Tempers sparked.

Lucy was avoiding everyone. She'd been sweet to Barnabas and his death hurt her. She shut herself in her room, only coming downstairs to entertain in the Long Room. Jeremiah Cathcart kept out of the way too. The last time I saw him he was burning Isaac's warped timber in a huge bonfire behind the coach house. He took his meals with Judd and slept in the hayloft. If Lucy slipped out after dark again I never heard her.

I thumped around the inn, paced corridors, tramped up and down stairs. Judd threw me out of the stables, Sally threw me out of the kitchen and 'Lizabeth made such a dour face about my working in the taproom that we nearly had a thunderstorm of our own behind the counter.

'Your miserable countenance is upsetting our customers,' Isaac told me. 'Take it elsewhere and try to pin some good humour onto it.'

Gregor brought in the midday stagecoach from Stonehill. The horses' flanks were glossy with the slow, persistent rain which had not let up since yesterday morning. The sky was luminous with threats.

Matthew changed the team. The animals were edgy and claimed his full attention. I opened the carriage door. Three passengers stepped down. A woman, a skinny clergyman and a gold bedecked city fop. I checked inside the coach. Empty. No Sailor Ben. No lawyer on his way to see his niece in Prestbury.

Blinking the drizzle out of my eyes I glanced up at Gregor. He lingered on the driver's perch while Sammy unloaded the baggage. A smoking pipe was clenched between his teeth. He seemed distracted, uncomfortable.

I waited until the coachman had taken both the baggage and its small gaggle of owners inside. Matthew hadn't yet led out the fresh team. I was alone in the yard with Gregor.

'Have you seen it?' I called up to him.

Gregor shifted on his seat. Something flickered in his tired eyes.

'Have you seen it?' I pressed. 'The turnpike?'

'Aye, I've seen it.'

I tried not to panic, not to let the moment slip away, to be swallowed up by the ugly black thing that was growing deep inside my stomach.

'Gregor, ten years or more you've been carrying passengers to Green Gallows. Tell me you won't use the turnpike, that you'll still bring the stage-coach down the South Road. You'll save the toll and your passengers shall be royally entertained. Isaac rightly prides himself on our hospitality.'

Gregor tapped his pipe on the side of the roof. Burnt tobacco fell in a black snow. ''Tis no use, girl. Our journeys are always posted at the coaching offices in Stonehill. The route, the times – everything. Drivers vie amongst themselves to see who can best match the timetable. The new road has caused great excitement. Oh, there are those who grumble about the toll-houses but they're gout-ridden old men who never leave their armchairs. People are no longer content with one trip a year to the next town or long journeys over bad roads, only to be finally baulked by a flooded stream or a felled tree.'

'I'll give you five guineas not to use the turnpike.'

He laughed but there was no cruelty in it. 'And

where would you fetch such a bribe?'

'Isaac will pay it. He'll pay double. There'll be something for your coachman too. A free meal, or ale perhaps?'

'You're not the only one whose trade is threatened. I have to do what I'm told or lose my job.'

He lived on the outskirts of Stonehill. The coaching company owned his house. He had never worked at anything else.

Any moment now Matthew would lead the horses out of the stables. 'Then who's behind it? Who made the decision to run a turnpike alongside the lykeway? We need to know who is killing us, Gregor. We need to find out who runs the Trust.'

He took a leather tobacco pouch out of his coat, refilled his pipe, lit it from a tinderbox and settled back on the seat.

'Stories, that's all I've heard. Names are thrown around like pots o' gin and the rumours are just as cheap. London is full of wolves, lass. They've torn the innards out of their city until there's nothing left to feed on, so now they're moving south and they'd as likely turn on one another if there's a morsel catches their eye, or a bigger bite of something that another has his eye on. Wolves in smart clothes and fine carriages.' He drew on his pipe. 'Or not so fine as the case may be.'

Gregor stared off towards the horizon. Fingers of blue-grey smoke pinched the sky from the road workings beyond the Chase. He said nothing more. From the stables came the jingle of harnesses. Matthew with the new team.

'Oh glory,' I whispered.

I couldn't tell Isaac. He wouldn't believe it. Not from my mouth. There was no proof, after all. Nothing you could pin a tail to. Yet I knew, and so did Gregor for all his talk of rumours.

For the rest of the afternoon I went about the yard thumping pails, banging doors, baring teeth at anyone unlucky enough to cross my path.

'What's got 'ee so worked up?' Matthew said, after I jumped when he brushed my arm. 'Are you still angry at me?'

I gestured vaguely at the leaden sky. 'I wish this weather would break. It has my teeth on edge.'

Matthew nodded and returned to his work but I knew my explanation hadn't satisfied him.

Later, Isaac, irked by my restlessness, put me in the taproom with 'Lizabeth. We circled each other like spitting cats. Every comment carried a barb, every gesture a slight. Some customers caught our mood and were amused no end by it, sometimes playing us off against one another or setting us to a task which required close work or both pairs of hands, laughing as the sparks flew.

'Lizabeth was too stupid to realise what they were doing. I was aware of my face growing redder and redder. Scenting victory, she flounced around the counter, cast triumphant glances, deliberately bumped into me when I was obliged to pass. Sensing a catfight, people egged her on. I was three heartbeats away from ripping her hair out by the roots when the stable-yard door opened and a group of mud-streaked labourers brought in a storm of their own.

They had to be looking for trouble. Isaac, on his ride over to the workings, had told the road gangs to stay away from Green Gallows. Tell a man not to do something and of course he'll do it.

They made no attempt to remove their coats or seat themselves. The biggest member of the group swaggered up to the bar, grinning like a dog with bad teeth. 'Lizabeth retreated, her back pressed against the ale barrels. I stuck to my place at the counter, quietly wiping down the woodwork. I met the labourer's flinty gaze when he slapped his callused palm down on the bar.

'Ale,' he said. 'Five pots. Now.'

I drew the first quickly and without fuss. The labourer beckoned over his cronies. 'Lizabeth sidled up and nudged me on the calf with the toe of her shoe.

'They're road workers,' she hissed in my ear. 'Don't give them anything.'

I poured the second jug and placed it, foaming, beside the first. I started to draw a third.

'Are you stupid? Pour those drinks away.'

I placed the third ale on the counter and started to draw a fourth.

'Right,' 'Lizabeth said, 'I'm going to fetch Mr Curtis.'

I had the fifth beer poured when Isaac barged into the taproom, 'Lizabeth, face flushed, tripped in behind him. Without a word he picked up the tankards I had poured and threw the ale in the workmen's faces.

'Get out,' he barked.

The big one thought to make an issue of it but his friend held him back. 'Don't let it bother you, Thomas. There's plenty places will be glad of our custom and there'll be plenty more when the new road opens.'

'That road won't open, not while I live,' Isaac snarled, and smacked his fist into the face of the nearest labourer.

I covered my face with my hands. Other customers shrank back to their tables.

The men fell on him. Isaac went down under a rain of punches. The big fellow had already shrugged off Isaac's blow and set to with his boot. When they were finished, Isaac's shirt was a crumpled blood pie. His nose streamed, his cheek was already swelling. They left him lying on the floorboards and strolled, laughing, towards the door. I suddenly realised that 'Lizabeth was screaming, had been since the fighting had started. Outside, rain hammered down on the yard.

The workman called Thomas paused, fished a coin out of his pocket and flipped it at Isaac. It jingled onto the floor beside his battered face.

'There,' Thomas said. 'That's for the ale. None can call us thieves.'

Isaac pulled himself to a sitting position. He spat blood. 'I don't want it.'

Thomas opened the door. Coats flapped in the whistling gale that flung itself into the taproom. He had to shout above the wind. 'Take it. You'll soon need all the money you can get.'

'Lizabeth ran off to fetch Mother. Not one to be thrown by the sight of cuts and bruises she set about Isaac's bloated face with linen, salted hot water and precious little sympathy.

'Looks worse than it is,' she said, dabbing Isaac's cheek and slapping his hand away when he tried to fend her off. 'Those fellows were playing with you. Their foreman probably sent them over.'

He groaned when she applied salt to the cut on his forehead. 'Stop fussing, husband. You'll be sore for a day or two and then off getting yourself into more trouble. 'Lizabeth, clean up that floor.'

The mop and pail were fetched from behind the counter. 'Lizabeth scooped up the coin, wiped it on the back of her apron and slipped it into the cuff of her sleeve. The mop ran over the floorboards in wide, lazy circles, leaving uneven streaks of blood and ale.

On his feet again, Isaac's first act was to have a go at me.

'You should know better than to serve road trash,' he growled.

'Sutcliffe is a member of the Turnpike Trust.'

'Eh?'

'Lord Sutcliffe. He is one of the Trust. He has an interest in the new road.'

I watched the rise and fall of Isaac's broad shoulders, the way shadows played across his face as 'Lizabeth moved in front of one window and then another, mop swish-swishing around the tables.

'How'd you know that?'

I bit my lip. 'One of the labourers was already drunk and started blabbing.'

'Lizabeth looked up and frowned. She opened her mouth as if to speak but then, remembering the coin I had watched her steal, went back to mopping up the bar.

Isaac slowly let out his breath. His eyes glimmered darkly. A big hand reached out and patted me on the shoulder.

'You've done well, girl. We just might have a way out of this after all.'

Chapter Six

'Rachel, fetch a riding habit. Take one of Lucy's, whichever can be made to fit. Judd will saddle up Mistral. We're going to London.'

Within the half-hour we were galloping through the murk. Drizzle pricked our faces as the horses gobbled up the miles. Soaked and mud-splattered, we stopped for the night at a small posting house. Isaac engaged a single room and made up a bed for me on the floor. 'Ain't got time to be dainty,' he explained. 'I'll look the other way if you want to use the pot.'

Nothing met with his approval. He all but hurled his supper in our bewildered landlord's face. 'The beds are lumpy, the food ain't fit for pigs and the place stinks like a privy,' he said within earshot of everyone. 'I'd dismiss any maid of mine who left rooms in such a state, or any cook who tried to serve swill like this to a paying customer.'

'You'll get us thrown out,' I said, fearful of spending a sodden night in the lane.

When I turned in, Isaac stayed in the taproom staring into the fire, an untouched jug of ale beside him. I didn't know whether he ever came to bed for I slept soundly despite the hard floor, and the next thing I knew he was nudging me awake with his boot.

'No time for breakfast,' he said. 'I've had the rogue who runs this bothy cut us some bread and ham. We can eat on the road.'

I was stiff and aching, but an hour in the saddle soon knocked the grogginess out of me. The skies had cleared and the countryside had a fresh, washed look. The road widened and traffic increased.

Eight miles short of the city we struck the new turnpike. This part was already open and busy with travellers. It had completely smothered the old South Road. Isaac refused to pay the toll, forcing us to resort to drovers' tracks for the rest of the journey. We lost an hour when a huddle of sheep blocked the lane. The drover just laughed at Isaac's red-faced threats.

Finally, London. Grey buildings belching smoke jostled together like rows of crumbling teeth. The streets were awash with sewage and fighting drunks. People spilled out of gin shops. Hawkers barked. Sedan chairs were whisked along pavements, red-faced bearers adding calls of 'By your leave' to the clamour. Tardy beggars found themselves bowled into the brimming gutter.

We crossed the Thames just south of St Paul's. On the embankment two enormous women, scarlet and riddled with the pox, scratched and clawed in the mud while jeering bystanders egged them on.

'Gerroff me! Gerroff or I'll 'ave the rest o' yer teeth out!'

Dogs barked and fought for scraps. Grubby, barefoot children bawled. Mothers breastfed while swilling gin. Men argued, played cheap card games, broke each other's faces with scarred fists, and baited animals. Carriages rattled past, splashing water in all directions. Rising behind the hovels, the cathedral pointed a stubby finger to the sky.

Through it all ran the grey, sluggish river, swelling with the tide, bloated on rubbish and drowned rats.

I clicked the reins and brought Mistral up beside Apollo. My fingers ached. I looked down and saw my knuckles white on the leather straps. Beggars swarmed around us, palms open, the limbless hopping or scrambling along the ground with spider-like agility. 'Please help, kind sir. A farthing, young miss, spare a farthing.'

I shrank back in the saddle. Isaac had been to London before and told me what could happen when you tossed an idle penny to the mob, of the riots that could follow as people scrabbled in the dirt or clawed your pockets in the hope of another prize.

The air was thick with scents – cooking food, horseshit, unwashed bodies. A thrum of sound and life – earnest, restless, desperate life. We spent the morning visiting inns and coaching houses. Isaac quaffed ales, slapped strangers on the back, pressed shillings into eager palms. Sutcliffe's patchwork carriage was well known around the streets of London. Not so well known was his lair.

'Didn't you get an address from his banker friends?' I asked wearily.

Isaac shook his head. 'We'll have to catch him on the hop, that's all.'

It was a hopeless task. My hair was blown into a tangle. My eyes stung and my rump ached from hours in the saddle. The cobbled areas of the city were not kind to Mistral's hooves, the clamour unsettled her and the lack of greenery and open spaces pressed upon her mood. She became sullen and unresponsive. Apollo caught it and sagged along, ignoring Isaac's impatient boot.

We tried some of the coffee shops hugging the river. There Isaac caught a whisper, a suggestion. A name passed from mouth to mouth. More coins left his purse. Something was muttered into his ear and we were on the move once again.

North of the river now. The streets began to widen. Our horses broke into a brisk canter. Isaac gave his mount rein, I followed. We passed the Gale Inn, home of the *Charger*, distinctive sign flapping silently on well-greased hooks. The gates were open. In the stable yard the famous coach was loading passengers. I wanted to dally for a closer look but Isaac waved me on.

'We've no business there,' he said.

Terraces of cream-coloured houses glowed in the sunshine. There were parks with clipped lawns on which young gentlemen promenaded with their doxies. A lily-shrouded pond bristled with ducks. There was a flower seller, wicker baskets brimming with reds and yellows. And opposite stood a sallow-faced man in a headscarf, his ears dripping gold, hawking jewellery and other trinkets from a bow-topped wagon. No gypsy he. The Romanies working the South Road dealt in horses, not worthless baubles.

I breathed deeply, savouring the scent of summer blooms. Water splashed from a fountain into a wide marble bowl. Cobbles gave way to paving stones. Grandly dressed couples, walking with their arms linked, gave us curious looks.

I reined in. Mistral halted, hooves scrabbling on the stonework. Isaac slowed Apollo, turned and clopped over.

'What's the matter?'

'Everyone is staring at us.'

'Tradesmen come and go as they please. I've as much a right to ride through this part of the city as anyone.'

'But...'

Isaac shook his head. 'An hour's delay brings that devil's road closer to my inn. If you've gone faint-hearted, lass, I'll give you a sovereign and you can wait for me at a tavern. I know a couple of good ones where you'll be looked after.'

I said nothing and clicked Mistral forward.

'Best be sure,' Isaac continued, catching up. 'I can't have you going soft on me once we find Sutcliffe.'

I forced a smile.

'I'm sure.'

'You shut this door in my face,' Isaac warned, 'and I'll put my fist through it. Don't give me any more excuses. Go and tell Lord Sutcliffe that I'm here. Curtis is my name, Isaac Curtis of Green Gallows Inn.'

The footman's expression remained poker stiff beneath his powdered wig. 'Lord Sutcliffe is not–'

Isaac held up his hand. 'His carriage is round the back. I saw it through the railings. He won't travel in anything else. It's been in my yard often enough.'

We were shown into a cramped room just off the main hall. A place where coachmen changed their boots. The address Isaac had been given brought us to a dead end road dominated by a squat, sprawling building of yellow sandstone. I'd squinted at it in the sunlight. A dozen tall windows, frames painted white, dark glass impenetrable. Others were bricked up. Something about a tax, I'd heard. No smoke from any of the narrow chimneys. No horses clopping in the lane.

The door was a polished midnight blue with a brass lion's-head knocker growling at its centre.

We don't belong here. The thought flitted through my mind.

I didn't know whether I was in a gambling club, bordello or opium den. The smell of the place was old and familiar. The gentry brought it with them in their carriages from London. Stale tobacco, sour brandy, suffocatingly thick French perfume.

Isaac fumed as the minutes ticked by on the mantel clock. Finally, the footman returned. He led us down a long, wide passage lined with paintings, through another door and into a yard. The door to Sutcliffe's carriage was open. We mounted the steps and crammed inside.

Sutcliffe was swaddled in blankets from the waist down. An embroidered silk dressing gown was wrapped around his thin upper body and a round felt cap – gold tassel dangling – perched on the crown of his head. Curtains were drawn across the narrow windows and candles burned from metal sconces screwed into the woodwork. On the floor between our feet, an untidy heap of leather bound ledgers spilled their innards across the thick rug. A half-empty glass of port stood on a small table.

Sutcliffe's eyes glittered within the hollows of his skull. He gestured expansively, gold rings catching the candlelight and sending yellow fireflies dancing across the walls.

'What's this, Curtis? What's this? In London to sample some of our city inns? If so, why come knocking on my door?'

Isaac's hat was a scrunched-up lump in his white, trembling fingers. 'I believe m'lord knows why I've come.'

Sutcliffe clicked a finger at the footman who was loitering outside the door. 'Metcalfe, fetch our guest a brandy. He has an attitude that wants mellowing, I think.'

'I don't want a drink.'

'It is either that or a ducking in the trough. Hot tempers are not welcome in this establishment. Take care I am not obliged to have yours cooled.'

Isaac inspected the carpet. 'I'm no tradesman. I am a landlord, entitled to some respect.'

'Quite so, quite so. I already know a great deal about who you are and what you believe your place is. However that does not explain your presence at my private club, nor excuse your insolence.'

Isaac leaned forward. Sutcliffe's expression did not change. What if Isaac were to attack him? He could never summon his manservant in time.

'The turnpike,' Isaac continued, voice quaking. 'The bastard road that is carving up the common land beyond Marrin's Chase. That will take every carriage from London and the coast a full six miles away from Green Gallows. From my inn.'

'Ah yes,' Sutcliffe clasped his hands together. 'I hear it makes good progress. The coast by mid-autumn is the latest speculation.'

'You said it would cost too much. You said your bankers wouldn't back it because it'd be ten years or longer before they saw a return on their money. Now I hear you're part of the very Trust that's going to leech me dry.'

'Have a care, dear fellow. These carriage walls are not so thick as you might imagine. You must understand my position. The Trust comprises a dozen members of whom I am merely one.'

'You have influence.'

'Influence, yes, but I do not control these men. I merely have an opinion and a vote like everyone else.'

'I have expanded Green Gallows on your word using money loaned by your friends.'

'Colleagues,' Sutcliffe corrected.

'Without the South Road the inn will shrivel up.'

'You may yet make your investment pay. Not everyone will take kindly to the turnpike tolls. Pack men and drovers will certainly not. They will still use the South Road.'

'Pack men and drovers have no use for supper on a silver trencher, nor the gold to spare for a night in a four-poster. Green Gallows has always been an inn fit for Quality. I'll not see it turned into a gin bothy, nor fill it with footpads and vagrants.' Isaac spread his hands. 'Build a connecting road from the turnpike. Put it about your London friends that it is worth making the diversion.'

'Worth what? A night scratching in a bug-ridden bed. A stale mutton pie and a jug of sour ale? That is the true measure of your inn, I think.' Sutcliffe fingered his neck-cloth. The bright material contrasted sharply with his withered grey flesh. 'My dear fellow, the world of commerce is littered with hazards. Circumstances change and the sharp-witted adapt to suit. You must make the best of this. Your first repayment on the loan is due at the end of this month, I believe. I presume you can meet it?'

'Aye, I can meet it. But what of the next month and the one after? Am I to dismiss my servants and sell up my stock? What use are stables with no horses or an inn with no maids? Am I to be ruined on the whim of a bunch of city dandies?'

Sutcliffe's voice remained level. 'The situation is not without remedy.'

A pause.

Isaac turned to me. Something different now gleamed in his eyes. 'Rachel, go and wait outside.'

'But...'

'Heed me now. Wait outside and no dallying at the door.'

He pinched my ear, which he hadn't done since I was *five*, and shoved me out of the carriage. Smarting, I turned to find the door slammed in my face. I stared at the polished oak. I wanted to be sick. Please don't let him say anything stupid to that horrible old man.

Fuming, I went back inside the building. I paced to the end of the long marble hall, then back again. A staircase wound upwards into a frescoed jungle of shadows and colour. Woman's laughter tinkled from some upstairs room.

A tall window illuminated the hallway, the glass old and rippled, distorting the view of the courtyard outside. Paintings of the dead and dusty gazed down from the butterscotch walls.

An open door begged a curious eye. I glimpsed men dozing in armchairs, discarded playing cards peppering the carpet like a thick fall of snow, table tops smothered in empty bottles and cigar stubs. Women in rainbow gowns littered the furniture, bodices open, gartered legs spread to all points of the compass. One shifted sleepily, pushed a snoring male head out of her lap and settled back on the settee. Her eyes opened. She winked dreamily and blew me a soft kiss.

I retreated, smothered in blushes.

Ten minutes later I'd had enough. I checked down the hall. The footman was nowhere in sight. I slipped back outside. Inside the carriage, Isaac was shouting.

'I want a share in the road. A share, do you hear? Get me elected to the Trust. You can do that.'

Sutcliffe's voice: 'I must insist on sampling the goods before the transaction is conducted. After all, Curtis, you would not purchase a horse without first looking in its mouth.'

Oh glory.

I couldn't wait to get out of London. The air was poison, the racket of drunks, hawkers and whores blistering to the ears. We had left the flower-lined terraces far behind. Everywhere, dogs were barking. Some lay dead on the street, black with flies, ignored by passers-by.

I set Mistral at a brisk canter. People hurled oaths as they dashed out of my way. I nearly collided with a sedan chair, leaving the bearers shaking their fists.

On the South Road, Isaac called to me to rein in. 'No hurry, lass,' he said affably. 'No hurry. 'Tis an easy journey back for us.'

He set a plodding pace, whistling most of the way. At the posting inn he tipped the ostler a shilling and ordered the best rooms from the landlord.

'What did you and Lord Sutcliffe talk about?' I asked over supper, pushing a chunk of mutton pie around the edge of my trencher.

Isaac's head was bent over the plate. He shoved forkfuls of steaming potatoes into his mouth. 'Not your business,' he said, between munches.

I stared at the crown of his head, at his black curly hair, and pushed my plate aside. Beneath the bluster lay guilt. I could smell it on him. He was like a boy who's stolen a slice of gooseberry tart then has to sit and face his supper with a swollen belly.

Isaac glanced up. 'Don't you like your food?'

'What did you promise Lord Sutcliffe, Isaac? *What did you promise him?*'

'Stop bawling. I'm getting tired of it. You'll have enough to be glad about in the months to come. In the meantime just be thankful we've still got a roof over our heads.'

Back at Green Gallows I stopped off in my room just long enough to change my dress then strode across to the coach house. Jeremiah had worked a miracle on the place. The floor had been swept, the walls scrubbed and a whole heap of junk carted outside and burned. He was fixing a broken hinge on one of the doors when I arrived. A slow grin slid across his mouth.

I shoved him inside. The hammer fell out of his hands and clattered on the flagstones.

'Hey, what's this?'

'I saw you with Lucy.' My throat was so tight I could hardly get the words out. 'I saw what you did. Isaac will kill you if he finds out.'

'He might,' Jeremiah said, 'then again he might not. I know you were watching at the window that day. And I know why you're here. It's taken you long enough.'

'Oh? Well I'm glad you know something.'

'There now. No need to go all pert on me. You thought I'd be easy, didn't you?'

'I don't know what you mean. Any more lip and I'll have Judd thrash you. You'll be sent away from Green Gallows – thrown out into the lane among the tinkers. I won't care one whit.'

'That ain't true either.' He took a step towards me. 'You can't hide things, Rachel. You ain't got the face for it. You won't see me take a hiding because that'd hurt you. And you won't lie to have me sent away 'cause that would hurt Lucy.'

'You've got a cheek insulting me like that.'

'Well listen to you.' He laughed, but there was no mockery in it. If I'd thought he was making fun of me, if I'd spotted the slightest glimmer of contempt in those dark eyes I swear, shaky-legged little coward that I usually was, I'd have torn his thick curls out by the roots. He had me. He had me and, worst of all, he knew it. Glory, I must have been trembling fit to clack my teeth together.

'Quite the little lady now,' he continued, 'all hot cheeks and umbrage. But the truth, little 'un, is that you've insulted me.'

He took in my expression, and something flitted across his features. Sadness? Resignation? Perhaps even resentment.

'Like I said, you thought I was easy. As easy as hitching up one of your horses. Lucy has turned the head of high-born dandies up and down the land. Oh, I know. Stables are full of talk, and not just these stables either. Must be hard on you. A carriage-door girl dressed in second-best clothes. No pretty rouge or cologne for you. You're out in the rain while she's in the Long Room in front of the fire.'

'They won't marry her,' I retorted. 'They look, is all. A pretty wench in any tavern would as likely catch their eye. Lords and ladies marry their sons off to other lords' and ladies' daughters. To get an heir, pay off gambling debts, save the face of a foppish boy who isn't man enough to hunt a wench on his own. They can't marry Lucy. They just want to fiddle with her petticoats and be ten miles down the Portsmouth road come dawn. Isaac hasn't realised that yet. But he will. He'll have to.'

'And that scares you, don't it? I ain't fooled. You hate it when those dandies smile and laugh with her, when their eyes follow her wherever she goes. You think on it every time you open a carriage door and the gentry inside stare right through you.

And here I am, with nothing to my name 'cept these blisters on my hands. You thought Lucy so far above me and my world that I'd be ready and waitin' for you. That I'd be willin' to take you into my arms at one snap of those fingers.'

'And what makes you think I'd want you?'

He spread his hands. 'If you don't, what are you doing here? Why are your cheeks scarlet and why are you trembling?'

He took another step towards me.

'Did you lie with her?'

His expression didn't flicker. 'Sisters can be close sometimes,' he said evenly. 'I know that. But there's some things you ain't got a right to hear. Special things. Between me and her.'

'Did you lie with Lucy?' I pressed.

He stepped back. 'You're scared. I can almost hear your knees knocking under that frock. But you'll have what you want, won't you? Should've saw that from the start. All right then. I lay with her. I had her in here, on the seat in that carriage. And another day I had her on the straw, her head tucked under my chin so I could feel her softness and warmth. Every sigh she uttered, every little movement of that golden hair was a joy. I can't tell you what it was like to feel her breath on my neck, to fancy I could hear her heart beating, to know she was full of life and to want to fill her with life in turn. There ain't no words I can use.'

He nodded. 'I touched her, and kissed her in all her gentle places. If I could've reached inside and pressed my lips against her heart I'd've done that too.'

He peered at me. 'Gone all coy have we? Well,

you wanted to know, and just remember 'twas you who forced me to tell.'

'How could you take my sister in a dirty, cluttered place like this?'

'She told me she wanted me in her bed. She was all set on smuggling me up the stairs when her father was asleep. Even though she knew he'd kill me and most likely her too if we were caught. Things like that are worth dying for, she said. And she was right. The way your sister looked at me that first time I thought I'd sprout wings and fly to heaven, and God forgive me if I blaspheme in saying so. I'd die for her. Do you begrudge that?'

I didn't reply. How could I? Jeremiah expected me to say no. It was the proper answer, but I couldn't be sure it was the truth.

'She turns my knees to water,' he continued earnestly. 'My veins burn, my head swims so I don't know whether it's Monday or Tuesday. I don't eat, I don't sleep and when I try to speak my mouth is stuffed with rocks. When I glimpse her through the parlour window or see her walking with your mama,' he held up his open hand and suddenly clenched it into a fist, 'my belly goes like that. Have you never felt such a thing? Is there nothing in your heart but ashes?'

'It's not right,' I whispered.

'No it's not, because now I've got to dreaming about things I can't have.'

'You could get a job in some stables up north,' I suggested, 'or maybe work as a farm hand. I've also heard there's work in Cornwall.'

He snorted. 'In a copper mine? Sorry, but I ain't one for grubbing in the dark.'

'You could go somewhere else.'
'No I couldn't.'
'Is what I saw your idea of love? You were like a terrier savaging a piece of meat.'
Something flickered in his eyes. I expected an angry retort, a denial. Instead he said: 'Give me your hand.'
'I'm not so easily charmed that I'd trust you, Jeremiah Cathcart.'
'Give me your hand,' he repeated. 'Trust me enough to know I won't hurt you.'
Reluctantly I offered my left hand, more curious than frightened now. He held it in the warm cup of his fingers. There was no pressure, yet my own fingers shook.
'What you saw was passion,' he said. 'When two people get close, when they feel that way about each other, nothing hurts or is wrong. But love can be gentle too.'
'Are you a poet as well as a farm boy?'
He chuckled. The sound seemed to rumble gently around the rafters. His grip slid up to my wrist.
'Open your hand,' he instructed. 'Wide, so the palm is flat.'
I obeyed, too caught up in the game to resist. Jeremiah brushed the middle of my palm with the tip of his index finger. He drew a lazy circle which widened to take in the ball of my thumb and the base of each quivering finger.
'Easy now,' he said, smiling.
I swallowed and closed my eyes. His flesh barely made contact with my own. My forearm shivered with goose-bumps.

Slowly the finger drew along the length of my thumb where it paused just below the nail before slipping back along the opposite side. His grip on my wrist, light as it was, did not relent. With his other hand he reached for the fastenings on his woollen shirt. Crude fastenings whittled from bits of wood and held together with strips of leather. One by one these were twisted, released. His eyes fixed on mine, that demon's smile flickering across his lips.

His shirt fell open.

Jeremiah grinned, willing my gaze to drop those few dangerous inches. I swallowed. His chest was pale skinned and smooth. So unlike the swarthy arms or sun-scorched face.

He drew my hand towards the gentle rise and fall. I tugged.

'No.' Still smiling. 'You don't want to do that.'

Fingers touched warm flesh. A sigh leaked out of my throat. My palm was pressed into the slight hollow between his ribs, fingers splayed out, tingling.

A steady heartbeat. Blood pumping like a river just under the surface of the earth.

'Feel that,' he whispered into my ear. 'That's a man's life, young Rachel. Strong and steady, ain't it? But when Lucy touched me there, you know what? It dipped and dived like a swallow. I thought I was going to swoon or just plain turn for the door and run. And what's your heart doin' right now, eh? What kind of merry jig is it playing even as I speak?'

He let go of my hand. I held it pressed against his flesh for a few lingering moments. A gasp of realisation. Blood rushing to my cheeks again. Then I pulled my fingers away from the warmth. The softness.

His hand, sliding easily through the syrupy air, quested for my bodice. A sharp intake of breath. A protest caught and trapped on the edge of my tongue.

'You can step back now,' he said softly. 'If you want to.'

His face seemed to quiver in the cool, still air. I breathed in deeply, eyelids fluttering. Catching a scent of that day's lunch. Or another girl's kisses. I was inhaling him. Drawing the warmth from his lungs into my own.

'Oh she's fast, little one, like you've got a hare running around in there,' he said, fingers pressed between my breasts. 'Is that something deeper than rouge I spy on your cheeks? And you're breathing like you've just run up a hill. Getting a taste for it are we? Getting a taste for love? Imagine this a hundred, nay, a thousand times stronger and then you might begin to understand why I look at Lucy the way I do.'

'Don't take your hand away.'

'I must, little sister. I can't have your heart snapping around my heels. You go and love someone who'll love you back.'

'How can I forget...' I gestured helplessly, 'this?'

'When you find the right one, Rachel, you'll forget soon enough.'

The parlour was empty, the fire low and guarded. Lucy's writing desk squatted in a narrow alcove set into the wall opposite the hearth. Isaac, fancying himself a carpenter, had built it from leftover parts of an old wardrobe. Square and clumsy, it was the one ugly piece of furniture in the room. Lucy used it dutifully, filling her fingers with splinters as she wrote.

I walked over to the desk and dragged out the stool. An oblong of cream paper lay in the centre of the vellum blotter. An inkpot sat on one side, a jar of crow quills on the other. Above the blotter was a shaker filled with fine sand and a red slab of sealing wax with candle and taper.

Seating myself, I plucked out one of the quills. Lucy had painstakingly taught me to write until I could manage big square letters. I was left-handed, a 'cack-hand' as Judd so charmingly put it, and if I was not careful the edge of my palm rubbed across the paper, smearing my sentences. I'd tried writing with my other hand but the finished page looked like a sparrow had run across it.

I dipped the quill in the ink. Immediately, black raindrops showered across the blotter. I wiped the quill on my handkerchief, utterly ruining it, and tried again.

'Rachel Curtis' I scratched onto the paper. Glory, what a blotchy mess. I wrote it again. Untidy but not too smudged. Encouraged, I wrote 'Lucy Curtis' then 'Judd', 'Isaac' and 'Mathew' then 'Matthew' again but with the right number of 't's.

Another dip of the quill. The sound of scratching on paper. A name.

'Jeremiah Cathcart'.

Beside it I wrote 'Rachel'.

Then beneath that I wrote 'Rachel Cathcart'

and a flowing script that, though a little shivery, was not too disgraceful.

I tilted my head to see how it looked, turned the paper, held it up to the light. I wrote the name again in big, bold strokes. I tried it in capitals – very pretty – then in narrow, scrunched up writing that could only be read by holding the paper at eye level.

A dozen more times I spelled it out until the quill broke apart, bleeding ink all over my fingers. I sprinkled blotting sand over the paper, shook it clean and examined what I'd written.

I tore the paper into strips, pulled back the guard and threw them on the fire. They burst into orange flame and were gone. I ran from the parlour, slamming the door behind me.

Dusk brought Will Davey riding into our yard. He was alone and unarmed. He had come, he said, to talk to Isaac about the ill-fated raid on the new road. He'd lived in Prestbury all his life and knew both Barnabas Pegg and his father. He was in no mood to arrest anyone.

Isaac showed the constable into the parlour and offered him brandy. The decanter was empty so guess who was sent to fetch a new bottle? When I returned from the cellar both men were seated in front of the hearth. I was in time to hear Mr Davey say that Colly Bruce had been taken on as toll-keeper by the Turnpike Trust.

'Colly Bruce, a bloody toll farmer,' Isaac spluttered. 'Might've known it. Only farmer he'll ever make. You've seen his place over at Four Trees. His farmhouse is a hovel, his brats in rags and his land choked with weeds. What stock he keeps is so scrawny if they died the flies would get naught off their carcasses.'

I served the brandy. Isaac swigged down most of his. Mr Davey left his glass on the arm of his chair. 'He's sold out to the Trust. Was one of the first to go, and he got five times what that patch of dirt was worth. Now they've pulled down his house and laid the stone for the new road.'

'Which is as likely the best use that pile o' rubble has ever been put to. So now he and that witch of his get a new toll keeper's cottage to fill with more of their buck-toothed bastards. He'll take money off my customers while I have to watch Green Gallows wither and die.'

'The Trust is buying up all the local farms. Families can stay on and work their smallholdings. You'll still catch all the village traffic. Farmers, merchants, craftsmen – anyone wanting to take their wares or their trade to Prestbury.'

'Local farms ain't my concern. We're not a posting house but a full-blooded coaching inn for long-distance carriages. A cart full of turnips or bleating sheep has no place at Green Gallows. Without regular traffic there'll be no money for the upkeep of the South Road. 'Twill become little better than a cart track, and nigh impassable come winter.'

'The Trust has bought the Coach and Horses Tavern. They're turning it into a posting house. Why not offer to landlord it?'

'I'll not call another man master. Green Gallows is mine to do with as I please.'

'They'll run you into debt, Curtis, then they'll buy you out at a pittance.'

'I'll burn the inn and salt the paddock if they do.'

'We've had turnpike roads for a hundred years. They'll not go away now. The last riots were thirty years ago. Those London people on the Trust don't want martyrs but they're planning to build a toll booth just outside Prestbury. You raise a hand against it or Colly Bruce and you'll as likely hang for it.'

Isaac swallowed the last of his brandy. 'It's all right, Will. It won't come to that. I've got plans of my own.'

I fetched Mr Davey's horse and saw him out of the gate. Everything seemed to be happening so quickly I didn't know where to turn next. As I walked back across the yard, Mother beckoned me from the window. 'I want to talk to you,' she said when I was inside. I made for the parlour door but she grasped my elbow. 'No. Upstairs.'

Her bedchamber was above the kitchen from where, during the day, scents of mutton and hot pastry leaked through the floorboards. A sparsely furnished room. A stool, an old leather armchair slowly bleeding its woollen innards onto the floor, a big square bed.

Mother seated herself on the mattress and patted the coverlet beside her. I went over and sat down.

'Now, Rachel, I want you to tell me all about Lucy and the new stableboy.'

Chapter Seven

I didn't bother with breakfast. I saw in the early coaches, pocketed the tips and sought refuge in the hayloft, where I slipped sixpence into my secret treasure trove beneath the windowsill.

A flicker of movement in the yard. I pressed my face against the window. Isaac and Judd were bundling Jeremiah into one of the hire chaises. His face was ashen. He didn't put up any kind of fight. Isaac climbed in after him while Judd hitched a pair between the shafts. A minute later he clambered up onto the driver's box. The carriage clattered out of the yard.

An hour later it was back. Isaac stepped down and closed the door. No one else got out. Wiping his knuckles on a tattered neckcloth, he tramped across the gravel while Judd unharnessed the horses. I fell back on the straw, shivering. A moment later the kitchen door slammed.

Jeremiah did not return that day. Nor the next. Lucy's face at the supper table that Thursday evening was ugly.

Sometime in the owl-hooting darkness I was dragged from a restless sleep by the latch turning on my door. The moon, peeping through the window at the end of the hall, threw ice-light down the passage, illuminating the figure standing in my doorway. Lucy, a silken ghost with a pinched face. Her hands were bunched into fists.

'You know where he's gone,' she said.

I shrank beneath the coverlet. Lucy advanced, bare feet whispering on the floor. 'Father told me he tried to steal some money and had to be sent packing but that's not true. You know what really happened. It was all over your face at supper. You only picked at your food where usually you would cram it into your mouth just as quickly as your fork could lift it. Father has done something. Something dreadful.'

Lucy grabbed the bottom of the coverlet and whipped it away. Cool air whispered around my legs. I curled up into a ball. 'Isaac and Judd took him away in one of the chaises,' I blurted. 'I don't know where they went, I swear to God, Lucy. They were only gone an hour. Perhaps they just frightened him, or paid him off.'

'You told him.' Her voice drew knife blades down my spine. 'You blabbed to Father. Had to stick your fat nose in didn't you, Rachel?'

I squirmed on the straw mattress. My sister had become a stranger, a snarling, spitting creature with hatred simmering in her dark eyes. Just then I would have done anything to get the real Lucy back.

'Mother saw you,' I told her. 'She saw the way you and Jeremiah looked at each other. You were stupid and careless to think no one would notice.'

'Me? Stupid? Fine words indeed coming from the prize turnip-head of Green Gallows.'

'You're the one who's stupid,' I retorted, a flash of anger replacing some of the fear. 'How could you dally with a stableboy knowing Isaac wants you to marry into the gentry? He doesn't parade you for hours in the Long Room just so you can run off with some penniless farmer's boy. You wanted to be caught, Lucy. You wanted Isaac to know that you're not happy, that you don't wish to wed one of those fancy fops in a lace-trimmed jacket.'

I wiped my nose with the back of my hand. I'd been crying and hadn't realised. 'And what about me? You never thought that I might like Jeremiah too? That in time he may come to like me?'

Lucy snorted. I picked up my pillow and threw it at her. It missed by half a league and thumped against the wall. 'Yes me. And why not? You have everything. I'm always left with the dregs.'

'I've told you again and again, Rachel, tried to explain it until my head aches and you still don't understand. Everything I have has been foisted on me. Mother even picks my nightshifts. This was the only thing, the only *person* in my entire life that I chose for myself. And you couldn't bear it, could you? You never bothered when lads took an interest in me before. But I didn't want them, that's the difference, isn't it? Your claws only came out when you saw my heart go soft. Well I hope you're satisfied. You couldn't have found a better way to hurt me.'

'At least you get some attention from Mother. I usually get ordered about like a scullery maid.'

'She only resents you because you're getting more like Father every day, and we both know her problem there, don't we?'

'Don't you start on that, Lucy.'

'Why not? It's the truth, isn't it?'

'You don't know the truth. Mother doesn't

even know it for sure.'

'We see it in their faces every day.'

'Then they both want us to be something we're not.'

Lucy's rosebud mouth curled into a sneer. 'You betrayed me to Mother because you wanted to sweeten her. You wanted a smile. No wonder she fusses over 'Lizabeth so much. You are so obvious in everything you do.'

'I am not.'

'Oh? I know about your cubbyhole in the hay-loft. Quite a little treasure trove you have in there. 'Tis a wonder some passing vagabond or drover hasn't had it out from under your nose.' She snatched the pillow off the floor and tossed it onto the end of the bed. 'If Jeremiah has been hurt...'

'Judd wouldn't let that happen.'

'We shall see, little sister. We shall see.'

'Where is Lucy?' Isaac barked, stabbing a potato with his fork. 'More guests due this evening and not a sign of her. She needs to practise her sing-ing, try on a new dress, a dozen other things.'

I forced a lump of beef down my throat. Lucy's lunch grew cold on its plate. Opposite, Mother sawed her own meat into neat squares.

'Perhaps she's by the pond,' I suggested, chok-ing down another mouthful of food. 'She may have forgotten the time. You know what a day-dreamer she is.'

He glanced at the window. 'It's going to rain again. I don't like her out in this weather. She ought to know better.'

I wiped my mouth with a napkin and pushed

my plate away. 'I'll go and look for her. She's forgotten, that's all.'

'No,' Isaac said, slamming down his fork. 'You stay where you are. I'll get her.'

Half an hour later he brought her in, soaked and snivelling. 'She was in the coach house,' Isaac explained. 'Now the rain's started and she's got us both a ducking.'

Mother stood up and grasped Lucy's arm. 'I'll take her upstairs and get her dried off.'

'Stay out of that place from now on,' Isaac warned Lucy as Mother led her from the parlour. 'There's nothing in there for you.'

Not any more, I thought.

Like a bad storm, Isaac gusted through the inn all the rest of the day, criticising, barking orders, yelling at 'Lizabeth to dust everything then dust it again. People fled before him like flustered chickens and, to make matters worse, Lucy went down with a fever. Isaac regarded her reddening nose and pink watery eyes with mounting dismay. When she sneezed three times in a row, he grabbed a wad of loose cotton out of Mother's sewing box.

'See this,' he barked, 'I'll bung your nose with it if you don't pack it in. You *shall* sing tonight. Sing as sweetly as an angel. I won't be put out by some girl's frippery.'

He threw the cotton into a corner and sat down heavily. A tear cut a pink track through Lucy's powdered cheek. Isaac's voice lost its brittle edge. His big hand plucked at a strand of Lucy's hair and he twirled it slowly between his fingers. A flicker of a grimace passed over her mouth.

'One day you'll ride in a carriage of your own with footmen to open the door for you,' he said. 'Maybe a chaise, or a landau so you can put the roof down when the sun's out and show the world your pretty hair. Farmers will doff their caps as you pass. Women will curtsy and call you m'lady. You'll eat out of porcelain brought by traders from the East. You'll be a queen, Lucy, you hear me? A queen.'

But there was only darkness in my sister's eyes.

Later I caught her sitting by the hearth in the kitchen, staring into the fire. I tried to talk to her. She wouldn't look at me. I said something else. I think I told her to grow up. She rounded on me then, and that was that. I don't remember much of what happened next, the things I yelled at her and she called me in return. I don't think I want to remember. It went on for some time, or maybe it just seemed that way. I was still shouting even after she ran out and slammed the door.

A minute later came the measured tread of heavy feet across the Long Room floorboards. They paused outside the kitchen door. I bit the end of my tongue and waited.

Isaac lumbered into the room. His sleeves were rolled up and a leather apron was tied around his thick waist. Both his hands and the apron were smothered in dust.

'What's this catfight between you and Lucy?' he demanded. 'I heard you howling at her when I was out in the yard. Damn near whole inn must've heard it.'

'She gives as good as she gets,' I said, 'especially when she can't have her own way.'

'Lucy can have what she wants. Scratch at her and you'll feel the hard end of my boot. She'll be the saving of this family. You'd do well to remember that.'

After he left I went to the cutlery drawer and cut smiles into my forearms with the knife Sally used to slice the carrots. She found me in the cupboard where the cheeses were kept, bloodied steel clutched in my hand. Thin fingers of crimson trickled between my knuckles. She stood watching me as the clock above the kitchen table ticked out heartbeats, then she prised open my trembling fingers and stole away the blade. I followed her into the scullery where she washed the knife in a bucket of water from the trough. Strips of linen soaked in salted water took care of my arms. Cowardice meant the wounds were shallow.

'Wear your long-sleeved gown,' Sally advised. 'If anyone does notice, tell them you went bramble-picking and were careless with the thorns.'

'Sally ... everything's going to be all right, isn't it?'

'Yes, lass,' she said without looking at me, 'things will be just fine.'

One day crumbled into another. Matthew tried everything to be alone with me but I saved my stable-yard chores for when he was busy changing the teams or exercising animals in the paddock. He wanted to know what was going on. I wanted to know too.

Lucy was a ghost whispering through the halls of Green Gallows on velvet slippers, silent save for the gentle rustling of her petticoats. The last day of August drew to a fiery close. The rain clouds had heaved themselves off to the coast and all afternoon a thick, indolent sun baked the earth dry, making a last defiant gesture before the first cool whispers of autumn began to rob it of its strength.

Since midday Isaac had tucked himself away in the parlour with Mother leaving the stable work to Matthew, the taproom to Sally and the carriages to me. I'd just seen off the Portsmouth stage and was holding a trinket Sailor Ben had given me. A straw poppet with a porcelain face. He said it came from Italy. I turned it over in my hands, not knowing what to do with it. Finally I took it into my bedchamber and dumped it on the mantelpiece. My room was an oven. I pushed the window open as wide as it would go, just in time to spot Lucy striding across the yard from the kitchen door. Matthew trotted along behind. They slipped into the stables. A few minutes later both rode out of the yard, Lucy on Mistral, Matthew astride one of the posted horses.

I was out of my room in a blink. 'Where have they gone?' I demanded of Judd, who was fixing a loose board on one of the stalls. He spat out a mouthful of nails and told me that Lucy had wanted to go riding.

'Can't blame her,' he said. 'First decent weather we've had in weeks.'

'Did she say where she was going?' I pressed.

The horsemaster shrugged. 'Ain't any of your concern.'

I groaned. 'I admit we've fallen out, but it was as much her doing as mine.'

Judd started hammering a new piece of wood

across the broken boarding. 'We all know what was done,' he said.

I stumbled down the dusty lane towards Marrin's Chase. Judd wouldn't saddle a horse for me. He said the tack room was locked and would stay that way until Lucy came back. He said I had no business going after anyone, that there was still work to be done in the yard. I called him an old fool. He told me he'd clip my ear if I ever said that again. I cried a bit, but it made no difference.

Well, I could still walk. Ahead was the Chase, green and brooding under the hot sun. Matthew was waiting at the lip of the old woodcutter's track. Mistral's reins were in one hand, his own mount's in the other. He frowned as I approached. Dust caked my skirts up to the knees, and the top of my stomacher was grubby with sweat.

'Where's my sister?'

Matthew pulled his battered tricorne down over his forehead to shield his eyes. 'She was hot. She favoured a walk in the shade of the trees. What're you doing here, Rachel?'

I ignored the question. 'You let her go in there alone, knowing the Chase is thick with poachers?'

''Tain't been no one skulking in these woods since the road crew cleared 'em out, as well 'ee knows,' he retorted. 'Lucy bid me stay here and promised she'd not venture far.'

I peered under the brim of his hat to try and see what lay in those shadowed eyes. He backed away.

'Matthew, if you're lying to me you'll fetch a hiding,' I warned.

He shook his head. 'Your sister is taking the air just as I said.'

I tried to shove past him. He dropped Mistral's reins and gripped my arm.

'Let me go. I'm going in after her.'

'No you're not.'

Curse it. No matter how much I wriggled I couldn't shake free. I aimed a swipe at his ear but he ducked it easily. More sweat was pouring off me and my breath was coming in short, dry gasps. Mistral stood in the lane, reins dragging in the dirt, watching us with round, docile eyes.

'Very well,' I stopped struggling, 'I'll just bide my time here until she comes back out.'

'You won't do that either. You'll turn on your tail and go back up that lane to Green Gallows. And you'll do it now.'

'I'll tell Isaac.'

Quick as a cat, Matthew had me by the wrist. His fingers burned hot fire against my flesh. When he spoke again his voice was low and full of winter.

'If you have any feelings for your sister you'll keep that mouth shut. You know what I mean, Rachel. We were just out riding, that's all.'

'Get out of my way.'

I tried to sound menacing. The hand holding my wrist trembled but didn't falter.

'I won't, and there's naught you can do to make me. Not this time.'

I tried to see past his shoulder but the open maw of the trail quickly dissolved into shadows after only a few yards. Matthew pushed me away.

'Go home, Rachel. Now.'

When Matthew returned from the Chase I didn't

speak to him for the rest of that afternoon. If chores forced us together we were careful to avoid meeting one another's gaze.

Lucy handed Mother a brilliant bunch of primroses freshly plucked from the woods.

'What were you doing going out that way?' Isaac said, frowning. 'Matthew ought to know better than to let you go riding by the Chase.'

'I wanted to pick blooms for Mama,' Lucy said. 'Those growing beside the lane are always withered and caked with dust. I did not stray far from the road and Matthew was with me the whole time.'

Mother spread the primroses across her lap in a yellow fan. 'They're lovely. I must find a vase.'

Isaac opened his mouth, then closed it. The subject of Lucy's trip to the woods was not raised again.

I had to see her. I *had* to. I waited until she'd gone upstairs then went to the washroom and grabbed a bundle of fresh linen. 'Lizabeth had been taking up Lucy's bedding and bringing down her pot usually late and with ill grace. The maid was out on the drying green now, hanging out last night's sheets.

Lucy's door was shut. I couldn't let this feud go on. It was stupid. I'd been warned not to bother her but she was my sister. We'd been a half-decent family once. Now we needed each other more than ever.

I swallowed, banged once on the door and pushed it open. Lucy sat on the edge of the bed. A book was open on her lap. I stepped inside.

'I brought you fresh bedding.'

'That's 'Lizabeth's job.'

'You know how hopeless she is. And sullen with it.'

'I'd rather she was guilty of ill humour than betrayal.'

'I don't want to fight any more. My life has been full of come-and-go friends. You were the only one who didn't disappear off down the lane or ride off on the next coach. Even when Isaac and Harriet tried to take you away you were still here.' I thumped my chest. 'Mother already knew about you and Jeremiah. You can't hide something like that, and I wasn't going to try and lie to her.'

'I'm your sister.'

'And I'm her daughter, whoever anyone thinks my father might be.'

Lucy regarded me for a moment then closed her book and tossed it onto the rumpled coverlet. 'You'd better put that linen down before you drop it. How was your trip to London?'

I laid the bedding on the fireside chair. 'Isaac has struck some sort of bargain with Lord Sutcliffe. I think it might have something to do with you, but I don't know what.'

'I've never seen Father like this. He's afraid, and it's rubbing off on Mama. He's always believed he deserves better things. Now he wants too much, from all of us.'

I went to the dresser and picked up her favourite brush, the handle whittled from horse bone into the shape of a prancing seahorse. Lucy sat up on the edge of the bed and I began to work on her hair, arm moving in long sweeping strokes. The bristles passed through it like fingers through water. My own black tresses were always coarse with grime after a day in the stable yard. When she brushed it, Lucy did so with a butterfly touch, patiently coaxing out the tugs, taking twice as long as I did with hers and handling my own brush – the oak-handled carpet beater I laughingly called it – with quiet deftness.

She sat in quiet contemplation, hands clasped in her lap, gazing into the hearth. Holding her hair was like trying to grasp sunbeams. It whispered and shimmered, forever spilling out of my hands like some golden nectar. This had always been our time, for warm thoughts and togetherness away from the bustle of Green Gallows.

I remembered Lucy's eighth birthday. She was given a porcelain doll. A tiny ghost face atop a sky-blue satin gown trimmed with lace.

'Gentlemen ran that in from France so I'm told, Lucy girl,' Isaac said, all soft-faced and fumbling smiles. 'Not another like it in the whole of England. Maybe not the whole world.'

I'd stared at the thing. I don't think either Isaac or Lucy even realised I was there. It had tiny white hands, so perfect I could see each sculpted fingernail. Glass eyes, as blue as the dress, yet warm and almost alive. Lucy held it to her chest as if it was a newborn and she had breasts to suckle it. Oh, I tried to smile, it was her day after all, and reached out hands to touch it, maybe hold it a little while. But Lucy snatched it away.

'You'll drop it,' she'd blurted. 'You're so clumsy.'

Isaac found me crammed into the bottom of the linen cupboard. A favourite skulking hole of mine until I grew too big to fit. My eyes were raw from a whole morning's worth of tears.

Isaac looked huge. He'd blocked out the light from the hallway. I could barely make out his features. I braced myself for sharp words. He'd say I'd spoiled Lucy's day, the way I'd stormed out of the parlour in a huff. His hand reached down. I braced myself.

Gently, his fingers stroked my hair.

'What use have you for dolls?' he'd said. 'You're a horsewoman, Rachel. No perfumed fancies for you. The smell of leather, oiled wood, the jingle of a harness and the crunch of hooves on gravel. That's your life, my sweet. What good would a china poppet do 'cept clutter up your dresser? Come now. Come outside with your papa.'

'No. I want a doll too.'

'You're just hurting because you think Lucy's got something and you ain't. But you have, my little raggins. You got something much better. You won't ever have a brother, or more sisters. Quack from Stonehill said your mama can't have any more. Took six shillings out o' my purse to tell me that.'

He tapped his temple. 'You're no dumpling, Rachel. Not in here. You know all about birthing. You've seen my horses put to stud often enough. Well, Harriet's belly is all dried up, see? Shrivelled like an apple fallen and left in the sun. Another child would kill her. So it's no boy for me. No son. I near drank myself to death in grief. Then you grew up. I saw you watch the stage come in, saw the way your eyes followed the ostlers, marked their every move. Every day you were at that window, staring, your lips working as if you were giving the men orders. I knew it was in your blood. Daresay if you weren't so young you could've hitched a team as good as any of those idle oafs. Fancy dolls and frilly laces are for Lucy. She'll marry a fine lord one day, and your mama will get her terraced town house with a darkie boy to bring her tea in a silver pot. I'd be a liar if I said I wanted otherwise. For too long I've broken my hands on leather and wood, too long not to want velvet against my own skin and a goose feather pillow to lay my head on at night. 'Tis my birthright, as I've always said. But you, Rachel. You were born to this. The lykeway and all that moves on and around it are what keeps your heart beating. My own father would've said as much. So don't go begrudging Lucy her little fancies because one day, raggins, you'll get Green Gallows, and that's worth more than any porcelain-faced poppet smuggled in on a boat from France.'

How could I understand? A child, living only for the moment and conscious only of my empty hands. I'd stopped bawling, for his sake and because I didn't want a clout around the ear. Survivor that I was, I already knew how far Isaac's patience could be stretched. But he'd chuckled rudely, scooped me out of my bolt-hole and slung me under his arm as easily as a sack of oats. I yelled and beat my small fists against his back as he carted me, legs swinging, down the passage to the stable yard door. But I was giggling wildly before Isaac's hand touched the latch and him laughing that big, booming laugh like thunderclouds knocking their heads together.

He'd set me down in front of a post horse, took

both my hands in his and laid them against the animal's flank.

'Feel that. What d'you think, eh? As soft as any velvet, smoother than any silk. But it's alive, Rachel. A living creature. Not some dead-spun material stitched together to adorn a little girl's toy. Feel him move. Hear him breathe. Sense the power in those muscles. Give him rein and he'll run you to the horizon and back. Still want a fancy gown? Nay, lass. Not you.'

I set the brush down. 'That beau of Mother's never really died. Not in her heart. Isaac was trying to steal me from him. To *make* me his daughter and help kill that cuckold's memory.'

Lucy settled back on the coverlet. 'Well, I've had enough of trying to fit into Father's schemes,' she finished. 'I have plans of my own.'

'Plans?'

But she didn't have to tell me. It was on her face.

'You're still seeing him,' I stated flatly. 'He's out there, somewhere in the woods, with perhaps a mouthful of promises and your kisses drying on his cheek. Oh glory, Lucy, this is a dangerous game to play.'

'Are you going to run to Mother and tattle on me again?'

'That's not fair.'

'No, I suppose not.'

She beckoned me over and slipped her hand into mine. The fingers were warm, comforting.

'I've gone too far to turn back now,' she said quietly.

'What will you do?'

'I can't tell you, Rachel. Please understand.'

So, she didn't fully trust me. I had only myself to blame. 'If Isaac finds out you're planning to defy him I don't know what he'll do to Jeremiah. Or to you.'

'I'd rather die than be his prize cow.'

'Don't say that.'

'It's true. Now give me a hug. I really need a hug.'

A week later, Lord Sutcliffe's patchwork coach rumbled into our stable yard.

In the days leading up to his arrival, everything Lucy did seemed to please Isaac. He smothered her in flowers carted all the way from Stonehill at huge cost, and each night had 'Lizabeth fill a scented hip bath in front of the parlour fire.

'Pick a dress,' Isaac told her. 'Any one that takes your fancy.'

'I don't want another dress,' Lucy protested. 'My cupboards are heaving with dresses.'

'You'll pick one,' he repeated. 'I'll take you to Stonehill tomorrow.'

'There are perfectly good merchants in Prestbury.'

'Not good enough. Not any more.'

I was working in the yard when Sutcliffe's monstrosity appeared. It halted in its usual place and Matthew ran out to whisk the horses away. He glanced at me, his expression full of unspoken questions. I ran inside to tell Isaac. He was at the table drinking port out of a fluted crystal glass. He practised raising the glass to his lips, sipping, then gently lowering his arm. No matter how many times he tried, that pretty glass always looked out of place in his mutton fist.

'Lord Sutcliffe is here,' I said.

He eyed the clock on the mantel and returned his attention to the glass. Mother's head was bent over her needlework. Lucy was reading a book. She looked paler than usual.

A fire was burning in the grate, a weak, spitting jumble of embers, more smoke than flame. Suspended on a hook above it, a copper kettle vented steam into the open throat of the chimney.

'Lucy,' Father muttered. 'Go and rouge your cheeks, then come and sing to me.' He stared into the hissing fire. 'I need something to warm my heart.'

Eight o'clock, and shadows began to take large bites out of the sunlit yard. Sutcliffe' s carriage squatted like a plump spider between the stables and the coach house, the shafts empty, the angular shadows it cast gradually softening into darkness. Guests taking the air gave it a wide berth.

'Why does he not take a room if he is so eager to stay?' I said, watching from the parlour window.

Isaac barely glanced at me. 'He never leaves his carriage. You know that.'

The coach rocked gently on its springs. The sound of squeaking leather carried across the yard, piercing the late evening air. Like a persistent drip it gnawed at my nerves.

'Lizabeth brought in a supper tray from the kitchen. 'Set it on the table,' Isaac told her. 'Lucy will take it out.'

The maid hesitated. Her gaze flicked to Lucy

then back to Isaac.

'There is still work to be done in the Long Room,' he continued. 'Our guests will be thirsty and there will be clearing up to do afterwards.'

'Lizabeth knew better than to disobey. She fled the parlour like a bashful puppy.

A moment of silence, then Isaac turned to Lucy.

'Take out Lord Sutcliffe's supper.'

Mother remained by the fire, head bowed, intent on her darning. I stared at my feet.

Lucy put down the book and rose from her chair. Isaac's eyes followed her. She picked up the tray awkwardly, hugging it to her chest. A teaspoon slid off and clattered onto the floor.

Isaac got up and opened the door. She passed through without looking at him. He closed it behind her then returned to the table, swigged port from his precious crystal goblet and began flicking through a deck of gambling cards. The smile deepened. Eyes glittered in the firelight.

I moved towards the window.

'Rachel,' Isaac said quietly.

I stopped, turned. 'Yes?'

'Come and take off my boots.'

I hesitated.

'Come on, daughter,' he continued in a sweet voice. 'Help your father.'

He stretched out a leg, his expression unreadable, his cheeks flushed with the port. I knelt and pulled off his boot. I put in its place by the fire and glanced at the window.

'Now the other one.'

I wrenched the boot off, forcing a grunt from

Isaac. 'Good,' he said. 'Now go help Sally in the kitchen. And stay away from the yard.'

I peeked out of the window on my way through the Long Room. The last of the summer's flies buzzed lazily above the carriage roof. The supper tray lay untouched on the gravel beside the lowered step. The door was closed, the curtain drawn.

The carriage shifted on its springs.

Eleven o' clock. Darkness. The inn asleep. My bed a rumpled pit of sweat and worries. Feet dragged across the yard. My ears strained. No mistaking it. The soft click of the latch followed by footfalls in the passageway.

Tinderbox sparked. My face was an orange moon in the mirror. Candle held aloft, I slipped out into the hall. My shadow bobbed along the walls. Dirt blown in from the yard scratched my bare feet.

From the top of the stairs came a gentle sound, like a whimper. Heart thudding, I padded up the first few steps. Shadows leapt from wall to ceiling.

Lucy was slumped in the corner beside her closed bedroom door. Both arms were clamped across her middle. Her head rested against the plasterwork. She reminded me of a sheet of fresh writing paper that someone had picked up and ripped to pieces. She did not look up, did not stir from that dark corner.

'Lucy...'

'Go back to bed.' That voice. Terrible. A crone's harsh croak.

I stepped closer, feeling helpless, foolish even. The light mercilessly picked out her features. I gasped and nearly dropped the candle. Red caked her chin and cheeks, drew ugly scarlet patterns across her throat and in the hollows of her eyes.

She's injured, I thought. *Oh dear God he's cut her.*

But it was rouge smeared over her face. Her hair hung in stringy tufts over her ears. Her bonnet was gone. The front of her gown was torn. A stain spread across her petticoat.

'What did he do to you?'

'What do you think he did,' she said in that awful, tired voice. 'Don't you know anything?'

I reached out, wanting to hold her, thinking that if I could caress some sanity back into the tangled haystack her hair had become then everything would be better.

'Don't touch me. I'm dirty. I don't want you to see me like this.'

'You're hurt. I can't just leave you.'

'You can't undo what's been done.'

The candle trembled in my grasp. 'I'll kill him.'

'No you won't,' Lucy said.

'Then let me help you up. You can't stay here all night.'

Her door was ajar, a candle flickering busily inside her bedchamber. 'Lizabeth's work I supposed. I managed to get Lucy inside. She lay, crucified, face down on the bed, embroidered coverlet rumpled about her like old sacking. Her hair fanned out in a damp, stringy crescent. One of her slippers was missing. The fire was banked high, the logs crammed higgledy-piggledy into the narrow fireplace. Glowing embers had fallen out of the grate and lay smoking in the hearth.

'Lucy?'

She stirred, gathered in her limbs, looked up. Resentment simmered in her eyes. All the blue had leaked out of them leaving dark, polished coals.

'Just fetch some hot water, will you? And fresh linen. I need to wash.'

Dawn. I tumbled out of bed, barked my shin on the wooden post and hobbled to the open window, one hand clamped around my throbbing leg. I nudged open the shutters and peered into the yard.

Lord Sutcliffe's carriage was gone.

Lucy was hunched at the parlour table taking birdlike nibbles of her breakfast. Isaac ate heartily, wolfed down bread and mashed oats with the appetite of a starved man. He nodded when I took my place and shoved a piled trencher in front of me. It was hard to look at him. Instead I tore off a chunk of bread and tried to catch Lucy's eye but she refused to be drawn. Isaac chatted to her between mouthfuls. She put down her fork, rose, curtsied and begged to be excused. Isaac nodded good naturedly towards the door and smiled as she whispered out.

I nearly choked on my bread. I poured some water into a cup and swallowed it down. Isaac slapped me on the shoulder.

'We'll need to get you a new dress too, Rachel,' he guffawed. 'Not a hand-me-down but one made to fit, by the finest seamstress in Stonehill,' he winked, 'or maybe even London.'

I put down the cup. ''Tis uncommon kind of you,' I heard my mouth saying, 'but a waste of good material, surely, to wear splashing about in the muddy yard.'

Isaac leaned back and slapped his thighs. Tears of mirth streamed from his round, tarnished-farthing eyes. 'Right you are too, my girl. Much too fine for opening carriage doors, but 'twas not what I had in mind. We've had a change in our fortunes. There'll be something fancy for all of us before the month is done.'

Lucy was waiting for me in the passage. Her back was to the wall, her head leaning against the grey plaster.

'Sutcliffe is coming back,' she said.

On Sunday Isaac accompanied Lucy to church. She was smothered in a pale green confection of satin and taffeta with a wide, ribbon-bedecked bonnet perched atop a tumbling white wig. The gown had arrived at Green Gallows yesterday afternoon courtesy of Lord Sutcliffe. Mother whooped when she saw the shimmering expanse of green material.

'Come, Lucy, you must try it on at once.'

It fitted perfectly.

And it wasn't the only thing to arrive. Oh no. Little trinkets kept sidling up to our doorstep when I was in the paddock, or busy in the wine cellar, or off on some errand. Before we left for church, Lucy caught me outside my bedchamber.

'Look,' she said, holding up her hand. Metal glimmered in the light seeping through the hallway's one window. A ring. A green jewel in a circlet of gold. Reflections threw emerald fireflies across Lucy's taut face.

'Lord Sutcliffe's groom delivered it. All the way from London. His poor horse was steaming and dead on its feet. The ring was barely out of the groom's pouch before Father crammed it onto my finger.'

I studied the ring as best I could in the bad light. I was no metalsmith but it looked poorly fashioned. Nothing a lady would want to wear or display proudly in front of friends. Lord Sutcliffe was a rich man. But this looked cheap.

'It doesn't seem worth much,' I ventured.

'No it doesn't, does it? Perhaps he was afraid we'd sell anything better. We're commoners, remember. Commoners in debt. And yet it's so appropriate. A crude ring for a cheap whore.'

'Why don't you take it off if you hate it so?'

Lucy clucked with impatience. 'Look more closely, sister.'

I stared at the puffed white flesh either side of the metal band.

'It's stuck,' Lucy confirmed. 'Even if I did manage to get it off, Father would probably nail it back onto my finger. I've been tagged like a farm beast without even the respectability of a marriage to hide behind.'

I travelled to church with Judd and Sally Button. I couldn't let Lucy face this by herself. Matthew drove, which was a rare privilege for him. As soon as we arrived, I scrambled out of the door, nearly catching my petticoats on the step. Lucy was on Isaac's arm, looking like a bride, with Mother walking serenely behind. Isaac was back in his powdered wig and velvet breeches, the humiliation of the night with the Grayses seemingly forgotten. Inside the church, whispers breezed around the aisles. Faces turned towards Lucy then quickly away again.

Mother sat Lucy near the front and settled beside her. I was stuck on the next pew, watching Lucy's stiff back. The muscles in her neck and shoulders were as taut as the strings of her spinet.

Old Buseridge wheezed into his pulpit. Sometime during the service the wind got up and rattled the ancient leaded glass in its panes. The door blew open and the first early-dead leaves of the infant autumn swirled through. Hats and wigs flew off. Two men, struggling, pushed it closed but the cold spirits were in. Women drew their shawls around their shoulders, men shivered, babies started bawling from the soiled depths of their swaddling.

I stumbled over my prayers. The service seemed to go on forever. When we finally emerged, sneezing, into the churchyard the wind had gone off to torment some other village. Left behind was a litter of twigs, torn leaves and a harvest of spiked green horse chestnuts, which the village urchins pounced on.

Mother stood in the middle of the path surrounded by a gaggle of twittering women. Lucy was at her side, prayer book clasped in her gloved hands, eyes downcast. Mother plucked at Lucy's gown with busy fingers, stroking the material, lifting it for the ladies' inspection.

Another, smaller, ring of people clustered around Isaac. Men who had abandoned their trades and farms to take jobs on the road. He told them there would be no more trouble. They shook his hand, clapped him on his broad shoulders. Coarse laughter scattered crows from the trees, bringing disrespect to this normally peaceful churchyard.

But though their mouths smiled, their eyes did not.

Standing apart from the group, Will Davey leaned against the lich-gate, no merriment, pretend or otherwise, anywhere on his face. He caught me watching and nodded curtly. I picked my way between the tombstones and scampered down the cinder path to the gate.

'Mr Davey.' I dipped my knees and managed a smile.

'Don't curtsy to me,' he said sharply. 'I'm not your papa and I ain't your master.'

The smile melted off my face. 'Oh.'

He gestured northwards towards the turnpike. 'There's your master. He's a greedy one, young Rachel. 'Twill take all we possess and more to fill his belly.'

His face was gaunt and scraggly. Shadows lurked under his eyes and in the hollows of his cheeks. Both hands were chapped and badly blistered. A filthy linen bandage loosely bound two fingers.

But I'd seen my own face in the looking glass recently and shadows wallowed there too.

'The turnpike is serving some village men well enough I hear.'

A flicker of anger in those dark eyes. Only once before in my life had I given lip to Mr Davey. He'd plucked me off my feet, thrown me across his thick leg and belted my rump while Isaac stood by and laughed. I'd howled of course, my thirteen-year-old pride cut to ribbons, though there had been nothing in the blows.

'Sometimes you talk like your sister and it don't sit well on your tongue,' he said. 'You've got sense tucked away in that fat head but you're too timid to put it to any use. Find yourself a husband, a good man, and get away from here. Let him take you to Cornwall where there's fishing or tin mining. Or even Dorset to start up a farm. I love this land as much as you but it's been injured and the blow is a mortal one. Already the wound is festering. It's poisoned your mama and papa and trapped your sister. Run away. Run away while you can. You ain't got much of a life. No friends stuck out here in the middle of nowhere with nothing but a few nags for company.'

'Friends arrive in coaches every day,' I countered. 'And I have my sister. I have Lucy.'

'She'll bring calamity to you, girl.'

'But I love her.'

Davey shifted against the post. 'Aye, I see that in your face. But trouble surrounds her, young Rachel. 'Tain't of her making, but it's there, and anything it brushes'll be stained for life.'

I gazed around the churchyard, at the laughing chattering women, the men smoking cigars Isaac had given them, and at Lucy, pale as the marble statue she stood beside. No one was talking to her.

'Don't go crying on me,' said Mr Davey. 'My words hurt because there's sense to 'em as well you know.'

'I'm not a piece of baggage. I won't let myself be carted off by any clod-headed farmhand who wants a wife.'

'Baggage is just what you are, Rachel, whether you find the notion sweet or not. I doubt you've much of a place in Isaac's grand new schemes. Put what faith you have left in God or whatever else you trust and don't get in the way.'

The trouble started in the kitchen.

I was on my way down from the guest rooms. We were between coaches and 'Lizabeth, silly cow, had stumbled on the stairs, spraining her ankle, so I had been told to help fetch the linen and take it to the washroom. My route took me through the kitchens where 'Lizabeth had been left by the hearth with wet strips of muslin swathed around her swollen flesh.

Shifting the bundle of linen onto one arm I lifted the latch and pushed the door open. It swung inwards, revealing 'Lizabeth's tear-splashed face and Isaac, glowering over her, seemingly ten foot tall compared to the slightly built girl.

His face was black, his arm raised. One swipe of that big hand was likely to split 'Lizabeth's skull open like an egg.

'I never stole it, I swear. Miss Lucy gave it to me.'

'Why should she want to give you something so valuable?' Isaac growled. 'It's for a lady, not some kitchen scrubber.'

'I don't know, really I don't. She put it around my neck herself and told me it was mine for keeps. I ain't never had anything as pretty as this before.'

I slipped past, not daring to breathe. Isaac noticed nothing except the quivering creature in front of him. 'Lizabeth was holding something against her breast, holding it so tightly her knuckles had gone white, but I recognised the gold chain that spilled from between her fingers. Oh yes.

I ran into the washroom, dumped the linen on top of the already stuffed wicker basket and left through the outside door. I slipped across the stable yard, around the corner of the inn and entered again through the door beside my bedchamber window. Along the passage, up the stairs three at a time and I arrived, out of breath, in Lucy's room.

She had her back to me and didn't turn round when I entered. She was seated at her dresser. A wooden-handled hairbrush, stained with age, was clutched in her right hand. Behind her the bed was strewn with clothes – fine gowns thrown one on top of the other, crumpling the material.

'Lucy', I said, coming to stand behind her 'why are you combing your hair with that old thing? Where are your good hairbrushes?'

She stared into the looking-glass, arm working the brush in long, stiff strokes.

'You gave your necklace, the one with the golden heart on it, to the scullery maid,' I pressed. 'That was a birthday gift, Lucy. Isaac paid two guineas for it.'

''Lizabeth has always liked it,' she replied without pausing. 'She always remarked on it whenever I wore it. Could not keep her eyes off it, in fact. Well now it's hers.'

I caught the brush. Lucy yanked it back out of my grasp. I sighed. 'Isaac thinks she stole it. He's in the kitchen with her now, about to blacken her face. Even if he lets her keep it you know she'll only lose it, or sell it, or get robbed in the lane on the way home. And even if none of those things happen her grasping lout of a father will have it out of her hands and peddled in the nearest gin tavern before the day is out. Now, what has happened to your good hairbrushes?'

Lucy gave her hair an idle flick and tossed the ancient trinket into the box on her dresser. 'I gave them to the milkmaid when she brought the morning delivery.'

'Why do such a thing? Don't we pay her enough for the sour milk her idle brother's cows put out?'

'She is going to be wed. I wanted her to have something nice.'

'I'd love to have a set of brushes like that.'

'They are no kinder to your hair than those fish-bones you use. If you want any of my possessions take them. They don't mean anything to me. They never did.'

I knelt beside her and tried to take her hand but she jerked it away. With trembling fingers, she flipped the top off her powder box, picked up the puff and savagely dabbed her face. Clouds of white powder filled the air.

'You told me you had plans,' I said after a while.

Lucy finished powdering her cheeks and started on her forehead. Wisps of hair fell over her skin and got caught in the white paste.

'Will you run away?' I pressed.

'That was our hope. We thought we'd go north, elope together like some of the couples in those silly novels Mother makes me read. Jeremiah has some family, distant cousins he hasn't seen in years. He hoped they would take us in for a while, at least until we were wed. He hoped to start up in business, perhaps run a stable. I don't know what I'd do. All I have is music, Latin and needlework. Become a governess perhaps. It was a dream we wanted to make work. Perhaps we would have succeeded.'

'And now?'

She put down the powder puff and stared at her reflection in the mirror. Suddenly she looked ten years older than me, not two.

'I could run away from Father but not from a man like Sutcliffe. I've learned enough about him to know that. He would hunt us down, no matter where we fled, and find us. I dread to think what he'd do to Jeremiah. Perhaps have him transported or even hanged. Sutcliffe could accuse him of any crime he liked and no one would go against his word. I can't let that happen. I have to set Jeremiah free.'

'I don't think he'd go, Lucy. I think he loves you too much.'

Lucy turned the mirror to the wall. 'I know, sister. I know.'

Flowers began to arrive at the inn. Every day brought more by coach, merchant's wagon or private messenger. Huge bunches of purple, pink and yellow that would never be found growing anywhere amid the quiet woods, hedgerows and meadows surrounding Green Gallows. With each delivery there was always a gilt-edged card bearing Lucy's name and a splash of red wax imprinted with Lord Sutcliffe's ring. Nothing more.

The parlour and Long Room became choked

with exotic ferns and drooping petals. The air was thick with their scent. 'Lizabeth's face broke out in an angry rash and she kept bursting into fits of coughing. I couldn't stop laughing at her and that only made things worse.

'Stop that braying, girl!' Isaac warned when 'Lizabeth's hacking had me on the floor, eyes streaming. He sent me from the parlour in disgrace but 'Lizabeth gained little satisfaction from it. I laughed all the way down the hall and into the stable yard. Through the parlour window I caught her plum red face watching me.

Oh, I could be wicked at times.

Then the guests began tugging at their neck cloths or sneezing delicately into embroidered kerchiefs. 'Been to Africa,' one man – a slave trader from Bristol – told Isaac. 'Worse than any faggy jungle in here. A fellow can't breathe.'

Opening the windows only attracted the last of the season's bugs. Despite 'Lizabeth's discomfort Mother sent her upstairs with an armful of blooms for Lucy's bedchamber. Ten minutes later the maid was back clutching a bunch of broken stems.

'She sat and pulled the heads off,' 'Lizabeth explained.

Mother was not at all put out. There were plenty of flowers and more would arrive tomorrow.

Later, Lucy caught me in the corridor and asked me if I wanted some. I chose bunches of pink and yellow orchids and together we took them into my room. I arranged them as best I could on the narrow window ledge.

'You were sick this morning,' I said quietly. 'I heard you in the privy.'

Lucy put down the blooms she'd been holding.

'That's the third time this week,' I continued. 'Isaac hasn't noticed yet but Mother soon will. The servants too.'

A deep flush sprouted at the base of her neck and began to work its way towards her face. 'It's nothing. A slice of bad beef or a spoonful of butter that has turned sour. Remember when you had that fish pie Mother bought from the tinker woman? You were ill for days. Even the smell of food was enough to set your stomach groaning.'

'You didn't eat your breakfast this morning. You sat there playing with your potato until it fell to pieces.'

'I wasn't hungry.'

'You had appetite enough at supper last night.'

'It was hot yesterday. I took too much sun. It has caught up with me, that's all.'

'Perhaps Sally can fix a draught…'

Lucy grabbed my arm. 'Tell no one about this, do you hear? No one. Not Sally, not Matthew and most certainly not Father, understand?'

Her eyes were grey, cloudy, brewing storms.

'Lucy, why are you letting them do this? They're squashing you, can't you see? Is that what you want?' I pulled my arm free. *'Is that what you want?'*

She pressed her hands against her face. I stared at the pile of orchids lying on the bed.

'Lucy...'

She took my hand and pressed it against her belly. I tried to draw away. Fingers locked around my wrist. Her eyes held mine. Unblinking, burning fever-like with anger, passion, Lord knew what. She was more alive now than I had seen her in weeks. More sure of herself. Almost terrifying in her power.

'What do you feel, Rachel?' she asked – no, demanded.

'Lucy,' I said uneasily. 'Let me go. You're hurting.'

'Tell me.'

Her embroidered stomacher jagged my fingertips. I closed my eyes, almost too afraid to breathe. My pulse thumped under the pressure of her hand. I felt, or imagined I felt, something stirring very deep within her body. Something that was as much a part of Lucy as her own blood – yet different too, detached, taking on a form of its own. Another heart. Another soul.

I swallowed. Something fluttered inside my own belly. For a second, the merest whisper of time between the mantel clock hauling its long arm from one second to the next, I was more jealous of Lucy than I had ever been in my life.

'Some say a woman knows she carries life from the moment of conception. But whose life, Rachel? *Whose?* Now I think I know what Mother must have felt and why she looks at you sometimes the way she does. Truth hurts, but not knowing is worse. I can be the unwed mother of Jeremiah's child, but I'll die before I carry Sutcliffe's bastard.'

Within a day the flowers had wilted. It was too hot in my cramped bedchamber, even with the shutters thrown wide. In the end their sickly odour was more than I could bear. Lucy caught me throwing them into the ash pit beside the kitchen door. Her white face remained expressionless. She came over and squeezed my hand before disappearing back inside.

Item by item, trinket by trinket, Lucy stripped herself of her life. Isaac tried to catch her, but Isaac could not be everywhere. It soon got to be a game among our tradespeople to see what treasures could be smuggled out.

'It does not matter, husband,' Mother said. 'Soon Lucy will have all manner of new things. Let her dispose of her old chattels as she wishes.'

But a glimmer of uncertainty flickered across Isaac's brooding features.

Later that week a letter arrived with Lucy's flowers. It was addressed to Isaac. He was a sluggard at reading and passed it to Mother who quickly scanned the single sheet of embossed paper. She scrunched the letter up and tossed it onto the fire. Her eyes were shining.

An hour before lunch I spied Mother and Lucy alone together in the parlour. Mother had a hold of Lucy's arm and was shaking it. Lucy's face was a damp pudding of tears. Neither of them noticed me.

That afternoon I saddled up Mistral and spurred her along the lane at a gallop. Sometime during that wild ride the wind snatched away my tricorne and sent it fluttering into the rough gorse that lined the road. I had no time to search for it. Eight miles out of Stonehill I reined in, dismounted and tethered Mistral to a gate. I climbed over it, scrambled to the crest of the Ridge and looked down on where they were building the turnpike. An ugly gash split the Downs in two.

Men swarmed around the wound. So much work in so little time. Livestock which had grazed undisturbed for years huddled in corners bleating woefully, the sound carrying on the breeze to the crest of the ridge. Farmer Blankerton had complained in the taproom that two of his ewes had gone missing. 'My stock don't wander,' he'd said gravely, 'lest it's into the belly of some bastard Mick with a shovel in his paws.'

A plague of highwaymen on it, I thought savagely.

Matthew was in the stable when I returned Mistral, lathered and panting, to her stall.

'What're you cryin' for?' he asked, putting down a pail of slops and coming over.

I wiped my face with the back of my hand. 'I got a faceful of grit, that's all.'

He shook his head. 'We've had rain these past two days. The lane ain't dusty.'

'Well, fine, so now I'm a liar.'

I threw him the reins. He led Mistral into her stall and began to unbuckle the saddle.

'I can't cover for 'ee if you go sneaking out again.'

'Since when has anyone cared what I did so long as there's no carriage door in want of opening or kitchen rubbish to dump in the ash pit?'

Matthew didn't answer. He slid off Mistral's harness, fumbled with the bit and cursed softly as it clattered onto the floor. I moved so I could see his face. He looked confused – frightened even. His hair was tousled and his breeches speckled with old straw.

'You're taking too many chances,' he said, 'and you're going to get us all into trouble.'

Something was wrong.

I knew that the moment I woke. The shadow cast on the floor by the window frame was too close to the foot of my bed. I had overslept.

I dragged myself out from under the rumpled quilt and stood, blinking the sleep from my eyes. A huddle of dead embers clung to the bottom of the fireplace. I glanced at the clock. Nearly half-past nine. I had been asleep for a lifetime.

I yawned and hugged myself, surprised that no one had come to rouse me. Voices sounded from somewhere outside. I splashed some cold water into the basin on the dresser and bathed my tired face. The beginnings of a headache simmered behind my forehead. Footsteps ran past my window, a figure momentarily blotting out the light. Then a raised voice, a shouted response. And someone crying. Deep, hacking sobs.

I frowned. It sounded like a man.

I pulled my nightshift over my head and fetched garments from the wardrobe. I was half into my gown when 'Lizabeth burst into my bedchamber to tell me that Lucy had been found hanged.

Chapter Eight

A small crowd was gathered around the signpost. The rope that had killed my sister dangled from the top spar. Judd had found her, just past daybreak, when he had stirred from his bed to ready the horses for the first changeover of the day. The animals had been skittish and Judd, whose sharp eyes noticed that a small ladder was missing from the back of the stalls went to investigate, suspecting some footpad at work in the grounds. He had found the ladder all right, lying on the gravel beneath the creaking sign. And the rope.

She had done it in the middle of the night. Her body was already cold, her face stiff and blue. Lord knows how she managed to tie that rope. How many attempts had it taken? Was she afraid that somebody would see her – afraid more of discovery than of death?

Judd had cut her down, cradling her body in his thick arms. Matthew ran inside to fetch one of the sheets from her bed to wrap her in. Together they'd brought her into the parlour and laid her out on the rug. It was not until then that they discovered the ring finger of her left hand was missing. It had been sliced off, probably with shears or perhaps one of the larger meat knives from the kitchen. Lucy had rid herself of Lord Sutcliffe's gift at last.

Isaac sat in the parlour staring at the lifeless body of my sister – his daughter – still clad in the blue evening gown she had worn at supper the night before. He leaned forward and gently kissed her forehead. Mother stood beside him, pulling her hair, spitting out the words *no, no, no* as if they had the power to punch life into Lucy's dead heart. Isaac's eyes closed, his lips moved. He covered up her face with the sheet and went outside. Through the window I saw him cross the yard from the woodshed, the axe Judd used to chop logs for the kitchen stove grasped in his knotted hands. Handled right it could cleave a thick stump with a single bite of its sharp steel tooth.

I ran outside. Isaac strode around to the front of the inn, looking neither to the left nor right. Nostrum sellers scattered in front of him. He tore off his waistcoat, spat into his hands and hefted the axe. The blade whistled through the air, a metal arc cutting the throat of the early morning. His biceps bulged as the axe head struck the base of the sign. But that post had stood, squeezing the necks of thieves and murderers, for a hundred years or more. Nature had, with tools of frost and gale, turned the wood to a brittle stone. The axe glanced off, barely chipping the knotted surface. Above, hinges creaked. The sign flapped. The end of the rope still dangled as though questing for another neck.

'Lizabeth went hysterical, screaming: 'She's dead! Dead, dead, DEAD!' and not even a sharp slap on the cheek from Sally could quieten her.

I looked at Matthew. He looked back. His lips formed a word but I couldn't make it out. I threw my arms around him and rested my head against his shoulder. His arms slid around my waist. What a sight we must have seemed, standing outside a stable filled with restless horses, just holding one another until the tears came. I clung to Matthew as I might a husband for there was not another rock anywhere in this raging slurry of grief and pain that my life at Green Gallows had become.

Sally spent the rest of the morning peeling potatoes over a huge iron pail. Peeling until her fingers were raw and there was a mountain of white, glistening spuds cut into mad shapes and dumped on top of the kitchen table. Food enough for a regiment of troops, and thick peel lying everywhere like muddied snow. Her eyes slitted into buttonholes, squeezing back the tears as another flayed potato plopped into that bucket. And I thought if she ran out, if there were no more vegetables to butcher, then she would start on her fingers, peeling flesh away from bone in bloody strips. Then she'd move on to her wrist and work her way up her arm until there was nothing left of her but a skinned horror in apron and mob cap. And perhaps she would not stop at her flesh but go on unravelling herself, chipping at muscle and bone, gouging when the knife finally blunted.

Mother would not allow the fire to be lit in the parlour or the curtains to be drawn. She went about looking like someone had slapped her. Later I spied her in Lucy's bedchamber. The wardrobe doors were open and Lucy's best gown, the one Sutcliffe sent her, was spread out on the bed. Mother was perched on the end. She had one of the gown's sleeves in her hands and was passing the material gently through her fingers.

I crept back downstairs. The clock said six minutes past ten. The Stonehill coach was due in another half-hour. I paced from room to room, touching things. A vase of drooping campions, a table in the Long Room, the mantelpiece above the parlour fire. I moved the small free-standing mirror two inches to the right. I turned one of the cushions on Isaac's armchair the other way up. I plucked a spent ember from the hearth and crushed it in my fist. I sought comfort in making any small change I could to the world because I was helpless to do anything about the larger change, the fact that yesterday my sister was breathing and now she was dead.

A starling twittered outside the window. I wanted to wring the song from its feathered throat. If I could I'd stop the clouds in their tracks, prevent the trees and flowers drawing sustenance from the life-giving earth. I wanted all the men working the fields to down tools and go home. Blacksmiths' forges should lie idle, the coals turning grey as they died, coaches should pull over to the side of the road and the gales howling over the crown of Marrin's Ridge should fade to a whisper. There should be no laughter, no toil or play. How could the world go on? How dare the world go on when Lucy had died?

I kept returning to the clock, willing the hands to stop moving. With each tick her body grew colder, her death became more real. I thought of Lucy as I had last seen her. She would only ever exist now in the past.

That afternoon Will Davey brought a casket from the village and nailed Lucy inside. Isaac locked her in the tack room at the back of the stable and refused to let anyone in. I tried not to think of the white, lifeless thing lying in the oak box.

'I'll not have my precious girl put into the ground in some pauper's crate,' Isaac said. 'She'll get a proper coffin with handles and her name on a brass plate. And flowers, I'll smother her in flowers.'

Mr Davey took him to one side and laid a hand

on his shoulder. ''Tis just for a day or two, Curtis. She'll get a right pretty coffin if you say so. But let her rest in peace for now. There's nowhere else to put her. Not with guests coming and going through your doors.'

'We ought to lay her out in the parlour, proper like, and have Parson Buseridge come to say a blessing.'

'Later, Isaac, later.' Davey shook him gently. 'For now let's give her what dignity we can.'

Isaac nodded and beckoned me over. He slid his big arm around me and buried his head on my shoulder. I felt his face nuzzle into my neck and a warm dampness on my skin, spreading from his eyes until the top of my gown was wet with his pain and grief. He reached up and drew his index finger down my cheek, tracing the line of my jaw.

'Why did the silly lass have to go and do something like that?' he whispered. 'You're all I've got left now.'

I pulled away and stared at him. For a second I didn't know who he was.

Mr Davey called back just before dusk. I took tea into the empty Long Room where he and Isaac sat at opposite sides of the fireplace. Isaac stared into the flames, unblinking. Mr Davey's face was heavy, his mouth set in a tight line. He gazed at the picture of Lucy above the fireplace, eyes lingering, moving to her shoulders, bosom, hands, slowly back up to her face again.

The two men said nothing for a while. Will took a pewter flask out of his jacket pocket, pulled out the stopper and poured a dark brew, brandy by the smell of it, into his tea. He held up the flask, eyebrows raised. Isaac said nothing. Will grimaced and poured a generous measure into Isaac's cup. The constable pocketed the flask again, picked up his teacup and leaned back in his chair.

There were questions, routine, delivered in a leaden voice, answered with a nod or shake of the head. Isaac drank his tea, likely cold now, and gazed into the empty cup.

'Lucy will be buried in the gown gifted to her by Lord Sutcliffe.'

'No,' I blurted. 'She won't.'

Both men stared at me.

'Lucy wouldn't have wanted that,' I continued.

'Leave the room, Rachel,' Isaac said quietly. 'This is men's business.'

'Lucy was my business too.'

'Rachel...'

I fled the Long Room. Only two guests were using the taproom and the kitchens were sleepy in that time between clearing up after lunch and getting ready for supper. I stole the biggest breadknife I could find, smuggled it out in the folds of my gown and ran upstairs. Mother was gone. 'Lizabeth had cleaned Lucy's bedchamber. It wouldn't have occurred to her that there was no need to do so any more. No point in straightening her scent bottles, laying out the day's garments or putting an empty pot beneath her bed.

I hauled that hideous gown back out of the wardrobe. The knife blade gleamed in the light filtering through the small window. A dozen swift strokes and the dress was fit only for hair ribbons.

A noise at the door. Isaac was framed in the

doorway, his dark, boxlike face expressionless. I faced him, breathing hard, knife still in my hand, the gown in tatters at my feet. Three steps would take him across the room. He could swat the knife out of my grasp as if it were a stalk of grass.

His eyes twitched, settled, then twitched again. I looked at the floor. The knife slid out of my fingers and landed soundlessly on the rug. When I dared to look up again the doorway was empty.

By eight o' clock the Long Room was still deserted. Will Davey had ridden back to Prestbury. No one wanted supper that night though Sally prepared it anyway, hands cutting and buttering and slicing up bread in haphazard piles. A handful of guests huddled in a corner of the shadowed taproom. Quietly supping ale, smoking, keeping their thoughts to themselves. The remainder shut themselves in their rooms.

Isaac stayed in the parlour with Mother, the pair clasping hands across the table. Out in the stables, Judd made friends with a gin jug. The chink of earthenware drifted across the yard.

I climbed stairs, haunted passageways and paced the narrow corridors between rooms, my feet like two tired fish slapping aimlessly on the floorboards. I remember eating at some point. No, not really eating, just spooning it up and swallowing. Beef broth. The taste clung to the roof of my mouth.

People who encountered me during these night-long whisperings looked away, embarrassed, or dropped their gaze and hurried past.

All the next day I was a gypsy in the grounds of Green Gallows. An itinerant ghoul resurrecting memories. Here I was at the patch of grass by the pond where Lucy had sat making daisy chains. Then beside the tree we had climbed as children. Lucy scrambling to greater heights than I would ever dare, giggling from the upper, sun-dappled branches: 'Come on, Rachel, come on. Just another few feet and you'll be on the crown of the world like me!' And I, quivering like a rabbit freshly caught in the poacher's snare, hugging the trunk with my eyes squeezed shut. Then in the yard where we had nearly fought over Jeremiah. From there down to the coach house, peering through the small window, populating the junk with passionate ghosts.

Back in the bowels of the inn I flitted from room to room, touching everything she had touched, lying on every empty guest bed we had shared together, imagining her beside me again, her hair against my cheek, the moonlight on her face, her breathing tick-tock regular.

Isaac locked her room. 'Nail it up,' Mother said, but Isaac replied that one grave was enough and he wouldn't make a tomb out of Lucy's bed-chamber. She was dead but I was the spectre, haunting all her inside and outside places. But to anyone asking I'd say, 'Do you know what I feel? Nothing.'

Nothing…

Another letter arrived from Lord Sutcliffe. This time there were no flowers.

'He's heard,' Isaac said, pacing the parlour floor. 'My girl not yet in her grave and already someone's taken word to him. All he has to do is nod and the banks will foreclose.'

'You should not have taken the loan,' Mother said. 'Your dreams have brought us to our knees.'

'I won't let them take Green Gallows. My grandfather built it on land no one else would touch. Tainted ground, they called it. My own da told me he'd rather give the inn to the parish than see it in my hands. Told me I'd have the business on its knees before the year was out. When he was on his deathbed I said I could make a go of it. Poxed to the gills he was, yet he laughed at me with his last breath. Well, I proved him a liar, didn't I? Made it into the best coaching inn this district has seen, aye, by the blood and blisters of these two hands, and these same hands will tear it down before it goes to fill the purse of some city fop.'

Mother covered her face with her hands. 'What are we to do?'

'Bury our daughter. Then we'll see.'

Mother nodded. But I saw the doors of Bedlam reflected in those wide eyes.

Bad news always finds an eager ear. Guests stayed in their rooms. Pedlars, who often scrambled for pitches in our yard on busy mornings, melted away. Men seeking casual work exchanged whispers at our gate then went home again.

Gregor brought the Portsmouth stage in bang on noon. He wore a weary, hangdog expression. Even the horses seemed lacklustre and idled between the shafts until Matthew came to change them. With Judd in his cups we were just able to manage.

'I heard what happened to your girl,' Gregor told Isaac, who had come out to meet him. 'One of the local coachmen told me. 'Tis a damn shame.'

'You coming to the funeral? My Lucy thought highly o' you.'

Gregor slowly climbed down from his perch. 'Can't oblige, Curtis. The company won't give me the time off. Here...' He plucked a slim leather purse out of the waistband of his breeches and dropped it into Isaac's hand. 'That's from me and Sammy. Put something on her grave, something for people to look at and remember. Do that for her.'

Isaac glanced at the purse, then met Gregor's steady gaze.

'You want me to get the team changed elsewhere tomorrow, Curtis? Hough Farm can do it if I give them enough notice. Their mares are little better than shires but they'll get this pile of wood to Portsmouth before the tide.'

Isaac thrust the purse into the pocket of his leather breeches. 'Nay, Gregor. You'll change your team here as always, and sup ale under my roof. Green Gallows has never shut its gates to a coach while I've been master here.'

I opened the carriage door and helped down my passengers. A swarthy clergyman, a sailor and a girl with a boil the size of a soup spoon eating into her nose. I checked inside the coach for stragglers then slammed the door. I'd never seen the Portsmouth stage so empty.

'Judd,' I said, 'harness Mistral for me.'

He squatted on a dusty bale, palms open, staring at his hands. How small he looked. How withered, as if the muscles had turned to ashes beneath his flesh.

'Judd, please.'

'No,' he said, without looking up.

I crouched and tried to grasp his fingers. He shrugged me off as if I were a bothersome fly. I sprawled on the floor, grimacing as my hand squelched into soft manure. Dirt everywhere – mud from the yard, frayed ribbons of old straw, piles of horse dung.

'He won't let me clean up,' Matthew had said. 'He's sat there since this morning with that gin jug between his feet. I don't even know if there's anything left in it.'

I brushed myself down and made for the tack room door. I managed three steps before Judd raised a heavy boot and kicked it shut, almost taking my nose off.

'You're not leaving.'

'Let Matthew do his job,' I pleaded. 'The stalls need to be cleaned out. You've worked with horses all your life, Judd. How can you bear to see them kept like this?'

'Put a fine saddle and a pretty harness on an old nag and it's still a nag just the same,' he muttered. The letters of each word blurred into the next so that it came out *sssaaddle* and *haarnesss.*

I stood in the lee of the doorway and peered into the yard. Rain played its own melodies on our battered home. It hissed on the gravel, drummed on the roof, flooded gutters and beat against the windows. Just crossing from kitchen door to stables had soaked me.

There was an old saddle lying in the corner of an empty stall next to a pile of sacking. The leather was cracked, the pommel scuffed and black with use. Grunting, I hefted it up and threw it over Mistral's back. She started, hooves sparking on the stone floor before settling. The fastenings were frayed, the tarnished metal buckle clumsy in my hands as I struggled to tighten it beneath her. Judd watched me, making no move to interfere. He had knocked over the gin jug without realising and clear, bitter-smelling liquid trickled onto the dirty floor.

'You ain't gettin' no harness,' he said woodenly.

'Don't need a harness,' I replied. 'Mistral knows me. She'll do what I want.'

'Won't get far on that saddle. 'Twill fall apart before you reach the gate.'

'Then I'll ride bareback.'

I led Mistral out of her stall, whispering soothing words into her ear. The yard was still empty. Good. I licked rainwater from my lips and ducked my head back inside. 'Don't let Isaac find you like this,' I warned. 'You're horsemaster of Green Gallows yet, Judd Button.'

He stared at the jug. A dark puddle spread away from his boots.

I grasped the pommel. A man's saddle, so I had to hitch my skirts and swing a leg over. Much better than Lucy's fancy side saddle. This way I could feel the horse move beneath me, sense its thoughts, know better when to rein in or when to give it slack.

I sent Mistral out of the yard at a brisk trot, heedless of the rain stinging my face. Perhaps another hour of this wet misery before the clouds split again. Once through the gate I spurred the mare on. She responded at once, surefooted in the muddy lane.

Luckily the rain had eased off by the time I reined in at Prestbury church. I tethered Mistral to the lich-gate and stumbled up the path to the parsonage, keeping my skirt hems out of the puddles. Old Buseridge was in his front garden trying to revive his drowned flower beds. He looked up as I opened the gate, a limp bloom clutched in his hand. Immediately his cheeks coloured. His eyes darted everywhere.

'Parson Buseridge.'

He coughed. 'Child?'

'You must bury Lucy beneath the willow tree, the one in the corner beside the dyke where the church's land joins Farmer Oldacre's. No one else has ever wanted that plot yet Lucy liked to sit there in the summer after the service. She enjoyed the shade and you can see the whole of Marrin's Chase and the Ridge beyond. It was always one of her favourite places even as a little girl.'

'She is not to be buried in the churchyard.'

I swallowed. 'But this is Lucy's parish. She was christened here. She has been to every one of your services, never missing a Sabbath even when down with a fever.'

Another cough. A clearing of the throat. 'She is a suicide. She cannot lie in consecrated ground.'

'Then what's to become of her?' I demanded, voice rising. 'Shall we chuck her in the river? Perhaps sink her in the marshes before the new turnpike swallows those up too? Or shall we dig up our own paddock and bury her there?'

'God is merciful. Your sister will lie within sight

of his forgiveness. She will be buried on the other side of the churchyard wall on the strip of common ground beside the lane.'

'That patch of mud is scarcely wide enough to bury a cat.'

He flapped both hands. 'She took her own life. The Church is very clear on the matter.'

'She was driven to it,' I countered. 'By the cravings of a lecher. I call that murder, Parson Buseridge.'

''Twas her own hand that placed the rope around her neck, child. I shall pray for her salvation but her mortal remains cannot lie in my churchyard.'

'You held her in your arms, watched her grow up. Her faith was always stronger than mine. She never forsook you or your Church.'

'I wish I could help you. Lucy was a very dear girl. This entire business was ... dreadful. Yes, dreadful. There is no point in denying it. But the law is very clear. All we can do is pray and hope for mercy.'

He waddled off, black hat bobbing like a raven's beak.

Sally met me at the kitchen door.

'Get that dress off,' she commanded. 'You're leaving puddles on my clean floor, and look at those muddy tracks.'

Gone was the glassy-eyed lunatic. The old Sally was back and she was standing for no nonsense. She picked up a warm towel from the hearth and briskly rubbed the weather from my face and hands. When she was finished my skin tingled.

Warmth and feeling crept back into my veins.

'You've killed your dress for sure this time, Rachel,' she said, holding up the garment for inspection. 'Not fit to make a sack let alone be worn in front of decent people.'

'Don't throw it out,' I said. 'Isaac will go radish if he learns.'

'Well I must patch it up somehow. Where have you been to get in such a state?'

'The parsonage.'

'Feel better for it?'

'It didn't do any good.'

'Thought not. Sit in front of the stove and I'll see what I can do about this gown...'

Sally did her best but a few stubborn streaks of dirt lingered, and the material felt washed out and lifeless. My shoes were like two mud-baked kippers. There was no time to scrape them clean. I knocked them against the kitchen step to dislodge the thicker clumps of mud and crammed my feet inside.

'Buseridge says Lucy can't be laid to rest inside his churchyard.'

'Just as well. 'Tis full of thieves and adulterers.'

'What will Mother do? She'll be heartbroken.'

Sally didn't reply.

Lucy was buried on Tuesday. Buseridge shut himself inside the parsonage and drew thick curtains across his parlour window.

Isaac stood at the head of the grave, up to his knees in nettles, trying not to look into the shallow hole where water was already pooling. He opened his mouth. Nothing came out. Rain drizzled onto his tongue.

A raggle-taggle group of mourners spilled into the lane, forming a rough horseshoe. Hats were clutched in hands, shawls drawn tightly at the throat. Prestbury folk mostly. Those who had loved her. Those who had barely known her but were moved by her death and appalled at the cause of it. Some of doubtful faith or none at all, staring into the sodden pit where the laughing girl they once knew was about to be swallowed up.

The gravediggers, wanting the job done, a job not seen as a proper burial because of the circumstances, set to with their shovels. As the first chunks of soil hit the top of the casket people murmured and began to leave. The coffin had barely been covered when Mother crumpled to the ground. She fell without fuss, like a statue with the feet sledge-hammered out from beneath it. Her face was a weeping stew of pain and grief. 'Help me,' she pleaded, voice a quavering violin string. 'Help me, help me, oh God, help me.'

She clutched at passing legs, snatched at coat-tails, plucked at cuffs with her bony, scuttling fingers. People gawped at her. She grabbed hold of someone's waistband. He shook himself free, straightened his breeches and moved on.

Matthew's arm slid around my shoulders. 'Come away, Rachel.'

I shrugged him off. I stared at Mother, wanting to help her yet not knowing how. Finally 'Lizabeth came, pulled Mother to her feet and led her to the carriage. Her cries were lost in the rain.

Village men filed slowly past me, faces expressionless, arms around wives. No children present.

Sons and daughters shut away, forbidden to see.

Some took my hand, gently squeezing my numb fingers. Others kissed my cheek with rain-lashed lips. The hardness that was present in their eyes as they stood beside that yawning pit in the dirt melted into sweet compassion. Will Davey raised my hand and placed a soft kiss just above the knuckles. His eyes met mine. He shook his head gently.

Isaac tried to shake hands with some of the men. A few clasped his thick palm with a curtness that would've sparked his anger at any other time. The rest looked at his open hand as if they would spit on it. Eyes were flint beneath dripping hats and bonnets.

We piled back into the carriage. During the journey back to Green Gallows, Isaac sat next to me on the upholstered bench, his thigh pressed against my gown. I flinched when his fingers squeezed my wrist. 'Stay close, daughter.' The words, like an animal growl at the back of his throat. 'Stay close now.'

I sneaked a sideways look at him. Opposite, Mother had drifted off into some kind of troubled twilight. Her eyes were closed, her flesh drawn tight over her cheekbones.

'There are no flowers,' I whispered.

Isaac looked at me sharply. 'What d'you say?'

'Flowers.' I swallowed. 'There are no flowers on Lucy's grave. We forgot to bring some.'

He squeezed me again. Pain jolted up my arm.

'Lucy ain't gone,' Isaac said. 'Not yet. We'll run the inn as if nothing has happened. Tender the coaches. Feed our guests. No mourning clothes.

I'll not drape my inn with the colours of the grave.'

That evening, the Southampton stagecoach, which always called in at Green Gallows before heading west, failed to turn up.

Our supper table was as silent as the lane outside. Somewhere a crow rasped. It seemed to be laughing at us.

'The stagecoach will come,' Isaac said. 'Eat your supper, Rachel. Good money has paid for that. I'll not see food wasted.'

I ate. Each mouthful of boiled potatoes stuck like pine cones in my throat.

'Sally left some pies out in the kitchen,' Mother said vaguely. 'I'd better go and cover them if they're not to be eaten.'

'You leave them where they are,' Isaac said. 'The carriage will be here soon, bringing empty bellies all the way from Stonehill. No one has had to wait for their supper at Green Gallows.'

I thought of Mistral, stamping impatiently in her stall with an empty belly of her own. Judd was drunk again and Matthew was too grief-wrecked to be of much use.

'Rachel, go put on your dress and hat. You must be ready to greet our guests.'

I put down my fork and left the table. Isaac's fingers slowly curled and uncurled. Both hands twitched like snared rabbits.

While I changed, Isaac went outside and waited by the gate. I saw him from my window. He stood hunched, staring at the muddy ribbon of road which we knew in our hearts would soon never see anything more grand than a farm wagon lumbering to and from Prestbury market. He waited until the blues of the day softened into darkening greys. Eventually either a stiff back or an ale-starved belly pulled him indoors. His tread upon the parlour floorboards was the step of a man with one foot on the gallows.

''Tis late, is all.' His gaze swept the room, daring us to argue.

Lightning flickered above the Ridge. Soon the rain began to fall in earnest.

Morning brought little respite but Sally glanced at the sky and said the sun was biding its time and would show its face before noon. Meantime the road coughed up a private carriage with two passengers. I got two sixpences by way of a tip and Judd, nursing a sore head, had something at last to distract him from the gin. Mother, clothes buttoned all wrong and hair like a bird's nest, went into a frenzy of activity, catering for two dozen instead of two.

'Damned lucky to find you,' said a powdered fop, peering at Isaac through a pair of gold-plated spectacles. 'Heard you were closing down. Be damned awkward should our horses collapse in their shafts what with the way Emily's driver pushes the beggarly beasts.'

The silk-bowed bundle of rouge and feathers clinging to the dandy's arm brayed with laughter. He petted her hand. Isaac's cheeks coloured.

'Green Gallows is not closing,' he said. 'Nor shall it ever.'

'That's not the story going round the posting inns, dear fellow. Would've preferred to try the new road myself but Emily, bless her, wanted a thrill. Likes the thumps and bumps of that pig track out there. Well, let's see if you can manage a passable breakfast. I have not eaten since supper in London and that damnable road gets the belly rumbling.'

They stayed until noon. Long enough for their horses to be rested, long enough for them to complain about the food, the sparsity of the Long Room, the uncomfortable chairs and the foul weather, though I don't know what they thought we could do about that. Isaac tried to persuade them to stay the night but his heart wasn't in it, and they left before the next rain shower. Our empty rooms stayed empty, the bedlinen neatly piled, the water in the ewers gathering films of dust.

Meanwhile the inn was being rid of the sickly-sweet stench that had choked it these past two weeks. No more bouquets arrived from London. Dying flowers were taken out and dumped in a pile beside the ash pit. Some were to be burned, others to be mashed up and used as compost for Sally's small vegetable patch. I could've had my pick of the fresher blooms. A few were still quite pretty. But Lucy hadn't liked them.

'Lizabeth spent a great deal of time with Mother. I'd catch them in the parlour or out in the grounds, slowly treading circles around the inn. 'Lizabeth was like a murmuring priest, holding Mother's hand, stroking her hair, nudging her in this direction or that. I could've brained her for such cheek, but Mother seemed to be drawing back from the edge of whatever deep and terrible thing had been about to swallow her.

A rumbling in the lane. The *Charger* crashed through the afternoon. I had forgotten all about it. The coachmen huddled on their perch. Blinds were drawn over the windows against the bad weather. All gone in a blur of wild-eyed horses and varnished, crested wood. A sea of mud was thrown into the air by those huge, hungry wheels. It fell on our front gate like a curtain.

You'll stop, I thought savagely. *By God you'll stop one day*.

Gregor was due in half an hour. The sky's grey face finally broke into a wide blue smile. The sun rolled out from behind the receding clouds and lit up the world. Steam wisped lazily off the sodden gravel. Puddles shrivelled.

I clasped my fingers behind my back and paced a slow circle around the yard. Matthew appeared at the stable door, looked around then slipped away again. Harnesses jingled faintly.

The last withering strips of rain cloud were fleeing towards the coast, leaving only a few cotton puffs to dot the sky. A flock of migrating birds formed a beautiful half-diamond against the blue curtain.

The taproom door swung open. 'Lizabeth appeared, rolling an empty ale barrel between her scrawny arms. She righted it, set it against the wall and glanced at me before disappearing back inside.

I continued to mark a circle.

He's late.

A soft peal of church bells drifted across the treetops. Parson Buseridge had them rung every day at one o' clock. A local tradition.

A spring could have collapsed or perhaps one of the leaders had thrown a shoe. A highwayman, fearing the loss of future income from the heavily protected turnpike, might have been emboldened to hold up the stage. The carriage might even have rutted down to the axle – though Gregor was really too experienced to let that happen – or one of the wheels could have split.

I broke off my aimless circling and strolled, skirts swishing, to the gate. The surface of the lane was like a mud pie crammed into a too-hot oven. Where it had dried, cracks spread jagged fingers from ditch to opposite bank. Wet patches glistened, withering under the sun's glare.

Gregor's driven over worse, I thought.

I peered down the lane in the direction of the Ridge. A swarm of gnats clouded a shimmering patch of air. A bird twittered – a lone voice in the drooping countryside. My face and neck were thick with sweat. I wished for my battered old tricorne but I'd left it on a hook on the back of the larder door.

'Glory, Gregor, where are you?'

I plucked a leaf from the hedge next to the gate and rubbed it absently between thumb and forefinger. Dirt smeared my skin. Every tree, bush and flower was coated in a thin spattering of dust. It grimed our windows, tainted 'Lizabeth's washing so that she often had to do it again, gritted our horses' eyes and left throats feeling dry and sore.

The road. Always the road. Daily the workings threw up whirling dust devils that were snatched by the wind and sucked up into the rain clouds, only to be dumped on our heads with each downpour.

I trudged back towards the stables. The occasional twitterings had silenced. Breezes had ghosted away to soothe other brows. An unnatural, heavy stillness lay over everything. Even the crunch of gravel under my shoes sounded muted.

The heat was making me light-headed. I sheltered beneath the gable where a dark tide of shadow, as sluggish as spilled pitch, was creeping across the yard. Matthew appeared at the stable door again. He spotted me and shrugged.

The encroaching shadow had conquered another foot of ground when Isaac blustered into the yard. He strode over, boots kicking up dust.

'No sign, daughter?'

'Not so much as a drover's cart.'

He fished in his jerkin and pulled out his pocket watch. The chain glittered in the sunlight. He popped open the lid. A bead of sweat slid down his nose, dangled from the tip then let go. I watched it fall. Slowly. Like a teardrop. It dashed itself on the hot gravel.

Isaac knew the time. He'd known it before taking out the watch. The heat of the day, the lengthening shadows, the number of notches the sun had cranked itself along the wide arc of the sky. He did not need a timepiece to tell him the coach was late.

He opened his mouth to say something. A slow trundling sounded from the lane. We glanced at one another. Our ears, attuned to the creaks and groans of road traffic, recognised the slow plod of dray horses, the rumble of a farmer's cart.

It lobbed into view beyond the hedge. Bertram the tinker waved from his perch. Behind him, his cart sagged under a loosely tied pile of firewood. His family, as the result of a favour to some long-buried member of the Marrin clan, had sole rights to glean storm wood from the thick sprout of trees biting into the crest of the Ridge. Good burning wood, not smoky or sizzling like the sap-choked rubbish growing on the edge of the common land. Winds from the north hit the Ridge hard and there was always plenty of wood to bloat Bertram's wagon.

'Ho, Bertram,' Isaac called out, running to the gate. 'Have you seen the Stonehill stage? 'Twas due a good two hours ago.'

Bertram sucked on a long-stemmed clay pipe, which he never actually lit, and pushed back the felt cap which hugged the bald crown of his skull.

'That I have, Curtis, that I have. Passed me at the Churchdeacon crossroads. Horses were in a lather, so they were.'

'Which way did it go?'

Bertram scratched his forehead with the end of his pipe.

'It took the turnpike, Curtis. The driver waved at the pikekeeper and the gate was opened without the horses having to break stride.'

'That turnpike wasn't due to open 'til the month was out.'

'The Prestbury stretch was finished two weeks ahead o' the due date. Colly Bruce dropped all toll charges for the first six days and he's got men on the crossroads persuading people to use the new road. Big men with hard faces, if you get what I'm telling you. Constable can't do nothing 'cause the law ain't been broke. Carriages are taking the turnpike at a gallop, Curtis. A gallop. Almost as fast as the *Charger*. I'm still on the lykeway 'cause they weren't sweet on having a farmer's wagon getting in the way.'

'Is everyone taking the turnpike?'

'Not everyone. Leastways not yet. I heard the *Charger* will keep using the South Road until the turnpike reaches the coast. And there's a few others ain't yet ready to bite Colly Bruce's bait. Got their noses up over the toll charges, or they've business in the villages.'

'But they still need to change their horses. Only the *Charger* can make the coast without posting here.'

'Ain't you heard? They're changing their teams at the Coach and Horses in Prestbury. The Turnpike Trust has built new stables and is offering half-price lodgings.'

The drover leaned over the side of his wagon and spat into the dirt. 'Lot o' work going on over at the Coach and Horses. I think they've got more 'n' just a posting house in mind for that place.'

Isaac turned to me. The creases of his face were full of dust. 'Go inside, daughter. There's nothing for you to do out here.'

By mid-week business had slackened almost to nothing and Isaac spent much of his time at the gate. Other times he stood at the edge of the common ground watching the long-distance stagecoaches hurl along the turnpike. Mother sent me out with some ale and a chunk of bread, which he hardly touched. As coach after coach failed to turn up, his eyes narrowed into dark slits.

'Someone's got a bad mouth,' he complained bitterly over dinner. None of us had much of an appetite. 'They've been puttin' it about that there's no welcome for travellers at Isaac Curtis's place.'

He ripped off a piece of mutton pie with his greasy fingers, stared at it then threw it onto his plate. 'That new turnpike won't work,' he continued. 'Drivers will end up flogging their horses into the ground for the sake of a few hours off their trip. You see if I'm wrong.'

'Mr Curtis, sir. The traders are packing up.' Matthew stood at the parlour door, panting like an overexcited child.

Isaac was checking the accounts. He looked up from his ledger. 'What?'

'They say they're going to work the Coach and Horses.'

'Is that right?' Isaac stood up and threw on his waistcoat. 'If there's any nonsense I'll sort it out.'

He strode across the yard. I went after him. Matthew also scurried along until Isaac turned and sent him back to the stables. The tinkers, hawkers and nostrum-sellers, who had returned to Green Gallows within a day of Lucy's death, were gathered by the gate. A jumble of wares lay at their feet. Goods being passed into the lane, carts were loaded, trinkets bundled up and stuffed into sacks.

'What's this?' Isaac demanded. 'My place not suit you any more?'

One fellow, a clay-pipe seller, tugged the brim of his hat. 'Beg pardon, Mr Curtis, but there's been a lot of building at the Coach and Horses. The turnpike goes right by it and there's a big yard with room enough for everyone. Colly Bruce says we can work it for free. The way we see it, we go where the coaches go.'

'Get out.' Isaac swept his hand in the direction of the lane. 'Get off my land the bloody lot of you. Go work at the Coach and Horses. Take their extra space and shove it up your arses. When there's no place left to go, when the Trust owns every bush, boulder and stick of fencing, see what happens then. As far as I'm concerned you can starve and be damned. Your women and brats too. I'll shoot you before I let you through my gate again.'

It rained torrents for three days. Sheets of water swept across the fields. Isaac went back to his post beside the gate. Eventually Mother had to fetch him in. He sat by the fire, a shivering, bedraggled creature with hollow eyes. Mother dried him and filled him full of hot coffee. He stared over the rim of the cup, hands shaking.

'What else can go wrong?' he said.

We found out the next day.

Chapter Nine

Sally flustered into the Long Room. 'Matthew has been arrested. Will Davey has taken him to Prestbury and is holding him in the gaol beneath the assizes.'

I was by the hearth, trying to coax some life out of a stubborn fire because 'Lizabeth had put her back out and couldn't be troubled to do it. Isaac was seated at one of the tables, a white fan of bills and other documents spread out before him. His quill crawled down one column of figures then trickled back up another.

'Arrested? What could that silly arse do to get himself arrested?'

'He took Mistral onto the turnpike and refused to pay the toll. When the pike keeper tried to bar his way, Matthew shoved him aside and rode through the gate. The keeper told Colly Bruce. Matthew had barely gone a mile before Bruce caught him. So now the lad's locked in a cell with a black eye and I don't doubt a cracked skull to go with it, and Mistral has been impounded. They're talking about a five-guinea fine or six months walking the treadmill if he don't pay. If Colly says Matthew tried to resist arrest it will mean more – maybe even Newgate.'

Isaac dropped the pen on top of the papers. 'Ain't I got enough troubles? If your gin-sodden husband had been fit to keep an eye on the lad then this wouldn't have happened.'

Sally swelled with anger. 'Is that so? You've treated Matthew like a mewling brat often enough. He couldn't fight, so he's tried to make a stand in the only way he knows how. You hate the road so Matthew has got it into his head that he hates it too. Poor boy has had his backside kicked so often he can't think for himself.'

'He'll get more than a sore rump when I'm done.'

'You won't lay a finger on him, Isaac Curtis. If five guineas is what Colly Bruce wants then five guineas you'll pay. And the toll charge on top of it if need be. 'Twas your pride that put that boy in gaol.'

Isaac took in Sally's shrewish expression. His Adam's apple bobbed as he swallowed. 'I'll get him out. But the fine will come out of his pay. And if my daughter's mare has been mistreated I'll stop him for that an' all. But there's one other thing, Mrs Button. Rachel comes with me, as always. But Judd comes too. I don't want him stinking out my stables. Get him sober within the hour.'

He turned to me. 'Rachel, take Apollo over to the coach house and hitch him to the gig. It's time we went calling on our new toll keeper.'

Going into that coach house was harder than I imagined. A mad part of me half expected to see Lucy and Jeremiah encircled in each other's arms. Whispering. Touching. I could feel their ghosts on the dusty floor, see a shift of ribbon in the light trickling through the too-small windows and for a moment I just sat on an old oak box and stared at the walls while Apollo chomped on a clump of wild grass growing by the door. Ten minutes later I returned to find Sally in the stable yard. Apollo had proved skittish, but the short walk and fresh air had calmed him and I'd been able to get the harness on without too much trouble. Sally, both sleeves rolled up, was plunging Judd's head into the trough. Water soaked her apron. Judd's shirt was drenched and his fair hair plastered against the glistening dome of his skull. More water streamed out of his mouth, nose and ears.

'Listen to me, Judd Button. Get your wits back about you or I'll see you drink this trough dry before I let you go.'

'Leave me alone, woman,' Judd spluttered. 'You're bringing shame on me.'

'Is there no shame in what you do? Should I leave you to squat in the sty you've let those stables become to fill your belly with poison and your breeches with shit? I'll bear most mistresses but not one that comes in an earthenware jug. I can't stop you dying if you're set on it. But not slow like this. And not in front of me.'

'This place is damned,' he said. 'And I ain't staying here a day longer.'

But stay he did, and within the hour was sober again.

With the three of us crammed into the gig, Isaac took us at a nerve-racking gallop to Prestbury. A mile outside the village the new turnpike cut across the South Road. Twice I thought the gig would spill us all into the ditch. At the Church-deacon crossroads we were told to climb out. A tinker was selling his wares from a bow-topped gypsy wagon. Isaac paid him a shilling to watch our horse.

'Don't aim to walk to the toll-house do ye?' Judd muttered, nursing a sore head. ''Tweren't no point in rushing here if we're to plod to Colly's.'

'I'm putting no carriage of mine nor scrap of boot leather on that road,' Isaac said, jaw set. 'If you haven't a mind to walk you can bide here with the tinker.'

'Might come back and find gig, horse and

tinker all gone,' Judd continued. 'Never met one in these parts who didn't have a horse thief's blood in 'em.'

We walked.

The journey was a hot tramp over rough ground. We had to watch our feet, wary of turning an ankle on a half-hidden boulder or slipping on some wedge of chalky muck gouged out of the road foundations and dumped beside the ditch. Isaac wouldn't look at the turnpike. He strode along the verge, soiling his boots with grim determination.

Less than a month since I had looked down on the site from the crest of the Ridge. Everywhere was evidence of the brutality with which the turnpike had been forced through the countryside. Tree stumps littered the ground like broken teeth. Blackened circles of ash, where the felled timber and gorse had been burned, bruised the ground. Some of the older trees had been uprooted altogether, leaving ragged holes. Dry walls had been demolished, their stones plundered, the ancient boundaries they'd once marked ghosted away.

As we approached the toll-booth the pike keeper swaggered out to meet us. His face was flushed, his teeth stuck with bits of meat. He eyed us warily, one twitching hand careful not to stray far from the wooden baton propped against the door frame.

'Ben Crake.' Isaac shook his head. 'You've been supplying eggs and cheese to Green Gallows since my father's time. I never thought you'd turn Judas.'

'This job pays better, Curtis,' the pikeman said. 'The way I see it, you won't have much use for my dairy come another month or so. The Coach and Horses get their supplies from the big market at Stonehill and bring it down on the turnpike. They haggle a price I can't afford to match. Working here has fixed my roof and filled my family's bellies. What brings you out to these parts?'

'I have business with Colly Bruce.'

Crake thought about it. 'Toll farmer's cottage is that way,' he said, gesturing. ''Bout another half-mile south. 'Twill cost you tuppence a head if yer want to pass through the pike though.'

'Colly Bruce can pay it,' Isaac said, shoving the pikeman aside.

It was a good house, built square, with windows in every wall. Isaac walked around it, noting the powder-grey stone. It had been fashioned after the style of the toll booth with white window frames, a green painted oak door and a sloping, tiled roof. A strip of garden hugged the front of the building with a gate and gravel path leading up to the front step. A dirty plume of smoke trailed from the clay chimney pot.

'The Trust like to look after their toll keepers,' Judd remarked. It was good to hear him talking like his old self, but I suspected that something in him had gone, broken, slipped away like spilled gin seeping into the cracks of the stable floor. 'That house is built to last.'

'Colly Bruce will make a hovel of it,' Isaac said.

He lifted the latch and nudged open the gate with his boot. We followed him up the path in single file. His fist thumped the door. Somewhere inside a brat was screaming. A woman's voice cursed, then scolded. Isaac and Judd glanced at one another. The door swung to. Jenny Bruce stood, blinking in the sunlight. A grubby urchin clung to her hip. Her belly was swollen with another. Greasy hair was tied back with a frayed strip of ribbon and a soiled apron hung loosely from her bulging midriff. She smelled of cheap gin and old vegetables. Wrinkles cracked her face, though I'd heard Colly had taken her as a wife when she was bare fifteen and that only three years ago.

From inside the house the bawling intensified. A horrible odour of sour meat, unwashed bodies and brimming pisspots wafted into our faces. The half-naked toddler let go of its mama's waist and ran, giggling, onto the strip of dirt that passed as Colly Bruce's garden.

Jenny Bruce wiped her hands on her apron and glanced uncertainly from Isaac to Judd then back again. She was barefoot, her toes callused, the nails black with grime.

'What is it that you'd be wanting at my door, Isaac Curtis?'

'I'll have words with your husband, Mrs Bruce. He's holding one of my men. I want him released before the afternoon is done.'

The word 'Mrs' seemed to curdle on Isaac's tongue. No one knew for sure whether Colly was church wed or not.

She looked him over, her expression thick with insolence. Isaac waited her out. Finally she yelled back over her shoulder into the house.

Colly's grizzled face split into a thick grin when he saw us. 'Well, well, look who's at my door. A fool, a drunk and a dumpling. Wantin' a job are ye, Curtis?'

'I've come for my stableboy,' Isaac said.

'Is that so? And what use would yer stableboy be to you now, in an inn with no customers?'

'I'll get my custom back.'

'Aye well, that remains to be seen, don't it?' Colly hitched up his breeches and pushed past us. We trailed after him. His splayed feet scuffed up puffs of chalky dust. Long, lank hair fell around his ears. He leaned on the gate, arms spread, gazing at the road, first in the direction of the Ridge then past the toll-booth and on to where the road curved around Marrin's Chase. Hot air shimmered above the drained marshes. Birds that preyed on the insect life had gone. There was a terrible quiet about the place.

'Ain't it a beauty,' Colly said. 'The stagecoaches do double time. You can see the dust they kick up a full mile before they hove into view. A whore-house, Curtis, that's all yer inn is fit for now. The Coach and Horses is on the lookout for furniture. Can't fill their rooms quick enough. They'll give a fair price for yer beds. 'Twon't be no use to you no more.'

'My furnishings ain't up for auction,' Isaac said quietly.

'Reckon you ought to be selling stuff while it's still yours to sell. That's a fine mare your lad was riding. My Jenny could use a beast like that to take her to Prestbury market. I'll see to the boy's fine, Curtis, if you can see yer way to letting me have that filly. Fair bargain. Trade always was a better way of doing things in these parts than peddling in coins.'

'I'll butcher that mare rather than let you have it,' Isaac said. 'You'll take the fine, honestly paid, and let the lad and my horse go.'

Colly turned away from the gate. He nudged his hat back on his head with a grimy thumb. 'So be it. I've no mind to argue. South Road ain't fit for much more 'n' driving pigs down now. Still, Curtis, that swill your skinny cook serves up would suit 'em. Daresay you won't go short o' custom after all.'

'Savour your moment, Bruce. I'll swallow your impudence to get that boy out of the lice-ridden hole into which you've had him thrown, but watch your tongue or this fancy new road will see blood spilled on it.'

The smile cheesed off Colly Bruce's face. His eyes hardened. He glanced past Isaac towards the cottage, but Isaac stood between him and the door.

'Ye'll get hung for assaulting a toll keeper, Curtis, or transported at best.'

'Aye, that I know. I don't need to be an educated man to say that's no fair trade for a black eye and maybe a few broken teeth so I'll not give you the satisfaction of it. But don't try my patience any more. 'Twould not be murder in the eyes of God to do away with the likes of you. I buried my daughter just the other day. I'll not stand any more lip.'

Colly glanced down. Isaac's fists seemed as big as tree stumps.

'All right, I'll fetch the ledger. Once ye've paid the fine, I'll give yer a chit to take to the Prestbury gaol and another to get that nag back if you want it.'

'You ain't holding onto a thing of mine, Bruce. If that horse was naught but a sack of dead bones I'd still see it out of your hands.'

Colly spent a moment swallowing that, then strode past Isaac into the house. The baby was still howling. He returned a moment later carrying a leather-bound book.

Isaac slapped coins into Colly's palm. The toll keeper counted them out, shovelled them back into his hand then counted again. The smug leer slipped back across his face.

'Ye're a ha'penny short.'

I fumbled in my tip pouch, found a sixpence and threw it at him. The coin struck his cheek and fell into the dirt.

'You can keep the change,' I said. 'Your child needs some clothes, or perhaps a tuppenny rag to bind her feet. 'Twill still leave you with three-pence ha'penny for the gin bothy.'

Isaac stared at me as if I was some bad-tempered stranger who had just blown off the road. A grin split Colly's face.

'Lord Sutcliffe himself is coming to inspect the new highway next Tuesday,' he sneered. 'Should be near enough open to all traffic by then. I'll wager the *Charger* will soon be making its last run down the South Road. Not that it ever stopped at your flea hole.'

He stooped and picked up the coin. 'Daresay his Lordship will be dropping by Green Gallows though. Heard he has a debt to collect.'

We walked back to the crossroads in silence, collected the gig and drove into Prestbury. The assizes lay a half-mile outside the village, a large building that served as a corn exchange when the courts were not in session. The turnkey shambled, coughing, out of the door which led to the cells. Gurney Tregas, who did all the dirty jobs around Prestbury, ones not even the parish labourers would take. Isaac passed him the chit from Colly and Gurney spent two minutes scrutinising it, eyes squinting in the sunlight. He couldn't read so far as I knew.

'Come on Gurney,' Judd said impatiently, 'Ye've had yer moment of glory. Now open up this bloody dungeon and let the lad go free.'

Tregas hawked and spat on the grass, then disappeared back inside. A moment later Matthew stumbled out, pale-faced and smelling of old straw. The assizes had been an inn once, and the cells below had served as an ice house. They were little better than brick-walled pits with no windows and poor air.

A large bruise purpled Matthew's left cheek. He shambled forward, blinking. Strips of raw flesh banded both wrists where they had put the chains on him. A smear of dried blood darkened his collar. His hair was matted.

'Look at the state of him,' Judd protested. 'I ought to break your head open for treating him this way, Tregas.'

'No use gettin' all black faced at me, Judd Button,' Tregas blustered. ''Tweren't my doing. 'Twas the road men. Said your stablehand tried to make off on horseback.'

Judd laughed in Tregas's face. 'Make off?

Matthew there couldn't swat a gnat if it was trying to bite him.' He turned towards the gig. 'Come on lad, we're going home. I don't care much for the smell of this place.'

Matthew said nothing on the way back to Green Gallows. Judd drove the gig and Isaac sat beside him, staring at the lane as it unwound beneath our wheels. Matthew sat on Isaac's legs, hugging himself, refusing to look at anyone. Back at the inn, Sally poured him a hot bath, filled him full of steak pie and then talked Isaac into letting him nap in one of the upstairs rooms. We now had a good half-dozen lying empty at any one time. The sound of Matthew's laboured snoring crept through the woodwork until well towards sundown. After supper, Sally asked me to take him up a tray with a hot potato and mug of ale. He was awake when I entered the room, propped up against some pillows with the coverlet lying loosely across his legs. He was bare-chested, ribs poking through his sallow flesh. A tuft of black hair nestled in the hollow above his heart. He made no move to cover himself as I laid the tray on the table beside the bed. His eyes followed my movements, glimmering in the semi-light.

'Well,' I said, setting down a fork on the tray beside his plate. 'Nothing to say for yourself?'

'Don't see what there is to say.' His voice was a husky whisper. The coverlet rustled gently as his legs shifted.

I fetched a knife out of my apron, dropped it beside the fork and straightened. 'Why'd you do it? You were lucky to get as far as you did, and lucky again not to get your ribs cracked. Those pikemen are brutes. Isaac said the Trust gave them clubs to belt footpads with but I'd not put it past them to use them as they pleased. And I'm sure Colly Bruce keeps a gun in the toll keeper's cottage.'

''Twas something I had to do, Rachel.' He searched my face, then shook his head. 'You ain't got a mind to understand.'

'What I understand is that you were trying to look a bigger man than you are. Now you're a fool in Isaac's eyes and lightened his pocket by five guineas into the bargain. Judd thought Isaac was going to shoot Mistral rather than pay the extra six shillings to get her back.'

'Judd doesn't see things straight any more.' Matthew looked up. 'Nor do you.'

'What d'you mean?'

''Twas not for Isaac that I did it. 'Twas for you.'

I regarded that sad face. When I was five years old he'd lured me to the log shed, stolen a kiss, and cried after I'd bloodied his lip.

'I know you're clever, Matthew. I've seen you fill a coach enough times. None can balance the stage like you.'

'Aye, I can fill a coach right enough,' he replied sullenly, 'and Jeremiah was good at shovelling shit out of the stables. He had the face of a crow and hands as big as the shovel he bore, yet he stole your hearts, you and your sister both. I'm near sixteen now and you've ran me around the maypole for long enough. All I ever got was, "Fetch that pail, Matthew. Sweep this up, Matthew." Judd says this, Isaac says that. Even 'Lizabeth takes to lordin' it over me whenever she gets the chance.'

'Lucy was kind to you.'

'Lucy would pet the dog that bit her. Sometimes her kindness hurt more than the worst oath you cast at me. Well, I'll not believe I'm so ugly or stupid that I have to be pitied. I'm as good a man as any your skirts'll ever draw. Better 'n' most.'

'You ought not to talk about Lucy like that. Nor Jeremiah. He's gone and you'd best forget him.'

'He's not gone and you know it. Mr Curtis only took him as far as the Ridge. Judd told me when he was sodden wi' gin. Mr Curtis swore to kill Jeremiah if he ever came within sight of Green Gallows again. But Jeremiah wasn't afraid. Judd says he stared Isaac out, and Isaac looked at his boots.'

'Judd's tongue is as addled as his head. You said so yourself. Jeremiah wouldn't dare to come back.'

'He was seein' Lucy even after Isaac warned him. You know that to be so.'

'A parting kiss. Sweethearts saying goodbye. Jeremiah is probably working on a farm somewhere in the north. Or perhaps looking after horses like he wanted. There's nothing to keep him here.'

Matthew shook his head. 'I've seen him.'

'Where? You've scarcely been out of the yard.'

'Sometimes up by the paddock, watching from the dyke. Sometimes standing on the edge of the Chase or moving between the trees. Watching. Always watching.'

'It was a tinker you saw. Or some poacher laying rabbit snares.'

‘’Twas Jeremiah, still wearing the clothes in which I last spied him, though barely a stitch holding them together now. Like a wild man, all rags and scraggy beard. His eyes were staring like he was waiting for someone. Someone who wasn’t ever going to come. I waved once, stupid like. He just slipped between the trees and was gone.’

I glanced out of the window. ‘You’re teasing me like you used to do when I was little. Scary stories to make a child shiver. You saw a tinker, nothing more. The Chase is festering with them. Not even Colly’s hired brutes will drive them out.’

Matthew’s expression was carved in flint. ‘I know what I saw. I’d best let Mr Curtis know.’

‘No.’ I caught Matthew’s arm. ‘Don’t tell him.’

On Tuesday Lord Sutcliffe’s patchwork coach clattered into Green Gallows’ yard. A watery sun clung to the treetops throwing a jaundiced light over everything. Matthew was still in bed and Judd was in the paddock exercising Mistral. Colly’s men had been rough with her. Lash marks striped her flanks and she was favouring one of her forelegs. I was cleaning out the stables. The mess was terrible. Lord knew how much gin Judd had drunk. Earthenware jugs were lying all over the place. It had taken me most of the morning just to get the straw changed. When I heard the carriage I ran to the door and nearly died when I saw who it was. Isaac walked across the yard to meet it. The door did not open, nor the curtain draw aside from the window. Words were exchanged, respectfully on Isaac’s part at first but as his temper began to fly so did his sentences, scattering through the air like starlings. I don't think he even noticed I was there.

'If you want Lucy, I'll give her to you.'

'Indeed?' Sutcliffe's voice leaked from behind the velvet drapes. 'Was it merely rumour then, that the girl strung herself up from your signpost, that she was seeing some farm boy and planned to elope?'

'Come to Green Gallows six weeks hence and you'll find your bride waiting. My life on it.'

'Your life it is then.'

The coach drew out, filling the air with dust and chips of gravel.

'Those were Isaac's words.' I propped my feet up on the stool next to the kitchen hearth. 'What did he mean? Can't he let my sister rest in peace?'

'I don't know what goes on inside your father's head any more,' Sally said, staring into the crackling embers. 'I wouldn't put it past him to try and resurrect the dead to try and save Green Gallows. I've seen a man sell out his wife and family just so he could hold onto a patch of dirt no bigger than my vegetable plot. When a man wants to keep something badly enough there's no telling what he'll stoop to.'

Copper pots dangled from their hooks, gleaming and arranged according to their size. The tables were cleared and washed, the utensils and cutlery packed away in their drawers. Next door, 'Lizabeth was standing, arms folded, in the empty taproom. Tankards were lined up on the shelf above her, corked bottles a regiment of green soldiers on the shelves, barrels standing sentry duty in their racks.

Sally sighed and got up from her stool. She walked over to the cupboard, brought out two bottles of red wine and brought them over.

'Here, take these to the church. Parson Buseridge will need them for the week's services. I know you're not sweet on him right now but we have to abide by our duties.'

I took the bottles and placed them in a basket. 'Sally, what's wrong? Have I upset you?'

She regarded me, arms folded. 'I don't think you realise just how much you sound like Lucy sometimes. You've learned much from her, I can see that. All those flowery words, the clever turn of phrase, the pretty voice. But heed my advice, Rachel, and don't talk that way again. Especially when your father's about.'

I took the gig to Prestbury church. Parson Buseridge accepted the bottles with muttered thanks and shut the parsonage door in my face. Isaac had been providing the wine, free of charge, to Prestbury church since he took over Green Gallows, a tradition which his father had started.

At the side of the lane two boys were playing on Lucy's grave.

'Gerroff,' I said, hands flapping. 'Get away from there.'

The eldest grinned gap-toothed insolence and spat at my feet.

'You're Will Sullivan,' I said, shaking with temper. 'My father does business with your papa. He'll skin your rump with his belt buckle if you don't shift.'

The grin tightened into a sneer. 'My da works on the road now. He don't care what we do. And you can't go tellin' us neither. You won't have nothing left before long. My da and his friends want your house. You'll be a tinker, living in a wagon in the lane.'

'You're fibbing,' I said. 'We're not leaving Green Gallows.'

He shoved me, his hands squeezing my breasts like some old lecher. I tumbled onto the grass, petticoats fluttering. The children laughed. A horrible sound in this peaceful, fresh afternoon.

Anger flared between my temples. My fingers scrabbled on the wall, found a loose stone, pulled it free. I clambered to my feet, rock clutched in my hand. 'I'll knock your bloody ears off, the pair of you.'

The boys' mother appeared, a bramble basket hooped over her arm. She rounded up the urchins and sent them scampering away. I think her sons were more afraid of her thick forearms than my rock.

I tried to thank her but she turned away and walked off down the lane. I crammed the rock back into the wall and shook out my skirts. A huge tear rent the material from hem to waist. Fresh mud stains added to those already darkening the once bright velvet.

When I arrived home I went to see Isaac about a new dress. 'I can't greet passengers looking like this,' I pointed out.

But Isaac just smiled. 'You won't need to,' he said. 'Not any more.'

The picture told me.

I must have passed it a thousand times in the year it had hung on the wall above the hearth. I never usually spared it more than a glance. 'Lizabeth dusted it regularly like everything else in the Long Room. As a token of respect, Mother had placed a length of black silk across the top of the frame, the only mark of mourning in the entire household. As I passed from taproom to parlour, I hesitated. It had been a fretful morning. Sally had suffered a disaster with her ovens, the pies had come out flat, the bread was soggy and weevils had infested an entire sack of wheat. When I had gone to her with my torn dress she'd waved me away irritably. Desperate and feeling horribly naked with my soiled petticoats on show for the world to see, I'd pinched a needle and length of thread from Mother's sewing basket and smuggled them into my room, but my clumsy fingers couldn't cope with the stitches. Finally I'd gone into the taproom and given 'Lizabeth tuppence for a few hairpins which I used to tack the velvet together. I was on my way back when I noticed that the strip of black silk had gone.

Painting had been another of Isaac's whims. He'd read in one of Mother's society magazines that artists were much in favour among the fashionable set and the Duke of such and such or Earl so and so had all taken up sketching, along with their ladies. The next day he returned from Stonehill with an expensive sketch pad and a dozen charcoal sticks.

'That pad will feed the fire before the week is out,' Sally predicted. Isaac drew Lucy over three afternoons, his brow furrowed, his fingers moving sluggishly across the paper. He showed me what he had done.

'Do you think Lucy will like it, Rachel? D'you think she will?'

The drawing was crude but honest. Pleased, Isaac had it framed. He would have gone on to do more but the stable-hands, who had heard about their employer's new hobby, sniggered and made girlish gestures behind his back. 'Why not try writing a bit o' poetry into the bargain?' Judd said, laughing. 'I hear 'tis all the rage in France these days.'

Isaac tried to shrug it off but his mouth tightened and his eyes grew hard. The sketch pad burned to ashes in the grate of the Long Room fire that night. In the kitchen, Sally nodded sagely over a supper of boiled potato and cheese while Isaac snapped the charcoal sticks between clenched fists.

He would have torn Lucy's portrait to strips but she told him she loved it, so he hung it on the Long Room wall for everyone to admire.

'A gypsy sketched it,' he told guests and warned me, jokingly, that if I said anything different he'd chain me to the back of a hurdle and drag me to the stocks in Prestbury market square.

I stood on tiptoe and squinted at the portrait. It was different. The eyes were darker. The cheeks had filled out and a small dimple had appeared on the chin. Other, cruder changes had been made. The breasts, the mouth, the hands. All had been altered in some way.

I backed away from the fireplace. The girl in the

portrait wasn't Lucy any more.
It was me.

I passed the remainder of the afternoon in a daze. With no coaches due, 'Lizabeth nagged me to help her with the guest rooms. I spent an hour amongst billowing sheets, listening to her prattle about the village and the cooper's lad she said she didn't like but whose name sent a flush into her cheeks. I kept thinking about the picture in the Long Room. Twice I let sheets fall onto the floor.

'Just as well those are for the wash,' 'Lizabeth remarked, eyeing the creased bundle at my feet.

I scooped them up, stuffed them into the laundry basket and carried it downstairs. 'Lizabeth fetched another pile and followed me to the washroom. I went in ahead and dumped the dirty washing into the tub. 'Lizabeth put the other basket on the floor and went out into the yard to tie up the clothes line. She was back a moment later. The smile on her face would curdle milk.

'Best take a look outside the kitchen door.'

'What new mischief is this, 'Lizabeth?'

'No mischief,' she replied. 'Go and see.'

I won't look, I thought. *I won't. I'll just go right on into the laundry room and put the rest of this linen in the tub. Then I'll go and see Sally about supper. I don't care what's happening outside. 'Tis just another of 'Lizabeth's spiteful pranks. I won't bite her baited hook.*

In the square of yard behind the kitchen, I found Matthew burning my clothes.

'What are you doing?'

Sweat beaded his forehead. His cheeks were

flushed, his mouth a tight line. He didn't look up but prodded the pile of blackened, stewing garments with a metal tipped pole.

'Mr Curtis bid me do it. "Burn the lot," he says. "Don't leave anything."'

'You went into my room? You fetched them out of my wardrobe?'

'Naw. Mr Curtis had 'Lizabeth do it, not that she needed much telling. Should've seen her face. All excited like. Bitch'd gladly set a torch to your bed had she one to hand.'

I eyed the smouldering heap. Little was recognisable. A button lying to one side in the ashes, a twist of velvet not yet caught by the flames, the husk of an old buckle. I could hear 'Lizabeth laughing in the wash house.

'Those clothes were all I had. What am I to wear now?'

Matthew planted the end of the pole in the dirt and leaned on it. Soot clung to his eyelashes. 'Reckon you don't want to ask that,' he said. 'I don't know anything for sure, but there's them that has an idea.'

'Put this on,' Isaac said after supper.

I stared at the dress. A bow-fronted confection of smouldering pink velvet and taffeta.

'I can't wear that. It's Lucy's.'

'Put it on.'

He threw the dress at me. It fell, like a pink rustling ghost, into my lap. The garment was new, the velvet soft beneath my fingers.

'I won't wear it,' I repeated. 'I don't want anything of Lucy's. It won't even fit.'

'Don't go coy on me, girl. You'll go upstairs to Lucy's bedchamber, you'll put on that dress and you'll make it fit.'

A tear stung the corner of my eye, slithered down my cheek, spilled a dark circle onto the material. Mother stared at the remains of her beef supper. Her mouth chewed and chewed until I imagined her gums bleeding behind those pinched lips.

Isaac's tone softened. 'Put it on, lass. You said you wanted a new dress. Well, now you have one. As fine as to be found promenaded in any London park.'

I scraped back my stool and stood up, Lucy's gown clutched against my chest.

He grinned. 'Good girl.'

Chapter Ten

I caught her scent as soon as I put on the dress. Whatever I did she was there. A whiff of old perfume, a hint of stale perspiration. Parts of Lucy that 'Lizabeth's slack scrubbing hadn't been able to wash away.

Isaac had given me the key to her bedchamber. I spent an hour pulling strands of hair from those brushes she hadn't given away. Lucy on the pillows, the sheets, on the dresser stool where the impression of her behind remained on the upholstery. Wisps of blonde hair littered her bonnets. The wicker basket beside the dresser was a tomb in which other parts of her were interred. Nail clippings, powder puffs smeared with faded rouge, coarser hair plucked from her eyebrows – the daily debris of Lucy's life.

I once overheard a gravedigger say to his crony: 'Long after they're dead the hair and nails keep growing. Dig 'em up after a few months and they look like witches. What's left o' them that is.'

I perched on the stool in front of the dressing-table mirror and waited for the guilt to come. All my life I'd admired Lucy's possessions – her collection of gowns, her ivory-handled fan, the fine Sunday-in-church wig, the perfume bottles clinking together in their small velvet-covered box. But I sat in my dead sister's clothes and could barely bring myself to touch a thing. I hated myself. I hated myself because I had let them force me into this. I felt the defiler, the desecrator. It should've been Lucy's garments Matthew burned, not mine.

When I walked into the parlour for supper, Mother and Isaac were huddled by the hearth, talking in whispers. They stopped and looked up when I came in. Isaac leaned back in the chair and lit a pipe. Mother's whole demeanour had changed. She appraised me with a market trader's eye, lips pursed, eyes taking in the clothes. I found myself sweating though it was cool in the parlour despite the fire. That stare. It was the way she used to look at Lucy.

Sally brought in the supper trolley. She glanced at me then looked away. I took my usual place at the table but Mother said: 'No, come sit by me, near the fire, you need a little colour in your cheeks.'

So I took Lucy's place, with Lucy's embroidered napkin folded into a pretty horse shape on the tablecloth in front of me. The cutlery was laid out the wrong way for me. Lucy was right handed. Absently, I made to switch them around but Mother tapped me on the back of my knuckles. 'No,' she said again. 'You will get used to it in no time.'

Sally stacked the soup plates next to Mother then slipped away. Mother ladled a measure of steaming liquid into one of the bowls. Carrot broth. No meat again. I tried not to wrinkle my nose.

'Lucy.'

It took me a moment to realise that Mother was speaking to me. 'I'm Rachel,' I said, stupidly.

'Lucy will you pass this plate into your father.'

I did not move from my seat. 'My name is Rachel.'

She waited. I tried a spoonful of soup but my hand was shaking so much I nudged the plate and broth slopped across the tablecloth. Mother dabbed it with a napkin and refilled the bowl. 'Lucy,' she said patiently. 'Take this plate to your father.'

I left my seat, walked around the table and placed the bowl in front of Isaac. Mother nodded and ladled out the rest of the broth. I sat down and stared at my own plate as though it contained a poison that would shrivel my tongue. Mother said be a good girl, Lucy, and eat it up, so I supped every last drop. After supper, Isaac pressed something into my hand. A sweetmeat wrapped up in a pink bow just the way Lucy used to like it.

From that day I was someone else. 'Lizabeth

pinned me into my sister's dresses, chuckling whenever her fumbling hands pricked me through the material. Isaac forced me to read Lucy's books until my head ached, and only let me eat if I used her favourite cutlery. I had to kneel on the kitchen floor, 'Lizabeth holding my head over a wooden tub, while Mother dyed my hair a brassy gold using a foul concoction of herbs and clay. They made me walk across the parlour, back and forth, and flicked a leather strap across the back of my knees if the steps weren't quite right. I had to speak like Lucy, choke on her words, force them into my mouth like a rotten apple until I could pronounce her fluid, sing-song soprano to perfection.

Her clothes were still tight so I starved until I could breathe again. I was too tall so the heels were knocked off my shoes. Outside I was Lucy, back from the dead. Inside, Rachel screamed.

'You will practise music now,' Mother said. Traffic on the road had dwindled away to a trickle. The Coach and Horses had won posting rights and now all letters went through there along with the lads who carried them. An air of quiet desperation settled over Green Gallows.

I sat in front of the spinet. Under the lid sat the row of black wooden keys. Isaac stood behind me. I could hear his breathing.

Lucy had taught me a couple of simple tunes so I played those. I hammered the keys until my fingers ached and the tips began to blister. I fought a battle with my enemy. I sweated and strangled notes from its wooden throat. I played like a demon, as if the keys were fashioned from flint and sparks flew whenever my flesh made contact. I played until my hands turned numb and I could barely see the keyboard.

I ate at the Long Room table. A treat for one night only. I feasted on rabbit pie and sweet potatoes drowned in rich gravy. No foggy, scum-coated lemonade to wash it down but wine – rich wine the colour of deepest ruby that smelled of oak casks and flowers and exotic fruits. I was pampered like a queen.

I felt like a whore.

For as long as I played the game I could have whatever I wanted. That was the trick. Not just dresses or pretty trinkets, but love too. Yet I couldn't bring myself to say or think 'I am Lucy'. It was always *Lucy*. The word torn, twisted out of shape, turned into something corrupt. *Lucy*. Always with that emphasis, that hint of a sneer. I flinched every time I heard it.

I was scared of what they were turning into. I was scared of what I was turning into. Not Lucy. Not Rachel either. A mongrel creature, some in-between person. They couldn't make me exactly like her.

Could they?

She'd had a two-inch scar, a white puckered line slicing her skin between eyebrow and temple. She was nine years old when she picked that up. I was seven, climbing the old beech tree at the bottom of the paddock and, snug within its spreading branches, daring her to follow. Lucy, who'd always been a better climber, gripped the brittle, unforgiving bark with her soft hands. Six feet up her petticoat snagged and, without thinking, she tried to shake it free. One hand wasn't enough to support even her slender weight, so she fell, too ladylike even to scream. Not a great height but a rock was lurking in the grass waiting to deliver a jagged kiss. She was knocked cold and I, thinking her dead, ran screaming for Judd.

They took her into the parlour and laid her out on the couch. Everyone was yelling and then, good luck, Hannah remembered that a surgeon had engaged a room in the inn.

'Not serious,' he declared. 'A cut to the head and some concussion, nothing more, although the wound will scar. Bind it with vinegar-soaked linen and put her to bed.'

I ran and hid in the back of the stables, not daring to return until after suppertime. Shivering and hungry, I crept inside, my clothes damp and spiked with straw. Mother was upstairs and Isaac had returned to running his business. I ate a few bits I found in the larder, stripped off my clothes and locked myself in my bedroom. I cried most of that night, remembering Lucy lying unconscious on the grass. I thought I'd killed her.

Lucy was not ashamed of her scar. It was a part of her, as much as her nose and eyes. A memento of a foolish adventure.

'We must plan for your birthday,' Mother said in the parlour after supper.

'My birthday was on the fourteenth of May.'

'Your birthday is next Tuesday.' Mother was sewing, her needle whispering rapidly in and out of the material. 'Pass me that thread will you, Lucy dear.'

No work for me on Tuesday. No carriage doors to open. No early-autumn breezes to blow the smell of Lucy's rouge from my cheeks. That night Isaac stood me on the rug in front of the parlour fire. While my birthday supper grew cold he turned me slowly around. Mother watched from her seat by the hearth, silently picking soot grains out of her hair. Her eyes, round as saucers, glimmered in the firelight. The smell of Isaac's cheap cologne mixed with the sour tang of ale on his breath.

For five minutes I was turned like an ox on a spit. My feet rubbed a flat circle on the woollen pile of the rug. Then Isaac took a slim leather case out of his back pocket. His best razor, the one he always saved for his Sunday shave. He unfolded the blade, a glittering steel finger sharp enough to slice the muggy air.

'Grit your teeth lass,' he said. 'This will only hurt for a second.'

Holding me firmly with his other hand he swept the razor across my temple. All I could remember before I fainted was the blade's burning kiss and my mother staring at me, saying nothing as my blood turned the rug to crimson.

Isaac would not allow the wound to be stitched. It formed a puckered scar which in time, he told me, would fade to a thin white thread just below the hairline.

That following Saturday I slipped into the kitchen. Sally fussed over bubbling pots, checked the meat on the turnspit twice, three times. She flapped and flustered, picking at this and that, fingers jabbing like crows' beaks. Not once did she willingly talk to me or look in my direction. Each time I tried to strike up a conversation it was: 'Must go, must dash. Water needs fetching, vegetables sliced. This to do, that to take care of.'

Her voice stretched out of her throat like a taut harp string. I touched her elbow and she flinched, no, she actually jumped an inch out of her shoes. She rubbed furiously at her arm as though bitten by some growling, foam-flecked dog.

I stepped out into the stable yard. Matthew was beside the coach house trying to shovel away a pile of mud swilled down by the rain. He spotted me and ran inside. I went after him, cornering him beside an old pile of broken wheels. He looked like he wanted to thump me.

'What have I done to put such a sour look on your face?' I demanded

He spat into the dirt. 'Go back inside. There's naught for you here.'

'I'm still your friend.'

A shake of the head. 'I don't know who you are. Not any more.'

That Sunday, Isaac bundled us into a chaise and took us to the service at Prestbury church. Half a mile down the lykeway the leader threw a shoe. Isaac had to send Matthew back to Green Gallows for the tool bag while he rooted about in the lane. By the time the animal was reshod and we arrived at church, Parson Buseridge was beginning his sermon. Mother's arm slipped through mine as we walked up the aisle to our usual pew.

The whispers began somewhere at the back. They sighed through the church, gathering strength like a gale rumbling across the Downs. Isaac's eyes roved over the heads of the congregation. Mother's lips pursed into a tighter and tighter knot.

Mostly I kept my face buried in my prayer book. A quick glance up was to catch a dozen faces suddenly looking away. The parson stammered twice during the sermon. After the service he wouldn't shake Isaac's hand. Women hurried away when they saw Mother approaching, leaving her alone and confused.

The churchyard was pregnant with chattering people. They milled around the front door and straggled along the black line of the cinder path. Everywhere were tokens of the change that had fallen like a silver-lined shroud over Prestbury. Here, a new shawl. There, a fine bonnet. For the men – new boots and breeches, or perhaps a neck cloth.

And here came Jenny Bruce, gliding up the path in a new gown of cream taffeta which, against the tombstones, glowed like polished ivory. Her mouth was buttered into a triumphant smile.

'My, that's a fancy dress you're wearing,' Isaac said, letting his eyes flick over the gown. 'Take more than a dandy bit of cloth to make a lady out of the likes of you.'

'Laugh all ye like, Mr Curtis,' she drawled, 'but you'll be dressin' yer own wife in rags soon enough, and yer brat too.'

Mother tugged on Isaac's arm.

'Let's go, husband. Let's go home now.'

Isaac took us both by the hand. His palm was sweating. We headed for the lich-gate, trying to keep our steps even. Matthew was already waiting by the horses.

Half-a-dozen paces from the gate, Will Davey stepped onto the path. Beneath the brim of his felt tricorne his eyes were sharp as glass.

'How can you bring her here?' he said, pointing at me. 'How can you parade her in that dress in front of us all?'

'I'd leave peaceably with my daughter, Davey.'

'And which daughter might that be? There's folk here say you're not so sure any more.'

Isaac pushed past, his face like parchment. We hurried after. A chunk of sharp flint caught me between the shoulder blades. I bit my lip and kept on walking. Another stone whistled past my ear. The coach seemed miles away.

We never said anything on the way home and we never went to church again. Mother entombed herself in her bedchamber and wouldn't come out. Not for sense nor supper. Isaac pleaded, pounded the door, paced the passage outside.

'For pity's sake, Harriet, how can you let the Bruce woman get the better of you? Why shut yourself away?'

'Get me a gown like Jenny Bruce's and you'll see my face soon enough,' she called through the door.

Isaac retreated to the parlour and his ale, muttering about the fickle nature of women. But Jenny Bruce had hurt him too.

Next morning a note was delivered to the inn. Lord Sutcliffe would arrive on the third Thursday of the next month. The message went on to remind Isaac of their agreement and, in a thinly veiled way, to warn of the consequences should those promises be broken. Isaac's face went the pallor of sour eggs as he read it aloud, then he looked at me and some of the colour returned to his cheeks. He smiled.

'Go and put some ribbons in your hair, Lucy,' he said. 'Then come and play the spinet. I've a mind to enjoy some soothing music before supper.'

I tied my hair into pretty ringlets and sat in front of the spinet while Isaac sprawled in the armchair next to the hearth, a tankard of ale perched on his belly. His eyes never left the smouldering fire, not even when I fudged a couple of notes. After half an hour my wrists felt numb and I closed the lid of the spinet. Isaac waved me away. He was still slumped in front of the hearth when I looked in on the parlour again two hours later.

A dizzy week followed in which I was made to practise everything again and again. My speech, my deportment, my mannerisms. Nothing they did could coax a decent song out of my croaky throat but they made me practise talking, rolling my vowels and snip-snipping away at the consonants until my throat hurt and my tongue felt like a lump of wet mud. My waist had slimmed, the fat had sloughed off my thighs and my chin no longer sagged when I bowed my head in a curtsy at the end of a dance. Isaac himself taught me, donning best waistcoat and breeches to lead me in an endless string of gavottes across the Long Room floor. I no longer tripped over my feet or squashed his toes.

Lucy's clothes now fitted me properly. Mother had spent hours doing the final alterations and at one point hired a seamstress from Stonehill to help her. The account she presented to Isaac when the sewing was done made him curse aloud, but he eyed the row of pretty dresses laid out across the parlour table and paid up.

I was hungry all the time. 'Too fond of Sally's pastry,' Isaac once said. I remembered the way Lucy had always pecked at her food, and the way I had wolfed it down.

The hunger chewed at my will. Unable to sleep one night because of my groaning innards, I stole into the larder and ate an entire chicken pie. When I tiptoed back into the kitchen, Mother was waiting for me in her nightshift, candle in hand. She made me stick my fingers down my throat and sick it all back up. Next day she stitched me into a tight bodice. It was hard to breathe. Every movement, every step had to be carefully thought out beforehand. For dinner I waved away mutton and potatoes and settled for a crust of bread and a few sips of weak broth.

I told Isaac I wanted to go for a ride, to take some air and practise on the side-saddle.

'D'you want Matthew to go with you? After what happened at church?'

'No, I'll not go near Prestbury,' I lied. 'I'll be safe enough on the lane. I want Mistral to find her legs after the way Colly's men treated her.'

I was at the church within the half-hour. Happy to be out, Mistral had cantered most of the way. Her leg had recovered and the marks on her flanks were fading. I tethered her to the lich-gate. I didn't care whether Buseridge saw me or not. I thought the parsonage curtains twitched but it could have been my imagination. Instead of turning up the path towards the church I slipped away to the left, to the patch of grass between road and wall, where my sister was buried.

Hardly anything to see now. The mound of turf had been flattened by the rain and melted into the surrounding grass. Above, the sun punched blue holes in the thinning cloud cover. A tiny black 'v' of tardy birds swam through air currents towards the south.

'They've tried to turn me into you, Lucy,' I whispered. 'But they won't win. I could never be like you.'

Someone was watching me. A village urchin peeking from the other side of the churchyard wall. Blood rushed into my cheeks. It was Tommy Wright, the gravedigger's son.

'Who ya talking to?' Tommy said. ''Tain't nobody around.'

'Lucy, my sister, is buried here.' I gestured at the grave.

Tommy scowled. 'We heard 'twas Rachel buried at this corner. Fat ugly Rachel, who'll burn in hell for takin' her own life.'

I stared at him. 'No. Lucy was beautiful. I'm the ugly one. I was always the ugly one.'

Crude laughter, like water burbling through a weed-choked ditch. 'You ain't Rachel. You're a pretty maid. Not a sack o' spuds like she was.'

'You saw me,' I persisted. 'You were there that day, helping your papa shovel dirt over my sister's coffin. You watched me stand beside her grave.'

He shook his head. 'You weren't the girl I saw.'

He walked off across the churchyard. I watched

him go, not knowing what to do.

Then, for the first time, Lucy whispered in my mind.

I was meant to find her.

Call it prayer, the hand of fate or just the devil cackling on my shoulder but I sent out a note to Stonehill on one of the few coaches that still called at our yard and, after two days of finger-wringing, a message came back. I knew enough people working the posting inns around that town for this small miracle to work and I blessed every one of them in my head when I read the few scratched lines that said so little yet told me everything I wanted to know.

Getting away from Green Gallows for the day was easier than I thought. Mother spent much of her time with 'Lizabeth, Matthew was avoiding me and Isaac shut himself in the parlour, going over the ledgers hour after hour as if the figures written there would miraculously change in his favour. I threw a cloak around Lucy's gown, sneaked Mistral out of the stables and rode pell-mell for Stonehill. Arriving in a flurry of dust and dead leaves, I tied the mare outside the posting house and took up position on a bench, my hood pulled low over my face. I doubted any of the coaching staff would recognise me in Lucy's frippery but I had no wish to get bogged down in awkward chit-chat should someone's eyes prove sharper than expected.

I had less than an hour to wait. She stepped off the London stage, giggling in a peach-blossom gown and bonnet hung with feathers.

'Come with me,' I said, beckoning towards the Stonehill posting house. A flight of steps clung to the back of the building. At the top was a room the coachmen sometimes used when they had to sleep over. It was always empty during the day.

'I don't usually entertain girls,' she said, tripping after me, 'besides, I have an appointment with someone.'

'Yes, a warehouse owner down by the canal. His wife won't be back from her sister's until tomorrow so you've plenty of time for your little frolic. Besides, you've been with him twice this week already so I've heard.' I closed the door and slid the bolt across. 'Don't pretend you don't remember me.'

Uncertainty flickered across her face. She might assume I was Lucy, yet her wits were sharp enough to know something was not the same. My height. My eyes? Had she heard who lay in the unmarked grave at the side of the lane by Prestbury church?

'Can't say I rightly do,' she trilled.

'Glory, but you've a nerve. You think our memories that short? We lost a servant that night. You sat at our table, ate our food, made an idiot of my father. You're no lady. You're a tuppenny whore out of the London gutters.'

Above, a flutter of wings. A pigeon caught in the rafters. 'Did Lord Grays look past his swollen breeches long enough to enjoy the entertainment you provided at our maid's expense?' I pressed. 'Did it put an extra shilling in your purse?'

Her stance altered subtly. 'How'd you like a hatpin through your heart, love?'

Still that cultured voice. But now I could see her face, her real face. Here was someone who had scratched and clawed her way through life. If I pushed too hard she'd bite.

I took out my bag of tip money and threw it at her feet. The neck mouthed open and a few coins jingled onto the rug. Sixpence had already gone to the landlord for the use of the room.

She let her gaze linger on the bag for a few seconds. 'How did you know where to find me?'

'Your movements are well known to the coachmen. Some of them are my friends.'

'I've broken no law and in any case no court would touch me. I have friends too, country girl. Loyal friends bought with my own sweat. If his grace wants a wife for the night, then I am a wife. I've been just about everything else at one time or another.' She hiked her gown up a few inches. 'You see these petticoats? Silk, trimmed with Italian lace. Three years on my back paid for it.'

Her eyes suddenly narrowed. 'You're not the girl that idiot fop was feeling up. You're the other one. The one who smelled of horses, who old Grays called the milkmaid. What are you doing with her dress on? Why that wig, and the paint on your face?' She planted both hands on her hips and tilted her head. 'What's the game?'

I nudged the purse with the toe of my slipper. 'I need some help.'

'What is it you're after?'

'I want to learn how to attract a man.'

'If you don't know how to do that by now, love,' she laughed, 'you never will.'

'I'm serious.'

She gestured with a silken glove. 'Speak demurely, flutter your eyelashes, blush when he catches your eye. Use your instincts. Even in this midden you can set men's tongues panting.'

Glory, I was a snick away from blushing right now. All my anger had dissolved. 'That is ... not what I meant.'

'Aha,' her tone changed again, 'you want him to lose his wits as he drops his breeches, eh? Well, that shouldn't be hard for a rosy-cheeked apple like you. Are you a virgin?'

'What?'

Another flick of the glove. 'I suppose you must be. Well, in order to heat some oaf's blood you might have to spill a little of your own. Are you ready for that, my dear?'

'I ... don't think it will come to that.'

Derision cut my ears. 'It always comes to that. He'll stroke your hair, cup your cheek, brush your lips lightly with his own so you don't notice until it's too late that he's poked your maidenhood into the gutter where you can't fetch it back, ever. But you have power too. The same power women have had since Eve.'

'Any grubby harlot can take off her clothes.'

'That's true, my love, but it's not about what you let a man see, it's about what you let him glimpse. Come here and let me show you...'

I stepped away from the door.

On the last Thursday of the month, Lord Sutcliffe returned to Green Gallows.

'Go and sit inside his coach,' Isaac instructed. 'He is an old man. He could use the company.

Just for a few minutes while Matthew waters the horses.'

I looked into Isaac's eyes where my doom lurked in circles of muddy brown, then I rose from the Long Room chair where I had waited most of the day. I crossed the yard, opened the carriage door and climbed inside. I'd taken care to smear scented powder beneath each nostril so that the smell which greeted me was filtered, bearable.

A papery voice. 'Close the door. Come and sit opposite. Gently now. Mind my legs.'

The door clunked shut with the finality of a coffin lid. I fumbled onto the seat. The upholstery creaked. I sensed him shifting, heard his shoes scuff the rug-smothered floor, the rustle of clothing. Something clinked in the darkness. Liquid gurgled from a decanter. As my eyes adjusted I could see his hunched figure just an arm's sweep away. How terribly small he looked. Something glittered in his hand. A glass filled with dark liquid. Port, from the sweet smell of it. He took a sip. The drink shimmered darkly, like his eyes, which did not leave my face.

'You are not my beloved Lucy,' Sutcliffe said finally.

'No.'

'Does your papa think me a fool?'

'He just wants to please you.'

'Those are her clothes, yes, and doubtless her perfume too. I watched as you crossed the yard. You walk just like her.'

He snapped his fingers. 'What would I find beneath that pretty wig? Lucy's golden tresses or hair black as a crow? Have they painted your head as well as the rest of you? Can you sing like her, play the spinet, charm the hearts out of the local rabble? No doubt, no doubt. You have the look of a performing dog, ready to roll over and play tricks at her master's whim.'

I licked my lips. 'What sort of tricks would my master have in mind?'

A dry chuckle. 'There is a trick tenant farmers use to fool a ewe into thinking an orphaned lamb is its own dead offspring. They cut the fleece from the corpse and tie it around the interloper. The ewe smells its own lamb and happily suckles the orphan. So there you sit, in a dead girl's clothes. Brass can gleam like gold if you polish it well enough.'

He placed the port glass on a narrow ledge beneath the curtained window. 'Do you taste like her, I wonder? What say I take a peck at those pretty lips and see if you're as savoury a morsel?'

A whisper of breath against my cheek, the brush of papery lips.

Pretend he is someone else. It's gloomy, like a tomb. You can hardly see him. He could be anyone. Anyone.

Jeremiah.

No.

A hand clamped my knee in a bony vice. Strong, so strong. I could not believe him capable of such a painful grip.

'I can make a woman of you, little girl, be in no doubt. Unless some stable urchin has already tumbled you in the straw. I should hate to think your father has sold me a lame filly.'

I pictured Tommy Wright, the gravedigger's son, his mouth smeared into a contemptuous grimace, the coldness in his eyes. I felt a flicker of Lucy's courage. It grew inside the foul belly of that ancient coach. I became her. The act was complete.

'I can be Lucy for you. I can be everything she was.'

'What makes you so willing, my little butterfly? Are you that afraid of your father? He had your sister quivering in her shoes. She would have whored herself on your parlour table had I asked her.'

'I am sick of paupery, of skivvying between stable yard, kitchen and taproom. Men only had eyes for my sister and now she has taken their hearts to the grave. They grumble, shake their heads and talk about how lovely she was. They don't spare me a second glance. They never did.'

'You'd catch enough fish now, looking as you do.'

'And be the wife of a penniless farrier or wheelwright? The smell of horseshit is never far from my nose. What world I know seldom reaches beyond Prestbury, Stonehill or Marrin's Ridge. I've smelled the rich scent of city people, felt the cut of their cloth as I helped them down from their carriages. Now I want gold in my purse and jewels dangling from my ears. I want the whisper of silk against my skin when I go to bed, the soft kiss of pearls against my throat. Never having to wear the same gown twice, to sup broth with a wooden spoon or curtsy to all and sundry until my knees crack. Green Gallows has had a grubby paw around my throat from the moment I was born. You are the only man Isaac respects. And perhaps fears. As your mistress I'd enjoy courtesy I could never know as his daughter.'

I brushed my hand along the top of his velvet

breeches, paused, slipped two fingers inside. I was rewarded with a sharp intake of breath.

'Only a whore sells herself so,' he said, voice tight.

'Whoring is a bargain like any other, struck between two people who have something the other wants. I'll be a whore if you wish, only give me what I ask.'

'A whore with a good head,' he mused, 'is a dangerous thing. Are you strong enough not to be broken by your own ambitions, I wonder? Well, we shall put that to the test.'

Sutcliffe grasped the hem of my gown and lifted. His face was poker hard as my petticoats slithered up towards my waist.

'No.' I halted the ebb of satin and lace. 'Not in the stable yard.'

A hiss of impatience. 'You fuss to no good cause. No one can see us. A wise customer must sample the trader's fruit before buying.'

'I know of a small clearing in the forest beneath Marrin's Ridge. It can be reached by carriage. There is an old woodcutters' track. Trees provide shelter on all sides. There are things we can do without being disturbed.'

He abruptly dropped my skirts and sat back. 'By devil, I'll play your game but the winnings had better be high, my dear.'

'Richer than you can imagine, my lord.'

'Very well. Go and fetch your father. We shall see whether you will make a fit companion. Please me, and you'll get the reward you desire. You shall wear gold and the finest silks, and your father may continue to lord it over his precious inn for as long as I see fit. Disappoint me and he won't work in this county again. You have seven days to reflect on it. And remember I shall expect a hot-blooded woman, not the clumsy fumblings of a milkmaid.'

'I shall not disappoint you, my lord.'

'See that you do not.'

I don't know what was on my face when I told Isaac that Sutcliffe wished to see him. I never could hide my feelings that well. What the dark of the carriage concealed would be all too evident in the breezy light of the kitchen.

'If you've put him off, girl, I'll whip you arse-naked all the way into Prestbury.' He stormed out of the door. I sat by the window and watched him cross the yard. Less than a minute inside the carriage and he was back out, blinking in the evening sunshine. His expression was impossible to read.

Sutcliffe might have been toying with me. In the dark stink of the carriage was that withered face laughing?

Isaac hated other men laughing at him.

No, surely not. I had felt his palm brush my stocking tops, heard the rustle of his breeches. He wanted me. He had to want me.

The kitchen door groaned inwards. Isaac's bulky frame blocked the light, his face in shadow. He walked to the table, drew out the bench and sat down. He began pulling off his boots.

Mother, having watched from the window seat in the Long Room, scurried into the kitchen. Her gaze flitted from Isaac to me, then back again.

'Serve *Lucy* her supper,' Isaac said, drawing deeply from his ale pot. 'Give her anything she wants.'

Chapter Eleven

'Lizabeth tossed the letter onto the bed and strolled over to the dressing table. She picked up a bottle of Lucy's best perfume (no, *my* best perfume) unstoppered it and dabbed a generous amount of the scent behind each ear. Replacing the stopper, she returned the bottle to the dresser.

I snatched up the letter. Lord Sutcliffe's seal was a bloodstain on the cream vellum. The wax was broken. Crimson flakes showered onto the rug.

'Have you opened this?' I jabbed the letter at 'Lizabeth. 'I know you can read. You've bragged about it often enough.'

'London's a long way off,' 'Lizabeth purred. 'Many rough miles for a letter to come. Seal could've broke almost any place.'

I grabbed her arm. 'You're lying. Green Gallows needs good maids. Not parish trash like you. Take that grin off your face or you'll carry it with you into the ditch.'

She shrugged herself free. 'You're not my mistress,' she said, and slipped from the room. I slammed the door behind her. My hands were shaking as I unfolded the letter. A dozen scratched words.

Thursday outside Prestbury Church. At noon. My coach will be waiting.

S.

I closed my eyes and crumpled the paper against my chest. 'Lucy,' I whispered.

Thursday. The sky was a glaring blue sheet. I rode sidesaddle to the church. I'd told Judd that I wanted to take some air. He'd nodded glumly and harnessed Mistral. I don't think he cared much what I did any more.

The day was hot and dank. Summer's last fling. Sweat beaded the lining of my feathered riding bonnet. Mistral clopped dispiritedly past the lich-gate. Sutcliffe' s carriage was backed into the small track that fed off the lane and bordered the churchyard wall. I flinched, my hands jerking on the reins. Mistral faltered and threw back her head. I patted her flank and made soothing sounds until she settled.

The track petered out after a few yards. Sutcliffe's coach lay between the wall and a jumble of drooping brambles. Fat, oily berries glistened in the sunlight. No one picked brambles on church land. They said it was robbing God.

A team of four waited patiently between the shafts. Tails flicked lazily at flies. The coachman looked up at my approach and climbed down from his roof perch. He grasped Mistral's bridle and helped me to dismount with the other.

'Two hours,' I said. 'No more.'

A shadow flitted across his face. He was not Sutcliffe's usual driver.

'Prestbury village is only half a league from here,' I said. 'There is a tavern there. The Coach and Horses. The ale is passable, and they serve a fine mutton pie.'

He hesitated, eyes flicking from me to the carriage.

'Village girls don't see many smart young men,' I prompted. 'The tavern is full of farmers and cowhands mostly. Nothing there to catch a wench's eye. A finely dressed fellow like yourself, however...'

One backwards glance and he was gone.

I tethered Mistral to the back of the coach then tapped on the door panel. It made a sound like old bones.

'Is that my little plum?' Sutcliffe's voice whispered through the curtain.

'Yes, my lord.'

A rasping cough. Phlegm snorted into a kerchief. 'Well, well. Thought you'd come over all a-quiver despite your petulant bravado this Sabbath past. So perhaps you do hate your life enough. No matter. Step inside and we shall see if you have the stomach to finish the game.'

I imagined the fetid pit behind the curtain. The heat. The smells.

'Not yet, my lord. We must go to the clearing that I told you about. There I have a special treat in store for you. Be patient. It will be worth the extra miles.'

Two years ago a violent squall struck Marrin's Chase, uprooting the older trees and hurling them rumble-tumble across one another. Time and weather had turned their dead trunks slate grey. Nettles smothered the brittle roots.

Guiding the team took all my concentration. I'd

buckled Mistral's side-saddle to one of the leaders and was hanging on for grim life. The woodcutter's trail was thick with bluebottles. Brambles scratched the horses' flanks, snagged my dress and scraped along the panels of the coach. A few tardy wasps buzzed drunkenly around the wheelers' tails and were swished away.

Dollops of old horse dung lay scattered across the track. The carriage wheels lurched over rock one moment then sank in thick loam the next. The trail narrowed. Trees, their bark infested with ivy, formed a jagged wall to the right while on the left gorse and wild bramble were piled in untidy heaps.

The leaders checked and snorted. I urged them on as quietly as possible. If the team refused to go any further or if a wheel bogged down I'd never get the coach turned.

I shifted in the saddle. Lucy's gown dragged on my body. Powder and rouge turned sticky and made my face a trap for insects. The horses plodded, heads low, gnats feathering their limp manes.

I itched in a hundred places. The breeze, cool and fresh in the lane, had been swallowed up by the thick undergrowth. The air was skillet-hot, the light a mottled patchwork of leafy greens and searing yellows.

The toothy remains of a woodcutter's cottage broke through the undergrowth. The roof had caved in, the windows were smashed, one wall was missing where the stone had been plundered. A path choked with dead bracken and spiky gorse wound up to the empty door frame. Beside it a mouldering woodpile sprouted moss and brown toadstools. The air was heavy with the scent of decay.

I eyed the path cautiously. Some of the bracken had been trampled. Clumps of bramble were snapped off or shoved aside. This was Lord Marrin's land but seldom patrolled, the light game barely worth poaching. Marrin's bailiffs spent most of their time in the forest beneath the Ridge which was rich in pheasant and deer.

I dismounted. The hem of my gown caught on the stirrup. White petticoats billowed around my stockinged knees. Blood swam back into my legs. I felt dizzy and rested my head against the saddle. If I faltered now...

The carriage door swung open. Sutcliffe appeared, blinking in the soft light. I lowered the steps. His descent was ponderous, his legs seemingly ready to crumble into dust.

'Are we there, my little plum?'

'Stand there,' I ordered. 'Give me your walking stick.'

I thought he might refuse but Sutcliffe willingly pressed the length of hickory into my gloved hand. His eyes were shining pennies, his breath coming in short, sharp gasps. I ran my fingers up the polished shaft. Blood spots appeared over his cheekbones. A fleck of foam spluttered at the corner of his mouth.

I turned away. Using the stick I beat the path wider. In the mulch beside a strangled beech tree was a footprint, a man's from the size of it, and fresh.

Keeping my back to Sutcliffe, I smothered it

under a heap of dead leaves. A tinker come looking for a hare or perhaps some herbs for a potion. No other reason to visit the cottage. With the roof gone it offered little shelter.

I paused, closed my eyes and took a deep breath. The sharp caw of a crow echoed above the canopy of leaves. A fly whizzed past my ear. I heard the hollow melody of a cuckoo and the dry rustle of grasshoppers.

When I turned back, Sutcliffe had wrapped his arms around the nearest tree trunk. Perspiration streamed down his cheeks.

'I ... I do not wish to venture any further.'

I regarded him for a moment: this wizened monkey who had killed my sister. He stood on quivering legs, lungs wheezing like leather bellows. What kind of world did we live in where a man such as this could wield so much power over people's lives, could provide them with money and comfort or shrug them into the ditch at a whim? Why did honest men like Isaac, who sometimes worked until his hands were raw, have to scrape to such a creature and bend their lives and the lives of their families in the hope of a little charity? In the hope of being noticed?

I searched deep inside myself for charity, the same charity Parson Buseridge preached from his pulpit. This from the mouth of the clergyman who had refused Lucy a decent Christian burial, who would not have the soil of his churchyard 'tainted' with a suicide, and who kept his curtains drawn when they lowered her into that rain-sodden hole beside the lane.

I smiled a deep, bloody smile and thrust out my

bosom just as the harlot had taught. I had found something deep within my heart right enough.

Charity was not its name.

'The trees cannot bite, my lord,' I purred, 'and their branches hide the sky.'

'That may be,' he spluttered. 'But a man should have four walls about him and a roof above his head. These things he can see and touch. He can control what lies within. Not out here, where the sun can bake your eyes in their sockets or a gale blow the ears from your head. Nature is mad. It does what it will whenever it fancies. We are all at its mercy. Only a babbling idiot thinks he can control it.'

'But my lord, the sun is high and the day at its peak. You will not see the Chase more beautiful.'

'The inside of my carriage holds comfort enough for me. You play a daring game, my little plum. Be careful not to push my good favour further than my patience.'

My mouth fell into its most beguiling smile. 'Games? Yes, those are what I have in mind, my lord. You are safe here. The path is narrow, the bushes high on either side. Yonder cottage might lack a roof but there are three stout walls and a soft floor lined with bracken. No one knows we are here. Your turnpike crew drove the poachers out weeks ago.'

'You seek to test my mettle? What an impudent pup.'

For a moment I thought he might waver. No fish had richer bait dangled before it. If I could not entice him further then all my schemes would fall apart. That horrible mottled coach was his domain. I could not move or breathe in it. But out here with the earth beneath my feet, the trees around me and the sky above, I was powerful.

I broke the stitching on my stomacher and let the gown fall about my ankles. I had picked this spot very carefully. Matthew brought me here last summer. We drank from half a jug of cider stolen from Sally's larder, me giggling like a milkmaid while Matthew smoked a cigar stub rescued from the taproom floor and made plans for the future that were bigger than his purse. Judd found out about it and gave Matthew a hiding. We were lucky not to have a footpad slit our throats, he said. I had been too frightened to return to the cottage but I'd never forgotten it.

Sutcliffe's hand trembled as he clasped my arm. His eyes never left the trail as I led him on. It took an eternity to get him down those dozen or so yards. Finally I helped him around a tumble of fallen stones and into the house. In the lee of its walls, some of the tension eased out of his body. A different kind of urgency replaced it. Still he hesitated even though the prize lay in his grasp.

I slid an arm around his skinny waist. His breath was hot and faltering on my neck, his balance uncertain on the broken branches that had fallen through the open roof and littered the floor.

He kissed my cheeks, my mouth, my neck. His breath was heavy with brandy, his eyes the windows of a fanatic. He pushed me against the wall. A withered hand fumbled under my petti-coats. The other grabbed my breast.

I wriggled free and cracked the walking stick across his skull.

He groaned and staggered backwards. I hit him again. His legs buckled and he fell soundlessly onto the decaying leaves. A splash of crimson spread across his silver hair. He twitched, rolled over. Blue eyes widened and turned dark.

I leaned against the ruined wall, breathing hard. A beetle scuttled across Sutcliffe's cheek. I kicked his lifeless husk. I had changed him. I had cheated the Nature he feared so much. I had wielded power. He was not a man any more, he was a corpse. Not a human being but a cadaver. He would not father sons. He would not break other people's lives the way he had broken my sister. The last vestiges of wrinkled skin clinging to his cheeks would turn black and rot.

I knelt and poked his arm. The flesh yielded like cream pudding. Leafy treetops were reflected in his eyes. The blood was terrifying. How could a human body contain so much? Had Sutcliffe perished at the first blow? Or a moment afterwards?

I shivered even in the muggy heat of the Chase. In one of his more ghoulish moments Judd had told Matthew about a stagecoach passenger whose throat had been slit by a highwayman because he had refused to part with an expensive ring. 'Blood spurted out o' his neck like water from the stable yard pump,' Judd had said, unaware of the wide-eyed eavesdropper in the hayloft.

I had to think quickly. A puddle of blood now fanned out from Sutcliffe's broken skull, saturating the carpet of leaves beneath. I had planned this so carefully, working through each act. Now my first instinct was to run.

No, I thought savagely. *They will know it was you.*

I pictured his driver supping ale in the Coach and Horses, perhaps with one eye on the clock.

I shook my head to clear it. *Think, Rachel, think.*

Desperately I rifled Sutcliffe's pockets. I removed his pocket watch. Gold. It must have cost a ransom. Now the rings from each hand, jerking them off with no time to care whether the flesh tore. No, better if it did. Everything must look just right.

I ripped off his neck cloth and put the plundered items in it. How long before the body grew cold, the limbs stiffened? I must have looked like a witch. Or a madwoman. Had I not bewitched him? Used trickery in order to lure him here?

I found his purse, a velvet bag bound with gold cord. I laughed disbelievingly at the paltry scattering of coins which spilled into my hand. One waistcoat pocket revealed a silver snuffbox, the other an engraved cigar case. I propped his cane against one of the cottage walls and brought my foot down hard, snapping it in two. The embossed silver cap joined my hoard.

Something glinted at the back of Sutcliffe's open mouth. A gold tooth nestled beside his right canine.

I squeezed my index finger and thumb between those thin lips, prising his jaws further apart. I grasped the tooth and tugged. It wouldn't budge.

'You have to do this,' I whispered, closing my eyes tight for a moment. 'They have to believe. A thief wouldn't leave such a morsel.'

I jerked the tooth back and forth in its socket. My wrist ached with the effort. It was stuck fast. Had the surgeon or whatever quack ministered to Sutcliffe drilled it into his jawbone? I had a horrible image of that mouth suddenly snapping shut, of those teeth cutting through my glove and sinking into the flesh beneath.

Sweat blurred my vision. Flies were everywhere. One settled on Sutcliffe's left eye, a black smudge against his pupil. I yelped and jerked backwards. With a snap, the tooth came away in my fingers. I stared at it. My stomach heaved. I bent over, arms wrapped around my belly. Gnats settled on my cheeks, bit the skin, took their fill. I had not the heart to bat them away. I could not kill anything else, however tiny.

I opened my eyes and the world swam back into focus. So little time. The sun was barely visible through the canopy of branches but I gauged that at least an hour and a half must have passed since I dispatched Sutcliffe's coachman to Prestbury. Scrambling to my feet, I realised I was still clutching the gold tooth. I dropped it amongst the other treasures then dashed back to the carriage. The horses waited, tails flicking to and fro. The door was still open. Fresh air had done little to purge the musty stench. I checked inside. Old newspapers, a half full brandy decanter, a small chest, the lid open, papers spilling out.

I searched for other items. A glass, sticky with fingerprints, a ring of dark sediment clinging to the bottom. Nothing else. Nothing a highwayman or footpad would want to take.

I ran back to the body half expecting to find it missing, to find that I really hadn't killed Sutcliffe and that he was even now lurking behind some bush or wall, bloodied and bent on revenge. He was an old man but I lacked even Matthew's strength. The large amount of blood might not mean anything. I'd once scratched my arm on a broken window pane and had bled into a towel for the next hour, wailing that I was going to die.

Of course he was still there. The Chase had grown still. Even the birds had been shocked into silence.

I wiped my face with my forearm then bent and grasped Sutcliffe's feet. One of his shoes slipped off and tumbled onto the leaves. I slid my hands up and tugged on his ankles. The body wouldn't shift. I grimaced and put my back into it. How could such a sack of bones weigh so much? My riding shoes scrabbled in the mulch. I dug in my heels and heaved. Just when I thought my arms would pop out of their sockets I was rewarded with movement. Once I had him going the rest was a little easier. Fresh blood spilled out of the wound and left a trail in the crushed bracken. His arms dragged along.

An uprooted tree lay on the other side of the clearing. It took an age to haul the corpse there, another five minutes of grunting to push him in. The earth was soft and powdery. It gave way underneath me and I tumbled headlong into the depression. I sprawled across the body, my face inches from Sutcliffe's. My scream sent crows flapping from the treetops. I scrambled, whimpering, out of the makeshift grave. Tremors ran up and down my body. The scent of his cologne filled my nostrils.

Wiping away tears with a muddy forearm I started to push soil into the hole. Tiny, pitiful handfuls. As much slipped through my fingers as fell on the body. The soft shadows of the glade began to deepen.

It was impossible. I could spend the next hour scavenging dirt to throw over the corpse. Scraps of his clothing had caught on the roots of the tree. Both feet poked over the rim of the hole, the buckle of the remaining shoe glinting in the muted sunlight. I had no stomach left to strip him. I could not stand the thought of touching that dead flesh again.

An apron of blood drenched the front of my petticoats. I fetched my gown, shook it free of leaves and pulled it back over my head. My fingers struggled with the fastenings. I prayed the stain wouldn't seep through the thick velvet.

The hoard. What to do with it? I weighed the bag in my hands. Maybe I could bury it. Or hide it in the ruins of the cottage.

I turned. Jeremiah Cathcart was standing in the middle of the glade, staring at me.

The whole world seemed to catch its breath. I had thought myself beyond further terror, beyond any kind of emotion at all. I didn't actually scream. My tongue stuck in my throat. Then the words came.

'How long have you been watching me?'

He reached out. I stepped back, stumbling over a clump of gorse. His clothes were ragged as Matthew had said, his hair wild. His eyes, once piercing and alert, were like two plates of dough.

I glanced towards the overgrown path. Jeremiah moved sluggishly as he closed the space between us. If I ran perhaps I could reach the trail. His hands didn't seem to know what to do with themselves. He said a word, whispered it, squeezed it out.

'Lucy?'

'No, Lucy is dead,' I blurted.

Denial on his face. Now the sentences poured out. 'That ain't right. Lucy is mine. I've a right to have her. Those are her clothes, and that,' he pointed at my left wrist, 'I gave her that bracelet. 'Twas my mother's and it near broke my heart to part with it. But there's naught I'd deny her. What sort of devil are you? You walk like Lucy and speak with her voice, every word, just as she would say it.'

He drew closer, nostrils sucking in long ribbons of air. 'You even smell like her.'

Wild hands snatched at my dress. His dirty face was a stew of desperation and anger. ''Twas someone else they buried beside Prestbury church. Please tell me that's so.' He gestured at Sutcliffe's half-filled grave. 'When you brought him here, when I saw you take your dress off, I thought to murder you both. Then I saw you kill him. He had a black heart and deserved to die. Lucy was going to run away with me. We'd go to St Lawrence. Get married in the church like she always wanted. I once worked on a farm in the parish. They would've taken me back. Good with my hands, that's what they always said. Vicar keeps his head in a brandy bottle so he'd wed us with no questions asked.'

He had gone, stepped over into some other world. There was no telling when he might slip back. He'd seen me murder Sutcliffe and that could send me to the gallows.

No, not this girl. Not after what I'd been through.

I reached out and snatched his limp fingers. 'Would you see me in prison? Would you see me hanged? This brute attacked me. You saved me, Jeremiah. You. I will speak for you. I will tell people what happened. They will believe me.'

His face darkened. 'I saved you?'

'Yes. Don't you remember? Sutcliffe tried to ravish me and you struck him over the head. You didn't mean to kill him. If anyone comes that is what you must tell them.'

I pressed the folded cloth containing my bloody hoard into his hand. 'Take this. I shall return for it soon, after I've explained everything to the local constable. Don't drop it or let it out of your sight for a moment.'

He stared at the bundle with his sad, slow eyes. I glanced towards the uprooted tree, at those ridiculous, hobbled feet poking over the lip of the hole. Then the disquiet left my mind and I felt powerful again. Immensely powerful. I was drunk with it. Jeremiah would walk on burning coals if I asked him to.

'Stay here,' I told him, struggling to remain calm, to soothe him. 'Don't leave the woods. I shall return later. Then we can be together. Do you understand? Together. I can be Lucy for you. We were sisters. Her blood runs in my veins. She doesn't have to be gone from your life. Not completely.'

Again that simpleton's nod.

I closed his fingers over the bag. 'Trust me.'

His eyes met mine. A light flickered somewhere deep inside.

'I trust you.'

I fled the clearing without looking back. My skin burned with gnat bites and nettle stings. I hardly noticed. Sutcliffe was dead. The monster was dead. It felt as if a shadow had been lifted from the world. And I might yet not hang for it.

I retrieved Mistral's saddle, untied her from the rear of the carriage and rode back to Green Gallows. There wasn't a God-made muscle in my body that didn't ache, not a pore of my flesh that wasn't stung or bitten. A bath, a blessed cool bath, that's all I wanted, scented with rose petals or a touch of lavender. Underneath my gown the blood had dried, making a stiff board of my petticoat.

At Green Gallows I dismounted near the gate and peeped through a chink in the hedge. The yard was an empty dust bowl. I batted a fly away from my ear and waited a few minutes. No one emerged from the stables or the Long Room door. On the patch of grass behind the kitchens, washing hung limply from the clothes line, the linen glaring in the harsh light. No carriages waited for their teams to be changed, no horses slaked their thirst at the trough.

I had to pretend nothing had happened. If someone remarked on my grubby appearance I'd say I took a tumble from the saddle or I tripped, or a low branch hit me. Anything.

I led Mistral into her stall. Movement in the shadows. Matthew stepped into the shaft of sunlight thrown through the open stable door. 'Good ride?' he said.

'Yes. Mistral has improved. She was able to take parts of the lane at a gallop. Blew me about a bit, though.'

He leaned against the stall. 'We had a caller. Someone looking for Lord Sutcliffe.'

'Oh? Did you tell him Sutcliffe is in London?'

'He said he was his coachman. He said Lord Sutcliffe went off with a young woman he met at Prestbury church. Took the carriage. He wondered if I knew where they had gone.'

'What did you say?'

Matthew shrugged, his eyes taking in my soiled gown. 'I didn't even know Sutcliffe was in these parts.'

I stared at him, fumbling for words. He walked out of the door without sparing me another glance.

Fine. I'd take Mistral's saddle off myself. I bent and reached for the buckle. I was still wearing my gloves. They were drenched in blood.

I managed to get inside without anyone else spotting me. I scurried into my room, closed the door and set a chair against it. Using a tinderbox Sailor Ben had given me I lit a candle then drew the shutters. In the semi-gloom I dragged off my gown and tossed it over the end of the bed. Dirt, bracken and leaves shivered onto the rug. Grimacing, I peeled off my bloodied petticoat, bundled it up and crammed it under the bed along with the gloves. I would burn them later. I went to the ewer and poured a generous measure of water into the bowl. It was stale and tepid, but felt like fresh dew on my parched skin. I bathed carefully, washing the stink of death from my body. Dried blood caked my nails where it had soaked through the gloves. I brushed the thorns and burrs out of my hair, wincing whenever the bristles caught. I looked into the mirror and a witch looked back. Red scratches criss-crossed my cheeks where the brambles had caught me. I did not look much like Lucy any more. I did not resemble anyone I knew.

The sun was well on its way to the horizon when Will Davey arrived at Green Gallows. Isaac brought him into the parlour. Thick forest loam caked the constable's boots, grass marks scuffed the knees of his breeches and his jacket was spiked with thorns. He took off his tricorne and dropped it onto the kitchen table. Both eyes were red and watery, his thick greying hair tousled and greasy-looking. Somewhere outside, dogs were barking. Isaac nudged a chair forward with the toe of his boot. Davey ignored it.

'Lord Sutcliffe has been murdered,' he said. 'We found him in the woods with his skull caved in.'

Isaac gaped at him.

'His coachman reported him missing,' Davey continued. 'My men are still searching Marrin's Chase. Others are posted around the outside. If the murderer is in there we'll catch him.'

'Who killed him?' Isaac blabbered. 'Why?'

'Looks like a robbery. The thief tried to hide the corpse. Maybe he had it in mind to steal the horses as well but was foiled by the narrowness of the lane. This was too scrappy for one of our highwayman friends or anyone who makes a living cutting throats and purses. According to the coachman, Sutcliffe was visited by a young woman. A woman dressed all in satin.'

The constable's mouth was an ugly thin line. 'Did Lord Sutcliffe visit here?'

'No,' Isaac said.

'But he was here a few days ago. His coach was seen in your yard.'

'Family business. You know better than to ask.'

'A man is dead, and not just any man. I'll ask what I please until this affair is settled.'

'As you like. We're guilty of no crime. Not in the eyes of the law.'

'In the eyes of the law, no,' Will Davey said. 'But I need to talk to your girl.'

Davey asked me many questions. I nodded at some, shook my head at others. At some point 'Lizabeth came in with hot coffee. Isaac and the constable talked a little more. Davey kept looking at me. I wanted to wither and die under that scrutiny, but I would not be sorry I killed Sutcliffe.

The constable put his hat back on and left the way he came. Isaac watched him cross the yard. No fool, that man, no fool. I feared him terribly.

Isaac lingered by the window for a while. Then he scraped a chair out from under the table and sat down. Fingers made a flesh cage across his face. A sound escaped his throat, low and guttural.

'Jesu,' he said. 'What are we to do now? The Trust holds the deeds to my inn. Lord Sutcliffe was the only one keeping the pack at bay. How will I tell your mother?'

'You promised me breakfast on a silver trencher,' Mother said when Isaac had plucked up the nerve to face her. 'A carriage of my own, with footmen and a maid to dress me each morning. That's what you said, Isaac Curtis.'

'We might find another gentleman in want of a young wife.'

''Twas a mistake to try to make venison out of a turnip.' She turned to me. 'Rachel, I am tired of your face. Go to your room.'

It was the first time she had called me Rachel since Lucy died.

I returned to my bedchamber and put the chair back in front of the door. The soiled clothes would have to be destroyed. I couldn't risk smuggling them out to the ash pit. I'd have to light a fire in the hearth and burn them that way. It would take ages but I had no choice. Lucy's writing paper would make good kindling. I took out the few sheets she left in her drawer, crumpled them up and dropped them into the grate.

There was a loud rap on the door. I jumped, knocking the pitcher off the edge of the dresser. It missed the rug and shattered on the floorboards, spraying the wall with water. A muffled query sounded from outside on the landing. The knob turned, the door was pushed. The chair slid then held firm.

'Who is it?'

''Lizabeth. Why have you barred the door? What are you up to in there?'

I jerked the chair away and pulled the door open. 'Lizabeth stood framed on the landing.

'I was sent to see if you wanted supper,' she said, eyes quickly taking in the mess on the floor. 'I heard a crash, then when I tried to open the door...'

'I was washing and dropped the pitcher. It was an accident.'

'Oh, so why the lit candle and drawn shutters?'

'What new mischief is this, 'Lizabeth? I don't much care for your tone.'

Her gaze flicked past me to the hearth and the paper lying in the grate. The candle sputtered, throwing shadows around the walls.

'I want Hannah's room.'

'You'll get nothing.'

'I heard Will Davey talking about Lord Sutcliffe,' she said. 'You'll not be so smart now with your fancy man murdered an' all. I'll get what I want. You'll see.'

Chapter Twelve

Sleep came hard and my dreams were drenched in blood.

Will Davey turned up just after daybreak. 'Lizabeth's banging on the door brought me out of my bed. I threw myself out from under the covers and splashed the last of the water in the basin over my face. Hands, working by themselves, fumbled a gown out of the wardrobe and pulled it on. My feet sought out a pair of slippers.

I rubbed my eyes with the corner of a towel and looked blearily around the room. Dirt streaked the rug although I'd managed to brush the worst of it off the night before. A dark ring circled the rim of the washing bowl. I'd thrown the contents out of the window before going to bed. Shivering, I draped the towel over it, pulled a brush through my tangled hair and went downstairs to the parlour.

'We've caught Lord Sutcliffe's killer,' the constable said, rubbing his own red-rimmed eyes. 'He was roaming the woods not far from where the body was discovered. We've held him in Prestbury assizes overnight. He goes by the name of Cathcart. Jeremiah Cathcart. I believe he used to work for you.'

'He did,' Isaac said, nodding. 'I took him on as an act of charity which he sought to abuse. In the end I had to send him packing. He was a surly oaf and impudent with it.'

'We found a pouch on him containing some of Lord Sutcliffe's valuables,' Davey continued. 'Even a gold tooth. It had been wrenched out of the fellow's mouth. We asked Cathcart outright if he'd done the deed and he said yes.'

'So you have a confession. What more do you need?'

'Cathcart is a broken man. There was a murder and a robbery right enough but I doubt it was his doing.'

'Don't rightly know what you mean, Davey.'

'He's going onto the gallows a mite too easily. Guilt stinks out a man's face, turns it sour. Cathcart is a surly brute as you said, and defiant, but I'll wager my back teeth that he's never had a drop of blood on his hands. He's hiding something. That I am sure of.'

I sat at the table and supped tea. Some dribbled down my chin and spattered onto the tablecloth.

'What will you do with him?' Isaac asked.

'He is to be tried in London. Then it'll be Tyburn Field, I suspect. I'll call again soon, Curtis. There's much about this affair that rankles. Don't you or any of your household leave the parish until I say otherwise. Good day.'

He picked up his hat and left. Isaac took himself off to the taproom. I was alone in the parlour. Mother had not joined us. I was glad of that. There had been too many dark things in her eyes since yesterday afternoon.

I stretched and yawned. Only a dull ache in my arms and back reminded me of the previous day's adventures. There was no guilt, no feeling of the world ending. I glanced through the window at the sunlit yard and everything looked beautiful.

Then I remembered the blood-drenched garments under my bed.

I fled the parlour and ran upstairs. My bedchamber door was ajar. I was sure I'd closed it. I burst in. Nothing had changed. The rug was still dirty, the window closed and shuttered. I fell to my knees, fumbled under the bed and hauled everything out.

The petticoat. The petticoat was missing.

I remembered scrunching up the gown and dumping it here, the gloves too. As for my shoes, they'd been buried at the bottom of the wardrobe. But the petticoat ... what had I done with that? I was sure that I'd put it under the bed with everything else.

I opened all the drawers and rifled their contents. Then I checked the wardrobe, under the mattress, even beneath the rug.

Nothing.

I sat back on my heels. 'Lizabeth was a lazy sow. She rarely cleaned under my bed. My gown was stained, true, though most of the marks were on the inside and around the hem. But the petticoat was stiff with blood. If 'Lizabeth had sneaked in here while I was in the parlour. If she had taken it...

I ripped the coverlet off the bed and bundled the clothes inside. I'd given up the notion of burning them. The hearth was too small and would smoke out the room. I managed to sneak downstairs and scuttle across the empty yard to the wash-house. It should be quiet. Only five guests in the inn. A trio of merchants due to meet a cargo in Southampton and a young couple who had spent most of their time locked in their room. All had arrived in hired carriages.

I pumped water into the tub and threw in some soap. The water was freezing, but I couldn't chance heating up a pot on the kitchen hearth. I scrubbed my knuckles pink trying to get the stains out of my dress. If I couldn't clean it I'd have to bury it, but how to explain that if I was caught?

'Oh, and who's this stranger in the washroom then?'

I spun around, my back to the sink, arms spread.

Sally stood in the doorway, a bundle of linen in her hand. Behind her was 'Lizabeth, holding another basket, grinning thickly.

'What've you got in there?' Sally said, eyes narrowing.

'Some garments I wanted cleaned.'

'Since when did you take it upon yourself to scrub your own clothes?'

'This is my best dress. I soiled it while out walking. I don't want Mother to get upset.'

'You've put that delicate fancy in the scrubbing tub? That's no way to treat fine cloth. Here, let me see. I might be able to save it yet.'

She tried to shove past me but I darted in front of her. 'No, I can do it. I've been very careful.'

'Nonsense. Some of that material is so fine 'twould be like trying to wash cobwebs. Let me past now.'

'No.'

Sally stared at me. Our breath was the only thing stirring the air. Water trickled down my arms and dripped from my fingertips onto the stone slabs. I was vaguely aware of an itch in the crook of my arm, of the gentle fizz of soapsuds slowly dissolving.

She dumped the linen into the empty basket beside the tub. 'So be it then, but you're getting soap all over that gown you're wearing so that's two dresses ruined for the price of one. Let me know when you've finished larking around so I can get on with some proper work, and don't come bawling to me after you've made a mess of things either.'

I watched Sally's retreating back. She had spoken to me differently. As if I was Rachel again. Not completely, but the softening was there. I'd seen the look on her face when she heard Sutcliffe had been murdered.

'Lizabeth stepped into the doorway, linen basket perched cockily on her hip. A towel slipped off the top and flapped into the dust. We eyed each other. I swooped, plucked up the towel, shook off the worst of the dirt and placed it back in the basket.

'Can't I do anything without you haunting me, 'Lizabeth?'

'There was blood on your petticoat.'

Oh dear God.

'You took it. You had no right. Give it back to me.'

'Seems to me there's things you had no right to do either,' 'Lizabeth said.

I bit my lip. 'Take your pick of Lucy's jewellery. But I want that garment back.'

She shook her head. Dirty blonde locks tumbled around her ears. 'Hannah's room,' she said.

'Isaac decides who sleeps where.'

'I don't reckon Mr Curtis is much able to decide which way to button his breeches right now. If you were to ask him I reckon he'd say aye without thinking too much about it.'

'Mind your place. You've no right to talk about him like that.'

'My place is to mind you. There was blood and it ain't your time. I know because I always do your linen. Not only was there blood but it was in the wrong place. And too much of it, like you'd slaughtered a cow. So tonight I sleep in Hannah's room or I reckon I will be doing some talking to Mr Curtis myself.'

'I'm not afraid of you.'

'Yes you are. You always were.'

Isaac stumbled out of the taproom later that afternoon. The stink hit us as soon as he sat down.

Stale beer. Sweat. Desperation. He didn't speak. No one spoke to him. He was like a dog tied to a rope. Stay outside the circle and remain safe from its snapping jaws. But how long was that rope? How far could it stretch?

Isaac could hold his drink. He'd seen bigger, better, men under the table. He rarely faltered or slurred his words. But what poisons were swimming around in that mind?

He thumped the table. We all jumped. Mother, myself, 'Lizabeth. Isaac kicked back his chair. It fetched up against the wall and took a chip out of the oak panelling. He strode to the window. The sun threw planks of yellow light across the varnished floorboards. Isaac shielded his eyes with his hand and peered into that empty, empty yard.

'Where are they? Why does no one work our property any more?'

'Lizabeth scuttled off to the kitchen. She returned with a trencher of bread and cheese. Food to soothe a surly temper.

Isaac swept it off the table. 'Lizabeth yelped. Isaac pushed her aside and banged out of the Long Room door. He saddled Apollo and galloped into the lane. An hour later he was back. Striding into the taproom he snatched a pewter jug from one of the hooks above the bar and filled it from the nearest ale barrel. He took the foaming mug to a table in the far corner, lit a pipe and sat smoking, peering through the blue haze into the shadowed depths of the room.

Matthew told me later what had happened. Isaac had been to the Coach and Horses Inn. A noisy hubbub of men and women filled the yard.

Craftsmen, nostrum sellers, pedlars. He'd dismounted, tethered Apollo and walked around, greeting everyone by name. Nobody would look him in the eye.

He stopped in front of Tom Butcher who'd been selling clay pipes at Green Gallows since Isaac was a pup. Isaac picked up one of the pipes and turned it over in his hands. Tom was trembling so much his wares had rattled in their tray.

'Only a ha'penny a day to work the Coach and Horses,' he blustered. 'No charge on Saturdays.'

'Come back to Green Gallows,' Isaac said quietly. 'For a farthing a day.'

Tom had shrugged his crooked shoulders.

'The coaches come here,' he said.

I wanted the day to be over. I just wished Isaac would pass out or fall asleep instead of prowling the inn like an angry circus bear. Tendons stood out like thick roots on his bare arms. No one could settle him. It was impossible to concentrate on anything. Mother tried darning but tossed it aside after only a few minutes. I did my best to keep busy but there were no chores left to do. An inn with few guests is an idle place. We had our own thunderstorm brewing right here under our roof, but when we heard a distant rumble from the direction of the Ridge it was no rain-packed storm cloud.

It was the thunder of carriage wheels.

Through habit I glanced at the clock. On time as always. I took one look at Isaac's face and knew immediately what he was going to do.

'No.'

He took the old army musket down from the wall. ''Tis time the *Charger* stopped at Green Gallows.'

Mother, fingers like crow's feet, snatched at his sleeve. 'Isaac, don't be foolish. You'll get yourself shot.'

'This is the finest coaching house in the country. Nobody passes it by, do you hear? Nobody.'

He went for the door. I reached it first.

I ran down the lane waving both arms. The *Charger* heaved around the corner, horses snorting like dragons. I was almost trampled into the mud but the coach was already slowing. Just in time I reached out and caught the harness of the leader. My arm was almost wrenched from its socket. I was dragged a full twenty feet down the lane, shoes gouging the mud. One flipped off and was lost.

The driver raised his whip. His face was slab grey under his tricorne. 'Get off the road, you gypsy slut. There's no pennies to be had here.'

'You have to stop,' I screamed. 'You have to stop now.'

The *Charger* lurched to a halt. I let go of the harness, limped to the side of the coach and pounded on the door. One of my knuckles split. I hardly felt it. A woman's powdered head poked out of the window. An oval face, thin mouth, wide, hazel eyes.

'What is the meaning of this?'

The enormity of what I'd done struck me. There would be rich people inside the coach. Gentry. Lords and ladies, prosperous merchants and bankers. I had barged into their lives. I had stretched out my hands and tried to stop the world revolving.

I could hear startled enquiries. Has a horse thrown a shoe? Is it a robber? Perhaps someone would get out with a pistol, expecting trouble. What would they say when they saw this half-shod, sodden wretch? My arm ached. My shoeless foot had gone numb. I clung to the oak panelling. If the coach tried to drive off I would hang on by my nails. Isaac's musket didn't work. I was sure it didn't, but the driver and the fellow sitting beside him, the big man with the hunting gun slung easily over one arm, would not know.

'M'lady,' I entreated. 'My father is waiting in the lane outside Green Gallows Inn. His head is burning with temper. He is determined the stage will pull in. Please m'lady, 'tis a fine inn with good ale and the best mutton pie in the county. There's always a warm fire burning in the hearth and my mother serves tea finer than any you'll find in a London parlour. I've stood beside the gate waving like a simpleton for months and not so much as a wink in return. It's not fair. It's never been fair. Dukes and duchesses have slept under our roof. Please ask the driver to call in. You must stop. Just this once.'

She would not do it. She had no reason to do it. The driver was climbing down from his perch. He'd thrash me then throw me into the ditch.

A frown creased the young woman's brow. 'You'll catch a fever standing there.' She gestured to the driver who was lumbering towards me, whip raised. 'Leave her alone. She is badly upset.'

The driver replaced the whip in its holder. 'Can't

wait long, miss, not if we're to catch the evening tide.'

She leaned further out of the window and lowered her voice. 'Your father, will he cause trouble?'

'He won't let you pass. Not this time. Too many years. He's not himself. He has a gun.'

Oh glory, why did I have to go and blurt that out?

Her expression sharpened. She glanced at the driver's mate. The rifle was a twig in his hands. He didn't need a weapon. He could pluck the moon out of the sky.

'Want me to go and take a look, miss?' he called down.

'He won't hurt anyone,' I continued, fingers white where they gripped the window. 'The gun isn't loaded. Even if it was I don't think it would fire. It's so ancient. I think it must have belonged to the old King Henry. Isaac is a gentle man. Gentle but proud. He's all bluster, like a dog that still barks even though its teeth have fallen out. The turnpike has strangled him. You understand that, don't you? About the road?'

I was gabbling like an old hen. I thought: *All they will see is the gun. Loaded or not he's armed and they'll hang him in chains before one of those horses sets a single hoof in our yard.*

'He'll be no trouble. I promise. He's just confused. Let me go to him. Let me tell him the *Charger* is calling at Green Gallows.'

She fixed me with an appraising look and yes, she did understand. That much was obvious in her face.

'Pull into the inn,' she told the driver.

The coachman looked as if he'd swallowed a

brick. 'But miss...'

'We can still make the tide with an hour to spare.'

He scratched his jowls. 'Where is this inn?'

I pointed. 'Just around that corner on the left-hand side. You've passed it often enough. Five minutes is all I'll need.'

I ran back up the lane. Isaac straddled the road beside the gate, gun at the ready, face as grey as the rain which plastered his black hair to his scalp. He seemed impossibly large.

'We have guests,' I panted. 'Go back inside and put the gun away. The *Charger* is stopping at Green Gallows.'

He did not budge. His stare was murderous. The rain heaved into a downpour. All his features seemed to melt into one another. If I could not shift him now...

I slapped his elbow. 'What kind of landlord can Isaac Curtis call himself if he is not ready to greet a coach?'

Slowly, achingly slowly, he uncocked the gun and hefted it onto his shoulder.

'I've never failed to welcome passengers yet,' he said.

It worked. For a while. The *Charger* rumbled into our yard while Judd and Matthew watched, disbelievingly, from the stable door. This was what I'd always wanted. Now here it was sitting in our yard. I had touched it. For the first time.

I pinned on a smile and lowered the steps. 'Lizabeth's face was a round, staring moon in the Long Room window. Mother appeared and shooed her away. Five passengers descended, grumbling, into the rain. They all gave me a thunderous look. The last passenger wouldn't budge. A rake of a woman, shawl coiled protectively around her shoulders.

'I ain't getting out,' she said. 'Not me. Six years I saved for this trip. Six years scrimping so I could visit my sister Hetty in style. She'll be waiting at the stage house. I want to see her face when she eyes me in the *Charger*. Me, Dorothy Cox, being driven like a lady.'

'The *Charger* will not be overly late,' my benefactor said. 'It has never missed a sailing. The roads are bad but we have time for a respite.'

She smiled cheerfully at this bitter shrew of a woman who, out of everyone, had the smallest body and the biggest mouth. I offered my hand. Shrew-woman favoured me with a look that would curdle milk and grudgingly climbed out of the carriage, batting my hand away.

'Get off with you. I can manage.'

The hazel-eyed girl and I exchanged glances. She grinned.

I settled our guests in the Long Room then went to see Isaac, who was in the parlour. He had taken down his wig, dusted it with fresh powder and straightened it on his head. He shrugged on his embroidered waistcoat and fastened the buttons. Fastened them too easily. How much weight had sloughed off him? I hadn't noticed before but he'd withered slowly like a flower in a drought.

Mother spent a frantic ten minutes polishing his riding boots. As our guests settled, still grumbling, into their chairs he made an entrance to be proud of. It was easy to fool the mind, to believe everything was as it should be. Back was the genial host of Green Gallows moving among his visitors. Lighting a cigar. Refilling a glass. Chuckling politely or nodding gravely when appropriate.

Sally, caught on the hop, served up dishes of cold pheasant, honey-glazed ham and trout followed by raspberries smothered in cream. The only decent food we had left. From the taproom, Mother brought out mugs and a pitcher of ale for the coachmen. The passengers' griping softened with each bottle of wine drunk, each sweetmeat eaten.

'Go and find 'Lizabeth.' Isaac whispered in my ear. 'We need her. Quickly now.'

But 'Lizabeth was not in any of the places 'Lizabeth was supposed to be. I searched from cellar to attic and that's where I caught her, in Hannah's room. She'd left the door open. Perhaps she was clumsy. Perhaps she didn't care. She was standing in front of the tall looking-glass. A birthday present from Sally and Judd. She hummed a tune. I didn't recognise the melody. She wore one of Lucy's gowns. A velvet confection the colour of cats' eyes, with garlands of white satin bows looped around the skirts. She ran her hands across the stomacher, tilted her head and turned. First this way. Then that.

Her face was powdered, her mouth a bloody gash of rouge. She smiled. A different smile. Not the kind that always grated on my nerves. This was a belonging smile, one that said: *This room is mine. This dress is mine.*

That wasn't right. The room was Hannah's. The dress was Lucy's.

No.

The dress was *mine.*

'What are you doing?'

She turned and eyed me lazily. 'Taking what belongs to me.'

Suddenly I was tired of her. Tired of this stupid girl and her petty schemes. I stepped towards her. Measured steps. I was conscious of the floorboards through my slippers. Every chip and knot. The slight rise towards the east window. My concentration was perfectly focused. Somewhere outside came the rasp of a crow. A bluebottle thumped against the window-pane then was gone.

I ran the tip of my tongue across my lips, savouring the moist, salty taste. 'Lizabeth stepped backwards. She had never backed off from me before.

'You are a bad maid, 'Lizabeth. Clumsy and slovenly. You don't like me. Well, that's fine because I don't like you. I never have. You've tried my patience enough these past few weeks.'

'I ain't afraid of you.'

I struck out. How easy it was to do it.

The flat of my palm smacked against the corner of her mouth. Her bottom lip split open. Blood blossomed across her face. She staggered backwards, fetching up against the window ledge. She did not look hurt or angry. Only surprised. She wiped her mouth with her fingers and stared at the blood. Then at me.

You hit me, her expression said. *You hit me!*

Hooked fingers scrabbled for my eyes. I jerked my head away and aimed a kick. Missed. My shin barked against the corner of Hannah's oak dresser. Pain burned up my leg. My back thumped against the bedpost, knocking the wind out of me. I clawed her hair. Caught. A clump ripped away in my fingers. She squealed. She cursed. She spat, scratched and bit like a tomcat. We rolled across the floor. The rug slid out from beneath our writhing bodies. The mirror toppled and shattered. Jagged slivers rained over us. 'Lizabeth grabbed one of the largest. She thrust it, a glittering dagger, at my face. She wanted to cut me. To put her mark on me like a cow. Even if I gave her Hannah's room it wouldn't be enough. I saw that in her greedy eyes. Her mind would be forever plotting. Hands always grasping. Want, want, want.

I rolled her onto her belly, jerked my knee into her back and tore the dress off her shoulders. Satin bows fluttered across the room. 'Lizabeth yelped. Glory, it was good to hear that. I grabbed a fistful of hair and smacked her head on the floor. Her arm lashed out wildly. I pinned it with my other knee and sank my teeth into the back of her hand. Fingers snapped open. I knocked the shard away. It skidded across the floor. Her hand was bleeding where the glass had sliced into her palm.

I got the dress the rest of the way off her. I don't know how. She kicked and thrashed like a landed trout.

'This is my sister's dress. This is Lucy's. You'll not touch anything of hers again. D'you hear? Never again.'

I turned her over, straddled her belly, grabbed another nest of hair. The fight had gone out of her but I wasn't done yet. I spat in my hand and rubbed her face. Wiped off Lucy's powder and rouge. 'Lizabeth did not cry. Did she know what tears were? Had that slut's face only ever had snide grins papered onto it?

I could've killed her too. What was another life? This one was just as rotten, just as full of bile as Sutcliffe's. Kill her. Cut her scrawny throat with the same piece of glass she'd tried to stick me with and dump her body in the pond. I'd find someone to blame it on. No one would care.

I stood up, chest heaving. Not enough air in the world to fill my aching lungs. 'Lizabeth lay on the floor, whimpering. A trickle of blood ran from the corner of her mouth. She made no move to get up.

Blood drummed in my ears. Everything hurt. Glass fragments glittered in my hair like dew. I bent down. I pulled Lucy's shoes off 'Lizabeth's feet. I undid the petticoats and let them drop either side of her hips. Large hips. Good for childbearing, Sally would have said with a laugh. I peeled off Lucy's silk stockings and draped them over the end of Hannah's bed.

'Get out,' I said. 'Get out and don't come back in here. Ever.'

She scrambled to her feet, stumbled, regained her balance and fled the room. Her footsteps pounded on the stairs. I sank to the floor, strands of 'Lizabeth's straw-coloured hair clutched between my fingers.

I hope that hurt, I silently mouthed. *I hope that hurt, you hateful sow.*

Lucy's gown lay in rags on the bare floorboards. I had sent 'Lizabeth running downstairs in her shift. The enormity of it struck me. She had run downstairs in her shift, fat behind squirming beneath the cotton. I laughed until my belly ached. I had given her a bloody lip. I had given her a bloody lip and she was in her shift. Oh glory.

I washed my face, brushed down my gown and returned to the Long Room. I told Isaac that 'Lizabeth was nowhere to be found. He eyed me curiously for a moment, then whispered, 'More brandy for Mr Polding. Hurry.'

Mr Polding? Ah yes, the portly fellow with the broken nose. He had complained almost as loudly as Shrew-woman when the *Charger* had rolled in. Now he sprawled in an armchair, gut stuffed with our food, roaring with laughter. An empty glass was clutched in his hand.

I hurried to fetch the decanter. When I returned, Isaac was talking to the hazel-eyed girl. Talking about the road.

'You have a fine establishment here, Mr Curtis,' she was saying.

'Oh? Pity your coaches never found time nor need to stop.'

Her smile never wavered. She went on sipping her tea. 'Even with most of the coach traffic using the turnpike good use could still be made of such a property.'

'Aye, so I've been told. I wasn't expecting the *Charger* on the lykeway. Not since the turnpike opened.'

'There is some dispute over the tolls. Until this is resolved the *Charger* will continue to use the South Road. This can only be for a short time however. Other coaches are already making the journey more quickly. We are surviving on our reputation.'

'You are welcome here, miss.'

'I am pleased to be here, sir.'

And that's when I found out who she was.

Mother took me aside and whispered into my ear. 'That's Chloe Gale,' she told me, awed. 'The daughter of the stagecoach company owner.' Mother had seen an etching of her in one of those London journals she was so fond of reading. Miss Gale had a reputation for clattering around city parks aboard a phaeton perch, a light, lethal carriage that, with one pothole, could have an inexperienced driver off the seat and in the gutter with a broken neck. 'Not married either,' Mother added.

I was astonished at my luck. If anyone else had been aboard that coach it would never have pulled into the inn. I'd be lying in the mud with a whipped back and Isaac likely shot.

Our guests had finished eating and the table had been cleared. They sat around smoking, drinking, talking contentedly. Miss Gale tried chatting to Mother. To every one of Chloe's breezy questions she simply nodded or gave a muttered response.

I didn't know where 'Lizabeth had run off to. I kept glancing towards the door expecting to see some hysterical, bloody faced creature in a torn shift come bursting in, finger jabbed accusingly at me, screaming, 'Murderess!' Most likely she was skulking in her bedchamber, but I wasn't certain. When I sent her packing from Hannah's room I should have gone after her and forced her to return my petticoat.

I stole a quick look at Chloe. I wouldn't ever get a favour like this again. Why was she doing it? It had nothing to do with feeling sorry for me. Could she scent something here? Did Green Gallows carry the smell of death in its wood and plaster bones? Did she hope to pounce, to glean the best of the pickings once the Turnpike Trust had savaged us and moved on?

A pretty thing she might be, but steel lurked in those hazel eyes. Steel enough to stop the *Charger* and to the devil with her paying passengers. It all seemed so unreal. As if, like a band of travelling players, we were acting out the final meal of the condemned before facing death in the morning.

No, it must be my imagination. 'Filling my cupboard with wolves' was how Lucy would've put it. I offered Chloe a glass of Madeira but she waved it away. 'I shall settle our account,' she said. 'The tide will be turning and we must reach the docks.'

Isaac presented her with the bill – handed it to her on a little silver plate like a footman might pass a gentleman's calling card to a lady. She paid for everything. And I didn't know how to thank her.

She clasped my hand. 'Goodbye...'

'Rachel,' I said. 'My name is Rachel.'

'Goodbye, Rachel.'

'Thank you for trusting me.'

'You have a face that people trust,' Chloe replied, smiling.

On impulse I embraced her. Both Isaac and Mother drew in their breaths, Isaac probably outraged that I'd taken such a liberty with a guest and having seemingly forgotten that not two hours before he'd stood ready to threaten the lot of them with an old army musket. Well let him be angry. I'd brought the *Charger* into our yard. I'd tussled with 'Lizabeth on the floor of Hannah's room and I'd hug the devil himself if I wanted to. Chloe's arms tightened around me then she drew back and kissed my cheek. As abruptly as she'd entered our lives she was gone.

Isaac slipped off his wig and dropped it onto the table. Removing his waistcoat he strolled towards the parlour door. He started whistling.

The shadow lifted a little. But the storm still rumbled above our rooftops. How long would this respite last? How long could it last?

I saw 'Lizabeth a couple of times over the next few days. She was quick to keep out of my way, refusing to look at or talk to me even when obliged to serve supper. Sally joked that one of the village lads must have tamed her. There wasn't a mark on her face. I was disappointed. I wanted a bruise, a swollen lip, anything to prove that I'd hurt her. I wanted to hear her lie, say that she'd fallen down the stairs, walked into a door, been kicked by a horse. Either she'd stolen some baking powder to plaster on her face – she'd raided the kitchen before when a gypsy lad she'd been seeing tired of her carping and blacked an eye – or I wasn't the hard-bitten fighter I'd thought myself.

Hannah's room was locked. I saw to that. The day after the fight I slipped upstairs with a key and a brush and swept up the remains of the shattered mirror. I scooped up Lucy's clothes, locked the room behind me, and took them down to the wash-house. Later I told Isaac that I'd knocked the mirror over while airing the room. He just grunted.

I still didn't trust 'Lizabeth. I knew better than to think she had been cowed for long. She was like an assassin, biding her time for the right moment to plunge in the knife. I waited until she took a pile of linen out into the yard then searched her poky room. I turned out all her drawers, opened her wardrobe, rifled the chest at the foot of her bed – did everything except lift the floorboards. No bloodstained petticoat.

I had to get rid of her. Quickly.

'With so much loss of business do we need a maid?' I asked Isaac. ''Lizabeth has an uncle who runs a farm in Dorset. Perhaps she should go there. I could do most of her work and with the taproom so quiet Sally could cope with the rest.'

'She looks after your mother,' Isaac replied. 'The *Charger* won't stop a second time but trade will pick up once word gets about that it called here.'

Trade wouldn't flow down the South Road again. The *Charger* might stop a hundred times and it wouldn't make any difference. The arteries had already been cut. I glanced at Mother, sitting in her usual chair beside the hearth. She knew. Her dark eyes said as much.

On Thursday evening a man in a hired chaise arrived at Green Gallows. I spotted him from the window. A thickness settled in the bottom of my stomach and I made no effort to run out and open the carriage door. The visitor glanced around the yard, eyes hooded beneath his tricorne. Twilight softened the sharp angles of the outbuildings. Moths were already clustering around the lantern above the stable door.

He was a busy-looking man. He stood on the threshold of the Long Room and shook the evening off his boots. Tan-coloured riding boots. They looked too big for him. He strode through the inn as if he owned it, his gaze sucking everything in. We knew who he was and why he was here. The walk, barely more than a dozen steps, told us.

Isaac took him into the parlour and locked the door. Mother and I sat in the Long Room watching the rain which had swept in off the Ridge, and listening to the clock ticking. Ten minutes later the door opened. The man, hugging a ledger to his chest, donned his tricorne and left. He did not spare us a glance. A minute later we heard the clop of hooves and wheels trundling towards the gate.

Isaac looked as if his throat had been cut. He fumbled for a chair and sat down. His head sagged.

'They are taking everything,' he said. 'I told him about the *Charger*, told him we needed more time, but he said we have defaulted on the loan and the bank won't wait.'

'Is there anything we can sell?' Mother asked.

Isaac looked up. 'I already sold both my daughters.'

Next morning I woke to find the inn deathly quiet. I stole downstairs in my nightshift. No breakfast smells wafting from the kitchen, no sound of horses being taken from the stables for exercise in the paddock. In the Long Room nothing had been disturbed. The remains of last night's supper littered the table. Unwashed trenchers swam in a pail of cold water.

Isaac was slumped in Mother's armchair. A tipped ale jug spread a crescent stain on the card table in front of him. His head rested on his folded arms. He was snoring.

Barefoot, I went outside, heedless of the sharp

gravel cutting into my soles. A leaden sky bled a persistent drizzle. Pulling a shawl over my nightshift I stole through the grounds.

Finally I tiptoed across the cool grass to the pond.

Mother was lying on her back in the water. Her bloodless face stared sightlessly at the underbelly of the sky. The rain intensified, hissing angrily on the surface of the pond. On her dead, drowned eyes.

I screamed until my voice cracked. Judd found me kneeling at the side of the water, hands clenched against my cheeks. He had to wade into the pond to fetch her body. It was bloated with water. Will Davey was fetched from Prestbury and had her stitched up in a sack before her shift had dried. The gravediggers dropped her in a hole beside Lucy and shovelled quicklime on top of her. There was no money for a casket. I wanted to sell some of Lucy's trinkets but the Trust owned everything. They owned my wet shoes, my mud-spattered gown and the black velvet bonnet with the lace veil. They owned the gig that brought me here, the horse that pulled it, even the straps on Matthew's boots.

There was barely enough room on the verge for another grave. Someone said Parson Buseridge had suggested opening up the same hole and laying Harriet on top of Lucy, the way pauper families were sometimes buried. The parsonage curtains were drawn as they had been during Lucy's funeral. My eyes narrowed to slits. It had rained then, too.

No money for another Curtis death. No husband at the graveside. Isaac wouldn't come even though I pleaded with him.

'See to your mother's burial,' he said before shutting himself in the parlour. 'Won't make no odds whether I go or not. She still loved him, right until the end.'

Judd and Sally slipped away from Green Gallows before the burial. I didn't know exactly when, suddenly they were just gone. Matthew said they were hoping for work on a farm. He wouldn't tell me where and I knew better than to press him.

I regarded the faces of the mourners. As soon as the first clumps of sod thumped onto Mother's cheap shroud people melted away like rainwater. The gravediggers, eager to get out of the wet, were already shovelling soil back into the shallow hole. Burying another suicide. One of them pushed his spade into the dirt and wiped his hands on his breeches as if they carried the plague.

I walked back towards the lane. Matthew had gone ahead to ready the gig. A figure stood by the lich-gate, its outline blurred by the rain. I walked down the path, cinders crumbling beneath my shoes. My breath misted in the air. Such a cold day.

Abruptly, the figure stepped in front of the gate, blocking my way. It was 'Lizabeth.

'Are you happy now she's dead?'

The accusation in her voice chilled me even more than the thickening rain.

''Lizabeth, this is not the time.'

'You killed her just as surely as if you pushed her head under the water yourself.'

'What do you mean by that?'

'I was more of a daughter to her than you ever were. You stole her dreams. Ruined any chance she had of getting the better life she deserved. You're a murderess twice over. And you're going to pay.'

''Lizabeth, wait.' I caught her arm but she shrugged free and ran through the lich-gate, petticoats swishing lumps of cinder against the tombstones.

Chapter Thirteen

'Tell me it ain't so.' Isaac shoved the petticoat under my face. 'Tell me this ain't his blood.'

His voice kept breaking into high-pitched notes. There was a terrible desperation in it.

'There's too much,' he continued when I didn't reply. 'I've seen your monthly linen. You've bled like a kitten ever since God made a woman of you.'

I backed off. 'I'm not sorry I killed him. I won't be sorry.'

'Why? You could have saved this family.'

'Look what he did to Lucy. You made her go into his carriage knowing what he would do. You made a whore of my sister and would've done the same to me. Go on, tell Will Davey. He wants the killer hanged. Now you can let the law do it. At Tyburn, in front of the mob.'

Isaac's voice seemed to shake the windows in their frames. I couldn't see 'Lizabeth but I knew she was in the taproom listening at the hatch.

'I'll save them the trouble.'

He hauled me out of the Long Room door and dragged me by the hair across the yard. I stumbled, fell to my knees. He pulled harder. Gravel scraped my shins, bit into the palms of my hands. Dirt filled my hair, ears, nostrils. Agonised tears blurred the world.

I whimpered, begged him to stop.

'Up. Get up!'

His boot thumped into my ribs. Air whistled out of my lungs. I clawed my way to my feet, staggering like a drunk. Fire seared across my scalp as his thick hand tore clumps of hair out by their roots. Tears and snot made a weeping sore of my face.

'Father ... please.'

'Father now, is it?' Isaac grunted. 'That makes a bloody change.'

I tried to say something else. He clipped me across the mouth. A searing jolt as my teeth dug into my tongue then the bitter copper-tang of blood. My left cheek was numb, the eye swelling closed. Ribs ached. Both knees were raw from scraping across the gravel.

This had gone beyond a beating. Some terrible purpose festered in his mind. We were outside the stable door. A length of rope hung from a rusty nail hammered into the stonework. One hand still grasping my hair, Isaac hooked the rope over his arm. I thought he was going to tether me like a horse. I didn't care. He could lead me around on a leash as long as he let go of my hair. *Please.*

Matthew ran out of the stables. 'Get off her. Leave her alone.'

Isaac didn't break stride. He shifted the rope

onto his shoulders and lashed out. His fist caught Matthew square in the face. Matthew went down without a sound. Isaac didn't wait to see if he got up again. He dragged me round to the front of the inn. Someone was there. A thin, birdlike man loitered at the open front door. One of our few remaining guests taking the air. His mouth fell open when he caught sight of us.

The axe scars around the base of the signpost were still fresh. Isaac viced my head between his thick legs and fiddled with the rope. A moment later a makeshift noose dropped in front of my face. I screamed. Isaac tightened his grip. The guest stood and dithered, looking horrified. I don't think Isaac even noticed he was there.

Do something, I silently pleaded.

Isaac's body jerked. Something whickered through the air. A crack as it struck wood followed by a dull thud from the grass nearby. He had thrown the rope over the cross spar. My innards clenched. I was going to wet myself like a mewling child.

He was trying to frighten me. I clung to the thought, dug my nails into it. This was just a scare. He couldn't really do it. I was his daughter. His *daughter*.

Isaac stepped back, releasing me. I fell onto my belly, burying my face in the grass. A stolen breath, two. He grabbed my hair, jerked my neck back and dropped the noose over my head. The rope scratched the soft flesh of my throat. It smelled of stale linseed oil, dust and old cobwebs.

The man by the door stepped forward, mouth working. Isaac pushed him to the ground. I closed my eyes. When I opened them again the man was gone. The front door was closed.

'No...'

'That's right, murderess,' Isaac's voice was a soft rumble inside my ear, 'you've ruined my life, tore apart everything I had or ever wanted. Spit your prayers into the dirt before I choke off that whining voice of yours. Go on.'

His knee slammed into my back. I jerked forward. Immediately the rope snapped tight. Hot blood blew a gale in my ears. Fireflies sparked and danced behind my eyelids. I felt Isaac shifting, grasping the loose end of the rope, getting ready to pull. He grunted, the rope-snake tightened its coils around my neck and I was hauled to my feet. My arms flailed the air.

Shouting, curses, the smack of a fist. Someone thumped into me, shoving my back against the signpost.

'Let her go, man. Let her go.'

Something warm splashed my cheek. Isaac bellowed and released the rope. I slid to my knees, wheezing. Hands grasped the noose, pulled it open, dragged it roughly over my head. My strangled throat sucked in air.

Breath on my face. A hint of brandy and expensive tobacco. Another, different voice: 'She'll live, thank God, but another moment with that thing around her neck and I wouldn't give tuppence for her life. Who is that brute?'

'The innkeeper. Her father. The one who stormed through the taproom last night and refused to serve us. Don't you recognise him?'

'Her father? Dear heaven. Can you hold him

until someone fetches the constable? We'll have to send word to Prestbury.'

'I heard one of the London gentry was murdered in these parts.'

'We damn near had another murder on our hands. Might still do if you can't keep this fellow subdued.'

'The fight's gone out of him so far as I can see. A sore head when he wakes up though. God, what an animal.'

'What about the girl? D'you reckon we ought to move her? Listen to the way she's breathing. God, I don't like it.'

'Help me get her inside. She's not going to die. Not now.'

My eyes opened a crack. The first thing I saw was the rope, coiled on the grass beside me. Three other men were in the front yard. One was the gentleman who had tried to intervene a few minutes ago. A second, taller fellow stood nearby, a handkerchief pressed to his face. The third, by far the largest of the trio, sat astride Isaac who was lying face down in a patch of dirt beside the signpost. Both his arms were pinned behind his back. Blood spurted from his nose. His eyes were glazed. His barrel chest heaved up and down, gulping air.

I tried to say something. Cramp gripped my throat. Getting to my feet was impossible. There was no life left in my legs. Dizziness and nausea kept spinning the world out of my reach. Someone suggested fetching a surgeon but no one wanted to pay.

'Give her laudanum and let her sleep it off.'

'What? And have her choke? I didn't get my face punched just to have the wench die on me now.'

'Let her sip some water then. Perhaps we can find a maid to make a poultice. Wipe her face at least.'

'I spent half the morning trying to find a chambermaid. No one seems to work here.'

'Well, let's get them both inside. We can manage that between us.'

Will Davey turned up with a hunting rifle and two bailiffs armed with staves. The gentleman in the blue coat let him into the kitchen. The gun was an old flintlock, roughly hewn from iron and as tall as a man. Davey once claimed it had seen action at Naseby against the Royalists. A lesser man would have needed a stand to fire it. Davey swung it about his shoulders like a boat hook.

Isaac wiped his face with a scrunched-up apron. His eyes settled on the end of that hovering gun barrel.

'You took your time getting here, Davey.'

The big man nodded. 'Heard there's been some trouble with your girl, Curtis.'

Davey's tone was even enough but his rifle remained poised in the air between himself and Isaac. The two bailiffs who had come in with him made no attempt to put down their staves. They stood by the door, watching.

I swallowed. Pain squeezed my neck. Isaac said nothing. He stared at some invisible point on the kitchen wall. I sat by the fire in Sally's old armchair, my feet propped on a stool. The traders had not wanted to let either of us out of their sight until the constable turned up. One had suggested tying Isaac up or locking him in the pantry. He had not even acknowledged my existence since the men had carried me inside. My rescuers seemed relaxed enough now, but they kept stealing glances at Isaac as if he were a fairground bear that had slipped its chains and would pounce at any moment.

Will laid a hand on Isaac's shoulder. 'You'll have to come with me.'

Isaac nodded. I reached out a hand, brushed fingers against his coarse hair.

'Father...'

'You never called me that before today,' he said. 'Not until I was set to kill you.'

Davey pushed back his hat. 'You going to be all right, Rachel? I can send my wife over to sit with you.'

'No.' I tried to shake my head. Another flare of pain warned me to keep still. 'I'll manage.'

'What about your maid? Elizabeth?'

I coughed. ''Lizabeth doesn't work here any more.'

'There's a good apothecary in Stonehill. I can send for some herbs and ointments.'

'It's all right, Mr Davey, you needn't worry over me. I can make a poultice with some things from the kitchen.' I coughed again. 'Sorry, but it hurts to talk.'

'Aye, lass. I'll take my leave. If you need anything send at once to the assizes. Word will get to me. This has been a terrible time.'

He straightened his hat, stooped under the door frame and left. The bailiffs followed with Isaac.

I was now mistress of Green Gallows.

My rescuers cleared out within the hour. Perhaps they hoped to get away without settling their tally on account of saving my life, but this was still an inn and a bill was a bill. I wrote a crude note demanding payment.

'This is an outrage,' the man in the blue breeches complained. 'You owe us your neck, young lady, or have you already forgotten?'

I shook my head, wincing at the pain. Their spokesman spluttered some more, paid up and the three left, muttering.

The small pile of sovereigns glinted on the table. I opened my reticule and swept the coins inside. I tramped upstairs to Isaac's bedchamber. The room was buzzing with flies. I opened the drawer of the bedside table and took out the key to the money box. Everyone knew where Isaac kept that key, but nothing was ever stolen from the box.

Back in the parlour I slid the box out of the cabinet beside the hearth. The key slipped into the lock and turned easily. I lifted the lid. Blinked. Closed it again. I shoved the box back into the cabinet and tossed the key onto the supper table. I left the room without bothering to close the door behind me.

A gust of warm, musty air breathed into my face when I slipped into my old bedchamber. Isaac had started using it to store empty beer barrels and the odour of stale hops hung heavily over the stripped bones of my former bed. Dust softened everything. The dried husks of dead bluebottles peppered the windowsill. Trinkets that had no place in Lucy's lace-trimmed sepulchre had been swept off the mantelpiece and loosely stacked in an old vegetable crate. I lifted one off the top and fingered it idly. An eyepiece from a telescope. Something else Sailor Ben had given me. He claimed to have won it from a captured Spanish privateer. Sailor Ben's tales, I suspected, were as fake as most of his teeth.

There was nothing here of any worth. I returned to the parlour to wash my hands. There was barely enough water left in the pitcher to cover the bottom of the bowl.

I couldn't remember how to make a poultice, though Sally had done it hundreds of times. No fresh water had been drawn that morning. I dragged the pail out from under the sink and took it into the yard. Above, a patch of blue sky was ringed by grey clouds. A huge eye. The eye of God, staring at me.

I slapped the bucket down in the empty trough and worked the pump. Pain howled down my neck and shoulders. I settled for half filling the pail and hauled it back inside. Twice I stumbled, spilling water. Scraping away a layer of ash with the poker I found some warm embers lurking at the bottom of the kitchen hearth. I tried to heat some water but my hands were shaking so badly I dropped the pot. More water slopped out, dousing the already struggling fire.

I settled for soaking a strip of linen in sour wine from the larder, though I didn't really know whether this would help or not. Laudanum was kept in the kitchen in case of calamities. I stared doubtfully at the small stoppered bottle. Finally I treated myself to a single drop. I was about to return the bottle to the cupboard, thought better of it and slipped it into my reticule.

I returned to the Long Room. I pulled up an armchair, used another as a footstool and eased back into the soft, leathery womb, gently pressing the makeshift poultice to my ravaged throat. I closed my eyes and let its coolness soothe me.

What now?

The petticoat.

I confronted 'Lizabeth in her room. She'd locked the door but I had all the spare keys.

'You've got half an hour to get out,' I rasped. 'Be sure to take your chattels with you or else they'll be sold to the first tinker that comes along.'

I paid her a shilling, which covered her wages and notice, and stood over her as she fumbled her meagre belongings into a small flour sack and tied it with string. Her fingers slipped on the knot, forcing her to do it again.

'You forgot something.' I dropped my bloodied petticoat, rescued from the corner of the Long Room, onto the bed in front of her. She stared at the garment as if it were her own shroud.

'What's the matter, 'Lizabeth? Don't you want it? You seemed to set great store by it before. It'll make a fine keepsake for you.'

She grabbed the flour sack and fled the room.

I scooped up the petticoat, carried it outside to the ash pit and burned it. It took me six attempts with Sally's flint to get it to light, even after soaking it in brandy. Once it caught I waited until every inch of material had been reduced to smouldering ruin. When nothing was left except a few restless ashes I pressed my palms to my face and wept. I was free. Isaac could babble all he wanted to. People would think him mad. He had tried to hang his own daughter. No one would believe that I had killed Sutcliffe. There was no proof. The last of that was even now being swept away by a strong afternoon breeze.

I stood up and wiped my hands on my gown. The yard was bitter with smoke. I couldn't stay here. Not another day. Back in the house I bundled an armful of Lucy's clothes into a large cloth bag. After dropping the keys on the parlour table I wrapped a silk scarf lightly around my bruised neck and pinned it with a cameo brooch.

I fetched Matthew out of the stables. He emerged, bleary eyed, into the sunshine. Half his face was hidden under a linen bandage. Clumps of fair, wispy hair clung to his chin.

'Are you all right?' I asked.

He gestured at the bandage. 'I think my nose is broke,' he said, only it came out *dose is boke*. 'One of Mr Davey's men put this on. Wasn't much use to you out there, was I?'

'Don't fret. It took three men to stop Isaac. Now hitch the gig.'

He eyed the bag. 'You're running away.'

'Never mind what I'm doing. You always wanted to be in charge of the stables. Well now you can be master of the whole inn if you choose. Just take me to Prestbury.'

He hooked his hands on his rope belt. 'No. If you want to go somewhere you can walk.'

'Matthew, please don't make me argue with you. My throat is very sore.'

'My days of running after you are done,' he

said. 'And don't think of taking Mistral either. Everything here belongs to the bank now. I won't be branded a horse thief on your account.'

'Matthew...'

But he was gone.

So I walked. I didn't bother to close the main gate behind me and I didn't look back. I tramped the six miles to Prestbury without a soul passing me on the road. Late weeds poked drooping heads between the wheel tracks. Two years, maybe three without traffic, and no one would ever know this was once a busy highway.

A solitary cloud puffed across the sky. Hedges pressed in on either side of the lane. I kept swapping the cloth bag from hand to hand. Finally, with both arms aching, I opened it up and heaved some of the more frivolous clothes into the ditch.

A mile later I arrived at Prestbury church. Both graves were all but invisible. I walked past without stopping. I was thirsty and hot. My feet hurt. Even with half the clothes turfed out, the bag was still a ton weight. I just wanted to curl up and fall asleep. I thought about the bottle of laudanum I'd pinched from the kitchen. Drink that and I wouldn't have to worry about my sore throat or aching arms. I wouldn't have to worry about anything. It would be so easy.

When did you ever have an easy life, Rachel? I thought, and pressed on. Two hours later I turned into the yard of the Coach and Horses Inn.

The turnpike had become the centre of the world. Everything here was new. Walls had been whitewashed and fresh thatch laid on the roof. The yard thrummed with life. Post boys swarmed around like red-coated flies.

I found a pedlar and hawked the last of Lucy's jewellery. It fetched enough money for a trip to London. I pushed my way inside the inn. A queue of chattering travellers snaked around the counter. After a wait I took the pedlar's coins and booked passage. I would take the local stage to Stonehill from where I would catch the London coach.

'You're in luck, miss,' the barkeep said cheerily. 'Stage from Portsmouth is due within the half hour. There'll likely be a seat on that.'

He smiled. A ragged scar broke his face in two. He was dressed in crisp jerkin and breeches. Gold glittered from one earlobe. I knew everyone in Prestbury, or thought I did. This fellow's rolling accent hailed from a place far north of these counties. I responded with a bitter twitch of my mouth, thanked him and slipped the receipt into my reticule. On the way to the door he called after me.

'Perhaps you'd care to wait in the Long Room. There's a fine quartet playing. Or if it's food you're after we serve some of the best in the county.'

I paused and glanced back over my shoulder. The landlord caught my look, shrugged and went back to serving his other customers.

From the taproom I bought a glass of lemonade and took it outside. I sat on a bench with my back to the wall. On a patch of land beyond the inn the bare rafters of new buildings jutted towards the sky. I picked out faces among the crowds. There was Jenny Holdman, the blacksmith's wife, selling wooden combs, and May Stoddart, the miller's daughter, dancing barefoot amidst a circle of whooping, clapping young men and her turned fourteen only last month. Mrs Grenfell, the washerwoman, had forsaken her linen basket and was hawking sugar sticks to noisy children. Purses jangled, money glinted as it passed from palm to palm. It seemed that just about everyone in Prestbury who could draw breath had come to work the Coach and Horses.

And there, oh glory, was the last person in the world I wanted to see.

The insolent grin, the creased face, the swagger. I pulled down the brim of my bonnet. He strutted around, slapped shoulders, issued orders, hailed people by name. Ostlers brought horses from the stables. Men who once worked our yard. Colly made a big show of examining teeth and hooves. *You could pin a horse's tail to a cow, call it a hunter and Colly Bruce wouldn't know better,* Judd had once said, laughing.

His shadow fell over me. I tried to shrink into the wall. Glory, he stank. Despite the fine clothes and the cologne. A sick, dead smell of stale gin and rotten carrots. It must ooze out of his pores.

'By God it's the Curtis brat, and looking like something out of a Portsmouth bawdy house. I thought something had curdled under my nose. Must be that whorish perfume your papa makes you wear.'

I looked up. Colly loomed over me, fists planted on hips, legs apart. Shadows darkened his face.

'You don't impress me, Colly Bruce.'

'Now hark at that,' he chuckled. 'Why the husky voice? You trying to sound more grown-up than you are? And who soaped the inside of your mouth with such fancy words? No doubt the same clod who thought puttin' that fine gown on you would make lamb out of mutton. You were always fat, Rachel. Fat and ugly. Under that face paint you still are. I'll always be able to sniff you out. What's more I heard you're broke. Not two pennies to scratch your arse with. But don't worry, if it's passage on a coach you want I'll let you ride free. As a special favour like, from one old friend to another.'

'You don't run the coaching companies.'

He spat into the dirt. 'As good as, leastways if they want to travel the road.'

A carriage rumbled into the yard, raising plumes of dust. I hardly saw it.

'I've paid my own fare.'

'Paid your fare have you? And what else can you buy, seein' as I've heard creditors were gathering at your door like a mob at a hanging? Curtis always thought himself a better man than I. But he's from a rotten line just like his hatchet-faced wife and your horsefly of a sister. Well she's gone and yer ma too. I told your papa to come to me if he wants work and the offer's still open. I need someone to heft shit out of the stables. Or is that too humble a job? Tell him to think hard on it. 'Tis the only way honest money will cross his palm in these parts again.'

'Shovel shit he might, Colly Bruce,' my voice was barely more than a whisper, 'but you'd still not be fit to tie his boots.'

Colly tipped back his head and laughed. I let hot anger wash over me, waited until its strength ebbed. He wouldn't know. Not yet. Word would spread, of course, was no doubt spreading now. Isaac Curtis was in prison. Isaac Curtis had tried to murder his only remaining daughter.

You've every right to laugh, Colly Bruce, but I'll not give you the satisfaction of realising that.

'Look.' He swept his hand around the yard. 'More coaches arrive every day. New houses and stables are going up faster than a man can spit. Tradesmen beg to sell their wares here. What's your high and mighty papa got now, eh? A stable with idle horses, weeds growing in his yard and ale turning sour in the barrel.'

I was on my feet in a wink. Oh, it still hurt to talk but my temper was up. 'You think you're so grand, Colly Bruce. But you're no different than any other lackey. Green Gallows was the best coaching house in this county. My father owned it and the land it stood on. You own nothing. Not your house, not your horses, not even the clothes you stand in. So don't go lording it over me. You who have to jump whenever your masters in the Trust bark from their fancy London clubs.'

'Y'hear that?' Colly brayed. 'Miss Muck here reckons I should be jealous of that forsaken hovel her papa ran into the ground. Why, I'm turnin' green at the very thought of it.'

People turned to stare. Laughter rippled around the yard.

Nearby was a damp patch where a horse had piddled onto the gravel. I scooped up a handful and threw it at Colly's grinning face. A few pebbles scraped the top of his waistcoat. The rest sailed harmlessly past.

I grabbed another handful but Colly was wise to me now. He ducked and weaved, beckoning with both hands. 'Come on, missy. Let's see if you can hit me. I'm right here. Shouldn't be too hard. Not for a little tramp like you.'

Suddenly he lunged and snatched at my skirts. I scrambled for balance. The gravel missile fell out of my hand and slopped down the front of my dress. Watching stable lads howled with glee. I fell backwards and landed on the bench with a thump, knocking over the lemonade glass.

Colly tossed sixpence into the dirt at my feet. 'Come into the stables awhile. You're an ugly sow but I'll take a tumble with ye. Won't be so bad in the dark, eh?' He chuckled. 'Make it good and I might even give you a shilling.'

He leaned over me. 'I once asked your sister. She turned me down, the fancy bitch, but you'll do. Aye, you'll do well enough.'

'Don't you touch me. Don't you ever put your paws anywhere near me.'

'This fellow troubling you?'

A tall figure, face dark against the sun. A coachman in fine red livery. I squinted. The voice was unfamiliar, as was the balanced, easy way he held himself. Like a cat coiled to pounce on a starling.

Colly snorted. 'Why don't you stick with that sorry bucket of nails you drive.'

'That I will, Mr Bruce, just as soon as you get back to your own concerns.'

The two men faced one another. Colly eased back on his heels. His shoulders relaxed. He laughed, scooped up the sixpence and trudged off to the stables. Other people had already gone back about their business.

My rescuer touched the brim of his tricorne. 'You waiting for someone, miss?'

'I ... I have a ticket for London. I was waiting for the Stonehill coach.'

He smiled pleasantly. 'That'll be me.'

'Where's Gregor?'

'He's on the evening run. Company runs two coaches a day since the new road opened. Everybody wants to travel.' He cast around at my feet. 'No luggage?'

'Only this.' I held up the cloth bag. He slipped it out of my grasp and gestured towards the carriage. Nostrum-sellers pushed their wares under my nose. The coachman eased them away good-naturedly as we crossed the yard. I knew most of them by name. They'd only remember the scruffy fat girl who held open carriage doors.

On the turnpike we made good time to Stonehill. The ride was nothing like the tooth-knocking experience of the South Road. At the posting house the driver helped me from the carriage. I tried to thank him but he had already turned to assist the other passengers while his colleague passed baggage down from the roof. I had an hour to wait for the London stage. The posting house's taproom was packed with merchants and stevedores down for the market. I avoided their rowdy stink and settled on a bench in the yard. I felt dizzy. I hadn't eaten since supper the night before. Even then I'd only nibbled on a piece of bread. A lion clawed my throat every time I swallowed. I loosened my scarf and examined myself in the small looking glass that I'd slipped into the bottom of my bag. A dark band snared my neck. I touched the bruised flesh and winced. I had to see a doctor. But how to explain it? How?

The London coach was a squeeze but I managed to find a space by the window. Outside, the countryside rolled by. The gentle swaying of the carriage together with the steady rhythm of the hooves pounding the road outside sent me into a torpor. I eased my head back against the seat and closed my eyes.

The stink of London carried on the wind. The stagecoach arrived on time. I stumbled down the steps. Both legs had gone to sleep. I wasn't organised and I didn't have a plan. Where exactly was I? Sick with hunger, I searched the skyline in a bid to get my bearings. I bumped into a passerby who cursed and shoved me out of the way. Nearby was the Thames. The smell that rose from its dark waters pervaded the streets. And over there, the dome of St Paul's. I took in the surrounding buildings: sagging terraces mostly, perhaps fashionable once, the masonry now cracked, the paint flaking. Crowds thronging the streets seemed ill-faced and surly though one or two fine carriages clattered through, scattering a swarm of ragged urchins.

I hailed a sedan chair. It was late afternoon and I had no stomach left for walking. Cream-coloured city buildings glared in the harsh light. The beginnings of a headache buzzed behind my eyes.

'The Rose Tavern,' I told the bearers. Isaac had mentioned it on our trip to the city together. I could think of nowhere else to go. The landlord of the Rose was polite and gracious. He showed me into a low-beamed room that overlooked a small cobbled stable yard. At this time of day it was in shadow and the room was blessedly cool.

A bird twittered from the rooftops. Insects thumped against the window.

Alone, I laid my bag on the floor beside the bed and, without undressing, rolled onto the patched quilt. Within seconds I had fallen into a deep sleep.

Jeremiah was to be tried that Thursday. I read it in a newspaper someone had left behind in the coffee house next to the tavern. Two aimless days I'd spent haunting the Rose and nearby park, dithering while my purse steadily dwindled. Drinking was painful, eating a nightmare. At the supper table I was sullen. Other guests avoided me. Stories blew around the inn like autumn breezes. I had eloped, I had been jilted, I was on the run from my husband, I was a ruined woman awaiting succour that would never come. Nothing was ever said to my face. The landlord and his busy wife remained as courteous as ever, but every glance and gesture held unspoken questions.

I cried myself to sleep. On my infrequent walks women gave me hostile glances and whispered to their husbands.

I awoke on the morning of the trial, sleepy and fog-headed. The sun crowned the patch of blue sky above the stable yard. I tumbled out of bed, knocking over the remains of last night's posset. I splashed water on my face, dragged a crumpled gown out of the wardrobe and threw it on.

Though I was too late for breakfast, the landlord offered me some bread and milk. I waved it away and asked the way to the courthouse.

'Going to the sessions, are you?' he said. 'Not much point. With old Moorcroft on the bench the verdicts are as good as given. Necks will stretch for sure.'

He drew me a crude map on the back of an old bill. Out in the street I made to hail a chair then changed my mind. I was on the dregs of my money. The landlord, rightly suspecting that all was not well in my world, had insisted that I settle my account daily. Nothing for it. I would have to brave the noisy city hordes and walk.

A small crowd had gathered outside the courthouse. I passed as just enough of a lady for the unwashed rabble clogging the back of the public gallery to let me through. What a grim sight I must have presented. My gown looked like a dozen goats had trampled over it, my bonnet was an ill-matching colour with a brim that drooped alarmingly and one of my heels had worked itself loose from the rest of the shoe, flapping when I walked.

I shook the dress and tried to smooth out some of the creases. It smelled of dust and dead moths. Inside the courtroom I pushed my way through the packed public gallery. A gaggle of women clustered near the rail. Most were intent on the proceedings. One woman eyed my dress and nudged her companion.

A door opened and Jeremiah was brought to the dock. He was pale but walked upright, flanked by two burly jailers. I took a deep breath. In my mind the killing was about to start again.

Chapter Fourteen

Judge Moorcroft was a thin, bitter man with a stare that could cut glass. A hanging judge who'd had women dragged through the streets behind hurdles, husbands pelted in the stocks and children beaten with hickory canes for selling flowers stolen from the park. Through his hands had passed the necks of more than a hundred offenders, necks that had been sent juddering skywards at Tyburn. Judge Moorcroft didn't believe in deportation. Why inflict one country's sinners on another? A man who was murderer or thief on the shores of England was just as likely to kill or steal horses elsewhere. His handiwork had filled a pauper's cemetery on the east side of London and many more graves would likely be dug. Isaac used to read the newspaper reports aloud in our parlour after dinner. Mother said the prisoners were getting no less than they deserved.

The courtroom reeked like an ostler's armpit. The air was thick enough to choke on. I shook my head to clear it. Jeremiah might see me in the crowd. He looked tired but alert. One eye was blacked and some teeth were missing. Was that the work of Will Davey's men or had it happened in prison? Suppose he named me as the killer? Suppose he yelled it out for everyone to hear? And even if he kept his silence that still left 'Lizabeth. Would she denounce me? She had no proof but someone might be nosy enough to start asking awkward questions.

I couldn't leave now even if I wanted to. People had flooded in behind me and the gallery was packed. All the windows were open but the room remained a furnace. One girl near to me fainted and had to be carried out over everyone's heads.

The trial was short. No sharp young buck of a lawyer wanted to try and make a name for himself defending Jeremiah Cathcart. The case was sewn. Sutcliffe's blood would taint anyone trying to save Jeremiah's neck from the noose. The four dusty owls seated at the bench knew this, as did the counsel and the jury. Cathcart had been found wandering the Chase. The look on his face, the makeshift grave, these were things that would keep Will Davey and his men gossiping over their supper and in ale houses for months to come.

Mr Davey himself was brought to the stand. I pulled my bonnet low over my face. The constable spoke for a while before being dismissed. Then a clerk dipped into his desk and produced a silver pocket watch. He dangled it on its chain for a moment then laid it down in plain view of the bench. Then he took out Sutcliffe's silk neckcloth, stained a dirty brown, the cameo still pinned to the material. It was placed beside the watch.

Moorcroft leaned forward and addressed Jeremiah. 'You took those things from Lord Sutcliffe?'

'Far less than he stole from me.'

The four men on the bench joined heads and muttered something among themselves.

He's going to be hanged, I thought wildly. *They can't possibly let him go.*

He had murdered one of the gentry. In the eyes of some it was the same as killing the King. Or God.

'In the face of this evidence,' Moorcroft continued, 'you freely admit to the crime?'

'That I do. I killed Sutcliffe. I knocked the miserable life out of his poxed body. Were he in front of me now I'd do it again. He deserved to die.'

A gasp swept through the courtroom. Jeremiah had damned himself as easily as if he'd taken a rope and tied it around his own neck.

Never insult the gentry, Isaac once said. *Never look them in the eye, answer back or throw their failings in their face. Remember always. Don't knock them off their perch. They bite.*

A flicker of distaste curled Moorcroft's mouth. He gestured with a lace-cuffed hand. 'So be it. You will hang at Tyburn Field. May God have mercy on your soul.'

Bailiffs appeared either side of Jeremiah and took hold of his arms. He offered no resistance as they bundled him out of the dock. The clerks started shuffling papers, already preparing for the next case.

'You can't hang him,' I whispered. 'You can't.'

People started jeering. Someone threw an egg. It caught Jeremiah on the back of the head and splattered yolk across his hair. He didn't turn round. Another egg missed and hit the wall.

I had to get outside. I couldn't stay here a second longer. I tried to claw my way through the crowd. Angry voices were raised. A scuffle broke out near the doors. Judge Moorcroft beckoned over another bailiff.

'Get this rabble out of my court.'

I was pushed into the street. My hat flew off, my reticule smacked onto the ground. The contents of my purse, no more than a few pennies now, scattered across the road. A flurry of limbs and filth-encrusted rags fell on them. I sat in the dirt, trying to catch my breath. I saw feet. Some bare, some in clogs, some bound in strips of leather. The women I had spied in the courtroom were fighting over somebody's shawl.

I struggled to get to my feet. A lump of mud hit the side of my face. I wiped my cheek and stared at the stain darkening my glove. Some of the women spat at each other. More words spilled into my aching brain, blurring into a continuous babble of hatred. One thought lay at the centre of it all, even as the mob fought around me. I should have spoken in court, denounced Jeremiah's confession as the stupid gesture it was. Yet I had said nothing. Done nothing. Now the blood of two men would stain my hands.

But I had felt a rope around my neck once, and I had no desire to feel it again.

A carriage rattled past. A cloud of spray splashed over me. Somebody laughed. A stone caught me a glancing blow just above the right temple. I barely noticed it. I felt cold and dead inside – shivering more from self-pity than from the filthy water soaking my dress.

The slam of a carriage door. Footsteps splashing through the mud. The sharp *zing* of a whip cutting through the air. A scream followed by a string of curses. Then a soft voice in my ear.

'Rachel? Rachel Curtis? Is that you?'

My face burned with pain. I could hardly move my neck. Blood trickled from the corner of my mouth.

'Chloe…'

A warm blanket enveloped me. 'Let me get you away from this rabble. My coachman will make sure there is no further trouble.'

Dazed, I allowed myself to be helped into the carriage. Warm, gentle hands fluttered around my head. They stroked my abused face, soothing, brushing away my lank, dripping hair.

'Chloe…' I said again.

'No, don't try to talk. Not yet. There's a lump the size of an egg on your cheek and more cuts than I dare count. You are lucky to be in one piece. When I saw you lying in the road I thought you were being robbed.'

She dabbed my face with her handkerchief. I had dragged mud across the carriage's goatskin rug. My fingernails were black with muck and my hair a tangled thatch. Chloe cradled me like a baby. She looked like an angel in a cream taffeta dress. I really thought I had died. Everything kept swimming in and out of focus. Cramp spiked my legs. I wanted to be sick but my belly was empty.

'They'll hang him,' I spluttered. 'They'll hang Jeremiah.'

Chloe shook her head. 'I heard about the trial. It was in all the society papers. I wanted to attend but one of my horses threw a shoe. Then a cart overturned in Baker Street and it took the oafs there half an hour to clear the road. Lord Sutcliffe was well known, if not well liked outside his own circle. Not many will shed tears over him. Members of his own Turnpike Trust are clawing at each other's throats over the disposition of his share in the venture. I actually met the fellow once. At a tea party. He arrived by coach and did not leave it all afternoon. He tried to entice me inside, can you believe it?'

I believed it.

'The thought of that yellowed, papery flesh touching me…' She shivered.

'He raped my sister. She took her life because of it.'

Chloe looked at me as if I'd slapped her. 'I understand there were stories,' she began, 'but…'

'But who would take the word of an innkeeper's daughter,' I finished for her.

The carriage lurched as one of the wheels struck a pothole. I sat up and peered out of the window. A fine drizzle had begun, blurring the passing buildings into a solid wall of grey. The city had a weary, washed-out look.

'Where are you taking me?'

Chloe brightened. She was a lively, utterly adorable girl. No dark shadows in the bright sunshine of her life. No growling, hissing demons to carve up her heart with their sharp, pitiless claws.

Or so I thought.

'Do you have lodgings?'

'Not any more. The last of my money went into the hands of that mob.'

'Then you will come to stay with me in my rooms above the coaching offices. You can be my guest for as long as you wish.'

'Won't your father object?'

'Papa is in no condition to object to anything.

He has remained bedridden these past two years and within the last few months has slipped into his own quiet shadow world. The surgeon says it is unlikely he shall ever emerge. Some sort of seizure was the culprit brought on by – who knows? Overwork, too much bad food, a fondness for brandy.'

'You sound as if you don't care.'

'My father was a strong man. I would not insult him with pity or sympathy. I run the business in his name, which would be enough to make him proud. This is the most peaceful I can remember seeing him, even from my childhood. Always a lion, head on fire with ideas and business ventures. He used to roar from room to room, arms stuffed with ledgers and accounts and bills of sale. It was like having all the windows open in a storm. He started this business before I was born. With an ancient curricle and a ribbed old nag he ferried farmers' wives to and from market. Ambition can be a terrible thing, as my mother found. It can crumple people up like old paper and blow them into the gutter.'

'Yes, I know.'

'I don't have a brother,' she continued, as if anticipating my next question. 'Mama died in childbirth – my birth. The fury of her life with Father had used up all her strength. She was quite worn out. A woman of twenty-eight with the body and mind of a fifty-year-old. She wanted to die, I think, after giving him the heir he craved. My mother was an honourable woman. She fulfilled her marital duties – the terms of the contract, so to speak. Father was always a stickler for things like that. It did not matter that I was a girl. To him it would just be another challenge. He knows me well. I have the coaching business in my blood, Rachel. You and I have that much in common. I cannot live without the musty scent of horses, the clatter of hooves on our stable yard, the rattle of carriage wheels.'

I regarded her wearily. 'Have your hands ever been covered with horseshit, has it ever been ground under your nails so that you can't be rid of it, no matter how hard you scrub? How many times have you stood in the pouring rain, holding open a carriage door for people who don't even notice you're there? How often have you had to nail a smile to your face in the hope of a penny tip? I'd worked half a day by the time you stirred from your bed, Chloe, and I thought it a good life. We have nothing in common.' I buried my face in my hands. 'Nothing.'

'I run the company,' she continued undeterred, 'and have done since Father's illness. The men obey me as they would him. It is a satisfactory arrangement.'

'I didn't know women could do such things.'

'Father remains titular head of the business which is enough to satisfy most of his peers. Others affect not to notice or keep their grumbles to themselves. So much is happening in the industry now; there is a fat slice of the pie for everyone with more to come. New roads criss-cross the country. Every farmer who can hammer together a cart is turning to coach-building and still there are too many orders and not enough materials. It is an exciting age in which we live, Rachel. Turnpikes and posting houses are opening up and down the country. Journeys are becoming smoother and safer. People who never ventured further than the lich-gate of the local church are now visiting other towns and cities. One day you shall be able to travel to Scotland as easily as you now can to Portsmouth or Southampton. I know the turnpike trusts have a monopoly on travel at the moment but that will change. Next year we'll have three times as many passengers. Profits will soar.'

'You sound like Colly Bruce.'

'What?'

'Nothing.'

I stared at the floor. The rug kept swimming in and out of focus. I blinked several times. Chloe's chirpy voice faded into a distant buzz. Dull pain as my head struck the inside of the carriage door. Darkness.

Whiteness. A ceiling. A mattress cradled my body in feathered comfort. Sheets felt soft against my skin. The room was bright and fresh. Lemon-coloured curtains billowed inwards like fat ladies' gowns. Paintings, little windows of wonder, beamed at me from every wall. The brass bedstead was polished so sharply I could see my haggard face in it. The wash bowl and ewer were porcelain, like milk fresh from the cow. And flowers, glorious flowers, as if someone had snatched a rainbow and thrown its colours around the room.

A hand rested on my forehead. Something cool touched my lips. A glass. I sipped the contents – water, laced with something sweet-smelling. A sallow face with ridged cheeks bent over me, eyes benign. Beneath his cologne, the scent of the apothecary.

'She fainted, nothing more. However she is very weak. She must be bathed and her bedlinen changed daily.'

'Yes doctor, thank you.' Chloe's voice, anxious. I tried to move my head. Muscles groaned.

'No food except warm broth and a little bread until she has regained some strength. The child is on the edge of a fever. Her body has suffered a terrible battering.'

'What is that mark on her neck? Has someone tried to strangle her?'

'Her throat has been badly bruised. A rope by the look of it. I've had to pronounce enough men dead after public executions to know.'

'Someone tried to hang her?'

'Or she tried to hang herself.'

Their voices dissolved into whispers. I closed my eyes and the room fell into darkness. When I awoke a second time, Chloe was seated beside the bed.

'How do you feel?'

I struggled to make my throat work. 'Safe.'

'In the carriage, you looked so hurt. I'm sorry I couldn't do more to help.'

I slid a hand out from under the covers. She took it readily. 'You've been so kind to me,' I whispered.

Her face brightened. 'Perhaps I ought to work on my conversation. I've never talked anyone into a swoon before. Now you must sleep. Get better, then we can decide what to do.'

'I can't go home.'

A nod. 'I thought not.'

She rose to leave but I grasped her arm. 'I may be in some sort of trouble.'

She pressed a finger to my lips. 'Say nothing. There's a terrible fear in your eyes. And sadness. When you're well we'll talk about it, not before.'

After Chloe left I lay on the bed for half an hour, staring at the pages of a book. *The Adventures of Tom Jones*. I found it hard to concentrate. Voices outside drew me to the window. It overlooked a cobbled yard. On the left was a row of stables. Doors, painted black and gleaming, were spaced evenly along the whitewashed brickwork. The end door was open. The voices were coming from in there.

I hooked my fingers under the window frame and lifted. It slid upwards. Familiar smells, like old friends, drifted into my nostrils. Just once, once in a hopelessly long time, the day seemed brighter, the colours more vivid.

I poured some water into a glass I found on the dresser. Garlands of roses were engraved around the rim. The drink was cloudy and tasted flat. I thought of the streams flowing out of Marrin's Chase, the water cold and fresh even in mid-summer.

I put down the glass.

Below, standing in the middle of the yard, was the *Charger*.

When I'd stood waving on the embankment at Green Gallows the coach seemed to fill the lane. Now it looked small. The shafts were empty and rested on the straw-flecked cobbles. Sunlight bounced off the varnished roof.

A stableboy strolled across the yard, bucket in one hand, cleaning linen in the other. He whistled softly. Dunking the linen in the soapy water he began to wash mud from the coach panels in long, easy strokes.

Thick laughter curdled across the yard. The boy glanced towards the open stable door, shook his head and went on slopping out the carriage. When it next left here it would pass Green Gallows on its run to the coast. It would pass the grass verge where my sister and mother mouldered in unmarked graves, and the prison where my father was being held. I had admired the *Charger* all my life.

I could take an axe to it.

My father. My father was in gaol. The place was little better than a pocket dungeon but it lacked the horrors of Newgate. Isaac would be unlikely to end up coughing his lungs into the straw the way I heard some wretches did. Gurney, the old turnkey, would watch him. Gurney would make sure Isaac had clean water and keep the maggots out of his bread.

I could not go back.

I saw Isaac's face in every shadow, in every trick of cloud over the moon. Sometimes he was pleading for forgiveness, other times he lumbered out of the pit of my nightmares with a noose in one hand and that dark, dead look in his eyes. Not my name on his spittle-flecked lips, but Lucy. *Lucy*.

Other faces. Colly Bruce's insolent triumph. 'Lizabeth's black accusation. And Jeremiah in the Chase, trusting, believing, even as I sold him out.

It was a while before I could pluck up the courage to look at myself in a mirror. I resembled a little Lucy doll that had been shaken, battered then trampled into the dirt. Dark roots spread out from the crown of my head, staining the blonde.

For two days I lay in that room, reading the books that Chloe brought me, peeping from the window into the yard, watching as the horses were brought out and hitched to the *Charger.* Through the open gates I glimpsed the busy street. The city chattered incessantly.

My bruises turned yellow and faded. Scabs dried and flaked off leaving pink blotches. Meals were brought on a tray by a flour-faced maid. Vegetable soup mostly, with a little bacon frazzled around the edges. Sometimes Chloe brought the tray. While I ate she perched on the end of the bed and talked about London, the weather, the river.

When I finished my meal she took the tray, kissed my cheek and said she had to visit her father. Edward Gale was confined in an attic room where he wouldn't be disturbed by noises from the street or yard. He was very close to death.

'Any other man would have given up the struggle weeks ago,' Chloe confided. 'He lives by willpower alone. But he will let go soon. Papa is too good a businessman to be a burden to anyone. He can die happy knowing that I am not betrothed.'

I dropped the piece of bread I'd been munching on. Crumbs peppered the bedspread.

'What do you mean?'

Chloe's eyes met mine. 'With no surviving family members I will inherit the business. The only way the Gale could slip out of my hands is if I marry before Papa dies. Papa is afraid some opportunistic young rake is going to charm me out of my senses while tricking me out of my property. This cannot happen after Papa has gone. Any children I might have would inherit. No husband can touch it.'

I'd forgotten all about my breakfast. 'I thought men took everything as a matter of right.'

'Papa spent a fortune drawing up this unholy arrangement with some very expensive city lawyers.' Chloe chuckled. 'Love him as I do, I don't think he ever fully understood my motives. The inheritance was never in danger.'

Another day passed. Two. I ate, bathed and rested. My body healed. But the dreams wouldn't go away. The doctor, a Londoner by the name of Peterson, looked in from time to time. Officially he was engaged to treat Chloe's father but he had already admitted to her that there was little more to be done. When she brought my supper tray she nailed a cheerful smile to her face. But her eyes were red.

Dr Peterson was a dark, impossibly tall man with arms like broomsticks and legs that seemed able to swallow up half the room with a single step. He towered over my bed, blocking out the light from the window and making me think of a swooping buzzard plummeting out of the clouds. But his smile was as gentle as summer rain.

The doctor chatted while he checked my bruises, rubbed balm into the remaining scratches and checked my brow for signs of fever. He was delighted with my hearty appetite and sent instructions to the kitchen that I was to have as much food as I wanted. Strength seeped back into my muscles like a slow, incoming tide.

But today, after glancing at my tongue and making sure that the bumps littering my head had finally subsided, Dr Peterson settled back on the edge of the bed and stroked his chin. The smile had gone.

'You are still not sleeping properly,' he said.

'No,' I said, taken aback.

'There are dark circles around your eyes. You are agitated, despite eating well, and there is a listlessness about your demeanour. I ought to prescribe laudanum but it dulls the senses. Even a little is not healthy for a girl of your age. If you were in pain it would be different. I shall prepare a herbal draught which will help you relax. Hopefully, natural sleep will follow but you must free your mind of anxiety.'

He leaned forward. 'Is there some matter you would like to discuss with me? I swear it shall not go beyond these walls.'

I stared at him. 'No.'

'Very well.' He rose, pressed his tricorne onto his head and scooped up his bag. 'I am a physician. I can heal ailments of the body. Problems of the spirit are beyond my skills. Good day.'

His footsteps thumped down the stairs. I glanced at my reticule which had been left on top of the dresser beside my bed. Inside nestled my little secret. No one had found it. I had checked earlier this morning.

I turned over on my side and pulled the covers up around my neck.

At the end of the week Chloe decided that I was well enough to be given a tour of her home. The Gale Inn was a narrow, L-shaped building hugging two sides of the square yard. The stables formed the third side with the tall pair of green wooden gates completing the square. What it lacked in breadth the building gained in height, being a full four storeys tall. To the restless pigeons fluttering above the chimney stacks it must have resembled a beckoning whitewashed finger. Spread over these four storeys was a large number of small, square rooms, many of which were empty.

That was the most curious thing about the Gale Inn. It wasn't an inn at all.

'When we first moved in I couldn't settle for months,' Chloe explained. 'I was only seven. A child. Father fell in love with it at once. Even then I knew he would end up dying here.'

Next door to the Gale was an apothecary's, which explained the strange odours that occasionally wafted through my open window. Flanking the stables was a combined coach house and blacksmith's.

'Oh, we don't own that,' Chloe said, flicking her hand. 'It's leased from an independent bank in the city. The chairman is an old friend of Papa's.'

Chloe showed me her drawing room. The furniture was neatly arranged around a walnut writing desk. This, she told me, was where she did the accounts. I expected the place to be heaving with books, letters and ledgers. But if Chloe wanted a book she fetched it from her father's study across the hall. Anything taken was returned immediately after use.

Apart from the colour, her bedchamber was a mirror image of my own. Ivory furniture was set against violet walls. A belly of white muslin hung from the top of the oak four-poster. Goatskin rugs made cream puddles on the dark carpeting. It didn't look like the sort of place anyone ever slept in.

I learned that I was occupying one of only two guest rooms in the Gale. Chloe didn't receive many overnight visitors. Guests due to catch the *Charger* stayed at local hostelries and were ferried here. The *Charger* left according to the tide, and as soon as the first passengers started arriving their bags were loaded onto the roof. A man called Arthur Briggs supervised the hitching of the team. Watching from my perch at the window, I felt Judd could've done it in half the time.

'We run some local services too,' Chloe explained. 'Though things are a little tight with all this new competition.'

'Why not open up more guest rooms, do everything under the one roof?'

'Father prided himself on running a coaching company. He was not an innkeeper. Oh...' Her hand fluttered to her mouth. 'I meant no offence. I am merely saying that Papa was a businessman. Passengers, not guests, were his trade.'

I grimaced. 'Being an innkeeper was never enough for Isaac. But why let other people gobble a slice of your pie, Chloe? You have everything you need right here.'

'I don't know how to manage an inn, nor do I have the experience to appoint someone suitable.

I am an unmarried young woman with a substantial business. The world is full of wolves. The Gale steals my every waking hour as it is.'

'Innkeeping isn't the hardest task in the world,' I said.

Chloe gestured dismissively but I could see that some of what I told her had caught. She opened a door and led me down a flight of steps into the kitchen. A warm place with a high ceiling and a generous hearth that sucked every scrap of smoke up the wide chimney. The cook was a strip of a girl with potato-coloured eyes and long, mousy hair that was slick with grease and leaked out of her mob cap like stuffing spilling out of a mattress. Her smock was crumpled but her hands and apron were clean.

'This is Kate,' Chloe announced.

The girl's eyes darted over my body. She seemed unsure whether to curtsy or not. I looked around. Vegetables smothered the table. Some had spilled onto the floor. Battered onions hung in rows from oak beams. On a platter by the washbasin, a badly plucked goose lay ready for the oven. It looked like a dog had chewed it. Next to it was a wicker basket piled with bread and slabs of cheese.

Chloe was about to say something when a maid appeared, curtsied and whispered in her ear. She regarded me apologetically. 'Rachel, I have to go. It is a business matter. I'll let Kate show you the kitchen then, if you like, you can have a quick look at the stables.'

The kitchen door closed. Kate and I glanced at one another, looked away. Kate fidgeted. I wrung my hands awkwardly.

'Not much of a kitchen,' she said finally.
'I've seen worse.'
'I hate cooking,' Kate confessed. 'I can't boil an egg without it bursting. Miss Gale says I'll get better in time but I've been here eight months and I still burn toast and boil potatoes dry. I'd sooner be a lady's maid and wear a nice frock like the housekeeper, Mrs Meecher.'
'If you hate cooking,' I said, 'why work as a cook?'
'I just do titbits for the passengers, and Miss Gale's meals. The men eat in town. My ma got me this job. She worked for Mr Gale as a maid. She says I'm no good for anything else.'
'Well you'll just have to find that out for yourself, won't you?' I winked and she grinned. Both front teeth were missing. She must have read something on my face because the grin galloped into a laugh.
'I lost them when I was eight,' she said. 'I was playing with a hoop in the kitchen, tripped and banged my face on the edge of a stool. Ma said it served me right.' She leaned forward, blushing slightly. 'If a boy ever courts me I'll keep my mouth shut forever.'
'Bet you can whistle though.'
'Better 'n' a dog handler. You like horses, don't you?'
'Yes. How did you know?'
'Every time you hear a clop of hooves your gaze flits to the door. You're not fussed about my kitchen. You're just being polite but I don't mind. Go on, you better go an' have a look at the stables.'
I laughed and lifted the latch. 'My family had a cook,' I said. 'She was one of my best friends.'

Her eyes widened. 'But ... but you're a lady.'

'Not that much of a lady. It was nice talking to you, Kate. I hope we can be friends too.'

Kate blushed to her roots. 'If you mean to take a peek in the stables then you'd better watch out for old Briggsy,' she warned. 'He doesn't like people poking around his yard. Especially girls.'

The early autumn sun made a dusty skillet of the yard. I shielded watering eyes with the flat of my hand. White paint glared on the walls.

I strolled across the cobbles, kicking at loose stalks of straw. A gaggle of stable lads larked around by the gate. One was sucking on a clay pipe. Blue smoke billowed around his face.

The boys eyed me with interest. One leaned over and whispered something into his fellow's ear. Both grinned. Although I had never heard anything directly, I knew there was gossip about me in the servants' quarters. They called me: 'That girl with the croaky voice.'

Laughter rattled through the open stable door. I peeped around the jamb, my eyes adjusting quickly to the gloom. Briggs, the horsemaster, squatted on the floor. Two liveried coachmen sat cross-legged in front of him. Small heaps of coins lay in disarray at their feet.

Briggs held up a wooden cup, shook it and tipped out its contents. A brace of dice rolled across the floor. Everyone leaned forward. The dice came to rest against the edge of a piece of sacking. A groan of dismay. A cackle from Briggs. He swept coins into his own pile, swelling the already large hoard.

'We'll have you yet, Arthur,' remarked one of

the coachmen, scooping up the dice and dropping them into the cup.

'You've more chance of tupping my wife,' Briggs replied, laughing, 'and she's been with her Maker these past three years.'

Behind them the straw in each stall was splattered with manure. Harnesses lay in a jumble in one corner. The animals were restless. One turned its head and eyed me dolefully. An open sack of feed had tipped over, spilling half its contents into the dirt.

I passed the water trough on the way back to the kitchen. Insects skittered across the surface. The water was murky. I bent and splashed my fingers, scattering flies.

A shout at my back. Briggs ran across the yard, boots kicking up tiny eddies of dust. He stopped close to me. Very close. My fingernails bit into my palms.

Judd and Matthew always had a friendly horse-and-leather reek about them that never quite went away, even when their breeches were fresh from the laundry tub. Arthur Briggs had the unsettling scent of wet chicken clinging to him. A man who works with his hands all day should at least whiff of honest sweat, a musky odour that the animals would know.

Briggs wore a round, wide-brimmed hat that had been stitched together from strips of mismatched leather. He did not take it off when he spoke to me. I imagined it never left his head. It threw a hood of shadow across his eyes. He had a languid, easy manner that bordered on lazy, and a grin packed full of crooked teeth that suggested a dangerous charm.

'And what might you be doing poking around my yard?' he said.

'I wanted to see the stables. Miss Gale said I could.'

'Women are good for a number of things, I'll grant that, but looking after horses ain't one of them. Why don't you go back inside, miss, put on a pretty dress and maybe play with a sewing needle. Real work gets done here. It's a man's place and guest of Miss Chloe that you are, you ain't welcome.'

Lumps of old manure littered the cobbled yard.

'Not that much work,' I said.

Chloe invited me to sup with her that evening. Soup to begin, followed by trout and then jam tarts. My stomach pinched at the taste. The soup was watery and the fish had been cooked into a dried husk but I was too hungry to care.

'You said you have been to London before, Rachel,' Chloe said, jabbing her fork into the trout.

'That's right. Isaac brought me here when he had … erm ... business with the coaching people.'

'What do you think of our city?'

I gestured with my spoon. 'There are too many buildings. People don't talk, they shove one another and shout all the time. Noise, nothing but noise. Even at night with the window firmly closed so that I am sweating in my bed, I can hear the drunks and the whores. Everything is dirty and smells, especially when the weather is hot and the wind blows in from the river. I have never known a stench like it, as if the air itself has been poisoned.'

The smile dropped off her face. 'We have parks, trees. Some have lakes with ducks and swans.'

'I could look out of a window at Green Gallows and see nothing but fields for miles. I look out of a window here and another window stares back. Behind that, no doubt, is another and still another beyond. So many windows yet so little to see. It's a wonder you don't just brick yourselves in.'

'You are very candid, and perhaps a little cynical, for your age.'

'I'm sorry, Chloe, I know you have been very kind but I've gone past any desire to please people for the sake of it. I say what I feel.'

She thrust a forkful of murdered fish into her mouth. The expression on her face when she swallowed was precious. 'And what do you think of the Gale?'

'Those stableboys idling by the gate – get one of them to sweep the yard. And make sure the water in the trough is fresh. It needs to be changed often.' I put down my spoon. 'One of your horses was limping. I'll wager the shoe was loose and a pebble or nail caught in the hoof.'

'It seems you have found much at fault with us, Rachel.'

'Your horsemaster is too fond of rolling dice, that's the only thing wrong here.'

'Briggs was the backbone of this place. Father's illness hit him hard.'

'He lets the animals suffer,' I said. 'That's wrong.'

'Really? And what else is wrong?'

‘As soon as the *Charger* draws in someone must be there to open the door. Someone pretty with a beguiling smile. Don’t wait for the driver to do it. Your passengers will have had a long journey. They’ll want fresh air and their feet on solid ground.’

I glanced out of the window. ‘Where did you say people stay when they come to London?’

‘In fashionable inns mostly. It depends on the season of course.’

‘You need a Long Room with music and dancing. Card tables for the gentlemen and a taproom for the merchants. More business is settled over a tankard of ale than in any bank or lending house.’

‘We are not in the hostelry trade. I told you that.’

‘And I told you that you have the rooms for it. The servants could be made to share.’

‘A little harsh on our staff.’

‘They would be comfortable enough and an extra three-pence a week will snuff out any grumbles. Money well earned for the extra work they would have to do.’

‘You are quite the businesswoman, Rachel. Papa would have taken pride in you.’

‘It’s enough that he was proud of you.’ I pushed aside the soup plate, skipped over the trout and tried a jam tart. It nearly broke my teeth. ‘There is one other thing,’ I said, spitting crumbs.

‘Yes?’

‘Please get someone else to do the cooking.’

We started taking walks in the park. A groom from the stables followed a discreet dozen paces behind.

Chloe never let us become separated. When I wanted to feed the ducks in the ornamental lake our feathered friends received a double dose of bread. When I paused to listen to a string quartet, Chloe developed a sudden liking for chamber music. I accepted a punnet of strawberries from a man selling them by the gate and there, like a white shadow, was Chloe, choking on the things as she tried to talk and swallow at the same time.

She paid for everything, fishing coins out of her purse as easily as a dandy taking a pinch from a silver snuffbox.

I discovered that I wasn't allowed to see any newspapers.

Oh I'd asked for them. Pleaded a couple of times. The maid always curtsied, looked apologetic and spun excuse after excuse.

'None were delivered today, miss... The passengers have taken them, miss... The scullery maid used them to kindle the fire, miss...'

'Then go and fetch one,' I said, exasperated. 'Here...'

I fumbled in my reticule and tossed the maid my last scattering of pennies. But when I returned to my room later the money lay in a neat pile on the dresser.

On Thursday evening, as dusk began to soften the outlines of the buildings beyond the stable yard gate, I told Chloe I was going for a stroll. She threw a wrap around her shoulders, pinned on a bonnet and followed me down the hall.

'Where are you going?' I said, pausing at the door.

'I am coming with you.'

'Oh? I don't remember inviting you. Suppose I have business to sort out? Suppose I'm meeting someone? Suppose I just want to chuck myself in the river and drown?'

'Rachel, please calm down.'

'Why should I? Whenever I put a foot outside that yard you're at my back.'

'People hear things. Gossip spreads quicker than the pox and I'd be a liar if I said there weren't stories circulating about you. Sutcliffe's murder came at a time when the society papers were starved of scandal. People have noticed that I've taken in a guest. Servants' tongues wag and questions are being asked. It has been ... awkward trying to protect you. I don't want you to get upset over anything you might read in the newspapers, especially about that boy whose trial you attended.'

'Am I a prisoner, Chloe?'

'Rachel, that isn't it. You're not some dark secret that I want to hide in a cupboard, but after what happened outside the courthouse I don't think you should wander around the city on your own.'

I wiped my face with a kerchief and stuffed it up my sleeve. 'I'm sorry to have become such a burden. Coming here wasn't entirely my choice. Just why are you so fond of me anyway?'

'Don't you remember that day, in the pouring rain on the road outside your father's inn? You clung to the window of the *Charger*, determined to bring the entire world to a halt just to buy a minute of my time. I thought you were very brave. I was moved.'

'Your admiration didn't buy my privacy. It didn't grant you the right to haunt me. I want a key for my door. And I want a key for the front door too, or I start packing my things now.'

'Do you wish to return home, to that inn? Word can be sent on the Portsmouth stage.'

'No.'

'Then you may stay here and work for me.'

'Thank you for your charity but I've no mind to become a scullery maid.'

'I had something entirely different in mind.'

Chloe turned. Her footsteps retreated down the hall.

I forgot about going for a walk. I went upstairs to my bed, scrunched up the covers and buried my face in them.

'I want my life back,' I sobbed. *'I want it back.'*

I must have lain like that for a good half-hour. Raised voices and laughter drew me to the window. I dabbed my eyes and peered into the yard. The same group of boys were back at the gate.

Grateful? Oh yes, I'd show Chloe how grateful I was.

I brushed my hair, pinched my cheeks to bring up the colour and put on one of the dresses Chloe had loaned me. I waited until I was sure the stairs were clear then slipped outside. The stable lads were still there. The eldest, a sandy-haired splint of a boy, towered a full head above the rest. I lingered beside the kitchen door until I caught his eye then beckoned him over. He came at a trot amid an earful of ribald taunts from his friends.

'What's your name?' I asked.

He shuffled and scratched the crown of his head. 'Thomas, miss.'

'Well, Thomas, I need a special favour. Out of all the boys here I think you are the only one who might be up to it. What do you say?'

'Depends on what that favour might be, miss.'

I stepped closer so that the hem of my skirts brushed against his feet. I smiled my brightest smile and slapped some coins into his palm.

'Get me a newspaper. Any London rag will do. Make sure you're not seen with it. I'll meet you here again before supper. Cook up any story you like for your fellows there, but this needs to be our secret. Can you do that, Thomas?'

I took his hand and squeezed it. He puffed up like a cockerel and swore he'd get me a paper if he had to run across the city for it. I let him go and he strutted back to his gawping friends. I didn't wait to hear what they said but slipped back inside. The kitchen was empty. No one spotted me as I tiptoed upstairs. I smiled. I felt free.

I spent the rest of the evening in my room reading the last few pages of *Tom Jones*. Then, while Kate was busy burning supper, I slipped out of the kitchen door on the pretext of needing to take the air. Thomas was already waiting in the shadows. He glanced around then slipped a package into my grasp. For a moment I thought he'd handed me a pound of bacon, then I realised he'd wrapped the newspaper in muslin tied with string. I tried not to smirk as I thanked him.

'What now, miss?' he said eagerly.

I kissed his cheek and sent him packing with the promise of a clip on the jaw if he ever told anyone. I was astonished at how easy it was. The power in red lips, a pretty dress, a coy expression and fluttering eyelashes. I felt as if, during my life, I had been denied some profound truth that was only just revealing itself. There was power in my body. It had cut Sutcliffe down more readily than a reaper's scythe. It had sent this poor boy scampering off on an errand which, if discovered, might cost him his job. But he'd been eager to go.

I regarded myself as if seeing my body for the first time. Why was it that men held the world in their pockets when women possessed such a potent weapon? It didn't make sense. I felt I could bend the chastity of a monk if I wanted to.

Power... Because of that power a man was dead. Another was soon to die. And my father was in prison. I had driven Isaac to attack me. It was my fault. I had smashed his dreams. I had provoked him beyond sanity. I should have let him hang me. I deserved a rope.

Guilt.

The thought fluttered around inside my mind. I made a mental grab for it, tried to squash it, but it darted out of reach.

After Thomas had disappeared into the stables I smuggled the paper up to my bedchamber and slid it under the mattress. I would read it after supper. I felt elated. It must have shown on my face because Chloe glanced at me curiously a couple of times at the meal table. I suppose she expected that I'd still to be angry with her. I downed my food quickly and then, pleading a headache, begged her leave. We had exchanged few words and I think she was relieved to let me go.

I closed my bedchamber door and slid the paper out from under the mattress. Using nail scissors to cut open the muslin, I spread the pages over the coverlet. Parliamentary business, overseas wars, social nonsense. What I wanted was near the back. I checked names and dates. A column caught my eye. The Southern Counties Turnpike Trust had held an important meeting. Following the brutal murder of Lord Sutcliffe, Lord Grays had been elected temporary chairman. There was to be a full General Meeting of all members in one month's time when nominations for a permanent successor would be accepted.

I scrunched the newspaper up, shoved it into the hearth and took a tinderbox to it. The paper blackened, curled then burst into flame. I waited until every scrap had been reduced to ashes then threw myself onto the bed and grinned at the ceiling.

You see, Lucy, I can be pretty too.

Chapter Fifteen

It was a fair morning for a hanging. A patchy sky, grey clouds impaled by sunbeams. A flutter of wind.

I hired a carriage to Tyburn Field and told the driver the Gale Inn would pay. Only the promise of a hefty tip stopped him grumbling. The journey was long and uncomfortable. The driver wrestled to keep his skittish horse in check.

I'd left the house a good hour before breakfast. Giving Chloe the slip was easy. I could imagine the flap when she found that I was missing. But I wasn't doing this just to spite her. Jeremiah Cathcart had taken my place on the gallows. I had to see for myself what that meant.

When we arrived at Tyburn the hanging yard was already full. The driver dropped me off on the outskirts. The place stank like a mire. The din hurt my ears. Everyone was yelling, jeering or laughing.

'Come back in a couple of hours,' I shouted up.

'I'll fetch my fare first, then we'll see.' The driver flicked the reins and the carriage disappeared behind the crowd.

What a dismal place: a swamp of mud and refuse. It probably never dried out even in the middle of summer. Humanity churned it up the way pigs turn over an acre of grass.

The mob was eager, straining to get a good view like gamblers at a cock fight. Bodies thumped against me. Water leaked into my shoes. I pushed through, shawl pulled up around my ears. The smell of baked potatoes wafted past my nose. Someone was selling them from a cart. Other people were hawking cheap ale and pastries. Dirty-faced urchins scampered everywhere. Commanding the yard was a raised platform where finely dressed gentlemen and their ladies were seated.

Someone shoved me in the back. I was squeezed between two rag-encrusted beggars and elbowed in the belly. In my shawl I was just another shape in the crowd, jostled, deafened by jeers and catcalls. Fighting for breath I started pushing people out of the way. Someone kicked me in the shin. I kicked them back.

A ripple of excitement stirred the crowd. I stood on tiptoe to see above the bobbing heads. I expected a gibbet like the one at Green Gallows. I wasn't ready for what I saw. A large skeletal thing like the wooden bones of a barn. They didn't execute a man on *that*, did they?

I imagined Jeremiah, weak but erect, being marched from the prison's bowels, flanked by scarlet-clad troopers. When his time came – tomorrow, next week, a month – I wanted him to die gloriously. Needed him to.

'Here they come.'

A cheer rose up. Everyone pushed forward. I had to go with the tide or risk getting trampled.

No rattle of drums, no soldiers resplendent in scarlet coats. Felons were brought out six at a time, driven in a cart with ropes already around their necks, and strung up together. Horses did the pulling, three ropes to each animal. Men were hanged alongside women. The bolder among them snatched a last few moments to make cocky speeches. Others screamed and begged for mercy, protesting their innocence to deaf ears. The rest were quiet, watchful, resigned.

Two minutes for the bored-looking parson to commend their sinning souls to God. Ten minutes or more dangling on the end of the rope, the weak surrendering their lives with a twitch and shudder, the fighters kicking their legs as if trying to fend off death. In the end everyone died in silence.

Twice the ropes stretched. A dozen people carted off to a common grave, to be buried together as they had died. One man was so old he had to be carried onto the gallows. Another was little more than a boy. When the hangman secured the rope he cried out for his mother. And now a third load, the last of the day.

A tired cob hauled the wagon into the yard. The prisoners resembled ghosts. Months crammed into squalid prison cells had leeched their bodies of colour. Everyone was filthy and ragged.

Beside me a woman prayed. A papist rosary was pressed against her lips. Another onlooker laughed and poked her in the ribs. 'Why waste your prayers on those wretches?' he demanded. 'Is your boy up there in the cart?'

'They could be anyone's son,' she said quietly, 'anyone's daughter. I'll pray for them all.'

First up on the platform was a skinny, hollow-eyed man. He stared straight ahead, mesmerised perhaps by the sight of the rope or the hangman's leather hood. My cheeks were wet. I wiped them and stared at the damp patch on my glove. The skinny man fetched a kick on the behind for not moving fast enough. He didn't speak or flinch as the noose was attached to the hauling rope. Perhaps he had already escaped, fled to some dark inner place. Women were screaming, family perhaps, or a wife and daughter. Someone else jeered, others laughed. A well-aimed cabbage, black with rot, caught him on the cheek and sent him staggering backwards. The rope brought him up short and the hangman quickly pushed him back into place.

Two young women were prodded out of the cart and onto the gallows. They could have been sisters. Dirty, straw-coloured hair, round faces, washed-out blue eyes that stared as if they were confronted by the slavering jaws of a pack of wolves. Someone behind me said that the girls had been picking pockets together around Westminster. Between them they had lightened the waistcoats of more than a hundred of London's gentlemen.

The hangman rubbed the breasts of one of the girls and, egged on by the mob, slid his hand over her crotch. Thick, silent tears slid down her face. Her sister kicked his shin. A rotten tomato splattered against her temple and she crumpled onto the planking. The hangman dragged her up by the hair and fastened the rope.

'Oh dear God,' the woman beside me gasped as they were hoisted up.

It should be you, said my treacherous mind.

I clasped my shawl around my own bruised neck, feeling again the rope's harsh bite. I stumbled through the baying crowd, blindly pushing people out of the way.

Jeremiah. This was Jeremiah's fate. What had I done?

Two dozen ragged steps and I fetched up against someone's chest. I tried to move out of the way but strong arms gripped me.

'No lass,' a thick voice said. 'You've done enough wandering for one day.'

I looked up. The grizzled face of Arthur Briggs glowered back.

'I cannot believe you went to that cesspit,' Chloe said. 'Why should you wish to do such a thing when you have made a new home – a new life – here?'

We circled each other like two fighting dogs. Chloe's parlour curtains were drawn, the door locked.

'I didn't even know you'd gone until some fellow turned up demanding payment for a carriage hire. I had to give him an extra shilling before he'd leave because you also took it upon yourself to offer a tip. A tip with my money. I don't spend hours huddled at my desk counting pennies just to indulge your macabre whims. If you want to go somewhere get Briggs or one of the stable hands to take you.'

'You wouldn't have let me go,' I countered.

'To Tyburn? You are right. Why this obsession with courtrooms and hangings? Do you like to watch people die? I stare death in the face every time I step into my father's bedchamber and it's ugly. I can't chase it away. I can't order it out like a maid or send it packing with a broom like I would a mouse. It's taken up residence in that place and dug roots deep into my father's heart. It's drawing the life out of him. Sucking it up until all that will be left under those bed covers, all that will remain of the man who bent this city to his will, will be a shrivelled husk.'

I regarded her angry, near-to-tears face. She gripped the back of the writing chair. Her knuckles showed white against the oak. So furious, although not just with me. I'd seen lots of pain in my yet-short life. Old as well as new.

'Is it my fault, Rachel? Because you think I am keeping you chained? Tyburn is a horrible place.

An open-air slaughterhouse. How could you go there? How could you stand and watch people executed? It's that stable hand, isn't it? Why is this man, this murderer, so important to you?'

'He was good to my sister.'

She regarded me shrewdly. 'Was he hanged today?'

'No.'

'Do you know where he is?'

'Newgate.'

'I daresay you will want to visit him in prison?'

I said nothing.

Chloe sighed. 'I will have Briggs take you in the gig. Perhaps this will help to purge your obsession.'

'I want no shadow at my back.'

'You can go in alone. Arthur will simply drive you there and bring you home. Grant me that much peace of mind.'

'Why are you being so helpful all of a sudden?'

'Because if I say no you will go anyway.'

Chloe let go of the chair, clasped her hands together. 'I have placed an order with the locksmith for an additional set of keys.' She fixed me with her hazel eyes. 'I am not giving in. I hope you understand that.'

I nodded. 'As I live here it only makes sense.'

'You will do more than live here, Rachel. Much more. Don't think you can always get your own way by going behind my back.'

She pulled back the curtains and stared through the window at the street. Breath fogged the glass.

'Papa will be dead by the end of the week.'

'Is that what the doctor told you?'

'No, but I can tell. We are of a kind.'

Edward Gale did indeed die, without my ever having laid eyes on him, in the early hours of Friday morning. One moment he was breathing. The next, the death rattle was in his throat. The maid was tending his linen. Her scream shivered down the backbone of the house.

I cried off going to the funeral. Chloe left, driven in a chaise by Mr Briggs, and was back two hours later, black skirts rustling. There was no reception for mourners.

'I still have a business to run,' Chloe explained.

She ordered her father's room stripped and his linen incinerated. Windows were flung wide and sulphur burned. His clothes were bundled out of the back door.

Chloe was now owner of the Gale Coaching Company.

There were few affairs to settle. 'He took a long time to die,' Chloe explained. 'There was plenty of time to prepare.'

'But were *you* prepared?' I asked.

In reply she dropped a thick bunch of keys on the drawing room table. 'There, as promised.'

I gawped at the jumble of glinting brass. There were at least a dozen keys on the ring. Chloe smiled at my expression.

'Your bedroom key is there,' she said, 'and a key to the front door just as you asked. There are also keys to the stables, the kitchen, the front gate and most of the other rooms in the house.'

'I ... I don't understand.'

'Really? I thought my intention clear.'

'No. I couldn't do it. Not that.'

'Why not? You have all these fine ideas but won't act on them? Do you believe they will fail?'

'No.'

She tilted her head. 'Then here's your chance to prove yourself. That's what you really wanted all along, isn't it?'

I clamped my hands over my ears. 'Stop it. Stop trying to get inside my head. You're too clever.'

'You are just as clever, Rachel. You can glance at a carriage, tell how old it is, who made it and how far it has travelled just by the thickness of the dust on its panels. I've seen you do it, in the yard, when you are taking the evening air. There's not a gig or curricle can pass our gate without catching your eye.'

'Your men would not take orders from me.'

'They have obeyed mine long enough. Those it doesn't suit can leave. Your talent will speak louder than your gender.'

I picked up the keys. The bunch felt heavy in my small hand. Chloe smiled.

'I will discuss your duties with you tomorrow… Coachmaster.'

'But ... but what about Mr Briggs?'

Chloe shook her head. 'Tomorrow.'

On the way down to lunch I met the housekeeper, Mrs Meecher, on the stairs. She was the sort of woman I wouldn't glance twice at in the street if it wasn't for the embroidered apron and lace-trimmed mob cap perched back on her head like a bishop's cap. My belly was rumbling horribly so I tried to slip quickly past her, but she stepped in my path. So much anger simmered in her blood-red eyes I thought she was going to slap me.

'Arthur is leaving,' she spat. 'He's in the stables clearing out his chattels. He won't listen to anyone. It's your doing.'

'Arthur ... Mr Briggs?'

'Yes, Mr Briggs. Mr bloody Briggs who's worked here from the time you were in swaddling. I don't know how you got Miss Gale's ear. I don't know what you said to her or what you did.'

This was all too sudden for me. 'I never asked her to dismiss Mr Briggs.'

'Oh, he's not dismissed, child. It would've been better if he had been.' She flicked tears away with her fingertips. 'We never had any trouble before you showed your face. Best for all if you just took what the mistress has given you and left. If Mr Gale had been well you'd have been out on your ear the day after you arrived.'

'Is that your opinion or do you speak for the other servants too?'

Meecher blushed. I pushed past her.

'Going to feed your greedy little face are you?' she called after me. 'By the time your belly's full he'll be gone.'

Arthur Briggs was already heading for the gate when I stumbled into the yard. A large canvas bag was stuffed under one arm. His face was inscrutable beneath the leather brim of his hat.

'Mr Briggs,' I called, 'don't go. Chloe ... Miss Gale needs you.'

He twisted round, boot heels crunching grit. 'Needs me does she? Is that why you're carrying the keys to the front gate? To my stables? Take 'em and stick 'em up your arse.'

'That's not fair. I never asked for this. You're just being pig-headed. If you weren't so sloppy in your duties I wouldn't need to have keys.'

'That may be,' Briggs said. 'But I never hurt anyone. What money I've got was honestly earned. From the face on you, anybody'd think I'd tried to rob Miss Gale. Well, that's not so. I'd never harm a hair on her head. I respected her father. He was a good man. Wise with folk and horses alike. It's not right for a woman to run a man's business. Miss Gale should have sold it to the Trust and gone and found herself a husband instead of turning her hand to something that isn't natural for a lady, no offence to her. I don't like it. None of the lads do. They don't respect me for taking orders from a girl. I've heard them laughing. I've lost enough sleep over it. Miss Gale's heart is in the right place but she knows nothing of men or of their pride. So now she reckons to put you in charge. Well, you better start hiring milkmaids because no London man will work in this bordello.'

'I've lived in a coaching inn all my life,' I retorted. 'I can do this.'

He hoisted his bag onto his shoulder. 'We'll see.'

Kate caught me as I passed the kitchen door and beckoned me inside. 'Heard Briggsy is leaving,' she said. 'Whole house is bleating about it.'

'I never made him go,' I said defensively.

'Harry Polding will go with him,' Katy said. 'Those two were press-ganged into the navy together. Served five years on a frigate. Better 'n' brothers now.'

'Harry Polding? But I was told he drives the *Charger*.'

Katy nodded. 'That'll hurt Miss Gale more than losing Briggsy.'

'We'll get another driver.'

'Might not be so easy as you think.'

'What do you mean?'

'Not for me to say.'

'Don't go all mysterious on me, Katy. I've already had Mrs Meecher spitting poison at me on the stairs.'

Katy grinned. 'Mr Briggs and Mrs Meecher are drinking out of each other's cup, if you see what I mean.'

'Really?'

'Everybody knows about it. Her husband runs the local circulating library. I met him once. He smelled of suet and old paper. I reckon if Briggsy tupped Ellen Meecher on the library floor Mr Meecher wouldn't look up from his precious books.'

She leaned forward. 'Sometimes, when all the coaches were out, Briggsy gave the stable lads a shilling and sent them to the gin house. Then he took Mrs Meecher into the hayloft. You could hear them at it if you passed through the yard. Most times though she sneaked him through the kitchen door and into one of the upstairs rooms. She knew I wouldn't say anything.'

'Because you were scared of Mr Briggs?'

'No, it's her I'm afeard of.'

'Mrs Meecher? She struck me as a bit of a dour kipper.'

'Oh yes but she's a real mare between the sheets. Husband couldn't satisfy her I'm told. If you've soured her temper she'll take it out on me. I only have to sneeze when she's in a mood and I fetch a clip.'

'If she does that she'll join her beau sooner than she thinks.'

The *Charger* rumbled into the yard at five o' clock, windows bristling with road-weary travellers. Harry Polding climbed down from the driver's perch, brushed his jacket and cast about the yard.

'Where's Arthur?'

One of the stable lads took him aside as the passengers dispersed. The boys had been drawing lots to see who would break the news. You could cut flint on Polding's expression. He was packed and ready to leave within the half hour. Chloe tried to pay him but he knocked her money onto the cobbles.

I was standing by the trough, outwardly calm, knees quivering beneath the folds of my gown. Out of his coachman's livery, Polding looked brutal. His gaze swept over me as he stormed towards the gate. I prayed I'd never meet him in the street, that wherever he lived it was far away and I'd never see that face again.

Chloe left Polding's wages scattered on the ground and went back inside the house. Thomas stooped and gathered it up. 'He's got a wife and three sons,' he explained. 'He'll need this.'

I ran after Chloe. 'What about the *Charger?* It's due to leave for Portsmouth again tomorrow.'

Chloe paused in the hall, hand on the doorknob to her drawing room.

'That's right, Rachel. The *Charger* leaves every day at eight, as you know. It is fully booked for tomorrow, I believe.'

'But ... but who will drive it? You can't trust one of your local coachmen with a team of six, not on a journey of that length. They'll have the *Charger* in a ditch.'

Chloe shrugged. 'Well, the trip will just have to be cancelled.'

'But,' I gestured helplessly, 'if word gets about that the *Charger* failed to leave on time...'

'We shall have a great many irate passengers on our hands,' Chloe finished, 'both here and in Portsmouth. Our reputation is likely to be tarnished beyond repair and revenue lost through cancelled bookings.'

'So ... what will you do about it?'

'Actually, Rachel, I'm more interested in what *you* propose to do about it.'

We stared at each other. Chloe's eyes glittered in the half-light. Though her hand still rested on the knob she made no move to open the drawing-room door.

'I shall need a carriage,' I said after a while.

'You may take my perch phaeton if you feel able to drive it.'

'I can drive it. And I shall need ten guineas.'

Chloe laughed and pushed the door wide. 'I'll give you twenty.'

It was good to be in the countryside again, in among rolling swards of grass with scarcely a building in sight save the odd squat farmhouse. Chloe had wanted to send Thomas with me. I said I'd go alone.

I took the turnpike to get the speed and paid a small ransom in tolls for my trouble. I swore I'd not do it again even if it meant driving all night back to London and breaking the axles on this spider-web coach.

Stonehill was winding down from a busy market day and the roads out of town were packed with tinkers, farmers and traders. The lucky pulled empty carts, their pockets jingling with the day's profits. Others had plenty to curse about. A gaggle of unsold geese flapped across my path. I saw a man tip half a sack of grain into the river rather than carry it home. A straggle-haired gypsy tried to peddle the last of her battered apples from her pitch on the verge.

Although my carriage drew a few admiring glances, the final part of the journey here had proved a different kind of hell. My horse remained bent on galloping at full pitch no matter the condition of the road or who happened to be on it at the time. Twice I had sent sheep, and furious shepherd, scattering into the ditch. Not only that but every man, no matter what sort of rickety cart he was driving, seemed determined to race me. A young woman in a pretty frock on a fast carriage seemed to slap some sort of mental gauntlet across their pride. Every encounter became a mad, dusty scramble. Each attempt to pass threatened to throw me from my perch and under the wheels.

I made it into Stonehill but only just. My jaws were aching and I realised I'd been gritting my teeth for the past two hours. My hair was blown into a thicket and studded with leaves. At the posting house I paid a mole-faced stableboy a shilling to see to the horse. My fingers shook as I handed him the reins.

I enquired in the taproom, received the information I wanted and begged a sip of water from the landlord. It might be a while yet before my knees stopped wobbling. I checked the clock above the hearth. His coach would have arrived an hour ago. He might not have left for home yet. Either way he was coming back to London with me. I wouldn't take no for an answer. I'd come too far, too fast and scared myself half to death. I was ready to give him all the money. Glory, I'd offer to bed him if that would swing his mind.

Mouth set, I waddled off to my destination, following the directions the innkeeper had given me. After three hours on the thin plank that served as the phaeton's driving perch any semblance of dignity had flown off with the sparrows. Chloe Gale must have been born with a lead bottom, I reflected, rubbing my tender flesh through the material of my dress.

The Coachman's Rest was tucked up one of Stonehill's back streets and lay within a spit of the stables. Heads turned as I stumbled through the door. Eyes pricked me from the dozen tables clustered around a crackling hearth. This was a man's place. A den of spit and whores, filthy jokes and strong ale. Dented copper jugs hung from low beams. The air was thick with pipe smoke and the stone floor was awash with wet straw and swill. Under one of the benches a pair of snub-nosed terriers scrabbled over a chicken bone.

The first thing I spotted was his hat: green and

riffled with old tassels. Clutching the purse of money I pushed through the mêlée. Someone pinched my thigh. I ignored it. A hand fumbled my rump. I slapped it away. Conversation was spiked with hearty laughter. In one corner a toothless fiddler sawed out a jolly tune. In another, dice rattled across the floor followed by cries of joy and dismay. Serving girls slipped between the tables, balancing foaming pots of ale in their hands with the grace of dancers. I thought of the empty Long Room at Green Gallows and the bare, barren rooms of the Gale, and felt a pang of envy.

His face looked thinner since I last saw him. He sat by the wall gazing vacantly into his ale mug. I fumbled inside the purse, counted out five guineas and dropped them on the table in front of him.

He stared at the coins glinting on the scarred oak, then his eyes flickered over me.

'I'm a coach driver,' he said evenly. 'I don't service bored women.'

I scraped back a stool and sat opposite. 'Take another look, Gregor.'

His mouth opened, then closed, then opened again. 'Good God, it's Rachel Curtis.' His expression hardened. 'Or do you answer to Lucy these days?'

'I only ever answered to Lucy because I'd starve if I didn't and those days are behind me now. I've come a long way at a speed no human soul was sensibly meant to travel and what I need from you is a hug and a moment of your time, if you think you can spare me both.'

'I think I'll manage that, aye,' he said, leaning

over the table and embracing me. 'What brings you here? You're the last person I ever thought to see in a place like this.'

I knitted my fingers together on the table top.

'Gregor,' I said. 'How would you like to drive the *Charger*?'

He put down his tankard. A white beard of ale foamed his mouth and chin.

'I'd like that,' he said. 'And I'd like to shove a gold crown on my head and call myself King George. Where have you been, Rachel? William Davey turned the parish upside down looking for you. Everyone has been talking about it.'

I told him some of what had happened. During the bone-juddering ride from London I'd managed to snatch time to think about what I would – and wouldn't – say. He listened in silence, callused fingers stroking the pewter belly of his tankard.

'When they took Isaac away there was nothing to keep me at Green Gallows,' I explained.

'You ran away?'

'Yes.'

'From Davey?'

'Will Davey's prize prisoner has been tried and sentenced. The constable has no use for me any more.'

His eyebrows arched. 'So now you're working at the Gale Inn? For Miss Chloe Gale herself? Landed on your feet there, girl. Not still opening carriage doors I take it?'

'No.' I flicked my hair back. 'We need a driver. Someone who can take the *Charger* to Portsmouth. Someone who knows every rut and pothole in the South Road. That's why I'm here.'

'You reckon I can do it?'

'I know you can do it.'

'What happened to the usual driver? He was a miserable bugger as I recall but he knew his trade.'

'There was a conflict of loyalties.'

'I see.'

I pulled another five guineas out of the purse and added it to the pile beside Gregor's ale pot. 'The *Charger* must leave London for the south coast tomorrow. I need you at the reins.'

He leaned back on his stool. A serving wench brought him another ale. He ordered apple juice for me. The wench glanced at me, eyed the pile of coins and raised her eyebrows questioningly. Gregor waved her away.

I watched as he drank. A trickle of dark liquid slid down his chin.

'You're serious, ain't you?' he said, belching. 'You breeze in here, throw money on the table and offer me a job every driver would give the gold in his teeth for. Yet not three weeks ago your papa was jailed and your innkeeping business ruined. Tell me this ain't some fever I'm suffering from or that Molly over there hasn't served me one sour ale pot too many. How did you find me anyway?'

'It wasn't hard. Everyone knows where you like to sup.'

He took another swig of ale and thumped the tankard down on the table. 'I daresay you're right. I'd never have known it was you. Not unless you told me. You've changed, Rachel. It's not just the clothes. You've got eyes that bite.'

I sighed. 'That road has changed us all. It has cut up our lives and thrown the pieces back together in all the wrong places. Good men suffer. Bad men grow fat.'

'Words right out of a London coffee house. The Rachel I knew never talked like that.'

'Does it disturb you?'

'No.' His tone softened. 'You speak just like the lady I always said you were.' He glanced at my hands still knotted together on the table top. They were blistered from struggling with the reins. 'And you're surviving.'

'Just.' I sipped my apple juice. It was a bit sharp but good enough to sluice the dust out of my mouth. My throat was almost healed. Only a faded yellow circle still marred the skin.

'What about you, Gregor?'

'The Turnpike Trust bought our coaching company.'

'I thought your master would never sell out. That was the rumour.'

'He sold out all right. They kept upping the tolls until we couldn't afford to pay. Seems like there's a toll-booth every ten feet down that bloody road. We couldn't go back to using the South Road. It would take too long and we'd need to post the horses.' He looked at me pointedly. 'Only posting house thereabouts is Green Gallows.'

'Is there any word?'

Gregor gave a dry smile. 'Can't let go, eh? That's no wonder. The Trust have taken it. There's a notice pinned to the gatepost, so I'm told. Nothing leaves or is delivered. No guests. Your stable lad is looking after the place. I don't know what will become of him.'

'That business with the tolls is piracy.'

Gregor shrugged. 'We use the turnpike all the time now. Because the Trust owns us we're exempt from the tolls. Bloody madness ain't it? We pay through our arses one day then breeze through the pike the next. They cut my wages because the journey's quicker. You're right about the road. It's been the ruin of us all.'

'You have no family, Gregor. There's nothing to leave behind.' I nudged the pile of coins. 'Settle your affairs. Take the rest as advance pay. Come to London with me. Drive the best coach in the country. Forget the turnpike. The *Charger* could take a cart track and still be first to Portsmouth.'

'I'll need a coachman.'

'I take it Sammy hasn't decided to swim back to Africa?'

Gregor chuckled. 'No, he has not. He might cause a stir among your genteel passengers though.'

'If anyone doesn't like it they can get out and walk. Now are you coming to London?'

Gregor pushed his tankard aside. 'How did you get here? A hired gig?'

'Miss Gale let me use her perch phaeton.'

He coughed and wiped his lips with a soiled napkin. 'Ye gods, lass, that's not a carriage. It's a coffin on wheels. Where is the thing? Not outside surely?'

'It's at the posting house. I paid a boy to look after it.'

'Well, you can sit inside for the trip back and let me risk my neck. I'll meet you at the posting house in an hour. And I'll have Sammy with me.'

Chloe got a surprise when Gregor drove the phaeton into the yard. She got a bigger one when she saw Sammy. I introduced them both, grimacing as pins and needles shot up both legs. A phaeton's cabin wasn't much bigger than an ale barrel. I'd nearly cracked both knees trying to get comfortable on the journey back with Sammy crammed in beside me. With the horse watered and rested, Gregor's driving style had proved lively. I felt no safer inside the carriage than I had on top of it.

Chloe took me aside. 'Did you use the whole purse?' she asked.

'Yes,' I lied. 'Gregor is worth it.'

'He'll need to be, otherwise your next task will be to soothe my banker's nerves.' She stared at Sammy. 'Who is that big dark fellow?'

'Sammy. Gregor's coachman.'

A frown furrowed her brow. 'Do we need him?'

'If you don't like my choice, Chloe, I'll send him back. And I'll go with him.'

She shook her head. 'I just hope you have not worn out my horse.'

'He's tired but had a good run even with the three of us to haul. It'll take more than a gallop to Stonehill and back to finish that one. He's a fine beast, Chloe. We had some good horses at Green Gallows but this one has the measure of them all.'

Chloe glanced over at the gelding. Thomas was already unhitching him. His flanks were coated in white foam but his eyes were bright and his ears pricked up. She was less taken with the state of her precious phaeton. A flurry of rain had found us just outside the city and spat mud all over the walnut panels. I scarcely had the pins out of my bonnet before she sent another stableboy, bucket and mop in hand, to swab it down.

Gregor and Sammy were billeted inside the inn. Gregor had Briggs's old room. Mrs Meecher just about choked when she heard that one. She screamed when she saw Sammy and swore she'd burn the house down rather than let a heathen into it. Sammy told her, in perfect English, that he was a practising Methodist. Meecher locked herself in her room for the rest of the day, much to Kate's delight, and didn't emerge until supper. The African stayed.

Now all we needed was a new horsemaster, and I had an idea about that too.

'His name is Judd Button,' I told Chloe after we'd supped. 'His wife is Sally. You'll not find a better cook or housekeeper.'

Chloe wiped her lips with a napkin. 'I'll send for them tomorrow. Are you sure they'll come?'

I nodded. 'They'll come.'

Judd and Sally Button stood in the middle of the sunlit yard, a thin canvas bag at their feet. After a few discreet enquires, Chloe had hired a chaise and driver to fetch them. 'You've had enough adventures for one week,' she told me. I wondered if it was really because she didn't want me to get her phaeton dirty again, but didn't press it. Gregor had already left on the *Charger* with Sammy beside him. Both men slipped easily into their new jobs and Chloe was clearly impressed. None of the passengers had looked twice at Sammy. 'Most of them have black houseboys or their fathers kept black slaves,' she explained, but I didn't tell Sammy that.

Judd's shirt flapped around his shoulders like a piece of loose sailcloth. Patched breeches hung like sacks on his legs. Everything they owned was carried in that square of canvas bound with rope.

'We sold everything else,' he said.

Sally looked more or less like Sally always did except that her dress was more ragged around the hem, and the crow's feet spreading out from her eyes were etched a little deeper. She greeted me with a hug and it was like embracing a hat-stand. Her kiss was paper-dry against my cheek.

I quickly had them stuffed to the gills on hot food then moved into a room on the ground floor with a window overlooking the yard. When they were settled, Chloe interviewed them separately in her drawing room.

She told me about it later over a glass of canary. Judd had been working as a farmhand on a small-holding owned by a friend of a distant cousin. He spent his days in the fields while Sally scrubbed out the kitchen, cleaned hearths and gutted chickens. Because the farmer was poor and the job given as a favour, Judd and Sally were paid half what the other hands received and had to sleep in the attic.

'I've learned to like potatoes,' Judd said grimly. 'Potatoes and sour corn.'

No stable or estate would employ Judd. They said it was his age. But news about Green Gallows had travelled. His nearest close relatives lived in York. He'd sent word to see if they would take him but had received no reply. A week after leaving

Green Gallows, Colly Bruce had paid a visit to the smallholding – a few boulder-ridden acres ten miles outside Stonehill. Colly had offered Judd the job of stable-hand at the Coach and Horses Inn.

''Tain't as grand as you're used to,' Colly said, 'but you'll get the smell of horseshit in your nose again. That's what you want, ain't it? As for that scrawny stick you're wed to, she can work in the kitchen. The scullery maid's sprained her ankle and Cook needs someone to fetch and carry. Think your doxy can heft a sack of flour?'

Colly had waited to see what Judd would do. Judd did nothing. Colly had laughed.

'I didn't take his bloody job,' Judd told Chloe. 'He didn't want me because I was good with horses. He wanted Sal and me because we'd worked at Green Gallows.'

I saw Judd afterwards in the servants' parlour. Neither he nor Sally would look me in the face. 'You're still too much like her,' Judd said. 'You're trying not to be, but it's no use. Isaac trained his little pup well.'

'Judd that's not kind.'

'I'll work for your new friend,' he said, 'because Sally deserves better than what she's got right now. Have you bought Matthew too?'

'He's still at Green Gallows as far as I know.'

'Always said he'd be there for life,' Judd muttered. 'He's a good coach boy but he's got fluff in his head. We both know it. So does he.'

Judd left for the stables. Sally hung back. 'We don't need your charity,' she said. 'I told Judd that, but he won't listen. He'll snatch whatever scraps anyone cares to throw him. We were little better than beggars at that farm. Lads a quarter of his age earned more than he did. What pride we had was left on the doorstep of your father's inn. I don't doubt you mean well and Judd will work hard. So will I. But inside he'll shrivel up with shame.'

'I asked Miss Gale to hire you both because we needed a horsemaster and a good cook. This isn't charity. You'll be paid a fair wage. I said you were the best and Miss Gale believed it. I hope neither of you plan to make a liar out of me.'

Sally shook her head. 'He won't go back to the farm for my sake. He wants me to eat well and sleep in a proper bedchamber, not a hayloft. If I say anything he'll just remind me of the bugs and the rat bites. But there's times when I think that's no worse than what we endured in the last few months at Green Gallows. Those are things you don't forget either.'

'Up, get up, Rachel. Your troopers await.'

The curtains were pulled wide. I sat up, blinking in the light. Sleep gritted my eyes.

'Troopers?'

'In the courtyard.' Chloe opened the wardrobe door, plucked out a gown and tossed it onto a chair. 'Don't wait for the maid. I will help you dress.'

'I need to wash.'

'You can wash later. Don't be so vain.' She scooped up the quilt and bundled it down to the bottom of the bed. Air whispered across my bare feet. She hustled me out of my warm cocoon, brushed the tugs from my hair in hurried strokes then dropped the dress over my head.

'Shoes now. Any pair will do. No stockings, it's mild out. You'll only take them off again later. Come, Rachel, don't be fussy.'

Green slippers, a blue dress, a straw bonnet pinned awkwardly to my abused hair. What a sight. I tried to hang back but Chloe was already pushing me out of the door. 'You're not the only one who's been making plans,' she said.

They were lined up in the courtyard. The coaching staff. All as sharp as pins in white wigs, green velvet jackets embroidered with gold, satin breeches and cream hose. Gregor and Sammy sported cravats which would be the envy of the keenest city dandy.

'There,' Chloe declared. 'All in bright new livery. Are they not magnificent?'

I walked along the line. I walked back.

'No good,' I said, shaking my head. 'Send the clothes back.'

Chloe looked as if I had slapped her. 'What?'

'Look at them,' I gestured, 'they are like the palace footmen in one of my sister's picture books. You can't send them out to work like this. In hot weather they'll cook and winter will have them blue with cold. This material,' I plucked a sleeve of the nearest jacket, 'too thin, too fine. These men are not serving at table. Coachmen have to live in their clothes, sometimes for days at a time. Garments need to be hardy. Vanity like this could kill.'

'I wanted them to look smart. I thought you would approve.'

'Smart, yes, but no need to turn them into fops. The first time Sammy there bends to lift a trunk he'll split his breeches. Have your uniforms, but of cotton and wool. They won't look so grubby, even after a long journey, and your driver will be grateful for it once the wind starts howling.'

Chloe was nearly in tears. 'I cannot send them back. They have already been paid for. The expense…'

I started across the yard.

'Where are you going?'

'If you won't listen I'm going back to bed.'

That afternoon the clothes were returned to the tailor. After some grumbling he refunded half the purchase price. Chloe sat in the drawing room and stared at the litter of coins glinting on the coffee table. 'That exercise has lightened my purse by forty guineas.'

'Money not squandered if you've learned something,' I pointed out.

'You are a cruel teacher, Rachel.'

'And you can be an awkward pupil.'

Chloe put down her teacup. 'What kind of life did you lead at that Green Gallows place?'

I picked at my sleeve. 'I was happy enough. The new road killed that.'

'That is hardly my fault.'

'No. I blame greed. I blame myself because I saw things rot before my eyes and could do nothing about it. I thought Lucy was the strong one but she let herself get trapped, and sometimes I hate her for that. Oh, I don't know. I thought I would be safe here. But I fear that road, and all the vermin it attracts, will push into my life again.'

'I've had my share of misery too.'

'Misery? I saw my sister buried and my mother

drowned. She was as close as you are now, lying belly up in a stagnant pond. How badly she must have wanted to die to kill herself like that.'

I banged the top of her writing desk with my fist. Inkpots jumped. A quill leapt from its holder and fluttered onto the floor. 'I never cried, never shed a tear for either of them. What kind of heartless witch does that make me?'

The room blurred. I found it hard to breathe. I slid off the chair, knocking over the neat piles of money. Coins rolled past my head as I struck the carpet. Papers feathered onto the floor.

Chloe knelt beside me. I was bawling like a cuffed two-year-old. Frantic footsteps thumped up the stairs. The door swung inwards. Mrs Meecher stood on the threshold, staring slack-jawed at the mess.

'Miss Gale...'

'Leave it for now,' Chloe said. 'Just go.'

Mrs Meecher glanced at me. She closed the door. I heard her big feet tramp back downstairs.

'I was never worth very much,' I sniffled. 'Not until Lucy died.'

Chloe helped me sit up. 'You have more value than you realise.'

We stayed like that for a few minutes, me on the floor with my back propped against her writing desk and her kneeling and holding my hand. Neither of us said anything. She gave me her kerchief to wipe my face and when I thought I could stand again she helped me up. I suppose I was tired. I mumbled thanks and an apology but Chloe just shook her head and gathered the spilled papers. I started picking up the coins.

Some had rolled under the furniture. Winkling them out gave me a chance to calm down. Afterwards I slipped upstairs with a hot posset and a newspaper. This time whenever I asked for one it arrived without fuss. The *Daily Register*. Thomas seemed disappointed when I told him there were no more errands.

Snuggling under the covers, I spread the paper out on the bed. There, by candlelight, with dogs barking in the street and a cooling breeze wafting through the curtains, I read that Jeremiah Cathcart would hang at the end of the week.

Chapter Sixteen

I stood in the dirt and rat droppings of Newgate. Like everyone else I'd paid sixpence to get in. To view the hopeless, the condemned. My fellow ghouls had gone off to view livelier fare – a mass poisoner, a girl not yet fifteen who had laced her family's wine with strychnine and watched, smiling, as they died at the supper table.

The turnkey touted the attractions of his jail like some trinket seller at the fair. 'Come and see Molly Ross. She's in this very jail, good people. The angel-faced killer. And here, John Allen the highwayman, slit the throats of a dozen coachmen in a three-year reign of terror. Hurry along now. The gallows grow impatient for fresh necks. See 'em before they're stretched. Hurry!'

I had trouble finding the cell. There were so

many, some packed with moaning bundles of grey rags. Skinny arms thrust out between the rusting bars. Fingers plucked my dress.

'Mercy, good lady. A little Christian mercy. Some food, or perhaps a drop o' gin…'

'I'm innocent, miss. 'Tis God's truth. Was my friend what killed him.'

'Miss, miss, I'm a rich man. Hire me a lawyer. Get me out of here and half my fortune is yours...'

I snatched my gown away and wished I'd brought some wax to plug my ears. The din was never-ending. A man banged his head against the bars, a litany of curses falling from his blistered lips. Another squatted in a corner, whimpering. Yet another urinated openly against the wall. People grew sick and vomited on the floor. Too many mouths ringed with dried blood. Too many sunken eyes, festering sores, matted beards and shaggy, dishevelled hair. I could taste the filth. I'd be lucky to get out of here without lice.

I struggled to remember the directions the turnkey had given me. 'Don't wander,' he'd warned. 'Don't go too near the cells. Some of these scum aren't against grabbing a pretty lady and giving them a good feel. Nothing to lose, y'see, and why not have a little touch of heaven when your soul is bound for hell?'

'How can you keep men and women in such a hole?' I'd asked. 'I wouldn't treat a dog like this.'

The turnkey's easy smile never wavered. 'If them what had been murdered and thieved against were here I daresay they'd give you reason enough. If you don't like the stink, douse a handkerchief with lavender and press it across your face.'

'How can you bear it?'

'Me? Twenty years I've worked the jails. I don't smell nothing.' He gestured. 'The man you want is down that way. Now I'll have that shilling you promised and will be back in ten minutes, no more.'

There were other cells, no bigger than cupboards, rank with damp and shit. I stopped at what I thought was the right place. The lantern flickering on the wall behind me barely lit the passage. In the cell a narrow window set high in the stonework bled a trickle of daylight onto the cold flagstones.

I edged closer. Nothing much to see. A mattress sewn together out of strips of sacking hugged one wall. The coarse material was badly stained and had burst in places, leaking straw onto the stone floor. A wooden bucket, filled with God knew what, sat in one corner. In the dark, in the stink, I could hear the scratching of rats.

Something stirred in the corner beside the mattress. A figure stood up and clutched the wall. A ragged blanket fell from its shoulders and tumbled onto the floor. It took an awkward step towards me. Another. I sensed eyes watching me. A hand lifting, reaching out. A word.

A name.

'Lucy…'

I could have fled. For a second I wanted to. A rush of guilt hit me like a fist in the belly. Instead I snatched the nearest lantern and hung it from a hook beside the door. Jeremiah's face was gaunt in the sour light. Not much had changed in the last month. Only a slight looseness of his once busy limbs betrayed the ravages of this shivering, hungry existence. Coarse whiskers sooted his chin. The same clothes he'd worn in court were filthy now and coming apart at the seams. His eyes were coals dipped in blood. They hardly blinked in the guttering light from the lantern.

I had thought long and hard about the deception I had played on him, about the lies I might still tell given the chance. But I hadn't come here for that. Neither was I looking for forgiveness or redemption. I suppose I just wanted him to understand.

'Take a look at me, Jeremiah,' I said. 'Lucy is dead. You have to let her go. You have to let me go.'

His tired eyes appraised me, soaking up my gown, my face. His fingers slipped between the grime encrusted bars. I stepped back.

'It was either me or you,' I continued. 'You've given me back life but I don't want it if it can't be my own. Under this dye my hair is black, not fair. I'm taller than Lucy. Isaac starved me into her dresses, but my face is still rounder, my nose full where hers was pert.' I rubbed my temple. 'Even this scar is fresh, and it's not quite in the right place. A botched job. See me for who I am.'

His voice was the rasp of a hawse against wood. 'I see well enough.'

I pressed forward. 'It's cold in here. The damp clutches your lungs. I hear it's two days before a new prisoner can get a proper sleep. Two days and two long nights shivering and jumping like a frightened rabbit at every sound. You must feel every flea bite, eat rancid scraps you would have choked on a week before.'

'I've had harder nights on the road, before I came to work for your papa.'

'Look at you. Our stables at Green Gallows were better kept than this hole. Glory, if you'd merely confessed to stealing Sutcliffe's pocket watch you'd spend your time in the day cell with the other common thieves.'

I edged back into the pool of light. 'Were you really so easily fooled, Jeremiah? Was Rachel Curtis so forgettable, your head so full of Lucy, that you could fall for such a trick?'

''Tweren't no court that sentenced me,' Jeremiah's voice was thick. 'This is your punishment, your judgement, 'cause I dared love your sister instead of you. So why don't you go and have the whole world slung into jail, 'cause everyone who met Lucy loved her. Now I've got to die but it don't matter none. I don't want to live without Lucy anyhow. But there's one thing I'll give thanks for. You killed the bastard that brought her to ruin. I saw you with my own eyes. I've always wanted to get 'em, the gentry I mean, for what they did to my da. To my family. But a coward is what I am. All talk and bluster. Lord God forgive me but I would've bent over and kissed my own arse had one of them ordered me to. When I saw you standing in the woods over his dead body I wished it was me holding that branch, me with his blood coating my hands. I never confessed to killing him to save your neck. I did it for myself.'

'They are going to hang you.'

He grinned, teeth sickly yellow in the poor light. 'Their gibbet shan't have me. I'll escape 'em.'

I nodded. He knew I'd understand. He would never escape these walls, but he could use his teeth to open veins in his wrists. More courage, then, than he'd given himself credit for.

'I'll be with her at last,' he said.

'Yes,' I agreed. 'You will be with her at last.'

He coughed. His whole body shivered.

'I'm thirsty. Can you get me some water? The bastard who runs this sty won't bring more until dusk.'

He passed me a wooden cup. I slipped away from his cell and found a water barrel at the end of the passage. I had to skim a layer of dust from the surface before dipping the vessel in. Halfway back I paused in a shadowed alcove and took the laudanum bottle out of my reticule. I twisted the stopper off and poured the entire contents into the cup. The water was brown and smelled like swill. He wouldn't notice what I'd done.

I passed the cup through the bars. Our fingers touched.

'Thank you,' he whispered.

He drank long and deeply. *Rest well*, I thought. *Forgive me. But you will sleep now. No pain. No more pain.*

Outside, a stiff wind had kicked up. The prison seemed to groan on its foundations. I clutched my bonnet and ran for the carriage waiting beyond the gate. Chloe knew where I'd gone. I'd told her before I'd left.

'I just want to see him, that's all,' I lied.

She'd smiled and said: 'I understand,' and hugged me. She hired a chaise and driver to take me because she did not want the staff to know. I'd slipped out of the gate on pretence of an errand and picked up the chaise outside the park. The driver set the horse off at a trot as soon as I was inside. On our return I had him drop me off at the park gates from where I hired a chair back to the Gale. Wind whistled between the buildings like air through a set of buck teeth. The first real shiver of autumn brought goosebumps out on my flesh.

With nightfall it would be colder still in Newgate. I wondered if Lucy's name, whispered in a dream, would be on Jeremiah's lips when his heart stopped.

I halted the chair just around the corner from our stable yard and paid off the bearers. The sun was weak and falling towards the rooftops. I dashed the few yards to the Gale, clinging to my bonnet. I had developed a talent for scuttling unseen across the yard. By the time I clambered upstairs and into my bedchamber my hands and feet were numb. My mind was numb too; and my heart.

I lit a candle and sat on the edge of the bed for an hour, watching the wax burn to a stub. The windows rattled in their frames. Ghostly voices boomed down the chimney. A maid came to light the fire. It wouldn't catch. Smoke billowed out of the hearth with every rogue gust of wind. I sent her away, scooped the coverlet off the bed and wrapped it around my shoulders.

There would be no funeral. Just a sack to stitch him up in and a pit like an open sore in the ground. He would be tossed in along with thieves and paupers, and have quicklime shovelled on top. Perhaps a word or two from a bored parson, a nod from the gravediggers before they hoisted their shovels and started filling in the hole.

I knew about death and burials because I grew

up beside the lykeway with an old gibbet creaking outside my front door. Coaches brought the curious wanting to know some of the history of Green Gallows. Isaac told them stories to make them shiver, to increase their appetite for port and a warm, safe bed. Tales of crime and punishment in both village and city until I, serving in the taproom and hearing every word, had my night populated with phantoms. How big my room suddenly became, the walls receding into darkness with who-knew-what lurking in the corners. Lying wide-eyed, face painted orange in the dying light from the fire and the coverlet drawn up to my nose, hearing the damned howl. Men hung in chains, men beheaded, disembowelled with red-hot pokers or garrotted. And behind it all the shadow of the plague, the terrible plague of more than a century ago. The death cart lumbering slowly down the lane, a procession of wailing mourners in tow.

Yes, I knew.

God might damn me but I saved Jeremiah from a horrible, choking death in front of a baying mob. I spared him the ordeal of squatting in a filthy cell, waiting as the blood ebbed out of his torn veins. I spared him the terrible shame of suicide. The burial in unconsecrated ground.

I stared into the mirror and Lucy gazed back. I ripped off the wig in a shower of pins. I soaked a strip of lace in the washbasin and scrubbed every trace of rouge from my face. Gold hair hung in lank threads either side of my head. Dark roots clung to the crown. It was like catching a glimpse of myself, the real me, behind some sort of badly done painting. And more than anything I wanted *me* back.

My belly ached. I hadn't eaten since breakfast. The clock on the mantel put the hour at a little past seven. I patted some life back into my raw cheeks and, without troubling to change, went downstairs to supper.

Chloe was already seated when I walked into the dining room. She eyed me over a steaming bowl of broth and gestured to Mrs Meecher.

'Set another place.'

I waited until the cutlery had been laid out then took my seat. Chloe said nothing as soup was ladled into my plate. Meecher withdrew and we were alone.

'I'm glad you decided to sup with me,' Chloe said at last.

'I'm hungry.'

'I could've had something sent to your room.'

I shook my head. 'I need company.'

Chloe sipped water out of a long-stemmed glass. 'A successful trip?'

'It was horrible.'

I stared at my broth. Chloe leaned over the table and poured me some water. 'Would you prefer something stronger? Papa didn't just keep books in his study.'

'No. I want my wits about me.'

'Then eat. You can't have had anything all day. The only well-fed things at Newgate are the rats.'

I picked up the spoon, dipped it into the soup and sipped the hot liquid. Warmth spread across my tongue. I gulped down the bowl. Chloe offered a plate.

'Beef pie,' she said. 'That woman you engaged to help Kate in the kitchen cooked it. It is really quite delicious.'

I cut myself a huge slab and scoffed it down. Better. I pushed away the empty plate and leaned back in the chair.

'What have you done to your face?' Chloe said. 'It looks sore.'

'Scrubbed it. I want a bath. I want to wash the stink of that place off my skin.'

'Very well. I will send Mrs Meecher up with the hip bath. Kate will bring hot water from the kitchen.'

She leaned forward. 'Rachel…'

'Please don't ask me, Chloe, whatever you do. Not tonight.'

She nodded and patted my hand. 'You must talk about it some time,' she said. 'It would be wrong to let it fester. You've enough wounds.'

When Mrs Meecher came to clear the plates away, Chloe gave instructions for my bath. The look the housekeeper gave me was priceless. It took her and Kate ten minutes to haul the tub up the stairs and by the time they'd wiggled it through the door of my bedchamber both women were puffing like old dray horses.

I was expecting something little bigger than an old tin bucket and so was delighted with the porcelain bath squatting in the middle of my rug. It could almost swallow me whole. Kate wanted to stay and undress me but I waved her away. I was no lady and I didn't need a maid.

Kate hauled pail after steaming pail of water up from the kitchen. The bath took an age to fill.

Finally she sprinkled in some rose petals and a drop of Chloe's scent.

I threw off my clothes and stepped in. The water slid over my body like warm oil. I settled myself and leaned back against the smooth porcelain. Ghostly wisps slithered upwards and caressed my face. I felt as though a thousand gentle hands were soothing the aches out of my muscles.

After a few minutes of bliss I opened one eye and glanced at Kate. She was laying out towels on the end of the bed. Folding and refolding. Arranging them perfectly then picking them up and doing it again. Her face was glum.

I sighed and slid deeper into the water. 'What ails you, Kate?' I said sleepily.

The rustling of towels stopped. 'That woman you brought in…'

'Sally.'

'That woman. She keeps telling me how to do things. In my own kitchen. This is right. That's wrong. Pour in more milk. Use less butter. I can't lift a spoon without her having something to say about it.'

'Sally Button has been a cook longer than you've been alive, Kate. Yes, it's your kitchen, but she's giving advice, not orders.'

'I know, but she wants to do all the cooking.'

'Why not let her then? I thought you hated it.'

Kate shrugged. 'But that ain't the point.'

I smiled, an easy thing to do in this deliciously warm bath. The irony was not lost on me. I wouldn't tell Chloe about my problems, but here I was listening to Kate's. Isaac would have laughed. 'All talk and no listen,' he once said of me. Before I could be a coachmaster it seemed I had to become a politician.

'Sally was cook at the inn where I used to live,' I explained. 'Some people, the landlord included, thought her the best in the county. She's had to swallow a lot of pride these past few weeks. I can't begin to tell you how much, and she's still hurting. Try to turn the other cheek when she orders you about. Leave her with the flour and the eggs. Let her use what pots and pans she wants. It's like binding a wound. Her cooking is all she has. She knows it's really your kitchen. She knows because I told her.'

Kate's face brightened. 'You did?'

'Yes. She thinks she's helping. Give her another week and she'll mellow. Both her and her husband have lived in the country all their lives. The city must be a big and frightening place for them. London scared me when I first saw it. I thought all these buildings must spread to the end of the world and I'd never see another field or piece of woodland.'

Kate picked up one of the towels and scrunched it between her fingers. 'I ought not to be talking to you like this. It's not my place.'

'You can talk to me any way you please. At Green Gallows Inn I fetched and carried just the same as you. Sally scolded me and clipped my ear more often than I care to mention, and I felt Judd's boot on my bottom more than once.'

Kate's hand flew to her mouth and she stifled a giggle. 'I think it's good what you're doing, looking after Miss Chloe like that.'

'You've got that wrong. Miss Gale is the one

looking after me.'

'I know what I said.'

I twisted in the bath to get a better look at her. She had put down the towel. Her eyes were bright.

'What makes you think these things, Kate?'

'I can't cook,' she said, 'but I'm not stupid, and I've got eyes. Her papa was so hard on her. He once had Miss Chloe on her knees in the stables, scrubbing the stalls in front of all the lads. Had her doing it in her best ball gown. I've seen her in tears trying to please Mr Gale, and him asking the impossible all the time. She can't run anything, not by herself. She's put you in charge so you can be kind to her. That's what she wants. Someone who's nice. She didn't have any real friends. Her papa never seemed to approve of anyone. I think he was the only man she ever danced with. They went everywhere together, so my mam told me. No suitor ever dared call. She needed someone to take his place once he'd gone.'

Kate shook her head. 'I had to go in there once. To Mr Gale's room. He was puking into a pot on the floor by the bed, like his whole gizzards were about to fall out. In between he snatched breaths like a drowning man might grab for twigs dipping into the river. She wants folks to think her papa was dying quietly and with dignity but we knew differently. She'll get it too. It's killed all her family. Then what's to become of us? That'll be for you to decide.'

'I ... I can't do that.'

'Not true,' said Kate. 'You're hard too. As hard as the cobbles in that yard. I saw it in your face the day you arrived.'

Next day Chloe asked me into her drawing room. I had slept badly and my eyes were sore. Chloe poured me a cup of tea and beckoned me to her writing desk. I stared at the pile of ledgers perched on the end. She caught my expression and chuckled.

'You keep the coaches running and I'll count the pennies. This is what I wanted to show you.'

Her plans for expanding local services. Six pages covered in neat handwriting. Soon we were both chattering away like a pair of milkmaids.

'Competition will remain tight,' Chloe pointed out. 'This industry is expanding so rapidly that every merchant and cart owner is setting up in business. But I have my name to trade on and more experience than most. Many of these routes will only require a two-horse team with no postings. Our current local services have turned in a modest profit but up until now we have relied on the *Charger*. It's very exclusivity makes it popular. People often ride on it for the very sake of doing so. It is a real mark on one's social card to go to a ball or tea party and say, "Oh yes, we journeyed on the *Charger* recently. You haven't? Oh, what a shame!"'

We glanced at one another and burst out laughing. 'It's true,' Chloe said. 'Riding on the *Charger* has little to do with travelling and everything to do with being seen. People often book passage, spend the night at the coast then return the following day. We have another establishment near the harbour. Not as grand as the Gale, but fashionable and well patronised by social climbers.

The *Charger* picks up and drops off there, and local services in the south make regular use of it. In London, as you rightly said, buildings jostle one another for every scrap of land. But outside the city there is a chance to grow.' She sipped her tea. 'Perhaps you would consider finding someone to manage it for me?'

'Surely you already have a manager?'

'Mr Grindle, the landlord, is an ale barrel on legs. And he's getting old. He did some favour for Papa years ago and that's why he was given the job. It wouldn't cost much to pension him off.'

'I'll give it some thought.'

She nodded. 'But you can see why the new turnpike will make little difference to our business. There will always be a clamour for tickets, God willing. And it all happened purely by accident.'

'By accident?'

'Yes, all because of one passenger. His name was Lord Wallcott, but we all called him Lord Muck. He travelled on the *Charger* each week and used every free moment to criticise and complain. Everything had to be perfect. He'd insist we swab down the carriage until it gleamed like a dandy's walking stick. Sometimes passengers were forced to wait. On rainy days, when the road turned into a pig's rooting patch, this became a real problem. Yet none of his peers dared go against him. He had a reputation as a gambler. Many men of note were in debt to him.

'One morning someone spilled some pastry crumbs on the floor. Have you ever seen an over-boiled kettle about to pop its lid? That was Lord Muck. I thought he'd drag the hapless passenger down the steps and heave him into the nearest gutter. He would not go anywhere until that carpet was clean, but every time he brushed out the crumbs the man with the pastry – a well-to-do farmer and therefore beneath Lord Muck's contempt – made a big show of dropping some more. It became a duel of wills. "My patience shall last longer than your pastry, sir," Lord Muck declared. "That may be, sir," the farmer replied, "but I have yet a mutton flap and a pork pie to work through."

'With that he laid aside his food, took out his snuffbox, helped himself to a generous pinch and promptly sneezed half of it over the upholstery. They'd have happily sat there until sunset if the driver hadn't fetched Papa. "The man is a scourge," Papa was told. "What is to be done about him? The *Charger* is already an hour late."

'Papa warned Lord Muck that if the *Charger* was delayed any further he would have to meet the cost of the other passengers' tickets. Lord Muck called Papa a glorified stableboy and told him to go shovel shit. Papa ripped up his ticket and had Arthur Briggs throw him into the street. He was banned from using the *Charger* and never recovered face. Every enemy, every rival of this man – and there were plenty – booked passage with us just to rub his nose in it. He became such a laughing stock, in fact, that he abandoned all his interests and left London for good. Word got about, the *Charger* became notorious and our fortunes were sealed. On a whim of human nature.'

We laughed some more and finished the tea. The tiredness had left my bones. Chloe talked some more about her plans. She was all for fitting out the rooms and opening them to guests as I had suggested.

'Where will you get the money?'

'The bank will lend it at a good rate of interest.'

'No. The Trust will get their claws into the Gale the same as they did with Green Gallows.'

'Don't be foolish. Mr Whittaker's bank is as solid as a rock.'

'Even a rock can be shattered with enough force. Raise the money some other way. Don't go into debt.'

Chloe took less than a minute to decide. Off to auction would go Edward Gale's most precious paintings. Chloe expected they would fetch a tidy sum, though she drew the line at selling his books. 'There are some treasures you just shouldn't let go,' she explained. 'I don't mind auctioning the pictures. It's what he would have done.'

When we had finished going over her plans, Chloe took something out of the desk drawer and handed it to me. A riding crop. A hickory shaft with a pearl-studded handle at one end and a small leather strap at the other. An ornament. A lady's toy. I doubted it could flick a gnat from a horse's ear.

'My mother's,' Chloe explained. 'She fancied herself a horsewoman, though she never went anywhere at more than walking pace and with a groom holding the reins.'

'What am I to do with it? 'Tis a lovely trinket, true, but of little use for serious riding.'

'Carry it as a mark of your authority.'

'I'm not hitting anyone with this.'

'I don't expect you to. Regard it as a badge of

office. It serves no purpose mouldering away at the back of a drawer.'

I gestured helplessly. 'Chloe, I'm just an innkeeper's daughter. I opened coach doors, fetched and carried with the servants, served ale in the taproom. Isaac thought he was as good as the gentry and suffered all his life because of it. I'm not getting ideas above my station. You're giving them to me. You're giving me authority the way Isaac gave me airs and graces because he thought I could be someone like you. But it won't work. It can't work. You're a different breed to me. You can't put a dray horse between carriage shafts and expect him to run like a thoroughbred.'

Chloe flicked a hand. 'I am not a lady either, Rachel. Oh, I am wealthy enough and Papa's money bought such breeding as was up for sale. But we were a family of cart-makers. Beneath the lace were splinters in our hands and dirt beneath our fingernails. The very best of society booked passage in our coaches months in advance, but our dinner table remained deserted and our invitations went unanswered. We serviced these people, we did not sup with them. Even their footmen looked down their noses at us.'

She shook her head. 'I can carry bags, clean up after a horse, open a carriage door. I have done it in the past and if the need arises I will do it again. But for now you will carry this. You are where I want you to be. In charge.'

Despite what Chloe had said, I felt a fool strutting about the yard with that crop tucked under my arm, but I knew she was watching me from her drawing-room window.

'Hey,' called a voice. 'What are you going to do with that, scratch your arse?'

Frank Hammond, an ostler and one of Briggs's dice monkeys. He bellowed with laughter. My fingers tightened around the crop. I imagined belting him across his fat mouth. He must have guessed my thoughts because he laughed all the harder.

I walked over to him. Hammond was lounging on an upturned water butt by the stable wall. He packed a wad of tobacco into a clay pipe and took his time over lighting it. Straw bales lay higgledy-piggledy on the cobbles. He rested his foot on one.

'Mr Hammond.'

He sucked on the pipe, tilted his head back and sent a blue ghost of acrid smoke billowing across the yard.

'That's my name. Don't go wearing it out.'

'Shouldn't you be getting these bales into the loft?'

He grinned. Smoke leaked from between the gaps in his teeth. 'In my own time.'

I glanced at the sky. Thick. Leaden. 'It might rain. The bales could be ruined.'

Hammond took another drag on his pipe.

'Mr Hammond, the straw...'

'The straw will stay where it is until I'm ready to shift it.'

'Miss Gale put me in charge.'

'Aww, go and tup yourself, you little country udder sucker. I'll not do what you say. Nor will anyone else. Miss Gale can't dismiss us all.'

But Miss Gale could.

She asked me at lunch why I was so miserable

and I blurted it all out. Hammond was sent packing from the yard within the hour. He told Chloe she was a harlot's bastard who'd slept with her father. Chloe told him not to expect a reference. His face was black when he stormed through the gates. Now I was a tittle-tattle and no one would speak to me.

'This is getting stupid,' I complained to Chloe. 'People are frightened to sneeze in case it costs them their job. Surely your papa, God rest him, was never this hard?'

'People didn't laugh at my father. Some worked for him a long time. They don't like change. But without it we can go nowhere. Whatever people might say about me I'm clever enough to know that.'

The coaching staff got their replacement uniforms. They paraded up and down the yard, bowing and laughing, and making elaborate gestures with their hands like city gentlemen. A suit for summer and one for winter, with a special overcoat to keep the rain out. Not as fancy as their last ill-found attempt at clothing, but the material was cut well enough and hardy. Chloe had reason to feel pleased.

For a while it seemed as if our little dream might work. Bookings for the *Charger* remained healthy. The waiting list grew. Word had it that some of the regular passengers were making wagers on who could reach the south coast first, one of the turnpike stagecoaches or Gregor McBain and his enormous darkie. I never knew one of our people to be out of pocket as a result of such a bet. Gregor's reputation soared.

Judd meanwhile worked like a devil. He had that yard turned upside down by the end of the week. At first the stable lads laughed at this country bumpkin in canvas breeches. Judd cuffed ears, kicked arses and swore so much and so loudly Chloe had to shut her drawing-room window. Soon everyone was calling him 'Mr Button'. The stables and yard became an ants' nest of activity. They were his lads, his team. Hands that once fumbled with harnesses had horses ready between the carriage shafts in a twinkling. There were no more gatherings beside the gate, no more ribald jokes or pipe smoke fouling the morning air.

He came to Miss Gale, cap in hand, to ask if they might each be paid an extra fourpence a week. She gave him the money. But she asked me first. Asked me in front of Judd. When I said yes, Judd nodded at her and put his cap back on. He turned and made to leave. Chloe called him back. She sat behind her walnut writing desk and waited until he took his cap back off and acknowledged me too. Then she let him go.

'Why did you make him do that?' I demanded. 'He has never done that to me in his life before. If we were at Green Gallows he would die of shame.'

'We are not at Green Gallows. He needs to know his place.'

'Judd is horsemaster, as agreed.'

She regarded me from under arched eyebrows. 'You still need to learn your place too.'

I bit my lower lip. 'What if I tell you all the stable doors need repainting?'

'The job will be done within the day.'

'What if I'm not as clever you want me to be?'

Chloe leaned forward in her chair. 'Let me ask you a question, Rachel. What keeps you awake at night? What is eating into your dreams? You were tossing and moaning deep into the small hours as if gripped with fever. I could hear you from my room. The servants have also remarked on it.'

I stared at her. ''Tis nothing. I've had bad dreams before.'

'Well whatever ghost is haunting you, you'd better exorcise it soon. I have enough demons to fight on the Trust without you letting another one in through the back door.'

'It's my business, is it not? Can't I even sleep without you telling me how I should do it?'

Chloe sighed and closed the ledger she had been flicking through. 'There's a sliver of anger embedded in you that's as hot as coal and sharp as broken glass. It is what drives you. I know that. I thought your visit to Tyburn and then to Newgate might lay some of these problems to rest. Instead they seemed to have picked the scabs off some not so very old wounds. You should take a look at your face sometimes, Rachel, when you think no one is watching. There's an expression there that puts a chill around my heart.'

She opened a drawer, took out a newspaper and dropped it onto the desk. 'Your friend in Newgate is dead.'

I swallowed. I was never good at faking surprise. 'He was not due to hang until tomorrow.'

'It seems he has cheated the rope. He was found dead in his cell. Poison is suspected though the jailer denies he had any means of obtaining some. Wretches die miserably in Newgate every day without even glimpsing the scaffold.'

She eyed me neutrally. 'People are in and out of the prison all the time. I suppose someone could slip a small vial through the bars, something that could be quickly swallowed. Relatives sometimes try to spare their loved ones the shame of a public execution. I do hope you will settle now, Rachel.'

After Chloe was finished with me I fetched two pitchers of water from the kitchen and locked myself in my bedchamber. Using herbs begged from the apothecary, I smothered the last of my blonde hair. When I finally stared, dripping, into the mirror a dark-haired girl looked back. I nearly cried with relief. I had reclaimed a part of myself. A piece of the person Isaac had shattered and glued back into that ghost mosaic of my sister.

I put a pebble in each shoe in a bid to sabotage my poise. I grunted and growled, trying to rid myself of Lucy's elegant speech. Each day I gorged myself on cakes and sweetmeats. One evening I overdid it and spent half an hour with my head over the privy, retching like a drunk until all my hard work was undone. I could do nothing about the scar except smother it in clouds of powder so that I went about with the face of a ghost.

'Why are you walking like that?' Chloe asked. 'You are clunking about the house, muttering to yourself like a simpleton.'

'My business,' I said.

Chloe shrugged. 'Well, keep your business within the walls of your room. The servants are beginning to wonder if you are ill.'

I knew Meecher was laughing behind my back, but I didn't care. Sally understood what I was up to. So did Judd.

It wasn't working. I got my hair back, but my waist remained stubbornly thin. My speech sounded false and faintly ludicrous; if I didn't concentrate I quickly slipped back into Lucy's flowery tones. And instead of walking with the old Rachel's sturdy confidence the pebbles in my shoes gave me a limp. Isaac had branded me. Branded me with my sister, in the head as well as on the body. I gave up, to Chloe's relief. There were plenty of duties to keep me distracted.

Then, at the beginning of October when coats were buttoned, scarves tied and the trees in the park lightened into the russet browns of autumn proper, everything fell apart.

Chapter Seventeen

Chloe put down her half-eaten cake. 'Something's wrong.'

I was getting used to her habits, the way we'd sit sipping tea and she'd suddenly look up, that frown pinching her forehead, and say 'Oh' before flitting off on some nearly forgotten errand. We shared a sort of bond. A chain of friendship and dependence. But it was a bond with a link missing. I would never understand her. Not fully. Nor she me.

'What's the matter?' I asked.

Chloe gazed out of the window. I was never allowed into her drawing room now unless it was to discuss business. I'd been given the use of a small parlour on the ground floor with a door opening into the stable yard where I could keep an eye on things. The room boasted a cast-iron hearth but the chimney was partly blocked and, when the wind blew up from the river, great snorts of brown smoke gusted out of the fireplace. Chloe offered to have a sweep's boy climb up and brush it out, but one glance up that narrow brick throat had my stomach flipping over. So I said no, the room was comfortable enough. October slipped into November, bringing with it the first flurry of sleet. Cold air hung like lead over the great belly of the city.

'This winter's going to bite,' Sally had warned, and asked Kate if she could order extra logs and kindling. Kate, pleased, told her yes, and Sally sent a lad running to the merchant. Sally did most of the organising and all of the cooking in the kitchen now, but asking Kate's permission from time to time seemed to satisfy the curious political arrangement they had worked out for themselves.

I liked my room, or my 'office' as I preferred to call it. It was cosy when the wind was blowing the right way. Chloe furnished me with a writing desk – oak, not walnut, and more practical than pretty. But it was mine and I felt grand seated behind it on the straight-backed chair she'd also had brought downstairs for me. A second chair placed opposite allowed me to interview people and it only took a moment to open the door and call someone in from the yard. Every day at noon, Kate brought in a tray of tea and buttered tarts. Dusk brought Judd, hat in hand, to report on the day's work. He never sat down. He never accepted tea. He still would not look me in the eye.

I was introduced to the tradesmen who dealt with the coaching side of our business – the blacksmiths, farriers and wheelwrights. I sat them in front of my desk and served them steaming cups of strong coffee, or warm ale if the weather was foul and they had the throat for it. They fidgeted, crossed their legs, uncrossed them, glanced at the door or out of the window. My questions often provoked a frown. Sometimes they met with a vague response, or no response at all.

'They all dealt with my father,' Chloe explained. 'Doing business with a woman tweaks their rough-shod sensibilities. I still have the same problem. But these people are good at their craft and they have a better head for profit than tradition. As long as their bills are met they will sit in your parlour and drink whatever you place in front of them. Don't be put off by their grouchy faces.'

She visited me most days, sometimes for just a few minutes, other times for an hour or more. We usually ignored the small calamities that were a daily feature of a busy stable yard. Judd had things sewn tight and I rarely had to interfere. Now the yard was quiet. The stables had been mucked and most of the horses were out. A pigeon cooed hollowly from some upstairs gable.

'Chloe?' I prompted.

She glanced at the clock. The frown deepened.

'The coach is late,' she said. 'The coach from the Royal.'

She stood up. A napkin slid off her lap and feathered onto the rug, scattering crumbs. Before

I knew it, cold air gusted in from the open door. I put down my teacup and hurried after her, skirts swishing.

The coach from the Royal? Hugh Gore would be driving that. I didn't know him that well. He'd sat on the edge of Arthur Briggs's dice circle, watching, not saying much. A bony man with a sharp nose and tufts of cotton-wool hair clinging to his pink scalp. Kate told me that a bout of flux had raddled his lungs as a lad. Instead of killing him it leeched the meat from his body. You could almost see death simmering in the hollows of his cheeks. He lived somewhere in the city, on the other side of the river. Despite his scarred lungs he smoked foul tobacco – the sweepings of the merchant's floor – that brought on an eye-popping cough.

The Royal was a well appointed inn which served carriages arriving from Edinburgh and Glasgow. Passengers travelling on to the south coast stayed overnight before catching the *Charger*. Hugh brought them to the Gale in a smart little coach. The journey, from the north of London, took an hour most days. He'd been due in at ten o'clock. It was now a half after.

Chloe stood by the gate, peering into the street. As I joined her, two carriages rumbled past, neither driven by Hugh Gore.

'Another five minutes,' Chloe said, 'then I'm taking the phaeton to look for them.'

'It might be anything,' I said. 'A damaged wheel, a thrown shoe…'

'The last time one of Hugh Gore's geldings lost a shoe he trotted back, picked the thing off the street and nailed it back on himself. My instincts don't lie, Rachel. Hugh's in trouble.'

'Perhaps...'

She silenced me with an impatient gesture. 'I know every step of that route. I know each rut, pothole and loose cobble between the Royal and this yard. I know almost to the second how long it should take a fresh team of horses to bring a coachload of passengers to the Gale. There is no market today. No spilled apple-carts, loose barrels or wandering geese to block the road. Something is wrong.'

I had no idea what to do. I paced the yard like an idiot, snatching glances at the gate. Gregor and Sammy would be getting ready to take the *Charger* out. Should I go and tell them?

'Rachel.'

Chloe waved me over. I came at a run.

'What's happened?'

'Shhhh.'

We heard it coming before we saw it. The beat was wrong, the rhythm of the horses' hooves too fast. They were galloping.

A minute later the carriage clattered into the yard. Metal sparked against the cobbles as the team scrambled to an untidy halt. The animals' flanks were white with foam, their eyes wide. The coach should have been packed with passengers. Nobody was aboard. Nobody.

Hugh Gore's face was a tureen of blood. He tried to climb down from the driver's seat, stumbled halfway and sprawled onto the cobbles. His coachman, Bill Mitchell, scrambled after and helped him up. Bill nursed a fat eye that was already turning purple. He had lost the heel off one boot. Hugh's hat was missing. His green jacket was ripped at the collar and stained with mud and manure. The left lens of his spectacles was starred into uselessness. Stinking lumps of horseshit coated the panels of his carriage, the wheels, the flanks of his frightened, sweating team.

Chloe knelt over Hugh, searching his injured face. Bill had managed to get him into a sitting position, though he looked ready to collapse himself.

''Tain't so bad,' Hugh said. 'Someone flicked a pebble and it nicked me on the temple. Got no right to be bleeding like this.'

'What happened?'

Bill wiped muck from his brow with a stained kerchief. 'Another coach pulled up at the Royal same time as us. Things turned ugly. Their driver started pelting us with manure, got the street urchins to join in. They must have been carrying buckets, knowing they'd catch us. A lump of it nearly took the leader's eye out.'

'Who was the driver?'

'Blackjack Jim.'

'The smuggler? This far from the docks?'

'Gallows fodder,' Bill informed me, catching my blank expression, 'released from Newgate on a bribe. I'd swear he smuggles brandy into the city in that damned carriage.'

'What about the waiting passengers?' Chloe said. 'Did no one send for a constable?'

'No constable came. The passengers got on the other coach.'

'Did you recognise it?'

'Aye, easy enough. It bore Grafton's mark.'

Chloe sucked air through her teeth. 'Grafton. Another company in the pocket of the Trust. I might have guessed. Such a petty trick.'

Hugh coughed and managed to struggle to his feet. 'That's not all. The other man with Blackjack Jim, that was Arthur Briggs. No doubt about it, though he was in Grafton's livery with his collar up and his hat pulled tight. He said naught, even as Billy was getting his eye blacked, and looked right through me like I wasn't there. He was my friend. My *friend*.'

'You said the passengers boarded the other coach,' I prompted. 'Why?'

Hugh's eyes flickered towards me. 'Blackjack Jim told them a team and six were waiting at the Rose and Crown, that they could ride the turnpike free to Portsmouth and only pay half fare on the tickets. All the time he was talking he slapped a hickory stick into his palm, fixing them with that devil's glare. 'Twas like a highwayman holding up a stage coach. None dared refuse his offer.'

'That's intimidation,' Chloe protested. 'Those people were booked to travel with us. Our reputation...'

'Don't count for a beggar's hovel when you've got a driver spitting his teeth into his beard and a carriage that stinks like the arse end of a horse,' Hugh finished.

Chloe pursed her lips. 'The third assault in a month. How long before someone gets hurt?'

I spun to face her. 'This has happened before?'

She didn't answer. Ostlers had come out of the stables and were standing about the yard. She beckoned the two nearest. 'Take him inside.

Make sure he gets warm brandy and a bath, then put him to bed and fetch the doctor.'

'Beg pardon, miss,' Hugh said, gaze flitting between Chloe and myself, 'but I've the evening stage to take out at seven.'

Chloe tried to smile reassuringly. 'The coach will remain where it is until this ugly business is resolved.'

I caught her arm. 'No, Chloe. It must run. I'll see to Hugh. Everything will be well.'

I waved the stable hands away. Taking an arm each, Billy and I helped Hugh into the kitchen. 'Sorry,' he kept saying. 'I'm so sorry.' We sat him on one of the tall-backed oak chairs that Kate used to warm her feet at the stove.

'Hot water and linen,' I told Sally. 'Kate, fetch lard out of the pantry to soothe Hugh's cuts.'

Sally took the kettle off the hook above the fire and poured steaming water into a large copper pan. Chloe poured the two men a generous dose of her best Madeira which quickly improved their humour.

'Nothing serious,' Sally said, gently wiping Hugh's face. 'Scratches mostly, and a few bruises. Looks worse than it is. No need for a doctor.'

With the men settled, I collared Chloe in her drawing room. She was staring through the window into the yard. The stable hands were already swabbing down Hugh's carriage.

'What did you mean when you said it was the third assault in a month?'

She turned. 'It has slowly been getting worse since Papa fell ill. Petty assaults, intimidation, difficulties with our suppliers,' she shook her head, 'and now this nonsense. Grown men brawling with one another in front of passengers. I would dismiss any driver of mine engaging in such tactics.'

She stepped away from the window. 'We take the passengers from the Royal. That's the way it is. That's the way it has always been. Grafton can't get away with this ... piracy. They've never stooped so low before. Some fat little scheme is festering in their minds.'

'Who is this Grafton fellow?'

'Another coach operator. A small fish with a nasty bite.'

I squeezed her arm. 'Is there anything in writing? Any contract or bond between you and the Royal?'

Chloe shook her head. 'Papa had a gentleman's agreement with the owner, Ted Millar. That was good enough for them. That was good enough for everyone. Papa and Mr Millar were old friends. They used to go to the cock-fighting together. It was Ted's prowess in backing good fighting birds that bought him the inn. He would not let a Grafton coach into his stable yard. He would not let them steal my passengers. There must be some misunderstanding. Tomorrow morning I will go and see him. He will talk to me. He used to bring me gifts when I was a little girl. His daughter supped in our parlour. Josephine is a fine woman, as her father is a good man. They would do nothing to hurt us. To hurt me.'

'I'll go with you.'

'No. One of us had better stay here.'

'Then take Judd. Or one of the stable hands. Someone dependable.'

She eyed me quizzically. 'You think me in need of protection, Rachel?'

I shrugged. 'After what happened at the Royal this morning, it seems wise. Those men might return.'

'They would not touch me,' Chloe was tight-lipped. 'They would not dare.'

But there was no conviction in her eyes.

Chloe left before breakfast and did not return until late afternoon. My nerves were ragged. Two passengers had arrived by sedan chair, keen to board the *Charger*, less keen to discover they would be the only ones travelling.

'Where are the others?' one demanded. 'A month, an entire infernal month I had to wait for the privilege of booking onto this donkey cart and here it is with enough room to stuff half of London between its doors. I require an explanation, madam.'

I'd been called any number of things in my life but never 'madam'. I mortared a smile onto my face and worked over every excuse that fell into my head. The pair – a Birmingham magistrate and an excise man from the Liverpool docks – were both dandied up in clothes that might impress socially but were hopeless for travelling.

The excise man cleared his throat. 'The coach *was* fully booked, was it not?'

'The passengers have travelled by other means,' I blurted, 'I am sure...'

'Other means? What other means? This,' he banged the panel again, 'is held to be the best carrier to the coast. Why would people of any distinction wish to travel by "other means"?'

I chose my next words carefully. 'They are booked into the Mermaid Inn for the night. If you board the *Charger* now you can greet them upon your arrival. Nothing is lost as you two gentlemen have engaged rooms there also.'

I opened the carriage door and waited. The magistrate dithered for a moment then grasped the door frame and hauled himself up the step, muttering. The excise man climbed in after him. It was all I could do not to slam the door. On the driver's perch, Gregor caught my eye and shrugged.

The magistrate leaned out of the window. 'A shoddy state of affairs. Very shoddy.'

'Our service cannot be bettered, sir.'

He favoured me with a withering stare. 'That remains to be seen.'

When Chloe's phaeton thundered into the yard I was in the stables talking with Judd. We both stepped outside to meet her. Her hair was windswept beneath the brim of her driving bonnet and grime scuffed both cheeks. She brought the phaeton to a groaning halt, threw Thomas the reins and clambered, tight-lipped, from the driver's perch. Without a glance at me she stormed across the yard, ripping off her gloves. Judd and I exchanged looks.

'I'd better go after her,' I said.

As if anticipating just that, Chloe did not take the stairs to her drawing room but turned into my parlour. I followed and closed the door. Chloe paced the rug, her eyes dark with storms. Suddenly she halted and slapped her gloves down on my desk.

'You saw Mr Millar?' I ventured.

'Oh I saw him right enough.'

I fumbled for something to say. 'How is he?'

She scooped up her gloves and twisted the leather between her fingers. 'Old. Beaten. Broken.'

I waited for her to continue. The only sound in the room was the creak of her abused gloves.

'I nearly didn't recognise him at first. He had thinned so much his breeches threatened to fall about his ankles. And his hair – so much grey. Ted Millar was always such a young-looking man. I remember the baker once mistook him for my beau. How we all laughed at that. Yet the person standing in his study had a face that belonged in the tomb.'

I pulled back a chair and sat down. Chloe buzzed around the other chair for a few moments then seated herself. She made no move to remove her bonnet.

'What happened?'

'His daughter has wed.'

I stared blankly at her.

'Josephine Millar, society plum and light of her dear papa's life, has gone and found herself a husband,' Chloe continued. 'Or rather a husband has been found for her. A quiet wedding. Out of town. Out of sight. The new man in her life is Augustus Rand. Does that name mean anything to you?'

'No,' I lied.

'No. It wouldn't. He is Lord Edward Grays's banker and Treasurer of the Southern Counties Turnpike Trust. Now do you see a glimmer of sense in what I am saying?'

I slumped back in my chair. Chloe continued:

'Young Augustus is a handsome lad. Josephine was bought, wed and bedded within a week. Another honest business falls to the Trust.'

'But why would Mr Millar consent to the wedding?'

I recognised the stupidity of those words as soon as I blurted them. Chloe confirmed my fears.

'You think the Trust could not obtain that consent? Half these men sit in Parliament. The Royal is a very select establishment. If Ted wants to keep his customers and his banker then of course he'll do what they say. Young Josephine was so besotted with Augustus, apparently, that she would have eloped had he asked her. As it was, Augustus threatened to take her abroad for good if Ted didn't open up his yard to "fair competition". It would break his heart never to see his girl again.'

'It was the same with Lucy. With Isaac. It's how the Trust get what they want.' I met Chloe's dark gaze. 'Now they want your business. They want the Gale.'

Chloe stood and pulled off her bonnet. Pins shivered onto the floor. 'Oh it's not my *business* that they want, Rachel. They have enough sovereigns festering in their pockets to keep their wives in pretty hats three lifetimes over. They want power. They want *me*.'

Next morning, two constables arrived in the yard to arrest Bill Mitchell.

'A writ?' Chloe stared at the two men. 'This company has never had a writ served on it.'

''Tis serious, miss. We are also here to arrest one

Hugh Gore for affray and disorderly conduct. He is known to work in this coach yard. You will hand him over along with the Mitchell fellow.'

'If you are referring to the incident outside the Royal, the other drivers were as much to blame.'

An edge to the constable's voice. 'We've witnesses that say otherwise, miss. Please give them up else we've a warrant to come in and fetch them.'

'Hugh is an old man and not in the best of health. Prison will kill him.' Chloe fumbled for her reticule. 'If there is a fine I will pay it.'

The men glanced at each other. ''Tis for the judge to decide. That fight nearly started a riot. This Gore fellow is lucky not to hang. Transportation's a likely bet. For him and his friend.'

'He won't last the voyage.'

'Then he should have thought of that before letting fly with his fists. Now bring him out or we'll have you an' all.'

'Me?'

'For obstruction. We ain't got all morning, miss.'

Thomas took the message indoors. A minute later Hugh and Bill shuffled out, bewildered, blinking in the sunlight. Hugh looked better now that his cuts had healed but his skin had a bleached pallor and he stumbled on the cobbles. Bill's face was a swamp of bruises. He winced as the constable caught him by the wrist and hauled him towards the gate.

'Come on you.'

A dark shadow loomed over the group. Sammy. Together with Gregor he had been readying the *Charger*. Now he stood in the constable's path, as immovable as a mountain.

The constable glared up at him. 'Don't give me any trouble now, ye black monkey.'

Sammy gestured with one big arm. 'Mr Bill is hurt. No need to go yanking him like a dog. He did not cause the fight.'

'Better call off your slave, miss.'

'He is not my slave,' Chloe said.

'I am not anybody's slave.' Sammy's voice boomed across the yard. 'I am a free man and can choose my friends. You will not hurt Mr Bill or Mr Hugh.'

The constable tipped back his hat and scratched his ear. His gaze slipped from Sammy to his colleague, then to Gregor seated atop the *Charger*. His other hand drifted towards the pistol tucked into his belt.

Gregor's face was in shadow. His fingers stroked the butt of the carriage whip. He could crack a fallen acorn open with the tip of that lash.

Sweat slimed the constable's top lip. 'I'm only doing my job. If these men don't come quietly troopers will be sent to fetch them and it'll go all the worse for everyone.'

He waved the warrant in front of Sammy's face. The coachman snatched at it with his teeth. The constable flinched. Sammy grinned widely then stepped aside.

The constable's shoulders relaxed. He turned back to the two Gale men. 'No manacles,' he said, 'if you promise to behave.'

'We won't make trouble,' Bill said. 'You have my word on it.'

The constable took Bill's arm. His colleague

took Hugh's. Both men were led from the yard.

Chloe was on the verge of tears. I slipped my arm around her shoulders and led her inside. 'I can't let them take Bill,' she whispered. 'He is known to the courts. He used to pick pockets outside Westminster Abbey – caught people as they left the services. Only Papa's willingness to employ him kept Bill off the prison barge. If he goes up in front of a magistrate again...'

'Why did Mr Gale help him?'

'Because Bill has a nose for the cock-fighting. Papa would steal a murderer from the gallows if he thought the felon would help him put a guinea on the right bird.' She fumbled for a handkerchief. 'They will be kept in Newgate until the trial. That could be weeks away. They'll come out pox-riddled and half starved.'

'Don't fret,' I said. 'We'll get them out.'

Chloe stared at me. 'Get them out? And how are we to do that? I hired you to run my yard. So far you've discharged your duties well. Are you now saying that you can work miracles? If so, they did naught for your stable-hand friend. Hugh and Bill will be locked up in the darkest cesspit in London while I sit and sip tea and exchange pleasantries with my bankers as I try to explain why the *Charger* ran near empty to the coast. The minds behind this charade want my men to suffer, want *me* to suffer. Hugh and Bill are paying for my stubbornness.'

I reached for Chloe's hand. 'I'll go and see them. Perhaps we can bribe the turnkey to allow a few comforts...'

She wrenched her arm away and headed for the

stairs. 'No,' she flung over her shoulder, 'you will not go to Newgate. Those men are my friends. I don't want either of them dying mysteriously in their cells.'

I told Judd to get everyone back to work then went up to my bedchamber. I stared out of the window. Black thoughts sloughed through my mind. As if catching my mood the clouds thickened and sank towards the rooftops. Thunder rumbled somewhere in the direction of St Paul's. I held up both hands and flexed my fingers. They were trembling. I gripped the edge of the dresser until my knuckles turned white. I waited, teeth clenched. One minute. Two. I let go. My hands ached. I let them drop into my lap.

This has to stop.

A surgeon would cut off a rotting limb so that the body might live. I had to do the same or be carted off, screaming, to the madhouse. I must sever the festering part of my mind, bury it deep and stitch up the wound. I would never completely forget, but I would live.

Glory, I would live.

I went in search of Chloe. Dusk fell so early now. The candles in the passageways had not yet been lit and I had to fumble in the gloom. Light seeped out from underneath the drawing-room door. I pressed my ear against the varnished wood. The scratch of a quill. Very faint. A sigh. The crumple of parchment.

I knocked on the door. The scratching stopped. A pause.

'Who is it?'

'Rachel.' I waited, twisting my fingers.

'Come in.'

The drawing room was a nest of flickering yellow light. The air was thick with the scent of hot wax. Candles were burned almost to stubs. Books lay open everywhere – ledgers, accounts, tradesmen's bills. In the middle of it all was Chloe, her haggard face pinched in concentration. Coins were stacked in small columns on the blotter in front of her.

'Profits down?' I ventured.

Red circles appeared on her cheeks. She banged the coins one by one into the money box and slammed down the lid. 'The light has almost gone,' she said, glancing out of the window. 'You'd do well to see to your stock.'

'My stock is safe in the hands of the man I hired to look after it. It's my employer I fear for.'

Chloe rubbed her eyes. 'I cannot afford to run services with no passengers. We shall not be able to bear the losses for long.'

'Is this more than just a ploy to drive you out of business?' I ventured. 'Do associates of the Trust bear you a grudge?'

'There has been a real scrabble since Lord Sutcliffe died. Too many men fighting for scraps of power. It may be months before the dust settles. In my dealings with the Trust I learned that they are very comfortable in their seat of power. Complacent even. They imagine that in the future no coach or sheep cart will be able to move in the south of England without paying dues. They may be right. They are a powerful concern. But they are still men. Sutcliffe's death proved that. In the meantime these assaults on my staff and against my property continue. The Trust's hired oafs like to start fights in public places. Today I discovered that Arthur Briggs has been picketing my men in the taverns and outside their homes. He wants them to stop working for you. No threats have been made but the implication is there, and I know he has been spreading rumours.'

'What did he say about me?'

'Someone definitely must have put him up to it. Briggs is not that sort of man.'

'What did he say about me, Chloe?'

She plucked up a copy of the *Daily Register*, flicked it open and ran her eyes down the printed columns.

'He called you gallows trash.'

I nodded. 'He has my measure.'

'The Trust carries a fat purse in one hand and a fatter stick in the other,' Chloe finished as if she hadn't heard. 'I've seen better men turned. Here,' she tossed the *Register* into my hands, 'see what those tuppenny hacks have said about us.'

The print was smudged. I held it close to one of the candles and read. The article painted a bloody picture of events at the Royal Inn. Hugh and Bill were held up as a pair of violent bullies who had frightened passengers and children, and prevented honest men from going about their lawful business. The scuffle had been exaggerated into a riot, the number involved blown up from a handful of onlookers to a crowd, and blame for starting the disturbance was placed squarely on the shoulders of the two Gale men. 'The culprits should be made an example of and prosecuted to the limit of the law,' the article finished.

I folded up the newspaper. 'This could be put to good use in the privy behind the stables.'

Chloe didn't reply.

'You're not giving up,' I told her.

'Of course I am not giving up. It is a game. A little charade of intimidation. Look.'

She dropped something onto the blotter. A gilt-edged card. Chloe's name was written on it in a flowing script.

'A while ago I was "invited" to join the Trust,' she explained. 'These invitations are repeated regularly, usually accompanied by a spiked axle or one of my horses going unaccountably lame. After such incidents the Trust is always quick to offer its "protection". Things settle down while they give me time to think about it. But these interludes are growing shorter. I fear I am trying their patience.'

She gestured at the card. 'The Trust members are holding a ball. To parade their wealth and remind us who really holds the purse strings. All the major coach operators will have been invited. I won't go. I won't pander to their vanity. They tried to get my father in their pocket and now they want me.'

She picked up the card and scissored it between her fingers. I was conscious that I was staring at it. Chloe seemed not to notice. She turned the small white oblong around and around in the weary candlelight. Abruptly she leaned over, dropped the card into the wastebasket, and stood up. 'You will forgive me if I do not sup with you tonight. I am in need of my bed. This business has exhausted me. Tomorrow will bring its own clutch of worries.'

She stepped away from her desk and started snuffing out the candles. While her back was turned I fished the invitation out of the basket and tucked it into my reticule. I bade her goodnight, kissed her cheek and quietly left. I took supper alone in the downstairs parlour. Candles threw shadows, a hundred dark reflections of me, across the walls. I looked bent, crooked. I fumbled in my bag, ran my finger along the edge of the invitation, and went on eating my broth. When I retired to my bedchamber and slid between the covers I fell instantly asleep.

Morning brought another visitor to the yard. Not a constable, thankfully, but a messenger with a letter for Chloe. We were taking tea in my parlour. Chloe seemed in good spirits but avoided talking about yesterday's events. She put down her teacup and broke the seal on the letter. Her dark eyes scanned the page.

'Our bank has been taken over. The new owners are refusing to renew the lease on our coach house and smithy.'

I caught my breath. 'Are you in debt to this bank?'

'Why no. There are no outstanding loans. Papa paid them off years ago.'

'Pull whatever's left of your funds out,' I said. 'Go elsewhere. Out of London altogether if need be.'

'But this family has banked with Whittaker's since before my grandfather's time.'

I thought of ravens wheeling in the sky. 'Get your money out,' I said. 'While you still can. Park your coaches in the street if you have to. And we can find another smithy.'

My next appointment for the day was in the kitchen.

I bided my time, watching the kitchen door from the window of my parlour. It opened a little after noon. Sally waddled across the yard and out of the gate, basket tucked under her arm. She had little patience with some of the tradesmen that called at the Gale. 'Little better than village footpads, most of 'em,' was her opinion. She preferred to fetch most meat and produce herself. Kate was hopeless at bartering and was fleeced daily. Sally, however, found she was getting to like these visits to the city markets. It was a new experience for her and many of the stallholders brought their wares from the southern counties. They shared her accent and her views, and their tongues were brimming with news and gossip. Some stayed in cheap hostels overnight and Judd often went over and shared a pipe with the men. In this odd way it helped them both settle into their new lives. Judd was never once in his cups as far as I was able to tell. Perhaps the horse trough in the yard, and Sally's steely gaze, gave him cause to think.

I closed the parlour door and passed back through the house. The kitchen smelled of warm linen and freshly washed vegetables. Sitting low in the hearth the fire was a warm glow whiskered with grey embers. Heat pulsed across the wooden floor.

Kate's face was slick with sweat. Wisps of hair escaped her mob cap and dangled about her ears. She looked around as I entered, bobbed a half curtsy and wiped her forehead with the back of one hand. The other gripped a pot of unpeeled potatoes. 'Just doing supper,' she explained. 'If I get it ready now I can go down to the river later and watch the boats.'

'I've never lived near a river before,' I said, seating myself near the turnspit and stretching out my legs. 'Or the sea. I've only seen pictures of that in books.'

'Wouldn't know there was a river here with all them buildings stacked around it,' Kate continued. ''Cept for the stink. It's worse on hot days. You were lucky not to be here July. Sun baked us for two whole weeks. People were retching and swooning from the smell, even those London born and bred. On the embankment folk chased rats the size of terriers out of their cellars.'

'Are there any rats here?'

Her eyes dropped. ''Spect so. I've never seen one, though I've heard scratchings beneath the floor. Every big house has them. Mrs Meecher deals with it 'cause I'm in terror of them. My sister got bit when she was a baby and she got sick and died. I won't go down the cellar. Not me. Not ever.'

'How does Mrs Meecher get rid of the rats?'

'Poison.' Kate lowered her voice to a whisper. 'She buys it from the apothecary.'

'We had rats in the country too. They'd get in the stables. Our ostlers used to set dogs on them. If my father managed to corner one he'd shoot it.'

'That's the way,' Kate said. 'Poison is too cruel. The rats creep off to die, y'see. You can only find the bodies by the stink. Molly, our washergirl, had a kitten and it ate some poisoned beef that Meecher put out. Molly cried for a week.'

She straddled a chair and began to attack the vegetables with long, clumsy strokes. More potato than peel was going into the bucket. It was a miracle the girl did not have her thumb off.

'Do you want a hand with those?'

She shook her head. 'I'm nearly finished. You'll only get muck all over your gown and then Molly will curse me 'cause she'll have to wash it.'

I laughed. Kate joined in. She popped the last potato into a bowl, dropped loose threads of peel into the bucket and stood up, wiping her hands on her apron.

'Is there a gun anywhere in the house?' I asked as casually as I could.

The end of the apron slipped from her fingers. 'You thinking of shooting someone, miss?'

'Oh no, it's just that my father kept an old army musket on the wall above the parlour fire. When we were little he told us it was to ward off highwaymen. He said that every gentleman keeps a pistol next to his brandy decanter. I wondered if it was true.'

Kate scooped an onion from the rack and started chopping it with a knife almost as big as her forearm. Her nose twitched.

'Mr Gale wasn't that sort of gentleman but yes, he did keep a gun. Molly found it when she was cleaning his study, not that he troubled much to hide it. An ornament maybe. You know, like his cane or his hat. A little silver thing. I don't know if it works. I don't know if it was ever fired. Might not even be there any more. A lot was cleared out after Mr Gale passed on.'

It had to be there. I knew every pin, quill and button that had been auctioned. And I knew where Chloe kept the study key.

'Are you sure you wouldn't like help with those vegetables?'

'Thank you, miss, but I'm sure.'

Although Chloe wouldn't let me go into her drawing room unaccompanied she never troubled to lock it. The door swung silently on its hinges. The curtains were pulled back. Weak sunlight spilled into the room.

Chloe had a headache and was napping in her bedchamber. It was at the top of the house on the same wing as her father's old room, so she wouldn't hear me scuttling about. I fished the study key out of the top drawer of her writing desk and slipped inside. Dust hung over everything. My slippers were muted on the thick rug.

The top drawer of Edward Gale's desk yielded only a pair of spectacles, an old snuffbox and a few chewed cigar ends. The second was stuffed with papers. Legal business, some personal letters, yellowed bills of sale marking old transactions. The last drawer gave up an etching of a lovely young woman in a flowing summer gown with her hair tied in ribbons. A rose was tucked under her chin, the stem clasped in one elegant hand. The resemblance to Chloe was haunting.

At the back of the drawer was the pistol, just as Kate had described it. I weighed it in the palm of my hand. Perhaps no more than a fancy paperweight, or something for slicing the ends off

Edward's cigars. I doubted it would frighten anyone very much.

I tucked it into my reticule, locked the study and returned the key to Chloe's desk. Friday promised to be a busy day and I had much to do between then and now.

I was going to a party.

Chapter Eighteen

Dark crescents hung under Chloe's eyes. She wrote letter after letter, scratching her crows' quills down to stubs. Light was always spilling out from under her drawing-room door whenever I retired to bed.

Builders were brought in, out-of-town jobbers who smelled of cheap gin and demanded money before lifting a hammer. They spent three roisterous days converting part of the lower rooms into a smithy, knocking a huge hole in the whitewashed wall to take a chimney for the new forge. One of the men made a lewd remark about Chloe. Judd took him inside the stables and knocked the wits out of him. Work went ahead quietly after that. We got our new blacksmith, and a farrier, and not too many questions were asked about who they were or where they came from.

Sally and Kate, meanwhile, had a blazing row after Kate dropped a dish of pastry. I heard the commotion from my parlour. I ran into the kitchen in time to see Sally slap Kate across the jaw, hard enough to split Kate's bottom lip. She stared white-faced at Sally, then at the blood dribbling onto her apron, and swooned clean away. I got one of the maids to put her to bed.

'Miss Gale is not to hear of this,' I warned.

The maid nodded. Sally spent the rest of the evening in front of the hearth, her face swimming with tears. 'I've never hit a lass, never in all my life,' she wailed. 'I don't know why I took such a turn.' But I knew. It was the same thing that had possessed all of us.

Friday loomed. My nerves were so bad I spent hours in the privy. Sally asked if I wanted a draught for a sour belly. 'What ails you?' she kept asking until I snapped at her and she left me to it, muttering. Everyone was on edge. The failing business. Hugh and Bill. The bank. Miss Chloe. Drivers were frightened to go out in case they found themselves beaten and intimidated, or falsely accused and dragged into Newgate to join the others. But nothing happened.

'I doubt we'll see any more trouble until after the ball,' Chloe said, 'when the Trust will growl because I've snubbed them.'

My appetite vanished. Chloe hadn't taken supper in the dining room for days so I used that as an excuse to stay in my bedchamber. A maid brought up a trencher piled with gammon and eggs. My stomach squirmed. I opened my window, put the plate on the ledge outside and let the pigeons feast.

The selection of gowns Chloe had given me seemed a little drab, the material too heavy. I could probably fluff one up a bit, but I'd never had

Mother's delicate touch when it came to sewing. Frustrated, I shut my eyes and grabbed the first one that came to hand. Yellow taffeta with lace cuffs and satin bows looped around the skirt. I draped it over the chair and tossed the others into the bottom of the wardrobe. I had no wig. Perhaps I could bleach my hair and tie it up with ribbons, or dust it with face powder. There was plenty of that, plus rouge, and I could cut out some star-shaped paper patches to press onto my cheeks. And I would need a fan. I could probably filch one from Chloe. She had dozens, some wooden, some crafted from bone. I'd spied them on her dresser when she first showed me her bedchamber. And a carriage, glory, I'd need a carriage. I couldn't walk to the Assembly Rooms. I didn't even know where they were and I had no money left for a chair.

The light had faded from the room. I took a taper from the fire and lit a candle. My head felt fuzzy. Tomorrow. I'd think about it again tomorrow. I'd decide what to do then.

As it happened, tomorrow supplied its own answer.

Chloe had settled on a new banker. A fellow called Renbold whose ill-fitting wooden teeth showered everything with spittle. He maintained an office in a corner of a decrepit warehouse on the south side of the river. She invited him to tea. His nose ran incessantly and, when introduced to me, his fingers lingered too long on mine. But he had neither the wit nor gumption to be anything other than honest. His was a family business that mostly handled shipping accounts and the whisper along the river was that, unsavoury as the man might be, he was to be trusted. Chloe needed men she could trust. So she agreed to transfer much of her assets across the water, but not all, so as not to raise too many eyebrows at Whittaker's Bank. Renbold was too small a fish to catch the eye of the Trust. We counted on that.

Friday morning she called me into her drawing room. A purse of money sat between us on the writing desk.

'Here,' she said, gesturing. 'The first offering to Renbold's coffers. You take it to him. It has been a long week and I am tired. Go this afternoon. Renbold is sending a landau but I won't put my money in the hands of a lackey and I don't want you going on your own. My drivers are all out seeking customers and I need Gregor for the *Charger.*' She sighed. 'I hope there are no more brawls. Another bloody nose will prove more than I can stomach.'

I slipped the purse into my reticule. 'You can trust me.'

Renbold's driver was half an hour late and surly with it. I climbed aboard the landau. It was a battered old cart of a thing, tethered to a wheezing nag with ribs like a corset. I had no notion why a supposedly successful banker would want to send such a horror.

I fingered the purse. The driver waited until I was seated then clicked the beast forward. We proceeded at a shambling pace. Street urchins pointed and laughed.

'Hey mister, yer horse is past it. Me dog could pull that cart better!'

Two streets later I ordered the driver to halt. 'I

have other business to attend to first,' I explained. 'There is no need for you to wait. I will engage a chair for the remainder of the journey.'

He gave me a dark look. "Tain't what I was told.'

I fumbled in the purse and dropped two shillings into his palm. Before he could say anything I clambered out of the landau. He stared at the money then at me. Slowly he pocketed the coins, straightened on his perch and clicked the reins. I lingered by the roadside until he was out of sight.

I was in the beating heart of fashionable London. Full of the places described in those dizzy magazines Chloe read in her drawing room. Pretty, terraced shops lined both sides of the road. Humanity thronged around me in loud, brightly coloured eddies. Sedan-bearers stomped along the pavements, cries of 'By your leave' sending pedestrians scuttling out of the way. I had to jump into the street to avoid being trampled. It had rained for two nights and the road was a swamp. I groaned as my feet splashed into a puddle.

I was no stranger to buying clothes. Mother's frequent trips to Stonehill had prepared me well, even though that place was a country hamlet full of hovels compared to these cream-painted streets. Fine carriages crowded the busy road. Everyone was driving or being driven, alighting only to slip through the polished door of some treasure box. Only maids, errand boys and tradesmen took to the pavements, jostling me, some cursing, others laughing as they poked me in the ribs.

'Forgot your carriage, love?' a thick voice yelled into my ear. A hand squeezed my behind before losing itself in the crowd.

I ducked inside the first dress shop I could find. Velvet confections filled the bay windows and spilled around the walls. Gowns so fine you'd have thought them sewn by angels. I dithered, feeling a frump in my mud-stained dress. Other customers stared at me. Whispers were exchanged.

I tucked myself in the corner. Trade was brisk. Ladies arrived in droves to collect gowns for the ball. It seemed that the whole of London society was attending. The proprietor, a tall, horse-toothed lady with a sprinkling of French in her accent, flitted from customer to customer, slipping quickly through a curtain to appear with another shimmering treasure.

I needed Lucy, needed her now. The proprietor's young assistant was eyeing me like I was a pig in a sack. She wanted to throw me out. It was all over her face. Shop girls always thought themselves a cut above.

I searched inside myself and found my sister. Her strength, her spirit, flowed through me. Such a strange feeling, like the little nips of strong brandy mother used to slip us whenever a chill frosted our ears. I could do this. I *would* do it.

A lull in the flow of trade. I smoothed down my clothes and approached the counter, side-stepping the assistant. 'I want a dress,' I said.

Horse-tooth was busy entering a column of figures into a cream-paged ledger. She did not look up.

'There is a cloth merchant in the market by the river,' she said. The French accent had gone.

'I want a dress,' I repeated. 'For the Trust ball.'

She dropped her quill and glared at me. 'The

ball? I think you have ideas above yourself my young milkmaid. Leave my salon or I shall have a constable on you.'

'Do I have to show you the invitation?'

A hollow laugh. 'Even if you *are* invited you will need to attend a fitting. Materials will have to be chosen and cut to size. It cannot be done in time.'

I grabbed her wrist and slapped the purse into her palm. 'I'll take one of the gowns on display. Anything will do. If you are any good at your job you'll be able to guess the size. If the fit isn't right I'll alter it myself. But I'll take it now.'

Horse-tooth weighed the purse in her fingers, then she tucked it under the counter and clapped her hands. 'Jenny, fetch a gown from the window. The turquoise one with the bows down the back. Wrap it up at once and bring it to me.'

The girl shot me a withering look. Horse-tooth turned back to me. A dour smile played across her lips. 'You might have to tuck the sleeves up a little but the fit will be good, I think. Now, we must find you a wig and some gloves…'

I hired a sedan to take me back to the Gale. I'd timed it so all the carriages would still be out. I hurried across the empty yard. My foot stubbed the corner of a loose cobble. A parcel slid out of my grasp and burst open. My new wig lay crumpled on the ground. Panicked, I glanced about me. All quiet. Tightening my grip on the other packages, I scooped up the wig, beat it against my thigh to shake off the dirt and, throwing dignity to the wind, ran for the safety of my parlour door.

Upstairs, my hands shook as I pulled open the parcels and spread their contents over my bed. Such treasure. Mother would have given her life to wear a gown like this. Even Lucy's finest paled beside it. I ran my hand across the material. A tingling sensation shimmied up my fingertips. The stitching was almost invisible. What would I look like with the dress on, wearing the gloves and silk stockings Horse-tooth had sold me? I imagined slipping my feet into the buckled satin shoes. She had even provided a small casket of white powder for the wig.

But I knew what I would look like.

One of *them*.

A costume. Think of it as a mask. A butterfly gown to transform a dumpy caterpillar for a night. It was their uniform: the uniform of the gentry.

I stripped off my travelling clothes and started pulling on the stockings. They were gossamer against my legs. I glanced at the scattering of coins on the dresser. Easily enough for a hire to the Assembly Rooms. Chloe would find out about the money, of course, but she'd started taking laudanum in a hot posset to help her sleep and spent long hours in bed.

A rap on the door. It gusted inwards. I was caught with my new stockings halfway up my knees. Gregor stood on the threshold, his tricorne dangling from his fingers. We stared at one another for a few moments. I snatched the coverlet off the bottom of the bed and wound it around me.

'Gregor...'

He never came in the house, never. Not even when Judd and some of the other men joined Sally in the evenings for hot broth or coffee around the kitchen hearth. I looked away, cheeks reddening. Clothes lay strewn across the mattress and on the floor. Rouge and powder littered the top of the dresser. The place resembled a brothel. Gregor took it all in with one sweep of his eyes. His mouth was a thin line.

'Where are you going?' he said.

'You're back early.'

He stepped into the room and swung the door closed behind him. 'Sammy took the *Charger*. One of the stable lads went as coachman. An easy job as we're so light on passengers.'

He skirted the bed, eyeing my gown. He dropped his tricorne onto the chair and picked up my new bonnet. He ran his fingers over the delicate material, rubbed the brim between thumb and forefinger as if testing the quality of tobacco or some exotic spice.

He let the bonnet fall on top of the dress. I shrank back under the coverlet.

'Gregor, you're scaring me.'

A smirk ghosted across his lips. 'I'm scaring you am I? Well that's a fine thing to say because you're scaring me too. So I'll ask you again: where are you going?'

'To the bank. The new bank. On the other side of the river. I'll hire a chair.'

'You were supposed to go to the bank this morning. I know Miss Gale gave you the money. Quite a fat purse it was, too. And a carriage arrived to take you there. Only you didn't go, did you? Two streets away you slipped the driver a juicy tip to keep his mouth shut, sent him packing then walked another two streets with that money bag stuffed inside your skirts. You're a clever girl, Rachel, but that was a damn stupid thing to do.'

'You followed me?'

'Aye, I followed you, at times close enough to touch your sleeve. Damn miracle you didn't have every cutpurse in London sniffing around. Only way in and out of the Gale Inn is through the main gate. How many other folk do you suppose saw you?'

'So what do you think I plan to do?'

He scooped up the dress, held the material to his nostrils, closed his eyes and inhaled. 'Expensive. Too good for the coffee houses or parading around the park. You can't go riding in it. Weather would whip it to shreds. You want to look pretty. You want to look like a lady. I'd say you plan to go to a ball. An important ball. I'd say you have a mind to visit our friends in the Turnpike Trust. I'd say also, Miss Rachel Curtis, that you're not done settling scores.'

I felt the blood drain from my face. 'How did you know about the ball?'

'Good God, lass, every driver north and south of the river knows about it. The talk has been about naught else. All their employers will be there. Everyone will rise or fall at the Trust's whim. I've never seen so many men nervous about their futures. Some will come away rich, some ruined. And you, you who used to serve ales from behind a taproom counter, are intent on walking into that rooks' nest as if you were Queen Charlotte herself. What do you intend to do? Get Hugh and Bill out of Newgate just by fluttering your fan at the first fancy-breeched vulture who happens to catch your eye?'

'I plan to do much more than that.'

'I'll daresay you do. And how shall you get there? Use more money from Miss Gale's purse to hire a carriage? I can't believe you'd try to sneak out in her phaeton. If the ride over didn't kill you the cold would. No, a coach and four, with a brace of liveried footmen and a driver dressed like a prince. Nothing else will do. Not if you want to impress. But your luck's in. Miss Gale is headed over the river to sweet-talk that weedy banker Renbold. He's invited her to dine at his apartments down by the docks. She's asked Judd to take her. She'll be leaving at seven.'

'She never told me about that.'

'Thought you'd just sneak out under her nose, eh? No, she didn't tell you. She doesn't care much for Renbold and doesn't like doing business with him. You can see it on her face plain as day. You ain't the only one with secrets.'

'How dare she.'

'How dare she? Hark at who's talking. I'd love to know what excuses you had cooked up to explain filching her cash. Go on, finish dressing. Paint your face and splash on some perfume. I'll knock on your door again in an hour. Make sure you're ready. We don't want any dilly-dallying if we're to get you to the Connaught Assembly Rooms on time.'

'I ... I don't understand. You mean...?'

'A coach and four will be waiting in the yard at half past seven. Thomas and one of the other lads will ride as footmen. A right pair of young dandies they'll look too.'

He grinned. 'Hugh and Bill are well liked. There's a lot of us don't take to what's been done, either to them or Miss Gale. She can't do aught about it. But I believe you can, and I've persuaded the others. Don't let me down.'

I threw myself at him, wrapping my arms around his scrawny, wonderful neck. I was oblivious to the coverlet slipping to the floor until Gregor eased out of my grasp and held me, chuckling, at arm's length.

'Cover your modesty, girl, or you'll have me in Newgate along with our two friends.'

'You're too good to me,' I said, rescuing the coverlet.

'You need looking out for. Judd won't do it. He sees your sister in your face, maybe your father too, and it scares him. Everyone's a little afraid of you, Rachel.' He pulled his tricorne back over his head. 'I'll see you at a half past the hour. The Assembly Rooms ain't far. You'll be there in no time at all.'

Chloe left at seven, just as Gregor said. I watched her from my bedchamber window. The lantern caught her features as she climbed into her phaeton, Judd at the reins. Her face was grim.

I'd worked out a way of doing up all the fastenings on my new clothes without the help of a maid. It still took the better part of an hour before I was finished. A couple of pins, a lift here, a tuck there, and the dress was snug. On went face powder, rouge, and finally the wig, dusted and fixed with more pins. I'd dipped into the jewellery box

Chloe had given me and chosen a pair of opal earrings plus a blue velvet choker faced with a porcelain cameo. A sprinkling of scent and I was ready.

A gentle knock on the door. Gregor stood on the threshold, hat in hand, resplendent in his *Charger* livery. He sucked air through his teeth. 'You'll do,' he said. 'God, lass, you'll do. The coach is waiting in the street so as not to get Meecher's nose twitching. Kate is in the larder and Sally's minding her own business.'

I threw a wrap around my shoulders, scooped up my gloves and blew out the candle. We slithered downstairs and across the yard. The moon kept its head below the rooftops. Gregor carried no lantern but the stars were bright.

A breeze carried the smell of wet varnish from the waiting carriage. 'Hugh and Billy's coach,' Gregor explained. 'We fancied it up a bit. Doubt they'd mind.'

He gestured at the two lads clinging to the back, also wearing coachman's livery. 'We didn't have any spare wigs for 'em so we put chalk in their hair and told 'em to keep their hats on tight. Tom there managed to swipe a couple of pairs of Miss Gale's stockings from the laundry basket. That's what we made the hose out of.'

'They're wearing Chloe's stockings?'

'Shush. Don't let 'em hear you laughing or they'll die of shame. Tom's got Sammy's breeches on, pinned about the knees, and Howard there is wearing an old pair of his da's, patched and dyed. We tied some ribbons and gold braid to the jackets to pretty them up. In the dark they'll pass well enough. No bugger ever spares coachmen a second glance anyhow.'

'You've been busy in those stables.'

'In the coach with you. If Miss Gale gets back before us, Sally will tell her you went to bed early. If she wants me, I'm in the tavern with the lads.' He opened the carriage door. 'Now, if m'lady would care to step inside...'

The first grey tendrils of fog were rising like thieves from the river when we drew up outside the Connaught Assembly Rooms. The journey had taken less than an hour. The state I was in it could have been forever. Several times I wanted to bang on the roof and tell Gregor to turn the coach about. Sight of the wide, imposing building, light flooding out of the tall windows, made my belly flip. Carriages were drawn up in a line beside the flagged area at the entrance. Gaily dressed figures drifted around the door. The air was full of laughter and excited chatter. The large number of unaccompanied women would make my task easier.

Gregor appeared, ducked down to lower the step then opened the door. 'Good luck, lass,' he said. 'We'll be round the back with the other coaches. When you want to leave just tell one of the footmen at the door and he'll come and fetch us.'

He reached up, took my satin-gloved fingers and helped me down the steps. 'You're beautiful,' he whispered. 'I always said you could be a lady and that's just what you are.' He nodded towards the Assembly Rooms. 'Finer than anything in there. I'm proud. Prouder than I've ever been of anyone in my life. Do what you have to, lass. We're all praying for you. I wish to God you were my daughter.'

He closed the carriage door and escorted me to the entrance of the Assembly Rooms. A tongue of yellow light spilled across the paving stones. He thought I was going to bargain with the Trust, use my youth, my charm to sway their old heads. Get Hugh and Bill out. Stop the fighting. Leave the Gale in peace. How proud would you be, Gregor, if you knew about the gun in my reticule?

He stopped at the door. 'Nervous? So am I. That's a den of wolves in there. I oughtn't let you go in. There's a lot I oughtn't do.'

'You couldn't stop me, Gregor.'

'I know. You're set on it. I'll go back to the coach.' He smiled thinly. 'Just call when you need me, like I said.'

He walked off into the dark.

Footmen swung open a set of double doors. A long hall, a thick press of people, a distant, fluting sound of music. I let myself get carried along with the flow. Candles burned everywhere from elaborate chandeliers. Thousands of candles, enough to light my old bedchamber for a lifetime. My nostrils were clogged with expensive perfume and a sour underscent of sweat. One ageing dandy was too free with the contents of his snuffbox. I caught a few grains and sneezed. Young men grinned and nudged one another.

The gentle tide of partygoers drifted to the left and through another set of doors. I stepped into the biggest room in the world. The far wall was barely visible through a haze of cigar smoke. A dozen marble pillars supported a lofty roof. Colours assaulted my senses. Music, smells, a busy hum of voices.

I was standing on a balcony with a wide staircase dropping away before me in a carpeted waterfall. Lining the wall behind the columns were rows of tables smothered in crisp white linen. Food was piled high on decorated silver trenchers, with po-faced servants in attendance. In front were chairs for the ladies. On a raised area near the windows a musical quintet scratched out a gavotte while couples danced on the polished floor.

A footman held out a hand swathed in a glove whiter than swan's feathers. Before I could think, before I could stop myself, I pressed the invitation into his palm. His eyes ran over it briefly then, to my utter horror, he turned and announced: 'Miss Chloe Gale,' in a voice that boomed across the room.

I had not thought to change it. Now I would be exposed as a fraud. I couldn't run. The press of guests behind me made that impossible. I expected everyone in the Assembly Rooms to turn and stare but the footman was already accepting other cards, reading out other names in that same bullish voice.

I grabbed the banister and eased myself down the stairs. I needed air, a seat, a sip of water. Anything. I'd come here with only a hazy notion of what I would do. Now even those vague plans deserted me. The gun felt like a lead brick in my reticule.

One of the young men from the upstairs hall pushed through the throng. I thought my ploy had failed and I was going to get thrown out, but he bowed and asked me to dance. I politely refused his invitation. I couldn't afford to let my nerves make a fool out of me. Surprisingly, he didn't seem to mind. It scratched my pride a little, but I supposed most people were there for more than just the gavotte. Perhaps he thought he'd try his luck again later.

I picked up a bread slice topped with trout and absently bit into it. The fish tasted thick and oily. I found a pitcher of water flavoured with lemon juice, poured myself a glass and gulped it down. The heat in the room was oppressive, the smoke a soiled fog. I wanted to be sick, to run home and curl up in a corner. Perhaps if I asked a footman he would fetch Gregor. They would let him in, wouldn't they, in order to escort me home? But how could I look at him? How could I meet his eyes after what he said to me out there in the darkness? He would not be proud any more. Nor the two lads, nor anyone who had helped plot this adventure. I stole a glance at one of the chisel-faced servants. He stared right through me. I baulked at the thought of asking him for anything.

How could Mother have yearned for such a life? These people would have hooked out her country roots in an instant and sliced her to pieces. *Perhaps you should have stayed with him*, I thought. *You wouldn't have had a bent farthing to your name but you would have been in love. It had to be better than this.*

'Excuse me, miss.'

A voice at my shoulder. I nearly dropped the glass of water. A small, squat man, smartly dressed in blue velvet, his wrinkled face a picture of cunning enquiry. He wore no wig, but had chestnut hair, streaked with grey, tied with a black ribbon at the nape of his neck. He bowed. 'I wonder if you might provide the solution to a question which is sorely vexing me?'

'Erm... How may I do that, sir?'

He stroked his chin. 'You were announced as Miss Chloe Gale. I heard it most distinctly. That footman is possessed of a voice which could frighten a horse out of its hide. And yet...' Another caress of his chin with one long, manicured fingernail. 'I have had the pleasure of meeting Miss Gale on a number of occasions and, presuming my memory serves me well enough, I am of the opinion that she looks nothing at all like you. Pray how shall we resolve this interesting conundrum?'

Stay calm. Stay calm. Put just the right hint of enquiry into my words. 'You were observing me, sir?'

'Observing? Gracious, m'lady, you make me sound like some manner of spy.'

'Peeping Tom, perhaps?'

He laughed and made an elaborate flourish with one ringed hand. 'As one of your hosts I would prove remiss in my duties if I did not take careful account of my guests. You presumably carried an invitation or you would not have been admitted. Yet you are not Miss Gale. My original question still begs an answer.'

He waited. And waited. Laughing crowds swirled around us. The quintet struck up another tune. A footman appeared at my elbow and offered a platter of sweetmeats. I shook my head.

He melted into the throng. But my inquisitor stuck to me like a barnacle on the underbelly of a rowboat. Host he might call himself but I'd wager he was there to winkle out gatecrashers, and one snap of those fingers would summon burly servants to escort me outside.

'Ho, Charles. Who's that you've got there? My, what a pretty catch. Don't keep her to yourself, man.'

Blessed interruption. I mouthed a quiet prayer of thanks and turned to my saviour.

It was Sailor Ben.

I stared at him, waiting to see if he would recognise me. Not a flicker in his eyes. I smiled and managed a convincing half curtsy.

'M'lady, you favour us with your presence.' He clasped my hand and placed a kiss between the knuckles. 'We have not had the pleasure of your company before. Certainly I would remember such exquisite beauty.'

Now was the time to see whether I could play the game. I snapped my fan open. The man called Charles had already merged back into the throng. 'I am a novice in the ways of the coaching industry, sir. I seek to learn the intricacies of the business. You are a member of the Trust?'

'Indeed I am, and very much at your service. You, ah, represent some male partner?'

I smiled hooked sunbeams. 'My interest is in the Gale Coaching Company.'

His expression clouded. 'You are in league with that young harpy? I see she has chosen not to favour us tonight. Yet I heard her name announced.'

'You speak unkindly of my employer, sir. Her indisposition was quite sudden. She asked me to attend in her stead. There was simply a misunderstanding with the name.'

'Ah. Indeed yes. No wonder Charles was buzzing around you. He is a little overzealous when dealing with unfamiliars. Forgive us, please, but it would be untruthful of me to say that our dealings with Miss Gale have not proved a trial.'

'Because she chooses to pursue her interests independently?'

'That is an admirable quality in anyone, let alone a woman of still tender years. But the nature of our business has changed. It is important that people of means channel their resources into joint enterprises. There is no place for individualists in the modern business world. Miss Gale must come to heel if she wishes to maintain a profitable organisation. Our terms have not been unreasonable.'

I fluttered my fan gently. The draught caught a wisp of loose hair poking out from under his wig. 'As I explained, sir, I am merely a novice. From your uniform I thought you a seaman.'

He gestured expansively. 'I have many interests, many indeed. I would be more than happy to share some of my own knowledge and experience. Over a glass of canary, perhaps...'

He drew me into a wood-panelled chamber and closed the door. Two leather armchairs were arranged before a small, flickering hearth. A table was laid out with a platter of sweetmeats, a wedge of cheese and a decanter. A writing desk hugged the far corner.

‘These chambers serve many purposes.’ His eyes glinted. ‘The adjoining room is furnished with a bed.’

‘I don’t take your meaning.’

‘There are many ways of conducting business. We have entertained a number of young women at these events. Some are sent by desperate husbands attempting to stave off a foreclosure, or to snatch a morsel from our collective purse.’

‘You speak very frankly, sir.’

‘That too, is in the nature of our business. Politics and diplomacy have their place but can prove an impediment in these fast-moving times.’ He filled two glasses from the decanter and passed one to me. ‘What exactly is your position within the Gale, if I may ask?’

I sniffed the liquid. Strong canary. ‘I am Miss Gale’s assistant. I am authorised to speak for her on a number of important matters.’

‘But I also sense a personal interest, is that correct?’

I nodded. ‘We are all receptive to opportunity, sir.’

‘Captain Beechcroft is my name but please call me Benjamin. You remind me of my daughter. She’s about your age and has a sharp head on her shoulders.’ He seated himself on one of the armchairs. At his invitation I took the other. ‘I’d heard that Edward’s girl had taken a filly under her wing. Stories circulate. Everyone prompts their share of gossip, newcomers especially so. It’s all hot air. Things are in turmoil since our chairman’s untimely demise. More urgent matters crave our attention.’

'I heard Lord Sutcliffe was murdered.'

'Indeed. Over an innkeeper's daughter. Some fancy he picked up during his business dealings. We had her father tied up pretty well. The girl was the final trophy, I daresay.' He chuckled. 'Stephen Sutcliffe was always torn between fine brandy and young women. He liked, and was indulged, his trinkets. The girl's father was a bit of a rough plank. Believed he could use his daughter to winkle his way into our circle. Quite impossible, of course.'

I conjured up a laugh. 'How so?'

'We have to be careful whom we wed, my dear. Many families wish to dip their fingers into our particular pie. Taking a country bumpkin for a bride is one way of tupping the wench but we don't want her father pushing his nose into our affairs. 'Twas the inn itself Sutcliffe wanted. I believe he wished to turn it into a family residence for himself. Good hunting ground around the old South Road, and old Lord Marrin was a regular gambling partner of his.'

'But was it not a working inn?'

'Hardly a problem, my dear. The father was up to his ears in debt to our banks. We would simply foreclose. He would be packed off to Portsmouth on some pretext and then pressed into the Navy. The Trust always acts legally, you understand. Another canary?'

I had drained my glass without realising it. I nodded. He finished his own drink, returned to the table and refilled both glasses. I watched the firelight play across the walls. The chamber was well soundproofed. Only a whisper of music filtered through the door.

I took a deep breath. 'We are also in need of a property in that area, with stables and a small acreage. The inn under discussion sounds as if it might suit.'

'For private use?'

'Of course.'

He sighed. ''Tis as well, my dear. With the opening of our new turnpike such places no longer have any commercial value. You have heard the tales concerning this particular establishment?'

I gestured with my fan, as if reading the society magazines was as second nature to me as drinking scented tea.

'Well,' he continued, 'the Trust invested a considerable sum in the property at Lord Sutcliffe's behest. We should need to recoup some of that capital before parting with the deeds.'

He mentioned a figure. I laughed.

'I can assure you, my dear, that figure represents only a small percentage of our expenditure. Selling Green Gallows at that price poses a considerable loss to the Trust.'

I laughed again. 'Come now, Captain Beechcroft. Who else would be willing to purchase such a lame nag? We've all heard the stories. Murder, cursed ground, madness, suicide. You would do well to give it away.'

'Impossible. Quite impossible.' He smiled.

'Then perhaps I have something else to offer.'

He poured himself another glass of canary. His eyes met mine.

'I am sure I could persuade Miss Gale to start using the turnpike,' I continued. 'That persuasion might extend to joining the Trust. Only stubbornness prevents her, and a belief that she is following her dead father's wishes.'

Sailor Ben dipped into his waistcoat pocket and consulted his watch. 'Ah yes, Edward Gale was a strong man. We met on several occasions. Never had any quarrel with the fellow, though I can't say I found him particularly agreeable. It will be hard for Miss Gale to embrace new ideas, living as she does in that place.'

'Better reason to obtain a country retreat. I can look after Miss Gale. She is tired. Two of her best coachmen have been locked up. Trade is slipping. She will join the Trust.'

'Very candid talk from an ... assistant.'

'As you said, Benjamin, I have interests of my own.'

'You are obviously not a Londoner.'

'No, I am from the southern counties.'

'And well spoken. A parson's daughter, perhaps? A former governess, though your age would suggest otherwise?'

I flicked my fan coyly across my face and said nothing.

'Very well, let us retire to the other room and discuss details.'

'No.'

'My dear, if you wish to barter with me then there are certain obligations that must be observed.'

'Perhaps, but not in this bordello. I have other things to attend to tonight.'

'You will come to my private residence if invited? Strictly business of course.'

'Of course.'

'Then we do understand one another.'

I put down my canary glass, gathered my skirts and stood up. Before I reached the door a hand on my arm restrained me.

'You are certain Miss Gale will join the Trust?' Sailor Ben's voice at my ear, low, brittle. 'Within the week?'

'Within the week.'

Chapter Nineteen

A solitary lantern burned outside the gate when we returned to the Gale. Gregor climbed down from the driver's perch and walked the horses into the starlit yard. The kitchen door opened, throwing a plank of light over the cobbles. It was Sally. I scrambled out of the carriage.

'You'd best come in,' she said, nodding towards the kitchen. 'Miss Gale is in her chambers and Meecher hasn't budged from the servants' parlour all evening.'

'How is Chloe?'

'She ain't in good humour, that's for sure. Fair stormed about the inn hunting for you. Wouldn't take my word that you'd gone to bed. Almost turned my kitchen inside out as if I'd stuffed you into a drawer along with the anchovies. Took laudanum to settle her for the night. A few drops in a posset, like she's been having all week. Wouldn't give tuppence for her temper tomorrow.'

'Put another drop or two in a cup of tea and send Kate up with it in the morning. I'll make sure you don't get into trouble. In the meantime you can close the kitchen for the night. I'm going to bed.'

Not bothering to fetch a candle, I pulled off my slippers and crept up to my room. No light shone under Chloe's bedchamber door. From the other side came the sound of gentle snoring. I slid into my own room and locked the door. Breath misted in the air, ghostly in the starlight that bled through the window. The curtains were still pulled wide, the fire in the hearth had blackened and died. I knelt and blew hopefully into the embers, catching a faceful of cold grey ash.

I lacked the heart to fetch tinder to rekindle it. I dragged the coverlet off the bed, wrapped it around me and sat on the edge of the mattress, staring out at the night. It was easy to become a little girl again, alone in the dark, scared.

Did you sleep soundly in your bed, Lucy? Or was it like this, sitting wide-eyed in the pitch black, going over the things you'd done and trying to decide whether you were right, knowing that it was already too late?

The morning dawned grey with the threat of rain. I yawned and sat up, the coverlet sliding off me onto the floor. I'd fallen asleep in my clothes. They were crumpled and stale-smelling.

Shaking my head to clear it of the night's fug, I crossed to the dresser, lifted the pitcher and shook it. Water sloshed around the bottom. I poured it into the bowl and dabbed some on my cheeks, washing off the rouge. My powdered wig lay on the floor beside the chair, though I couldn't remember taking it off. I yawned and stretched, then dragged a brush through the tangled thatch of my hair. Ow! That left my scalp stinging. Tossing the brush onto the bed, I peeled off my garments, opened the wardrobe and selected a fresh day gown. 'Not too bad,' was my opinion of the reflection in the looking-glass.

A flurry of raindrops spattered against the window. The clock on the mantel put the hour at a little after ten. I'd hoped to rise at seven.

Unease gnawed at my belly. I opened the door and peered into the corridor. The doors to Chloe's bedchamber and her drawing room were closed. I ducked back inside, crammed my feet into some slippers and crept downstairs. In the hall I met Mrs Meecher. Her face was dour.

'Why didn't the maid come in to make up the fire?' I demanded. 'My bedchamber was as cold as a tomb.'

'Miss Gale's instructions.'

'Where is Miss Gale now?'

'Sleeping. Just as well, isn't it?' And she was off.

The kitchen was empty. Scraps lay on a plate beside the cutting board. Vegetables, a morsel of dried bread and a crust of beef pie. I stuffed everything into my mouth and washed it down with water drunk straight from the jug.

Plans. So many plans to make. I had to see Sailor Ben, see him alone, but how? He could provide the lever I needed to open a crack in the Trust's implacable wall, but I had to know more. And there was so little time. If I could keep my nerve I could handle Chloe. She had enjoyed a rich life in this cosy haven in the city. I imagined I could still smell the rich loam of Marrin's Chase beneath my fingernails where I had tried to dig Sutcliffe's grave with my bare hands – could still feel Isaac's rope tighten around my neck. I had stepped over a threshold and a door had closed behind me forever. If I stopped now I might as well dig my own tomb at the corner of Prestbury churchyard.

I pushed open the door to my parlour, still tossing schemes around inside my head. Chloe was seated behind my desk, in my chair, the contents of each drawer spread out on the blotter before her. She was in her day gown. Her dark eyes glittered as they fixed on me. After a second of nerve-stretching silence she gestured at the chair opposite. I sat.

'You took it. You took the money. *My* money.'

'Yes.'

'You had no right.'

'I had every right. I don't get paid for working here. I get three meals a day, a bed and a small parlour. I'm worth more than that, Chloe.'

'I placed my trust in you and was rewarded with deceit. Mr Renbold must be wondering what manner of business I run if my own employees rob me. When he inquired as to the whereabouts of the promised funds I didn't know what to say. As far as I was concerned they had been delivered safely. By you. It was utterly humiliating. I had to send Judd over that very night on horseback with every penny I could scrape out of the bottom of my money box. Of course by that time you were already engaged elsewhere. I can surmise where the money went.'

'I had business to attend to.'

'You went to the Ball. You snatched that invitation out of the basket when my back was turned and went to the Ball.'

'One of us had to. The Trust want the *Charger* to use the turnpike. They believe it will raise their profile. I think it's also a matter of male pride, which will cost us naught.'

'And I daresay they also "desire" that I join the Trust.'

'Yes. They want you to join the Trust.'

'My father would not have wished it.'

'Your father is dead.'

She stared at me for a moment. 'The things he said about that nest of racketeers are true, and truth doesn't die. You've sold yourself, Rachel, better than your own papa ever managed, and now you'd sell me too. Why? Because of some godforsaken acreage next to a road that no one but myself and a gaggle of peasants are willing to use any more? So you can be better than the father who always put his own ambitions first? Or better than the sister who was given everything while you wallowed in her shadow, wearing second-best gowns as you stood in the yard in the rain, grinning at coach passengers who barely saw you were there?'

A sharp crack as my palm slapped across her cheek. Her eyes widened. Colour drained from her face. I stared at my hand as if it was some ugly, foreign thing that had sprouted from the end of my wrist. A smile crept across Chloe's mouth. I'd split her lip. A crimson finger of blood trickled down her chin.

'Why so upset, Rachel? Were you hoping I'd drink your drugged tea? That would have made it easier, yes? Easier to have me sign all the documents and undertakings when still dull-witted. Don't look so surprised. I am not a child. I know what goes on under my own roof. Quite the little group of allies you have garnered for yourself, but Meecher has worked at the Gale for twenty years and Papa brought the maid in when she was still a snot-nosed child.'

She pressed a kerchief to her mouth. A red flower blossomed in the centre of the lace.

'Your anger drives you, I know, but it can bite. If you lose control, the gallows may yet have your neck. I've never pretended to myself that you would be satisfied to live here and work for me. I saw what was in your face that day I plucked you from the street outside the court. There's a large part of me that wants to throw you back into the gutter with the few chattels you brought with you. But I agree that your flinty heart may be of use to me yet. What sum of money will you need to see this game of yours to the end?'

'Chloe, I'm sorry. I'm so sorry…'

'How much money?'

I took a deep breath. 'Not much if you can provide me with the use of a carriage whenever I need it and someone dependable to drive.'

'Not Gregor. I need him for the *Charger*. You can use Judd. He has left the yard well enough managed to be absent from his duties for a while. And you are better off with your own man, I think. Frankly, I ought to dismiss them all but who else will work for me at short notice, the way things are? You have done a neat job of trussing me up.'

She slid back the chair and stood up. 'I am

offering you this because if I don't you will take it anyway. You're off the leash. There's no stopping you. And yet I'll humour you because I believe you are my only chance for survival. You think you know the Trust? I know them better. They are a pack of dogs. If they suspect betrayal they can turn on a man and tear him to pieces. They'll think nothing of savaging one of their own. If you want revenge on them for something they did to your family, take it with my blessing. But I want my men out of prison, I want the Gale and I want to be left alone. It is not that I lack the courage or the wits to fend for myself. I lack the anger.'

She placed a key on the blotter. 'This opens my money box which you'll find in the bottom drawer of my writing desk. I've withdrawn more funds from Whittaker's so take what you need. I don't want to know your plans, Gallows Girl. I am too weary to care. Papa's death hurt. It still hurts. I can't fight you and the Trust at the same time.'

Her lip had stopped bleeding. Would I ever see any colour in those fragile cheeks again? 'Papa never hit me, not once, no matter what I did,' she whispered. 'I don't know what pained me more, the blow or the knowledge that you and I can no longer be friends.'

She walked to the door, opened it and paused on the threshold. 'If you need anything else you may pass your request through Mrs Meecher. If it is personal, you may leave a note in my drawing room. From now on I shall sup alone. You may eat where you please.'

'There is one thing I want.'

Her eyebrow arched.

'I want the maid to light the fire in my bedchamber,' I said. 'And I want her to do it now.'

Sailor Ben owned a grand set of apartments not far from St Paul's. I sat in his parlour, nibbled cakes and sipped Chinese tea. His invitation had arrived two days after the Ball. I wore the same gown but had trimmed it with different coloured ribbons. One of Chloe's bonnets was perched on my head.

My host had no living wife or mistress as far as I could tell. When I knocked he answered the door himself. Everything in the house was spotless and neat.

We'd been making idle chat for about half an hour. So far my nerves were holding. Ben put down his teacup.

'Now my dear, we have a bargain to seal, I believe.'

'You must have collected some interesting things from your years at sea,' I replied.

He coughed. Cake crumbs spilled out of his mouth. 'Erm … yes. Just a few mementoes.'

'May I see them?'

I waited. His pupils widened slightly.

'Well, of course, I would be delighted to show you. They are in my study.'

He rose and led me upstairs into an oak-panelled room that overlooked a small garden at the back of the house. A snatch of lawn embraced by flower beds. The grass looked as though it had been cut with nail scissors.

Sailor Ben stood in front of a well-stocked bookcase and pored over the titles.

'You're not interested in my trinkets, Rachel,' he said. 'I tipped you with enough playthings whenever you saw me off the Portsmouth coach.'

I stared at the back of his head. So much had happened in the past few weeks I thought I'd gone beyond shock.

'When did you realise it was me?'

'I had my suspicions from the beginning. You look and sound very different, of course. But you resemble your sister too much for it to be a coincidence.'

'Then why play silly games with me?'

'I was curious to see how far you would take this charade.' He turned and seated himself behind a mahogany desk, spreading his palms across the polished top. 'I've no doubt your presence at the ball was well engineered. You've learned, my little doxy, learned a great deal. You could almost pass for a lady. You didn't acquire that skill by opening carriage doors, but then peasants do possess a degree of guile from birth.'

There was a seat in front of the desk. I took it. I had to wait a minute to get my wits back. The door was right behind me. Maybe I could run for it, but what would be the point? I'd been stupid to think things could be this easy. Sailor Ben was playing with me, but I could still win.

'The Turnpike Trust taught me the meaning of guile.'

He nodded. 'Well said. Now remind me what you hoped to gain by coming here today.'

I swallowed. 'Stop harassing the Gale. Leave Chloe's staff and property alone.'

'Anything else?'

'I want Hugh Gore and his coachman released from Newgate.'

'Very noble. And for yourself? There is something for yourself, is there not?'

'Green Gallows. I want Green Gallows back. My father worked for it, my mother and sister died for it. I nearly died for it. Both the inn and the land it stands on belong to me. You have no right to it. You never had any right.'

'Ah yes, the inn. Given that I have the power to grant these requests, what good reason would I have for doing so? I now think it most unlikely that I can entice you into my bed. As for your promise that Miss Gale will join the Trust? That may just be another part of your little deception.'

'If you don't do what I ask I'll kill you.'

'Indeed?'

I scrabbled in my reticule, dug out Edward Gale's pistol and aimed it at Sailor Ben's forehead. My hands were shaking badly. 'I'll shoot, Ben. Be in no doubt.'

'You have to cock the hammer.'

'What?'

'You need to ease back the hammer so that, when the trigger is pulled, the flint will strike the metal plate and ignite the gunpowder. Only then will you succeed in putting a lead ball through my brain.'

He rose slowly to his feet. 'You don't look much of a murderess with that dandy's toy in your hand. Such fury in those pretty eyes though. Such fear. I suspect a great many things have sparked that temper. I daresay I ought to detain you and send for a constable. You'd not escape the noose a second time.'

My thumb fumbled for the hammer. In one fluid movement, Sailor Ben leaned across the table and snatched the gun out of my hand.

'Look at it,' he snorted. ''Twould probably blow up in your face. Did you even check to see it was primed? No, I thought not.' He opened a desk drawer and tossed the pistol inside.

'Have me arrested if you want,' I said. 'Just give me back my father's land.'

''Tis true that I took over administration of the area,' he admitted, 'but, speaking frankly, many of Lord Sutcliffe's interests were built on debt and riddled with corruption. With his death, everything collapsed. It may take accountants and lawyers months to sift through such accounts as there are. As Lord Grays has taken over chairmanship of the Trust, albeit temporarily, Sutcliffe's property interests passed into his hands.'

'Lord Grays? But at the ball you said...'

Sailor Ben's eyebrows arched. 'I merely countered one deception with another.'

I struggled to maintain my composure. 'Tell me where he goes, what he does and who he sees...'

'My dear, you are in no position to demand anything. You have just threatened to kill me. I would be perfectly justified in fetching my own pistol and shooting you where you sit. I am now convinced that you murdered Stephen Sutcliffe. It was no farmer's boy. A man would not have been so clumsy.'

I pressed my fingers over my eyes and rubbed. My temples were beginning to throb.

'What happened to the body?' I whispered.

'They paid someone to drag it out of the woods and bring it to London. He was entombed in some family mausoleum at Highgate. He had no surviving kin. The Trust took everything, including that rat's nest he drove around in. Only a handful of people turned up at his interment. As much to see him put away as mourn, I suspect. You did everyone a favour, Rachel, except that boy who was jailed in your stead. Who was he? Some country simpleton you duped with your charms, or did you frighten him into doing your bidding, the same way you tried to scare me?'

'No... No.'

'So, the vexing question remains, what am I to do with you?'

'Anything. I'll do anything you ask, just help me get Green Gallows back.'

'Is it really so important to you, that little hovel in the country? It barely accounts for a half dozen acres.'

'I don't care if I never set foot on it again. It's just that... It's just that...' I gestured helplessly. 'You must want something too, or you would have sent for the constable already.'

Ben nodded. 'I want the chairmanship of the Trust. Grays is a brandy sot and a philanderer. His wife is bedridden. She hasn't been out of her room in two years. The last of a family racked by one malady after another. Weak blood, generations of it, killed them all off. She inherited everything and, through some legal trickery, still holds the purse strings. Grays is not a self-made man, he is a woman-made man, if you understand my meaning. I believe that new roads are good for this country. They will open up opportunities for commerce, allow greater freedom of movement, the spread of trade and knowledge. Many of my colleagues on the Trust share these ideals. Does that surprise you? Sutcliffe, with Grays's backing, held us in thrall. A powerful man, and a most blackly evil one. Now that power has passed entirely to Grays, but he has a fat belly and a fat heart to go with it. Profit at any cost. Profit without thought. Anna, his wife, has threatened to divorce and dispossess him should he ever be caught with his wick in another candle, so to speak. She is far less tolerant than most Trust members' spouses and could prove a powerful tool. Up to now Grays has proved very astute at ducking the consequences of his adulteries. He has a ravenous appetite but while he was in Sutcliffe's pocket we were all too afraid to move against him. So we closed our ears and turned a blind eye while his whores disappeared back into whatever rat holes had bred them. Now if we could find one, just one, it would give us a lever to prise him out of his comfortable seat, but he has been especially careful since Sutcliffe's mur– death.'

He sat down again, steepled his fingers and rested his chin on the tips. His expression softened. 'I know Lord Grays spent a night at Green Gallows. He would not have come alone.'

'I think I may be able to help you,' I said.

Judd was silent during the ride back to the Gale. I needed the quiet, needed time to think. Things had taken a different turn. Ben said if we were to do this then we had to move quickly. I didn't entirely trust him; how could I have faith in anyone connected with the Trust? He was using me. Just as I'd planned to use him. Whether our little plot worked or not, he'd promised the Gale would be left in peace. 'Just games,' he'd said. 'That's all. Elaborate games. No real malice was directed at Miss Gale. The case of her two coachmen would never be brought to court.'

That was good enough.

I climbed down from the carriage and trod across the yard while Judd unharnessed the horse. Sally was in the kitchen and warmed some broth, which I gulped down. It was the first hot food I'd enjoyed in more than a day, my stomach had been so knotted with nerves. It was still early afternoon with plenty of time to get started. Sailor Ben had provided me with a list of what I needed. That list was tucked inside my sleeve.

First I bathed, then napped for an hour before putting on some fresh garments. Nothing too fancy. Instead of using a wig I tied back my hair with a ribbon and pinned on a bonnet. I settled for a dusting of face powder with a hint of rouge. Perfect.

An air of peace had settled over the Gale. Sally and Kate made a big show of making up after their little war in the kitchen. I'd no doubt the hugs were sincere and the kitchen was a better place for it. However Kate remained a bit wary of the other woman. True, they worked and supped together, and still swapped gossip over mugs of steaming tea by the hearth. But a spark of unease, fright even, flickered over Kate's face whenever Sally moved unexpectedly. Mrs Meecher, to my knowledge, had never hit Kate hard enough to draw blood.

Judd had the stables to himself. He sat on an upturned crate, working oil into a leather harness with busy strokes. I told him what I wanted.

'I won't take you,' Judd said. 'Not for any money. Not for the price of this job. I've been a churchgoing man all my life. If Sally found out she'd never speak to me again.'

'That's the second time you've defied me this year, Judd Button.'

'Let's pray there won't be need of a third.'

Clucking impatiently, I went in search of a sedan chair. Sailor Ben would have to help me.

In the yard I bumped into Chloe. She had just climbed down from her perch phaeton. We stopped and stared at one another for a moment, a breeze kicking up little whorls of dust on the cobbles between us. A couple of dead leaves were caught in Chloe's hair. Her eyes were full of winter.

'My, don't you look sharp,' she said, tight-lipped. 'Another ball?'

'No,' I replied. 'I'm going to a brothel.'

'I am pleased you have found your true vocation.'

I felt her eyes on me when I walked into the street and hailed a chair. I did not look back. I could not bear to.

'Far be it from me to turn an honest, God-fearing man like your Judd to the ways of Satan,' Sailor Ben laughed when I told him what had happened. 'I think we can spare you a gig and a dependable driver, one not so easily corrupted by the ways of the flesh.'

'You won't come with me?'

'Rot me, girl, I can't be seen going into those places, not in daylight. My man will keep an eye on you, and his face is unknown to those who matter. There are only a limited number of establishments involved. Most conduct all their business under their own roof. Only a few "rent out" as it were, and Grays would not have approached a street girl. In these parts a pox-free harlot is as rare as an honest banker.' He laughed again.

He sent for his driver, a lumbering ape of a man who answered to the name of Calthorpe. I'd seen enough sailors off the Portsmouth coach to know where this fellow had spent most of his working life. The sea had weathered that square-jawed face as surely as it works a piece of driftwood. He stood a good head taller than Ben and had to stoop when going through a doorway. Beneath his liveried jacket I imagined a broad, sweeping back scarred by the bite of the cat.

Ben introduced us in his study. Calthorpe swept low, scooped up my quivering fingers and favoured them with a gentle kiss.

'Delighted to make your acquaintance, m'lady.'

I stared. That voice. Gentle and cultured. Not the brutal grunts I'd expected. He bowed again then left to fetch the gig. Ben's stables were two streets away.

'Don't let him scare you,' Ben remarked drily. 'You need a man like that where you're going.'

'He spoke like ... like...'

'Like a gentleman?' Ben chuckled. 'Calthorpe was a captain once, like me. Twenty-five years he served in His Majesty's Navy. From snot-nosed midshipman to command of his own vessel. He's seen more than his share of campaigning.' He shook his head. 'Greed turns the finest of men. That's something you learn quickly, whether in the heart of London or out on some godforsaken ocean.'

'What did he do?'

Ben poured himself a measure of canary. He took a sip and eyed me over the rim of the glass.

'If he's to drive me around this city,' I pressed, 'then I've a right to know.'

'He started smuggling,' Ben said, 'stuffing the gunwales of his ship with enough contraband to hang him and all his crew. I don't know who put him up to it. I don't know who paid him. I only know that the harbourmaster's son rumbled them and was found dead-eyed and cut about the throat within the foul walls of some dockside den. The scandal was terrible. Calthorpe and I had enjoyed a card game or two in the past so I offered him a job and a place to live. That was five years ago, and he's done me more service than I'd care to talk about.'

I glanced at the list of addresses. Calthorpe arrived with the gig and a minute later we were out on the streets.

Daylight. This dirty business had to be conducted by day when there would be no gentleman clients to make enquiries. A young lady, arriving with a driver and asking questions, might provoke a shiver of panic. 'Members of Parliament and even minor royalty are known to use these places,' Ben had warned. 'It wouldn't do for some of them to be caught with their breeches about their ankles.'

We visited one sagging palace after another, always to be greeted by some crinkled, over-rouged matron. I promised discretion and made sure they caught the cut of my purse. Most treated me with an indifferent civility, as though I were in a bakery purchasing bread. Some girls fitted the description I gave, but none were the person I sought. Even if she wore a different gown with a change of hairpiece I was confident I could spot her.

Number five on the list. An elegant sandstone building jostling for space in a busy crescent. Outwardly the home of a prosperous merchant or banker. A black polished door. White-framed windows. A brass knob gleaming in the cooling sun. I checked Ben's list twice to make sure we had the right address. I glanced at Calthorpe, upright and grim at the reins. He nodded.

On the third knock the door was opened by a dandied footman. I showed him my purse and he let me in. That's how it was. No questions. No nonsense. I waited in the lobby. A white-haired ghost-figure drifted down the stairs towards me. The footman whispered in her ear. The pale face cracked into a smile.

'Our house is usually closed at this time of the day,' she purred. 'Most of the girls are asleep, you understand?'

I nodded and fumbled for my purse but already she was sending maids to rouse her charges. She wore a long, flowing gown of saffron, but I couldn't stop gawking at her hair. Not white with age – from her unlined face she had no more than ten years on me – but a shocking, bleached hue. She caught me staring. Pink eyes glittered with amusement.

'I ... I'm sorry,' I stammered. 'I didn't mean to stare.'

'You've never seen the likes of me before, I'll wager,' she observed with a wry laugh. 'My kind is rare in such a business, but some men have a taste for the unusual. Come, seat yourself. Already I sense the girls stirring. Enjoy a glass of Madeira while my little seeds blossom into flowers.'

I gulped down the drink and didn't protest when she refilled my glass. Erotic paintings lined the walls, bold, gaudy, framed in gilt. Curtains smothered every corner, softening the angles of the high-ceilinged room. A carpet, as thick as meadow grass, cocooned my feet. I had to resist the urge to nudge off my slippers and dig my toes into the soft pile.

A figure appeared at my elbow. A footman bearing a platter of sweetmeats. No, a girl. Bewigged and in breeches, yet no mistaking the feminine form beneath the male garments. Did that make her a footwoman? My road-weary brain giggled. I snatched one of the treats and washed it down with more Madeira. This was the most comfortable I'd been in hours.

The albino slipped out from behind a curtain.

'My daughters are ready,' she announced, ringing a brass handbell.

A parade of young women glided down the stairs. Damned women, Mother would have called them. I stifled a yawn. It was getting late. Calthorpe was not a gentle driver. I longed to rub my aching muscles. At a guess I'd put us six miles from the Gale. A good hour in these busy streets.

The line trailed to an end. I was all for giving up. And then suddenly there she stood, as beautiful and insolent as she had appeared that day at Stonehill. When she had taught me how to be a woman, how to heat a man's blood, and I had seduced Lord Sutcliffe into the depths of Marrin's Chase and murdered him.

The hair was different – now a fiery red. Dark rouge drew in her cheeks, and painted lines around her eyes gave her a feline elegance. But that pert nose was the same, as were the butterfly hands and small, rounded bosom.

I stood up and pointed.

'This one.'

The boy-girl servant led us into a private salon. As soon as we were alone I closed the door and faced the girl I had chosen.

'Remember me?'

Her polite smile broke into a toothy grin. 'Well, look who it is. My eager pupil. Do you need more lessons or have you come looking for work? Daresay we can have you gainfully employed in no time.'

'Got another job for you,' I said, plucking the purse from my reticule and dangling it in front of her eyes.

'A new client?'

'An old one.'

That Saturday I renewed my acquaintance with Lord Grays. I'd sent a note to his chambers the previous day, mentioning my acquaintance with

Captain Beechcroft and expressing a wish to meet the Trust's new caretaker chairman. I signed it Miss R. Curtis to spike his curiosity, and sprinkled the paper with scent.

Of course he couldn't resist.

'Does Grays suspect that you have your eye on the chairmanship?' I asked as we rode in Ben's landau.

'He suspects everyone of everything. He'll laugh and clap my back, entertain me in his house and give me the pick of his stables, all the while watching for a knife in the ribs. I'm depending on you to distract him.'

I checked my rouge in a pocket looking glass and smoothed a few wayward wrinkles out of my gown. Ben had picked the dress from a large wardrobe of feminine clothes he kept in an antechamber beside his bedroom. 'I am a widower,' he explained. 'I do a great deal of entertaining. My women dress to please me.'

A bonnet, wrap and gloves perfected the outfit. I would never look prettier, I reflected. Tucking the mirror back inside my reticule I regarded our hireling seated opposite. Her real name, I had found out at last, was Ellie. She was a true professional. Despite all my preening I would forever be the frump compared to her. Amusement sparkled in her eyes. This was just another game. She did not know what was at stake. She had played so many parts, been so many things to so many people, that it had all become meaningless.

We pulled up outside the first house in a sweeping crescent bordered by a park on one side and a row of sycamore trees on the other. I mounted the steps while Calthorpe tucked the landau down a side road. A footman promptly answered my knock and showed me into a study off the hall. Books, documents and ledgers swamped the small oak desk. A large candlestick, veined with melted wax, sprouted out of the chaos littering a marble mantelpiece. Light seeped through a tall bay window.

Lord Grays shuffled into the study in a pair of satin slippers. His dressing gown was open at the waist, his belly a pale moon spilling over the tasselled belt. A velvet skullcap hugged his thinning silver hair. His eyes were red and gritted with sleep.

'I was surprised to receive your message,' he said, gesturing expansively at a velvet draped chaise. 'Please sit down. Move that clutter onto the floor. It won't hurt it to sit on the rug for a while. Excuse me for not helping you, but my back has been grumbling of late. I don't normally receive guests at this hour but I am always charmed to make the acquaintance of a young lady, whatever the time of day.'

'I represent the Gale,' I said, sweeping up my skirts and seating myself.

His hand hovered over the canary decanter. 'So your letter informed me. Normally I deal with Miss Gale directly and would be as well to bang my skull against the nearest pillar for all the profit it serves. Does your presence here signal a warming of attitude? You seem much more pleasant of aspect than that sour kipper. Will you join me in a glass? No? Quite right m'dear. Much too early in the day, but age brings its privileges.'

I leaned forward, clasping my hands above my knees. 'You do not recollect me?'

Grays frowned. He poured a measure of canary. 'Forgive me. The nature of my business brings me into contact with many personable young women in all corners of the county. We met at a ball perhaps, or tea party?' He tapped his temple. 'Do me the kindness of refreshing my sadly fallible memory.'

'Your banker treated my sister like a whore.'

The glass paused halfway towards his mouth. He placed it back on the table. It made a little 'clink' as it struck the side of the decanter. He glanced towards the door.

'Don't summon the footman,' I said. 'We have business, you and I, and neither of us shall leave this room until that business is done.'

His brain fumbled for memories. No wig that night. No rouge. Just a country clod in a battered dress. *How many harlots since, Lord Grays? How many bought faces?*

'You sat at our table,' I continued. 'We ate and drank with you. We gave you the best of our house while you humbled my father and made my mother look a fool. We lost one of our best maids at your whim and the roof over our heads because of your trickery. Some might argue that was business. I call it theft.'

He slid behind his desk, kicked a pile of books out of the way and sat down. 'Who are you? By God tell me. I'll not have this sort of talk in my own house.'

'Curtis. Does that name mean anything to you?'

His expression sharpened. 'Sutcliffe's doxy. No,

her sister. I do recollect. You were as insolent then as you are now. Well, if you've come to me in hope of a handout, my young wastrel, the trip was in vain.'

'I wouldn't ask for that even if I were in need of it.'

Grays sighed. 'Your father was a victim of his own stupidity, believing that he could simply buy his way into our association with that goose of a girl.'

'Lord Sutcliffe thought her fine enough.'

'As creatures go, yes, but so is a good horse, and the horse is a mite more useful.'

My hands tightened around my reticule. He caught something in my face and laughed. 'So what do you propose to do, m'dear. Threaten revenge? Go for my throat with a paper knife? I've had all of that and more. You do the Gale no favours by coming here, if you do indeed represent that business as you say.'

He stood up, hand questing for the bell pull on the wall behind his desk.

'Don't summon the footman,' I repeated.

We both heard the sharp rap on the front door, the manservant's steady tread along the hall carpet, the door opening, voices. A moment later, Ellie swished into the study, the flustered servant chirping protests at her back. Lithe as a cat, she shut the door in his squawking face and blew his lordship a soft kiss with one gloved hand.

'Delighted to meet you again, m'lord,' she cooed in a dove-sweet voice. 'Or should I still call you "husband"?'

Grays's face blanched. He glared at me. 'What

do you mean bringing that harlot into my house?'

'I thought your wife might like to meet her,' I explained demurely. 'Your real wife.'

'Aha. So that's your game, my pretty little tease. Well go ahead, go ahead,' he gestured towards the door, a fat smile on his mouth, 'take your little toy upstairs to Anna's bedchamber. My servant will show you the way, and he'll be glad to open the door for you when she laughs you both into the gutter.' He chuckled meatily. 'You are but one of a hundred becoming faces that have tried to charm their way into my circle, and this just another one of a hundred tricks. My wife may be bedridden, but nothing ails her wits. She would not take the word of a whore. She knows their mouths can be bought as easily as their bodies and that I have no shortage of enemies who covet my wealth and position.'

'Her wealth,' I reminded him.

'No matter, no matter. You obviously have some intimacy with my affairs. I am curious as to who sent you. This enterprise cannot be of your own concoction. What bungling fool thought to prise favour out of me? Own up and I might not feel so disposed towards having my footman thrash you.'

'A sovereign sent your loyal footman scuttling into the pantry. Everything can indeed be bought, Lord Grays, including your reputation. Ellie here will show you what I mean.'

Ellie was only too glad to. She pushed Grays back in his chair and swung her leg over him as easily as she might settle herself into a pony's saddle. Skirts billowed around his legs.

'Get off me!'

'Well now, you didn't complain the last time I did it, m'lord. Why, you practically dragged me on top of you. The bruise on my thigh took a week to fade, and here's your flag starting to climb its pole all over again.'

The tip of a thin finger traced the line of Grays's jaw and tapped him gently on his dimpled chin. 'I've worked your body, m'lord. Worked it well. Just like a flesher with a shank of beef. I know all your little ins and outs. Better than your wife, maybe. Perhaps I can describe you to her? The little pox marks on the end of your quill? Now there's something she'd like to know about. I'll wager 'tis been a while since she scribed anything with that particular pen. And what about the curious scar that's so far up the crack of your noble arse your cheeks need to be pulled apart to see it? Wonder what manner of implement could have caused that, m'lord? If your wife hasn't the stomach to take a peek then perhaps she'll insist that her surgeon examines you. I'd be pleased to direct his attention to one or two other little oddities.'

Grays snorted. 'Any bribed valet could have told you that. It won't wash, m'dear.'

'Maybe, maybe not. But what d'you suppose might heat your dear Anna's temper the most? The idea that you tupped a whore behind her back, or the fact that you passed me off as your wife? There's enough can testify to that and willin' to do it without having their palms oiled. You even took me to church. Is Lady Grays likely to think the parson's lying an' all?'

He sat back down with a thump. 'Damnation. That pink-eyed witch assured me of discretion.

I'll have her bordello burned down and all her whores with it.'

'There are men of greater importance than I who might object to that.' Sailor Ben was in the doorway, leaning against the jamb. His face was languid, his tone even.

'Beechcroft, this is your doing?'

Sailor Ben shook his head and gestured at me. 'She's already got me on the hook, Grays. Just as she's about to land you. Best not fight it. She has made some powerful friends.'

'You think me fool enough to be taken in by such a caper? You always overestimated yourself. I should have guessed you'd be behind this nonsense. Go back to Portsmouth and keep your affairs in the docks where they belong.'

Ben chuckled softly. 'An old trick this may be, but we have the right bait for the right fish, I think. No need to hear it from my lips. Young Ellie here has already told you. And I am witness to the fact that you have been carousing with a harlot in your own study while your wife lies in her sickbed upstairs.'

Grays squirmed free of Ellie's hold. Laughing, she let him go. 'Well presumably you are all in this for something?' he spluttered. 'You cannot have money. The release of funds from Lord Sutcliffe's estate requires the signature of all the trustees. I have no personal wealth, as this little strumpet,' he wagged a finger at me, 'so rightly pointed out.'

'Money?' Sailor Ben laughed. 'The last thing we want is money.'

He turned to us and bowed. 'If you two ladies

would care to wait outside in the landau, Lord Grays and I shall discuss business. I do not believe this will take long.'

Chapter Twenty

'He gave in to everything?'

Sailor Ben settled back on the landau's seat. One hand toyed with the end of his pigtail. 'How could he not, after that little stunt your pet harlot pulled? Still, it was not as difficult as you might suppose. Grays enjoys the esteem of the chairmanship but does not care for the work that goes with it. He has made the best of his brief term as Acting Chairman and can retire to other, less taxing matters with no loss of face. The issue should go to a vote of course, and so it shall at the next Trustees' meeting, but my nomination, with Grays's backing, is unlikely to be opposed. Grays himself nets a tidy sum by way of a thank you and can return to his distractions without incurring the wrath of his wife.'

He'd taken me to a coffee house while Calthorpe returned Ellie to the brothel. There she was to pack some chattels and leave the city for a while. 'As a precaution,' Ben explained. 'However we will need to keep her within reach in case Grays decides to renege. I think it unlikely but pride is a plague upon us all.'

Ellie would go to Chelsea where her brother owned a fruit stall. The brother didn't know

Ellie's true occupation. He believed she worked as a maid in a town house. Ellie was advised to dress soberly for the trip and take the first available coach. If necessary she could be fetched back within a day.

Outside the window London went about its business. I was glad this part of it was over. The gun still nestled at the bottom of my reticule. First chance I got I'd slip it back into Edward Gale's desk. Sailor Ben had promised me the deeds to Green Gallows by the end of the month. Hugh Gore and his coachman would be out of Newgate much sooner.

I slipped Ben a sideways glance. He took a silver flask out of his jacket pocket, uncorked it and took a generous swig. He caught me looking and offered the flask. 'Rum,' he said. 'Another naval tradition I haven't quite been able to surrender. Try it. It'll warm your belly and we have cause to celebrate.'

I shook my head. 'When we've sealed your part of this bargain.'

Ben laughed and pocketed the flask. 'No wonder Chloe Gale thought she could make use of that hard head of yours. You must have proved quite an asset to her.'

'She doesn't seem to think so. I've lost her friendship and she no longer trusts me. I won't be turned out, but it's going to prove hard living under her roof for a while.'

'I could provide you with comfortable apartments.'

'The Gale suits me well enough, thank you.'

'Permit me to provide an allowance then. No,' he

raised his hand, 'hear me out. You can regard it as a wage. Fair remuneration for all your efforts. I maintain accounts at a number of reputable dress shops and milliners. Make use of them as you please. If you prefer, fittings can be arranged at the Gale.'

'Glory, they'd never stomach such vanity.'

'Then come and live with me. By all means keep your little bolt-hole at the inn if that gives you comfort, but mine is a large house and even a sea-weary old widower gets tired hearing the echo of his own feet.'

'I'll not be your mistress, Ben. Nor will I climb into anyone else's bed.'

He chuckled. 'Rot me, no, I'd not ask that of you. At my side, however, you could prove enough of a distraction to leave people unguarded. Your wits are also sharp enough to pick up things that others might miss. I'm willing to make quite an investment in you, Rachel. I'd also like to make you my ward, at least until you come of age. Stay tonight and think about it. I will send word to the Gale. Chloe's business will not suffer while I am Chairman of the Trust, I promise. That surely will give her cause for warmth.'

Hugh and Bill were released that Tuesday. I went to fetch them in Sailor Ben's landau, Calthorpe at the reins. I brought thick slices of ham, a round of bread, a little cheese and a flask of wine. Good wine to enrich weakened blood. I found them standing in the mud outside Newgate. They didn't recognise me. They didn't seem to recognise anything. The coachman's clothes in which they'd been arrested were torn and soiled. The silver buttons were missing, as were the buckles on their shoes. Billy had a terrible festering gash above his right eye. I later learned that one of the other prisoners had taken a fancy to the pin in Billy's neckcloth. Billy did not want to part with it. The inmate had gone at him with a carved rat bone. It nearly took his eye out. Hugh broke three of the prisoner's rotting teeth before he laid off. A riot had nearly started. Jailers piled into the cell brandishing staves. One man fetched a broken jaw. Another had his skull split open. He died in the night.

Calthorpe helped the men aboard. They eyed him distrustfully, but took his hand and climbed up. I gave them the sack of food. They gulped it all down, even the muslin wrapping the cheese came in. Billy nearly sicked it back up again. When his stomach had settled I took them to the Gale. I did not return them to their homes and families. I wanted Chloe to see me set them both down alive in the yard. I wanted Judd to see. And Thomas. And bitter-faced old Meecher from her upstairs window.

Just my luck.

Grey clouds spread across the sky and dumped a torrent of water on our heads. Calthorpe struggled to raise the hood of the landau but it stuck fast. I threw a blanket around my shoulders and shivered for the rest of the journey. Calthorpe drove the horses as fast as he dared. When we arrived at the Gale, the yard was empty. I ferreted Kate out from the larder where she was stacking pots of jam. 'Miss Chloe isn't here,' she told me.

'Judd has taken her to Renbold's. Thomas has got a day off and gone to the river with his doxy, and Sally is at the flesher's. You back to stay, miss?'

'I've brought Hugh and Billy, fresh out of jail and in need of a seat by the hearth. Make sure they have a change of clothes and send word to their families.'

'Yes miss,' she said. 'I'll see it's done. Are Hugh and Billy out for good?'

I nodded. 'For good. Tell Miss Gale when she returns that I brought them here. Make sure she knows, won't you, Kate?'

'You brought them,' she repeated. 'Yes, miss.'

I went home to Sailor Ben and was rewarded with a basin of hot, scented water for my feet and a generous measure of brandy. I had a room that was three times the size of my chamber in the Gale and a four-poster as big as a barn. Dinner brought exotic dishes that Ben had discovered on his travels around the world. Some were garnished with spices that had me gulping water, others melted on my tongue or filled my mouth with sweet fruits.

Calthorpe took me riding around the park on a fine piebald from Sailor Ben's stables. He was always a shadow clopping steadily a few paces at my back. A breeze threw a brassy carpet of dead leaves across the bridleway that turned to burnished gold when the sun came out. The air was fresh and pricked the lungs. I felt safe.

Then I had to earn my keep.

'What do you want me to do?' I said when told this. 'Scrub the scullery?'

Ben laughed. 'Socialising can be hard work. By

the end of the month you will be quite weary of parties.'

'I'm going back to the Gale soon.'

He smiled and flicked a speck of dust from the sleeve of his jacket.

I met them all.

In the coffee houses, at tea parties, at balls or the opera. Everyone who counted for anything in the Trust. In their dens, their lairs, we tracked them down, Ben at his most charming and me on his arm, smiling.

People stared. Others whispered into friends' or partners' ears. Men smiled and bowed, eager to place a kiss on my hand. Women mostly favoured me with a frosty glare or a look of intrigue. I lost count of the number of liveried footmen who glided up and pressed a card into my palm. A quick read of the inscription, a glance around the room. Ah, there he was. A smile that was a little too wide, a slight inclination of the head. Glory, what a dusty fossil…

The rest was easy.

'I hear you are skilled at cards, Sir Edward… Is that a new phaeton, Lord Harman? I understand they are very dangerous. It must require great courage to handle such a device... A pleasure to make your acquaintance, Lord Campbell. I have always wanted to meet a Scot. I hear they are a particularly hardy breed…'

I made powerful friends and prised the lid off all their secrets.

On Friday morning, during breakfast, Sailor Ben handed me the deeds to Green Gallows.

I stared at the oblong of paper, the blob of red

wax imprinted with the seal of the Trust's lawyers. I turned it over in my hands. I ran my finger along the edges. Ben sat watching me, a faint smile on his lips. He was dressed to perfection in a blue riding suit and calf-high leather boots that caught the light and glittered whenever he moved. His pigtail had been tied up into a series of plaited loops that clung to the nape of his neck.

'Well, you have got your little country retreat,' he said. 'Now all you need is a dowry.'

I choked on my tea. 'Dowry? I've no plans to wed.'

'My colleagues remark on the fact that you are not married, that you have no beau or gentleman callers,' Ben continued, passing me a napkin. 'I told you that you had the potential to prove a great asset. I have been giving some consideration to your future and have arranged a suitable marriage partner for you.'

'What?'

'His name is Viscount Rochefort. A Frenchman by birth, though he has spent some thirty years on these shores. His business interests, both here and abroad, merit our attention.'

'But ... but I don't know him.'

'You met him at Lady Coloughon's tea party. He expressed great interest in you. Were the Trust to find him a suitable bride his membership, and all the advantages it brought, would be assured.'

'I don't remember. One tea party seems much the same as another. He must be quite old.'

'He is forty-eight, in fair health and his command of English is faultless. Come, Rachel, don't quibble. By all accounts he is an excellent catch.'

I dropped the envelope. A tear slid down my cheek. I felt its slow progress. 'Ben, tell me this is a jest. I don't want to marry an old Frenchman. I want to marry a man I love. There must be enough eligible young bachelors in London society for that to be possible?'

He nodded. 'True, there is no shortage of young rakes whose fortunes outmatch their wits. But those, my dear, are earmarked for equally empty-headed fillies. Marrying for something as ephemeral as love is a poor business arrangement. Surely if you learned anything of our methods then you must know that this is the way we have always done things?'

A second tear joined the first. I wiped them away. Sailor Ben could not mask his disappointment.

'I thought you more hard-headed than that. If you wish to continue to enjoy the privileges your new position bestows then you must follow my instructions. In this matter I am your better. You will sup with Viscount Rochefort tomorrow evening and a marriage contract shall be drawn up. I understand the Viscount already has an heir – the fruit of some previous union now dissolved. I do not believe his marital demands on you shall prove onerous.'

He reached down and squeezed my knee. 'Run with the pack, girl, run with it. Only then can you hope to win the hunt.'

I spent the day in my room staring at the wall. I refused lunch and waved away Ben's housekeeper when she tried to bring me tea. She went without complaint. Her face carried an *I know why you're in a mood but you'll get over it* expression.

I couldn't touch anything. Not the dresser, not the perfumes, not the expensive set of ivory-handled hair-brushes. The fine gowns Ben's city accounts had bought me hung unused in the wardrobe.

When dusk leadened the sky I dressed in the one set of garments I had brought with me from the Gale and went downstairs. Ben was in the back parlour smoking his pipe. A glass of rum sat on the fireside table and a book was open in his lap. He looked up as I came in, tapped his pipe out on the hearth and slipped the volume back into its place on the shelf. His face was flushed and genial.

'I'll hook your fish,' I told him, 'in exchange for a favour.'

His eyebrows raised. 'Another one?'

'Precious little to ask in exchange for what I'm giving you, and a favour that will better the Trust's interests.'

He smiled. 'This is all very mysterious, Rachel. Can it not wait until after my election to the chairmanship?'

'No. If I am to wed, as you desire, then there are a few ghosts I need to lay to rest. It will cost you nothing and use very little of your time.'

He inclined his head. 'I am at your service.'

'Colly Bruce. Does that name mean anything to you?'

'It sounds familiar though I cannot say I am intimate with it.'

'The Trust appointed him as a toll farmer for

the Prestbury section of the turnpike. This was partly done to hurt my father, or so he believes. Bruce works from the Coach and Horses Inn. I know him of old. He fancies himself a farrier but is bad with animals. Gypsies sell him lame stock that would make other dealers' beards turn grey. He has whipped three poor beasts to death. The chaises that he rents are so poorly looked after that a fair-sized pothole would crack their axles. He has a fancy for gin, a quick hand for beating his woman and is a turnip when it comes to business. People were nearly killed when one of those tin-tack boxes of his overturned. The local wheelwright said the woodwork was so rotten and riddled with worms you could crumble it between your fingers. Bruce has no nose for the trade.'

Ben's eyes searched my face. 'My, you really don't like this fellow, do you?'

'I don't like his habits. I don't like his manners or his talk. He skulks around always looking for trouble. He enjoys causing injury. You see it in his eyes or the way he grins. Colly Bruce grins a lot.'

'You wish him dismissed?'

'I want him sent to Portsmouth. On any errand, it doesn't matter. I want him sent to Portsmouth and taken by the press gang.'

'Indeed?'

'Your sailor friends can do it.'

'Was that the only request, or is there something else?'

'I wish to visit Green Gallows, to survey my property. Will you lend me your carriage?'

Ben chuckled. 'My carriage is a little trinket that's good for trotting around London parks. The

South Road will split its axles within a mile. Why do you think I always used the local stagecoaches? You will have to travel by similar means. In fact, it might pay to book passage aboard the *Charger*. With your influence I am sure you can persuade it to stop at your inn. I shall send word today. You can board it at the Gale in the morning.'

He refilled his pipe with a wad of fresh tobacco and lit it with a taper from the hearth. Clouds of blue smoke billowed towards the ceiling. 'Do not tarry away too long, my little dove. We cannot keep your prospective groom waiting.'

Chloe was waiting when Calthorpe dropped me off at the Gale's main gate. The day had dawned bright with a stiff wind blowing from the north, biting ears and noses. She invited me to her drawing room. I accepted. Mrs Meecher laid a platter of tea and sweetmeats on the walnut writing desk and withdrew. Chloe filled two cups and whitened the tea with fresh cream. She took a sip, settled back and appraised my travelling gown and the cloth valise I'd brought with me. Small lines had cut into the soft flesh beneath her eyes. She popped a sweetmeat into her mouth. I waited until she had finished eating. My own tea cooled in its cup.

'You are running away,' she said finally, wiping her hands on a napkin.

'Yes.'

'Where will you go?'

'Green Gallows first. After that, who knows.'

'Will you tell me why?'

I told her.

'Hmmm. I thought it might come to that. The gentry are well bred, Rachel. They choose just the right stud for their mares in the manner of a skilled horsemaster. You are no more ill used in that respect than any well-born woman. You should feel pleased. It means you have been accepted into their ranks.'

'I don't want it.'

'No?'

'No. I'm not Isaac or Harriet. I never dragged myself through each day dreaming of meals on china plates or a house with more rooms than there are days in the year. I've slept on old sacking before and I can do it again.'

She smiled thinly. 'You always got what you wanted.'

'No, not always, but I've kept my promise to you. The Trust won't trouble you any more. Hugh and Billy are out of jail and your business will be left to thrive. Send the *Charger* down the turnpike and it travels toll free. I guarantee it.'

'I believe you for once. And I am grateful for my coachmen's release. Perhaps there is something I can do for you.'

'You did enough.'

'Not quite. You know my views on marriage. Local tongues have dubbed me the South Road Spinster. This is a very rich bed in which I lie and I am not overkeen to tip it over. Papa raised me well in that respect. But you? Is there someone who would turn your heart?'

Jeremiah, rotting in his rat-infested cell, Lucy's name forever on his lips.

'No.' I shook my head. 'No one. There never

will be anyone. The price does not suit.'

Chloe leaned over her desk. 'Put that in writing and I'll give you a tenth of the business. If you are still unmarried in a year you'll get a third. Five years and you'll become a partner, equal in everything.'

'Why?'

She caught my expression. 'Nothing sinister. No impropriety. I need help, Rachel. I still cannot manage the business alone, and there are many who say I am not as strong as Papa. Recent events have proved the truth of that. Yet who can I trust? The forest is riddled with wolves. Every month I continue to receive marriage proposals from predators with their eyes on my fortune. If you agree, my lawyers can draw the papers up and you can sign when you return from your little pilgrimage. It will prove a very solid document. Your new friends might be irked but they will recover, though I fear you may not find yourself invited to many of their parties in future.'

'You already had this planned,' I accused.

'As I told you many times, I know these people. And I believe I have learned one or two things about you into the bargain.'

With the scratch of a quill I would sign my life away. Never to wed within these shores. Never to allow any velvet clad wolf to sink his teeth into my life and property. An unnatural pact for the rest of my natural life.

'Don't look so glum,' Chloe said encouragingly. 'Sometimes you'll suffer an ache. Treat it like a bad tooth. Men will never seem more attractive, even the ogres. But when your belly flutters, keep your mind on the profits and your body in a nunnery. Either that or be a brood mare for whatever pet monkey the Trust picks for you. Take a sip of tea and tell me what you want to do.'

I rode the *Charger*. On the turnpike for the first time. Wheels a blur, horses working up a lather. Buildings gave way to hedgerows and frost-glazed meadows.

Two other passengers. A young man dressed for the town, gently snoozing, hair a soft chestnut cradle about his face. Beside him an older, pinched woman outrageously periwigged in red with a green ball gown that clashed terribly with the hair. She gazed uninterestedly out of the window, layers of rouge and powder smoothing all expression from her face. Her baggage, all eight cases, was tied to the roof. Sammy had been sweating by the time that lot was safely stowed.

I fingered the handle of my valise. My mouth was dry. The carriage lurched over a rare bump and the young man stirred. His eyes opened briefly, exposing a hint of blue to the grey world outside. He glanced at me then dozed off again, the flicker of a smile on his lips.

I wondered if he had ever broken a girl's heart, ever been forced to abandon someone, or would be forced to wed a woman he didn't love. Was that also how it worked for males born to the Quality? I'd never know the likes of him as a husband. Every man I took would be as a lover only, to enjoy fleetingly until someone else culled his heart.

Could I accept Chloe's pact? Could I?

Stonehill slid by the windows. Six miles later

the carriage lurched as the team turned onto the Churchdeacon crossroads. The red-haired lady frowned.

'We have left the turnpike. We were not due to stop until the coast.'

I fixed her with a steady gaze. 'We are not stopping. We are merely taking another route. 'Tis only for a few miles. We shall rejoin at Prestbury.'

'What other route? There are none to speak of.'

'There is if you know where to look.'

'The old South Road? We'd need shire horses to haul the carriage over the ruts. Why are we here?'

'This was once the main road south. The *Charger* is no stranger to these parts.'

'But it will mean a delay. Non-stop, that's what my ticket says.'

'I work for the Gale. You'll be refunded half your ticket price. An extra hour or so won't hurt.'

'Half it is then, but tarry more than an hour and I'll have the lot.'

I sighed inwardly. The crossroads had already edged out of sight behind us. We were on the South Road. Already, the hedgerows either side had encroached on the lane. Brambles, leeched of colour by the cold winter, scratched against the wooden panels. Soon, we were on the long rise up to the top of the Ridge and coasting down the other side. I swallowed and closed my eyes. I was not ready to see Green Gallows. Not yet. When I opened them again, the dark spire of Prestbury church was looming towards us.

I tapped the roof, leaned out of the window and shouted up: 'Pull over here, by the churchyard.'

The *Charger* clattered to a halt. I grabbed my

valise, opened the door and jumped lightly onto the verge. 'Don't forget, half the ticket price!' the painted lady called after me. I slammed the door. The horses snorted, their breath white plumes in the sharp air.

'Leave me,' I instructed Gregor. 'I have an errand here, then I'll walk to the Coach and Horses and hire a chaise.'

'Will you be all right, Rachel?'

'This place, these fields,' I gestured, 'were my home once. You'd best go. I've already made the *Charger* late.'

All traces of the two graves had been smothered by grass and dead weeds. A snaggled rock embedded in the dyke was the only clue as to where Lucy lay. I stood on the road before the patch of washed-out green. I needed no Bible, no prayer book or tokens. Just my voice. And my love.

'The *Charger* stopped, Lucy, as I always told you it would. Just a little while longer and my business will be done. Rest well, sister.'

I stooped and laid a hand on the grass. The ground was cold. The previous night's frost hadn't yet thawed. My knees creaked a little as I rose. I felt like an old woman.

Mother's grave. 'I could have loved you more,' I whispered, 'if you'd only let me in. It didn't matter who my father was. You never understood that.'

Jackdaws wheeled in lowering circles around the church spire. Someone was watching me from the parsonage window. A pale moon face. White wig. Dark clerical garb.

I gathered up my skirts, opened the gate and strode up the path. The lawn on either side was immaculately clipped, the flower beds cleared and ready for the following spring. Parson Buseridge's housekeeper answered my knock. I pushed past her into the study, where the parson had retreated from the window and was flicking through a book. Ecclesiastical texts, from the wording on the spine. He was holding it upside down.

'You know who I am,' I said, 'and normally I'd not set foot, not one foot, inside this house. But a wrong has to be righted and you are going to see to it. You are to see to it now.'

He tried to close the book. It flapped in his hands and tumbled onto the floor. Behind me I heard the housekeeper say: 'She just barged in, sir. There was naught I could do to stop her. Shall I fetch one of the gravediggers?'

'Leave your lackeys to their bothy,' I continued. 'My business is with you.'

'And what, pray tell, might that business be since you clearly have no manners nor respect for the cloth?'

'Ha! If I hadn't been trained so well I'd spit on your shoes for saying that, Parson. Don't dirty the word "respect" with your pompous tongue. You'll fetch your holy water or incense or whatever it is you use, go out there and bless the ground in which my sister lies.'

He gawped at me. Behind the round lenses of his spectacles his eyes were bright and priggish. 'She is a suicide. She must remain in unconsecrated soil.'

'Lucy was murdered, as plainly as if she'd been dragged to the gibbet and had the noose forced around her throat. It doesn't matter whose hand was on the rope.'

'Even so, I shall not consecrate a patch of verge. I have no authority to do so, and you, young lady, have no right to demand it of me.'

'If you won't perform the ceremony outside the churchyard wall, then you must bring Lucy inside. This land is owned by the Southern Counties Turnpike Trust. I'm not without influence in the company.'

'Nonsense. It is Church property.'

'And the lane which passes it? The fields and villages nearby? The stream which serves your well? What if the road were to close, your well to dry up, your congregation to find their souls better served elsewhere? A preacher without a flock is no use to his Church. You'd be left with crows for parishioners.'

'She was buried in quicklime and must lie where she is,' the parson blustered. 'No grave-digger hereabouts will touch her remains. Then there is the stigma...' He gestured helplessly. 'Even after centuries of teaching, the Church has not succeeded in freeing men's minds of superstition. Old customs cling like rotting ivy.'

'Lucy is not under quicklime. She's in a casket. If you'd attended to her burying like the Christian you profess to be you would have known. Knock down the wall. Rebuild it at the edge of the lane. Then bless the ground. No one will find demons in a churchyard.'

'It cannot be done. There are deeds, church records. The boundaries are clearly marked.' He shook his head. 'The Rachel Curtis I knew would never speak such insolence to her betters.'

'The Rachel Curtis you knew was buried with her sister.'

'You are a devil.'

'I am. A creature moulded by other people's greed. Do what I say, Parson. I'll not ask you a second time.'

Colly Bruce was not at the Coach and Horses. I hired a gig and made the ostler wait while I looked it over. Satisfied that it would manage the few miles required of it I set the horse at a brisk trot to Prestbury goal.

The turnkey shook his head. 'His daughter? His daughter you say? Weren't it you he tried to murder?'

Yes, I was his daughter. Yes it was me he'd attacked.

The turnkey rubbed his chin. 'You're sure there'll be no trouble?'

'No,' I said. 'No trouble at all.'

Lantern swinging, he took me down to the cells. They were dirty and stank of piddle, but a palace in comparison with the sty that was Newgate.

A small window was set into the thick oak door. 'Who are you?' Isaac said, peering through the bars.

'I'm Rachel, your daughter.'

'I don't have any daughters,' he said.

I turned to the jailer. His gaze shifted from me to Isaac and back again.

'Let me in,' I said.

On a table was a candle and some leatherwork. Isaac had been working on a pair of boots, painstakingly stitching the pieces together. The turnkey fetched a stool and I seated myself. He glanced once at Isaac then left, slamming the door and locking it. I could hear his wheezy breath lingering in the corridor outside.

'Are they treating you fair?' I asked.

Isaac ran his fingers through his hair. His belly was thinner, his eyes tired. 'Why did you come here?'

'I wanted to see if you hated me.'

'I don't hate you. I thought you'd gone for good.'

'Really?'

'I never lied to you in my life. Neither you, your sister nor your mother. I've never lied to anyone. I just want what's mine.'

I took a deep breath. 'I work for the Gale coaching company and have strong connections within the Turnpike Trust. I have used those connections to secure the deeds to Green Gallows. It is out of their hands. Forever.'

He stared at me. 'Now I must call you a liar.'

I fished in my reticule and brought out a bound sheaf of documents. I broke the seal and spread the papers out on the table. 'Take a look.'

He swept the leatherwork onto the floor and snatched at the papers. As he read each one, slowly tracing the words with his finger, belief spread across his face.

'Now I can finish what I started.' Flecks of spittle flew from his mouth. 'I'll open a smithy, get some horses. The gypsies will do a deal. There's always something those beggars want. I'll steal business right out from under Colly Bruce's nose. You can get me out of here, Rachel. You can get me out today. There's nothing I can't do, not now that Green Gallows is mine again. This time it will be different. This time there will be no Trust to bleed me dry. I can buy land. Open other inns. Beat those London upstarts at their own game.'

I took the papers from his quivering hands and gathered them up.

'No, Father. Green Gallows is mine.'

'What?'

'You read the deeds, saw the name on them. Green Gallows belongs to me. If you put one foot on that property you do so by my grace, otherwise you will be trespassing.'

He laughed. He cursed. He beat his fists against his temples, spat in the dirt at my feet and called me a selfish whore. Then he started crying. The turnkey's face appeared at the door. His gaze flicked warily from me to Isaac.

'I need a manager to work a posting house on the coast,' I continued. 'The job is yours if you wish it.'

'Work for you?' He spat again. 'Not while Green Gallows stands. I'll stay in here until my teeth rot in their sockets.'

'If you have a change of heart you may send a message to me at the Gale Inn as I shall be there for the next few days. I'll arrange it with the jailer. As soon as I receive word I will plead your innocence. I will tell Mr Davey that we had a misunderstanding, that you were upset because Mother died, and that the merchants exaggerated the situation. Mr Davey knows the type. He'll believe me when I say that there was a terrible row, that you were rough with me but never had murder in your heart. I'll say that I was upset, angry and afraid, that I fled to London. I'll even say that I provoked you. The constable will understand. He's a family man. I'm offering you a life, which is more than you were willing to give me. I've no doubt Mr Davey will secure your release.'

'What kind of witch are you?'

I smiled thinly. 'I am what you made me, Father.'

'Father, eh?' He grunted. 'Each time you call me that it chills my blood.'

It was dark when I arrived at Green Gallows.

The moon was high and full, silvering the land. The gate stood open; the lantern tacked to the post had not been lit. Gravel scrunched under the wheels as I pulled up outside the stables. A soft yellow light glowed within. Opposite, the dark bulk of the inn stood out against the stars. Woodsmoke drifted in the bitter air.

I tethered my horse and peeked inside the stables. The stalls were empty apart from one scraggy-looking mare chomping oats at the end of the row. Beneath the window an upturned barrel served as a makeshift table. The remains of a supper was spread out on top of it. Breadcrumbs, a rind of cheese, an ale tankard. Above, the hatch to the hayloft was closed and bolted.

I lit a spare lantern, went back outside and tried the front door of the house. Locked, as were the Long Room, kitchen and taproom entrances. All the ground-floor windows were boarded up. The sign had been removed from its gibbet. The marks hacked into the wood by Isaac's axe were plain in the moonlight.

Matthew was standing by the pond, staring into its black depths. My shoes crunched on the frost-brittle grass. Perhaps it was that which made him turn, or the bobbing glow of my lantern.

'Can I help you, m'lady? If it's a room you want there's plenty to choose from. There are always empty rooms at Green Gallows.'

He looked unwashed, bewildered. I smiled warmly. At first he frowned, perhaps suspecting a trick. Then his eyes widened and ... there! A spark of recognition or perhaps a stirring of some memory, a long-buried hurt.

'Are you well, Matthew?'

He staggered, grasping his stomach as though he'd been struck.

'I ... I thought 'ee dead.'

'The girl you knew is dead. That Rachel was fat, slovenly, frightened of shadows. She's gone and won't be missed. I am who I want to be, nothing less.'

'Why did you come back? There's nothing for 'ee here.'

'Nothing? To my father this was everything. And look at you, Matthew, coachmaster at last. It's what you always wanted. To be in charge.'

He sighed. 'I'm in charge of naught. The chaises are gone and the stables are empty, 'cept for one old nag what was too sickly to take. The bailiffs even went in and had the linen off most of the beds.'

His eyes had a brittle, glassy look. In the shadowed yard it was hard to tell what else was lurking on his gaunt face.

'So the inn is still open to travellers?'

'Still open, aye. I'll never turn away a coach, nor fail to service a waiting team. My stables might be empty but there's a bed at Green Gallows, with a warm fire and supper if you want it. I hold a set of keys. They pay me, like, to look after the place. There's always work.'

Pushing a broom in and out of empty stalls, cleaning floors that had been swept a dozen times already. Oh Matthew.

He grasped my wrist, his voice suddenly puppy-dog eager. 'Have you come home, Rachel? Have you come back to be with me? We could work hard. Buy Green Gallows back from the Trust. Turn part of it into a farm. Not much land here, I know, but we could have geese and pigs. I could run a smithy. We could open the taproom for the drovers. Would you like that, Rachel? Isaac won't bother us no more, and Judd's gone. Just you and I now.'

His grasp tightened. 'They say Sutcliffe had gold in his coach. That Jeremiah Cathcart took it and hid it in the woods. Maybe we could search for it.'

I gently disentangled my wrist. 'You'd like that, would you, Matthew? To have gold? To have the land and the inn? To be rich and own everything?'

He nodded feverishly. 'Aye. 'Twould be grand. I'd be as good as any that sit in the front pew at church. I'd hold my head up and walk among the squires. People would say: "There goes Matthew Collins, landowner, farmer and innkeeper, and him started so humble."'

'And what of me, Matthew Collins?'

He frowned. 'Why, you'd have fine gowns and a horse of your own. Maybe a carriage one day.'

I surveyed the empty, moonlit yard. This childhood place. This island the world had visited. Ghosts walked. Carriage wheels echoed. Horses snorted as they were backed into shafts. Pedlars hawked their nostrums. People loved and fought, shed tears and died. This was the core of everything that had turned rotten in our lives. Even I had wanted it, lusted after it.

'Rachel?' The first note of uncertainty. 'What d'you have a mind to do?'

'I'm going to burn Green Gallows to the ground,' I said.

I took Matthew in my carriage. He lay on the seat, his head in my lap. His face was streaked with tears. With my free hand I caressed his hair.

Fire populated the land beyond the Chase with flickering orange ghosts. I did not look back.

I called in at the Coach and Horses and engaged a room. I booked another for Matthew and had a fussing maid put him to bed. He went without protest and was fast asleep when I looked in.

Not long after daybreak I returned to the blackened husk of Green Gallows. Sparks had flown from the blaze, carried by a southerly breeze, and wafted through the open stable door, finding a ready feast in piles of dry, dusty straw. Fire had leaped from rafter to rafter, roof to roof, swallowing up the coach house. Charred spars of timber jutted towards the leaden sky like broken, rotted teeth. Only the signpost was untouched.

The old gallows.

Half a dozen tinkers' caravans were drawn up at the gate. Every year they came to Prestbury common to sit out the winter. The blaze would have been seen for miles. Figures, wraith-like, picked their way among the smoking ruins. A pair of dogs started barking over some titbit unearthed from the shattered kitchen. They leapt for one another and collided in a tangle of fur while the men stood around laughing.

I did not see a villager, not one, anywhere nearby.

In Prestbury, I called at the courthouse and posted the land for sale. My asking price was one penny. A gentleman from Liverpool bought it that same day, a shipping owner who wished to expand his interests along the south coast and sought a suitable plot to build a family home. He couldn't believe his luck, the clerk told me.

On returning to the tavern I found Colly Bruce. He was bullying some of the stable lads. I tapped his shoulder and he turned, snarling at the interruption. I wore only a plain travelling gown.

'So yer back,' he said. 'What in God's teeth do ye want this time?'

My voice was satin. 'Mr Bruce, I would like a word with you regarding your future. Perhaps we should go inside…'

He had a small office tacked onto the stables that stank like a midden and was full of clutter. I handed him the envelope Ben had entrusted to me. Colly glanced at the wax seal bearing the imprint of the Turnpike Trust and tore it open. He stared at the letter and flushed. He couldn't read. I offered but Colly shook his head. He sent one of the stableboys to fetch the innkeeper's son, who wanted to be a clerk and was learning his letters. The lad read it out slowly, hesitating over some of the words, but the missive's intent was clear enough. Colly went white with rage. He snatched the sheet of paper and crumpled it up in his fist.

'This is your doing,' he said.

'I hope the sea air mellows your temper, Mr Bruce.'

'What d'ye mean by that?'

I walked out of the office and bumped into the horsemaster, who was standing by the door. A fat grin wrinkled his face.

'Do you know Matthew Collins?' I asked. 'He worked the yard at Green Gallows Inn.'

'Young Matthew? Aye, met him many times at Prestbury market, Judd Button too.'

'Can you give him a job and a place to stay? He's fine with animals and has a keen eye for balancing a carriage.'

The fellow looked past my shoulder at Bruce and nodded. 'I'll do it on your say so, miss. Good hands are always welcome.'

I bought a bunch of flowers from one of the hawkers in the yard. They'd been grown in a hothouse and the price made me wince. Wrapping them carefully, I turned in my gig and hired a mare and side-saddle. I cantered down to Prestbury churchyard and divided the bouquet. Half went on Lucy's grave, the other on Mother's.

Unburdened, I tore off my bonnet and let the horse have free rein. At Green Gallows, the tinkers' vans had gone. I didn't stop. I galloped all the way to the crest of Marrin's Ridge before checking my mount. I climbed down, breathing hard. Lather coated the animal's flanks, but she was bright-eyed and enjoying the crisp air as much as I. Below, the land spread out in a patchwork of greens, browns and greys. The dark bulk of Marrin's Chase thrust out of the ground like a wooden molehill. To the west was the turnpike, black specks moving along its length. A wisp of smoke still rose, like a pencil stroke against the sky, from Green Gallows. Further east were the cream buildings of Marrin's Hall, together with its park and gardens. And directly south lay the scattered houses of Prestbury village, seemingly growing in number by the day.

I spread my cloak on the grass and sat, knees bunched under my chin. *What now, Rachel Curtis?* I asked myself. Return to Sailor Ben and be married off as a society chattel? Or fall in with Chloe and never marry at all? More choices than some women enjoyed in their lives. More choice even than Lucy had. Yet watching that line of smoke I had a glimmer, for the first time, of what Lucy had been searching for all those times she'd stood by the gate or paddock wall, staring down the lane. Green Gallows was the rope that had bound me to both Ben and Chloe. That rope had now turned to ashes.

A pounding of hooves on grass. Another rider was making his way up the Ridge, his mount taking the slope at a brisk pace. A large dark hunter, the horseman in perfect control. His scarlet jacket was a bright flag against the muted winter countryside. Soon I felt the thunder of hooves rippling through the ground beneath me. He crested the Ridge and halted his beast next to mine. One effortless movement had him dismounted and at my side, hat in hand.

'My compliments, m'lady,' he boomed, in a thick northern accent. 'I watched you tackle the Ridge. A fine display of horsemanship.'

I matched his gaze. He did not flinch, nor take offence, but grinned widely. Gold glinted from within the hollows of his generous mouth. Despite the aches in my bones and the specks of soot still clinging to my scarecrow hair, I smiled in return.

'You're very kind, sir.'

His eyes took in my clothing. 'You have come far? From London perhaps? I am a visitor to these parts myself. This road,' he gestured at the distant turnpike, 'has opened up many new business opportunities.'

'No, I live in this parish. I was visiting my sister's grave. She is buried in Prestbury churchyard. I put some flowers there.'

'I am sorry to hear that. Was she taken by illness?'

'Her heart was broken.'

'Oh.' He stared awkwardly at the ground.

'May I ask you something?'

'Of course.'

'Do you think you are a good man?'

His eyes widened then he chuckled, but without mockery. 'Well, yes. I am no saint, what man can say he is? I try to do my best where possible. Sometimes I don't succeed. I dislike failure but can live with it most of the time. It is how we learn, and how we better ourselves. Why, do you not consider yourself a good woman?'

I rested my chin on my knees. 'I don't know.'

'Permit me to say that seems rather cynical for one so young.'

'Young? I already feel as if I've lived a lifetime.'

'I take my hat off to you for your frankness. Thompson's my name. Bernard Thompson.'

'I'm Rachel Curtis.'

He gazed out over the flatlands. 'There's been a fire.'

'It was an old building. Old and rotten. Someone should have torn it down years ago.'

He slapped his crop against his thigh. 'Well, as long as the ground is good. That's the important thing, eh? It's beautiful here, and restful.'

I didn't answer. I leaned back, braced my arms behind me and stared up at the sky. Puff clouds swam in the brittle blue of winter. I heard Thompson shuffling on the grass, his boots making small *swish swish* noises.

'Please don't misunderstand me,' he said after a moment, 'but there are things in your eyes that are troubling. Are you in any kind of distress?'

I turned my head and smiled again. It slid so easily onto my face I felt my skin warm with the simple beauty of it.

'Do not concern yourself, sir. I, like my sister, am at peace.'

The publishers hope that this book has given you enjoyable reading. Large Print Books are especially designed to be as easy to see and hold as possible. If you wish a complete list of our books please ask at your local library or write directly to:

Magna Large Print Books
Magna House, Long Preston,
Skipton, North Yorkshire.
BD23 4ND

This Large Print Book for the partially sighted, who cannot read normal print, is published under the auspices of

THE ULVERSCROFT FOUNDATION

THE ULVERSCROFT FOUNDATION

... we hope that you have enjoyed this Large Print Book. Please think for a moment about those people who have worse eyesight problems than you ... and are unable to even read or enjoy Large Print, without great difficulty.

You can help them by sending a donation, large or small to:

The Ulverscroft Foundation,
1, The Green, Bradgate Road,
Anstey, Leicestershire, LE7 7FU,
England.
or request a copy of our brochure for more details.

The Foundation will use all your help to assist those people who are handicapped by various sight problems and need special attention.

Thank you very much for your help.